HIS DARK MISTRESS

MINDY SATURN

Published by A Horse Called Alpha

ISBN-13:   978-0615994796
ISBN-10:   0615994792

For JJ, who always believes.

The bartender returned from throwing out the last of the drunks and looked at the woman still sitting at the bar. Outside, the sun was beginning to rise. He should have been closed hours ago, but he had let the regulars stay when it had become obvious she wasn't going to move — and he hadn't wanted to end up alone with her if he could help it.

He knew her by reputation, knew better than to push her whether or not she wanted it. She smiled to herself as he stood awkwardly.

"Um," he said.

She snorted, a chest-deep noise that reverberated in her nose, and she looked around her hair at him. He had the look of a man who knew how to use a baseball bat in a fight. She respected such men. In a smooth, quick motion, she tossed back the shot sitting on the bar in front of her and slid a bill out of her jacket pocket.

"Half for you, half for the rest of the bottle," she said. He hustled behind the bar, eying the hundred under her fingertips, and put his hand under the bar. She read his eye.

"The other one," she said. His hand moved and returned with the bottle of whiskey. She took it silently and left, her long jacket cracking at the influx of fresh air from outside as she opened the front door.

The whiskey sloshed in the bottle as the woman strode across the street. The coffee shop she was headed toward was still empty. She heard the door to the bar bolt behind her as the bell on the coffee shop jingled.

Beth would be here in fifteen minutes. The woman was as predictable as a clock. The Custom House clock would strike seven and Beth would walk through that door. The dark woman picked a seat at a booth and threw herself into it, propping her feet on the opposite bench and opening the bottle. She took a sullen drink of it.

"I'm sorry, booths are for paying customers only," the skinny kid with the unfortunate complexion called from the register. The woman looked at him, took another drink, then stood. He took a step back from the register as she approached. She slapped a twenty dollar bill on the counter and snatched one of the promotional mugs off of a hook above the display case, then returned to her booth and poured a full cup of liquor, leaving the bottle on the table.

The kid edged out to her table with a few dollars and a stack of coins, then vanished into the back. The woman put her feet up on the bench across from her again and settled in to wait for a blond reporter named Beth.

HIS DARK MISTRESS

Beth was in the middle of her post-story ritual. She had slept in till eight, then bought every newspaper or magazine she had seen on a casual walk in to work. Now the periodicals lay stacked on her chair behind her, and she was systematically filing all of the chaotic paperwork from her last story. Post-it notes stuck related printouts to clippings, where she was lucky, and made multi-colored mosaics of indecipherable quasi-English where she wasn't. One by one, she went through the pieces of paper on her desk and read them, nodding to herself silently. She had gotten it. She had captured everything she wanted to capture; she had said what she wanted to say. She told *the story*. Finally, a little after lunchtime, her desk was empty. This was when her job frightened her most. The empty desk. No story. Her friend, Kelly, hot-shot political writer, said that she always had three or four things going, so when she finished a story, she never hit the moment of 'what now' that Beth did. In fact, Kelly claimed, that was *normal* for a reporter. That wasn't how Beth worked. She only did one thing – that *one thing* – until it was done, to the negligence of everything else. She had no room in her head for anything else until the ceremonial cleansing of her desk.

David approached slowly, giving Beth an opportunity to glare him off, but she was staring at the broad expanse of clean wood. It was done.

"You ready for lunch?" he asked.

"Mmm," Beth said, glancing at the pile of news that she was dying to paw through. David glowered, guiding her shoulder away from her desk.

"Food first," he said. "I've got the comments from up top on your article."

Beth sighed, glancing over her shoulder, then wove her arm through David's elbow. He would give her space, but only so much. He thought that she needed positive reinforcement for her work, and satisfaction that her contributions were recognized by the senior editors. Investigative journalism of the vein that she practiced was a tenuous profession at best. She was on fire if she turned in four articles a year, and that made her and her kind the first to be forgotten and the first to be cut from the payroll when such things were necessary. David thought that that should make Beth insecure for some reason.

Lunch was a quick trip to the lunchroom downstairs, where Beth watched cable news and nodded at what she thought were appropriate intervals. Dave was proud of her, that was all she needed to know. Well, if she'd thought about it, that would be all she needed to know. Instead, she was preoccupied with a developing story on a murder trial in Baltimore, a news report on financial legislation going through Congress, and a behavioral study about only children. The national news stream was displaced by a local press conference for the mayor, and Beth glanced back at David. She was busted. He narrowed his eyes.

"Good job," he said.

"Feel better?" she asked, resisting the urge to look back up at the TV. His mouth twitched in a suppressed smile.

"No, but it'll have to do." He threw his napkin onto the plate in front of him, only half-playing at frustration. "Go read your papers."

Beth waited a polite two seconds before blotting her mouth with her napkin and bolting from the cafeteria back up to her desk. The stack of papers started on the floor to one side, unread, and landed, disheveled, on the other side. The desk stayed clean. There would be something.

Sometimes it took weeks. She would become increasingly short-tempered as she went through newspapers, magazines, press releases, everything she could get her hands on. Then her days would get shorter. She would get out, walk the city, and talk to people. Eat at new restaurants, go to museums. Anything to put things together that busy people missed. She was off schedule and off story, and she didn't sleep well.

Two pages in, though, something itched. She absentmindedly pulled a stack of post-its out of her desk drawer and set them on the smooth, reflective surface of her desk. She didn't need to look to find them or the pen. She just kept reading. Words would come.

It would be something. Words that perhaps she didn't understand yet. They just itched. A question that she could clearly see the answer to, but where the truth was equally obviously hiding. She read on. The itch grew.

Shoes. Expensive shoes.

She had seen them, but she couldn't remember. The itch grew worse, and she wasn't reading words any more. She turned the page in a magazine, glancing distractedly at the models. In a celebrity gossip magazine, the models wore *nice* shoes, but they didn't wear really expensive shoes. Not yet. She needed a fashion magazine.

High end.

Expensive shoes. And a manicure.

Polish to match a skirt suit in... what was it? Wine? Burgundy? Heaven help her why she knew it, but they were twenty-five hundred dollar shoes made by Louboutin. The skirt suit was... Beth slapped her forehead.

Armani. She hated herself a little for knowing that. She was a reporter, it was her job, on and on, but she tended to believe that men in leather jackets and jeans knew a lot more than society women in haute fashion. About everything. The men who collected their trash knew most of their secrets, and the women who tended their children knew the rest. Beth didn't get information from rich women. She got it from the people they paid.

So. Armani suit, Louboutin shoes. Now she just had to put a head on top and maybe she would be able to figure out what was bothering her.

She had lots of false starts, like this. She was used to it. She would just float one thing and then another until something became a real story. She had no illusions that this was the one.

Except the part of her brain that had already figured it out. It was jumping up and down and screaming at her to catch up.

She dropped the magazine into the discard pile and shoved her chair back. She was halfway down the hall by the time the chair hit the far wall.

The culture magazine owned by her parent company was housed in the top two floors of her building. She jabbed at the elevator button and waited ten seconds before heading for the stairs. The elevator dinged behind her and she made a quick analysis before returning to it. As the doors closed, she was already regretting it. There was nothing to look at but her reflection in the elevator doors. Her mind was racing, but to the same effect as a cat on a marble floor. She needed something she could get traction on, or, lacking that, at least a set of stairs to be in the way. She glared at her reflection as her mind spun, grasping for threads that didn't even exist.

The doors dinged open again on the sixth floor, and a man Beth didn't know started to get on, but unfortunately his height was not far enough from her own, and he found himself substituting for the target of her glare.

"Sorry... I'll... get the next one," he said, backing away. Beth's eyes dropped to the floor, trying to remember where the image had come from. The suit... the hair! She knew the hair, and she couldn't remember what she was remembering.

The elevator finally reached the eighth story and Beth left it with the driving force of an avalanche. She should have taken the stairs.

Janet was at her desk.

"Burgundy skirt suit by Armani, knee-high boots from Louboutin. Does that mean anything to you?" Beth asked.

Janet looked up at her as though she was telling a bad joke.

"That's what the mayor wore in her press release two hours ago."

Beth's hand slapped over her mouth on autopilot. Janet watched her with mild impatience.

"Can I help you?" she finally asked.

"Do you have a picture?" Beth asked.

"Two hours ago," Janet reiterated. Beth was too distracted to completely understand what Janet was telling her, but fortunately, she was also too distracted to be belligerent about it.

"Kelly will have them," she said.

"Two hours," Janet called after her.

Beth took the stairs back down.

"Stuart, where's Kelly?" she called as she made it to the far end of her own floor, where the political news reporters lived. "In with David," Stuart answered as Beth walked past. Beth made a neat turn on her heel and plowed her way through the office maze cross-country to David's office. She didn't knock.

"Hey, Babs," she said dismissively. "Kelly, the mayor's press release this afternoon?"

"Snooze," Kelly answered, leaning sideways in her chair to be able to see Beth and still keep an eye on David.

"Hi, Beth," David started.

"Do you have pictures from it yet?" Beth persisted.

"It was two hours ago," David said.

"Why does everyone keep saying that? How long does it take to develop a picture?"

"Twenty to twenty-five seconds," Kelly said.

"Really?" David asked.

"No," Kelly told him. "Find Keith from the photographer's pool. He'll get them printed up for you if you need them," she said, turning to Beth. She winked, then swiveled in her chair to casually face David again.

"Thanks," Beth said, changing course with yet more commitment. Something wasn't right. She might have remembered to pull the door to David's office closed behind her, but she wouldn't have put money on it.

Three minutes later, she was standing outside a dark room, alternately leaning against a wall and sitting on a desk belonging to an unfortunate intern.

The shoes, the hair, the skirt, the nails. They added up to something, but bugger all if Beth could put together what. She tapped her fingers on the side of the desk, then moved back to the wall. After a minute, she realized that she was staring at a very uncomfortable intern, and she looked back at the carpet.

"Keith developing a photo for you?" the girl asked. Beth looked up at her and grunted. She closed her eyes and tried to picture what she remembered from the press conference. As far as Beth was concerned, mayors came and went. She voted, sure, but they were temporary. Stories had roots. And legs.

The door next to her opened, and Keith held out a slightly damp photo.

"Do you want the rest of them when they're done?" he asked. Keith was a good guy.

"This is fine," Beth called over her shoulder as she headed for the staircase.

She couldn't have sworn how she got there, but she ended up back at her desk, sitting and staring at the photo.

"Yup, that's the mayor," she muttered at it, cueing the frantic but mute portion of her brain to spit it out already.

The woman was so well-pressed that she would have competed with a cardboard cutout. Always did. Mayor Suzanne Cromwell hadn't come from much, and the backroom snigger was that she was overcompensating for it in the way she dressed. She had gone to finishing school. If she had cared, Beth would have had to make a note to look up exactly what that meant after 1960. Her accent was tutored American-nondescript, her posture was perfect. Beth stared at the picture, rocking slowly.

It was the hand. The fingernails wouldn't have been on the list, if it weren't for the hand. Beth nodded. That's it. Out with it.

The mayor never fidgeted. She didn't have any speechmaking gestures that the pundits could mock. She didn't sweat, nor did she stutter. Her pauses were empty of unattached vowels.

Beth wouldn't have noticed it if Cromwell hadn't kept reaching up to touch the pin at her right collarbone. Even in the photo, her hand was midway between its assigned, symmetric place at her side and the glittering accessory. Beth wrinkled her nose. It was actually a bit gaudy for the mayor's wardrobe. It was a red flower with great red rhinestones for petals, long, thin, green stones shaped as leaves and scattered, smaller white stones for a center and between the ends of the petals. It was something Beth's mother would have worn at least two decades ago on a print dress. On the Armani, it looked dignified and well-set, because that's what expensive clothes did for you.

Until you looked at it.

Slowly, Beth's fingers made their way to touch her lips. She set the photo gently on her desk, her mind at rest. Her hand found the pen and set the pad of post-its at the right angle. She wrote in careful, neat letters, without looking at it, still gazing at the photo. The first post-it note.

She put the pen away, peeled the post-it and stuck it to the center of the desk, putting away the pad before carefully aligning the photo next to the post-it, and sat back in her chair, staring quietly at the post-it.

What if they're real?

Beth straightened her hair as she got out of her car. She had gotten a name for a reputable gemologist about four hours away and, hoping that she had gotten far enough out of Boston for the man to not recognize the piece from television, she walked into his office. A friendly and slightly bored-looking receptionist looked up at her as the door closed behind her.

"Can I help you?" the woman asked.

"I had an appointment with Dr. Wells?" Beth said.

"Mrs. Coolidge?" the woman asked, checking a calendar. Beth smiled.

"Yes," she said.

"I'll tell him you're here," the woman said and stood. "Please make yourself comfortable."

Beth wandered to the wall, looking at the pictures of gems and the various small stones under glass. It had to have been a happy profession, she thought, for people who were deeply interested in small details. Cheerful colors, at least.

"Samantha," a soft masculine voice said behind her. Beth turned.

"Dr. Wells?" she asked, offering her hand.

"Please, call me Alan," he answered. "Come on back, where I have better light."

Beth looked up at the track lights illuminating each wall, and shrugged.

"You only have a picture?" he asked as he settled in behind a desk in what Beth would only remember as a brilliant white room. Beth nodded, putting the manila folder onto his desk. He pulled out the cropped and enlarged photos Beth had chosen.

"So what is your interest in this piece?" he asked, holding up the first as though he were reading an x-ray.

"It was my mother's," Beth said. "She always had money stashed away somewhere, but it didn't turn up in the estate. My sister says that the pin is just sentimental, but she won't let me get it appraised, so I'm wondering if it's worth more than we thought."

Dr. Wells was frowning, and he put the first picture on his desk to hold up the second, without lifting his fingertips from the first.

"You need to find their papers," he said.

"Papers?" Beth asked.

"Every one of these rubies should have papers, somewhere. If your mother knew what she had, she kept them somewhere," he said, putting the photo flat on the desk and bending over it. "How big would you estimate this pin is?"

Beth leaned forward and put her fingers on the picture, demonstrating height.

"Maybe about half as big as the picture."

The man whistled.

"I would love to take a look at these in person, but they appear to be untreated, near-perfect, natural, pigeon-blood rubies. Matching. Without a loupe and good light, I can't say what quality the diamonds are, or even for sure if they are diamonds, and the emeralds are flawless, but just there for show..."

Beth waited.

"I should have heard about these stones," he said, looking up at Beth. "And I don't recognize the jeweler."

Beth twisted her mouth, and shrugged.

"I wish I could tell you more about it. I don't remember how long she had been wearing it, and I don't know where she got it. Maybe my sister will know, if I can get her to tell me."

He looked back down at the photo.

"I told you on the phone that a lot of the time, the designer will contribute a lot of the value of the piece," he said. "I was wrong, here. A jeweler couldn't touch the value of those rubies."

He looked up at her and squinted. Beth did her best to look innocent and clueless, an expression she had perfected over the years – people over-shared with the dumb, but were cagey with the clever. He shuffled the photos back into the folder and handed it to her, apparently having made up his mind.

"You need to get this appraised. Get a court order, do whatever you need to. Your mother wouldn't want your sister to keep it to herself," he said, slightly paternally. "Bring it back to me, if you want, or get another appraiser to look at it, but get someone to look at it." He paused. "It could be worth millions."

Beth faked the catch in her breath out of habit, but a moment later her mind caught up, and she realized what she had heard.

"What do you mean?"

"The rubies, all on their own, are potentially worth six to eight million dollars. Any self-respecting jeweler with access to that quality stone would put most of the cost into the diamonds. Even at that size, they could be worth close to a million apiece," he said.

Beth tore open the folder and counted.

"Fifteen million dollars?" she asked.

"Could be a lot less; there could be inclusions I can't see, but you need to know that for sure. Even if it is a lot less, you need to find the papers for the stones, and you need to get it insured. And for heaven's sake, don't let your sister wear it."

Beth didn't have to completely fake stunned as she thanked him and excused herself. She was itching for a pen and a post-it note. Five-thousand dollar boots was one thing. A fifteen-million dollar brooch was certainly outside of the mayor's price range, and even if it weren't, Beth couldn't come up for a reason that the woman would put that kind of money into a gaudy accessory instead of, say, a giant house and a status-car. Beth sat in her own vehicle and opened the folder again to look at the pin.

"Where did you come from?" she asked the jewelry, before starting the ignition and heading back to her desk and her post-its.

She knew by the time she got back to the newspaper what her next step was, but she stopped by her desk anyway to post-it the photos to her desk with a simple '$$$' notation. The details were in her head; the notes were just to capture the thread. She looked down at the pictures and frowned. After the gemologist's reaction, she couldn't go showing around those photos without grabbing more attention than she wanted. She bit the inside of her lip, then walked over to the printer to steal a sheet of paper out of the tray. She looked hard at the brooch, then turned away and quickly sketched it from memory on the desk beside hers. She looked back at the pin and frowned. She was probably too accurate by half, since she had spent so much time analyzing it, but she justified that people who genuinely cared about such things would have a better memory than hers. She dug through her desk drawer to find a green pen, then colored in the gems in her drawing.

David stuck his head out of his office.

"You on something already?" he asked. She glanced up.

"Mmm? Oh. Yeah, I think so," she said. He raised his eyebrows at her. She grinned.

"This plays, it could be huge," she said. He nodded.

"Nose to the grindstone, good work people, all that," he said, absently waving his hand at her as he went back into his office. Beth grinned at his back and folded her sketch in half, sliding it into her purse as she spun to head to the elevators.

She made her way to the parking garage, heading through late rush-hour traffic to a hotel downtown where she had a standing relationship with the head concierge. She street parked a few blocks away and walked to the service entrance.

"Looking for Casper," she said to one of the valets on break.

"He's at the desk," the kid told her, resuming his quick meal. Beth made her way through the guts of the hotel unchallenged and emerged minutes later in the front lobby. Casper finished a quiet conversation with a woman carrying a small dog in her purse and made eye contact with Beth. He motioned to the bar.

"What can I do for you, love?" he asked, motioning to the bartender as he sat. The heavyset man slid a pair of water glasses in front of the pair of them wordlessly and went back to his other bartender-y work. Beth waited for Casper to take a sip of his drink before she pulled out the paper. Casper looked at it with curiosity, then grimaced at Beth.

"Aw, Luce, tell me you've got better taste than that," he said. She shrugged.

"A mother in my daughter's play group got it as an anniversary gift, and I want one," Beth said petulantly.

"If you've got a daughter, I've got a unicorn in the back room she can have," Casper said, then sighed and looked at the drawing again.

Beth waited.

"Couple'a guys do this kind of work. You want the one you want to talk to, or the one you don't want to talk to?"

"Pretend I'm not sure," Beth said. Casper looked at her a moment longer, then pulled a pen out of his pocket and wrote a name down under the sketch.

"This is the guy you want to talk to. The one you should stay away from is a guy named Petey Croft. Has a jewelry shop on Washington Street that does a pretty fair business, but he'll take as much money from you as he thinks he can get. Shop smart," Casper said, taking a deep drink of his water. Beth politely sipped hers. Casper watched her, and she raised her eyebrows at him.

"I like you," Casper said to her. "You're cute and you look me in the eye when you ask me a question. This," he said, using his index finger to push the sketch back over to Beth, "is not a tourist's game. Be careful."

Beth nodded, eyes wide with the faux ignorance she knew he could see through.

"It's just a jewelry store," she said. He grunted, then stood and walked back up to the concierge desk without looking back. Beth took her time, finishing her water, as she looked at the neat script under the pin. Petey Croft. She repeated it in her mind, feeling it out. She was dying to head straight over, but figured this might be something better chased in the morning, after she had had a night to think on it.

She looked back at the drawing of the pin, a feeling of smugness creeping over her. Plain sight didn't work so well, when she was around. She'd spotted it, and she had her thread. She could afford to take her time at it from here to make sure she didn't miss anything. She nodded to herself.

By the next morning, she had abandoned the frontal assault. She headed to the jewelry store shortly after it opened, but she wore a baseball cap and just browsed quickly, nodded at the counter attendant, then left. Nothing in the cases even vaguely resembled the cost that Dr. Wells had suggested, though Beth could see why Casper had identified the style. The jewelry that Mr. Croft was selling in his storefront was aspirational. It was intended to sell to people who wanted to look affluent, but who were so far off that they couldn't themselves tell the difference. Mayor Cromwell should not have been one of these.

Beth wandered a little way down the street, finding a friendly-enough cafe where she could sit and read a book for a few hours and inauspiciously watch who came and left the jewelry shop. She wasn't sure what she was looking for yet, but she had decided that knowing where to look was the important part right now.

It wasn't much to watch. Beth counted three customers by three, and found the store empty when she wandered past at five-thirty. The next day was much the same. She bought a specialty coffee to keep her waitress from getting testy, accumulating a twenty-five dollar tab as she carefully didn't watch the jewelry store. She pulled her university cap low over her eyes and turned pages in her novel at reasonable spaces, the full force of her will urging *something* to happen. Now.

... Now.

... Now.

The third day, her waitress was a perky redhead with frizzled curls that wouldn't stay put. After the lunch rush, as it were, the woman apparently became bored and came to sit with Beth.

"BU student?" she asked. Beth shrugged. Dressed in big enough clothes, she could pass for twenty.

"Dunno," she said. The woman frowned.

"On probation?" she asked.

"Don't really like it. My parents won't let me quit," Beth said. She had to have *some* story for showing up suddenly and drinking coffee all day for days at a time, after all.

"It's not for everyone," the woman said sagely. "My sister went for a while, but it cost too much and she was making pretty good money managing the stock room at Nieman Marcus, you know."

"Mmm," Beth said, trying to look more convincingly interested in her book. Three men had just gone into the jeweler's.

"You're just taking some time to think. They can't hold that against you," the woman said. Beth looked up at her helplessly.

"You just stick to your guns, hon. Do what's right for you. You want another coffee?" Beth eyed the jewelry store, then looked back at the waitress.

"I think just the check. Maybe I'll walk for a bit."

The woman pressed her lips together in apparent pride and nodded.

"You get everything worked out in your own head. Don't let anyone tell you what you're supposed to be," she said. Beth resisted raising her eyebrows at the woman to accelerate her, instead making a show of bookmarking her page as she snuck another glance at the jewelry store. What could three men be shopping together for at a store like that?

She slung her bag over her shoulder as the waitress returned with her check, and only glanced at the bill long enough to know that her twenty would cover it before handing it back.

"Thank you," Beth said. The woman patted her hand.

"You come back any time you need to talk," the woman told her. "You just ask for Bridgette."

Beth nodded and pulled the hat down a little lower as she navigated the tables back to the street. The three men stood out enough from normal that she wanted to get a closer look at them, even if she hadn't been trying to escape Bridgette. She glanced into the store as she breezed past it, but it was as empty as ever. She smiled to herself. Special customers. Men who did their business in the back room. They were much more likely to be the kind of men who knew about million dollar rubies than the young woman standing, as always, behind the counter gazing off into space.

Beth rounded a corner and found the most inconspicuous spot she could to watch the street without being in direct sight of the front of the shop, then crossed her fingers that the three men would continue down the street rather than returning the way they had come.

Her luck held.

About twenty minutes later, all three men walked past her. The first two were larger builds, wearing leather jackets and walking with the demeanor of stupid men who expected fear from everyone else. The third man had much more wit to his expression, as though there were a real possibility that he might have noticed Beth watching them. Beth squinted her eyes at them after they were past, then made a quick decision and followed. Two blocks later, a car pulled over and the clever man got in, while the two brutes went into a camera store. Beth crossed the street to give herself a shot at memorizing the car's license plate, then stayed as long as she dared in front of the camera store. The pair weren't long, here, but they went in to an Asian grocer three doors down from that, and Beth knew she couldn't stay any longer without risking one of them noticing her more than once.

She returned to her coffee shop the next morning to watch customers again, on the lookout for any of the three men or the car, but for a week, nothing else of interest happened.

Beth was nearly ready to abandon the entire project, Bridgette had become such a nuisance. The woman had decided that Beth needed an ally against a pushy, manipulative world, and Beth couldn't escape her advice for more than an hour or so at a stretch during the coffee shop's busiest times.

"I don't know why you waste so much money on these fancy coffees," Bridgette told her that morning. "You can just get the bottomless cup, if you want. I don't mind."

The other waitress, a sniffy college student named Linda, did mind, and Beth knew it. She shrugged at Bridgette.

"I like them," she said, flipping the page in this, her fifth novel at the coffee shop. Bridgette sat.

"Honey, life is going to get hard for you, if it isn't already. You don't need to go looking out for everybody but yourself."

Beth rubbed her forehead. Signs did not work on this woman, but the coffee shop was the best spot on the street for watching the jewelry store. There was no escaping her. Bridgette patted her knee.

"I've got a customer, but you think about that, okay?"

Beth looked tiredly up at the jewelry store, only the ragged edge of her journalistic instincts grabbing hold of what she needed to see. She sat up a little, but it took another second.

There. Down the block three or four storefronts. Leather jackets.

Beth stood, began to motion for Bridgette, then threw her book into her backpack and grabbed Linda.

"I need to go," she said, putting cash into Linda's hand as she quickly crossed the street to follow the tall pair of leather jackets the two blocks to the camera store.

And then the Asian grocer. Beth looked at her watch.

Well, they weren't prompt, but this could be a routine.

Beth hung out long enough to see the third stop on the block, then headed home. She had her next thread.

It had been three months. Beth sat in her apartment with a bottle of wine and looked over the map she was developing, spread over her desk. Absent-mindedly, she turned on the computer to her left and picked up the bottle.

It was a good map.

It met her requirements for quality, it just needed to be a part of something. It would help tell a great story, just as soon as she could figure out that part.

Turbo and Tank. She picked up the picture she had snapped of the two of them and looked at it quietly, taking a drink. It wouldn't be fair to call either one of them the brains, but Tank was the brawn, that much was clear. Beth had peeked into an alley behind a restaurant once about a week earlier, and it had looked like Turbo was picking at his fingers with a pocket knife while Tank did the hard work of extortion. Beth had seen the third man once more, but hadn't yet settled on a handle for him. He tended to look angry, but Beth was sympathetic. Tank and Turbo were only just barely motivated enough to show up and take money from their merchants a couple of times a week, and that, it appeared, only because of the promise that Tank might get a chance to hit someone. They had been back at the jewelry store once that Beth had seen, but she had started picking them up later in the route, in order to get the rest of it mapped out without attracting attention, so she couldn't be sure how central it actually was to their world.

She tapped a password into her computer and took another drink, still looking at the photo. As the modem sang, Beth walked in to the kitchen to get a bag of chips. She narrowly avoided exploding the bag, again, as she walked back and sat down to find an IM from David.

BabyBoy2317: Doritos and wine for dinner again?
AzuraThena: ...
AzuraThena: yes
AzuraThena: working late in an empty office again?
BabyBoy2317: Where else would I be?

Beth smiled to herself and turned back to her map, licking her fingers and reaching for the wine again. The computer behind her beeped, but she ignored it, looking at the map. Nothing here was pulling her forward. It seemed inconceivable that illegal activity operating out of a jewelry store that more than likely crafted a multi-million dollar piece for the mayor of a major city could be a dead end, but that's all she saw. It was a protection racket. Boring, dull, barely news on an empty page. In off days, she had shopped in the stores they visited, talked to a friend at the police office, even researched where the pair of them most likely bought their jackets, but there wasn't anything there that itched. She looked back at the computer.

BabyBoy2317: They turn up today?
AzuraThena: same as last time. waited at the park until the car picked them up.
BabyBoy2317: You sound stuck.
AzuraThena: i think i am.
BabyBoy2317: No progress on the car?
AzuraThena: too soon
BabyBoy2317: You're tearing your hair out, aren't you?
AzuraThena: little bit

There was a pause.

BabyBoy2317: I hate to even suggest it, but…
BabyBoy2317: Have you thought about chasing this from the mayor's side?
AzuraThena: what do you mean?
BabyBoy2317: You think these guys are connected to the mayor… Maybe you should be asking how she's connected back to them, instead.
AzuraThena: even i thought that was a bad idea.
BabyBoy2317: I know. It probably is. I just hate you being stuck for this long.

Beth took a long drink of the wine and looked at the cursor on the screen, then back at her map. It was such a pretty map. Thorough. It was bound to prove something convincing, eventually. This was why she was good at what she did. She would eventually find the next strand, and she would resume the chase. Without David reminding her, she would never really stop to think that she could end up stuck.

AzuraThena: you worry too much

Sure, she knew that following the mayor was probably a bad idea, but she had thought about it (and she hadn't denied it to David, technically). It was the obvious lead. The mayor was up to something; finding out what, exactly, would be much easier if Beth was digging through courthouse trash, talking to the janitors at the mayor's office, and following her chauffeur. Well, she considered, maybe it would be easier. Maybe there would be too much to find to sort out who did what. At any rate, she would have no shortage of leads. The problems were multiple, though. Point A, the mayor had security who frowned at stalkers. Sometimes they did something about them. Point B, there were lots of people watching the mayor. The odds of Beth getting caught by someone who would then start destroying leads were so high that they were almost unavoidable. Beth hated puzzling together shredded paper. It meant she was tardy. Point C, Tank and Turbo already had handles, and she was liking the direction her story was going. She wanted an awful lot for them to be involved, because men like that made good bad guys, and the more clever men they tended to work for made great bad guys. Financial scandal was certainly front page news, but Beth was due for a good villain.

BabyBoy2317: Given how little I know about what you do, I suspect that isn't remotely possible.
AzuraThena: thats why i dont tell you
AzuraThena: i want an ulcer-free editor

She still had the car. Her friend at the RMV would be at least a few more days to get a shot at the plate Beth had given him, but a car was a trackable asset. You couldn't hide who you were without being obvious that you were trying to hide, which was only more interesting. In the meantime, Beth would just have to continue to be patient. She snorted and tipped back the bottle of wine again.

Maybe it could be done. If all she did was watch.

A city government was a big thing to run, full of conflicting interests. There were at least half as many idealists as there were power-hungry megalomaniacs running around, and sometimes it's hard to tell which is which. A woman coming from outside the traditional ruling class might not have the same trusted connections from within city hall…

Beth reached for the bag of Doritos and ignored the beep on the computer.

There are two times for doing things you don't want people you don't trust to know about – behind a closed door and after hours. The closed door was probably a big enough barrier, for now, for Beth, but after hours… that held promise. A woman who didn't want her enemies to know what she was doing might be so busy watching for the enemies she knew that she didn't notice the enemy she didn't know. Or something. The bottle of wine appeared to be empty. Beth went for another.

With that and the Doritos, she reclined on the couch and thought it through. The pin had to come not only from somewhere, but from someone. Would they give it to her at her office? Beth rejected that somewhat instinctively. Paranoia liked dark corners. What would Mayor Cromwell have done that would be worth that much? Would she have been able to do it all at once, or would it be an ongoing action? Beth went and got a post-it from her desk drawer and stuck it to the bottle of wine so that she could write on it. *What can a mayor do that is worth that much money?* she wrote, and looked at it. *Building permit/zoning.* She thought. And drank. *Police.* The mayor had some voice in how police resources were allocated, certainly, but that would mostly be an affirmative voice: do this here, now, rather than don't be here, don't do that. She could get people promoted ahead of schedule, but was that worth millions of dollars? Could a strategic asset on the police force be worth that much money to someone in the city? Beth resolved to check recent promotions, as well as recently-approved building permits, but it wasn't a very good list, yet. *Cabinet.* It would take a massive ego indeed to spend that much to get into power, but it was possible. The number of people in the city with that kind of assets and high-level involvement in government seemed small enough to be worth looking at, anyway. *Future acts in another office.* Beth grimaced at this one. Proving someone had agreed to do something someday was more than tricky, and certainly Beth's patience would have run out by the time the mayor announced candidacy, ran for, and won an office. And that was overlooking that she would have to start another list of motives. She would be seriously disappointed if she had to start another list.

Beth looked hard at the list for a long time. She couldn't come up with anything else to add to it. The building permit seemed like the most likely – there was serious money there, and it was something she could do with plausible deniability, as long as no one figured out *what* the bribe was. She tapped that line with the pen, ringing the wine bottle slightly. If that were it, the deed was done, and what was needed was the legwork at city hall to find the paperwork. It was the right place to start in the morning. Quietly. But Beth's reporter instinct was for go-see-do, and she knew that her real plan was to follow the mayor tomorrow night. And the next night. Until she had a better lead. She went back to the computer.

BabyBoy2317: And I want a reporter who is in one piece.
BabyBoy2317: And knows what she's working on.
BabyBoy2317: Have you considered that you might be working on two stories, here?
BabyBoy2317: You have one coincidence between them, sure, but what if there are two stories, and you're just spinning your wheels trying to make them fit together?
BabyBoy2317: If they are separate, which one do you really want to chase?
BabyBoy2317: I'm talking to an empty chair again, aren't I?
BabyBoy2317: Listen, just be safe, okay? There will always be another story.
AzuraThena: im going to take your advice
BabyBoy2317: Wait. What?
AzuraThena: thanks for helping me think it through
BabyBoy2317: Which part are you considering advice?
AzuraThena: i need to get to bed. don't work too late.
BabyBoy2317: This is because I said there would be another story, isn't it?

Beth logged off and powered down the computer, then peeled the post-it off of the wine bottle and stuck it to the map. They went together; she knew they did. Beth would be thorough and eliminate everything on the list that wasn't related. But she would find the thread. There was always a thread.

A lot of reporters complain about paperwork. They are people people, as a rule, and would rather be out getting the story from human voices. Ones that actually talk out loud. Beth had started years ago with the same attitude, but had worked with a forensic accountant named Adam who, aside from exhibiting undiagnosed symptoms of Asbergers, was an inspiring model on how to appreciate a stack of papers. He had told her that papers, especially dusty ones, had more to say than any person, and that they would never lie to her, or forget. He saw the details on a piece of paper the way she saw a story, and at first as a discipline, and later as a passion, she had learned to appreciate them.

Not that she was as idealistic as he. People wrote paperwork, and people lied, but they at least didn't get a chance to revise and cover after she found the lie. They only got one shot at it, and she would take what she could get.

The problem with paperwork was that there tended to only be a few copies, and someone almost always wanted to know that you were looking at them, if they were of any interest at all. It was hard not to tip off the authors – the selfsame source of the lies and the coverups – and give them a chance to start eliminating anything else she hadn't looked at yet. Or anyone she hadn't yet talked to.

The only thing about her job that frightened Beth was the idea that she might get someone killed someday.

So Beth cast a wide net. She looked at franchise lawsuits all morning, and eminent domain filings for the first several hours after lunch. Only at three did she finally pull the first few building permits she wanted to look at, alongside several public park blueprints. From a quick glance at the list of filed documents, she probably had two weeks' worth of work to do to get through all of them inconspicuously.

At three thirty, she admitted to herself that her passionate appreciation of paperwork was still a lie.

At five, she returned the materials and headed out, putting her notes away in her bag. She suspected that the systematic trademark infringement by a certain group of restaurateurs would never make a large enough piece of work to justify a story for herself or anyone, but she duly noted the details and the sources, anyway. The building permits didn't turn up anything interesting.

She went and got Chinese takeout and made her way to the mayor's house, wondering for a moment if she should feel a little creepy. Stalking lowlifes was one thing. Sitting outside the mayor's house on a hunch was quite another. She shrugged and leaned over to get the camera out of her glove box. Lowlifes were lowlifes, even if they had nice titles.

The mayor got home at eight. Beth wrote down her license plate number.

Reflecting around midnight, at least Bridgette wasn't there. She was actually going to have to take up reading, if things didn't pick up soon. Beth yawned into her fist and started up the car. She scolded herself passively that she always expected things to happen on the first day. Kelly, ace politico, said that something happened every day that was worth reporting. Beth conceded that that was what made Kelly an ace, but she suspected some of the other reporters in the office who believed the same thing were prone to sensationalism to get something that qualified as a story. Then there were those who were confused as to what constituted a 'story' in the first place… There was a reason Beth only read the papers cover to cover seasonally.

Tomorrow something would happen. Beth willed it so, and the animal at the base of her skull refused to believe that her force of will wasn't enough to bring it into being.

The animal at the base of her skull was often disappointed, and only truly sated by Doritos and wine.

Nothing happened the next day. Or the next.

On the third day, Beth found a small-time scam that a building inspector was running to support what she thought she could prove in an hour's work was a gambling habit. The mayor went to a party.

On the fourth day, as Beth was resigned back to gritty discipline to make it through the stacks of city documents, she got a call at home about the black car Turbo and Tank rode in. She didn't normally check her messages three times a day, but not only had she been expecting this call; she was in deep denial about being bored out of her mind. She checked the documents back in with the clerk and headed home to call her contact.

"It's registered to a business," Gary told her. He would sometimes run searches for non-police city officials, and he would wait until a request came in that had enough characters in common with Beth's query that he could legitimately claim it was a typo. He told her once that he was sloppy with his typing everywhere to give himself credibility. Beth wondered what his boss was like.

"I'm ready," Beth said, leaning over a fresh post-it. He told her the name, and she immediately recognized it as one of the warehouses working at the docks. She raised an eyebrow and nodded. That made enough sense to make her happy, but her story had just taken a step to the complicated. A lot more questions than answers, but – she nodded decisively – these were better questions.

"Beth?" Gary asked.

"I've got it. Thanks, Gary."

She hung up and leaned on the counter for a minute longer, looking at the post-it, then shrugged. Onward.

She headed to City Hall to follow the mayor home, then sat down the street from her house again. This was the end of this, she promised herself. Better leads awaited – ones with fewer legal considerations. At eight, half a dozen well-dressed couples showed up. Beth took pictures, recognizing several of them as city corporate leaders. It was well-known that Mayor Cromwell kept company with money. The party lasted until two, at which point the mayor mysteriously... shut off the lights and went to bed. Beth wrote it down in her notebook, yawned, and headed home. Tomorrow.

The docks were so predictable she almost wanted to turn her nose up at the lead. She had been here before and the guard knew her as an art student at BU.

"Back again?" he asked as she walked up to the gate. She smiled and held up the camera.

"Hi, Gerald."

"How did you do with the stuff you shot last fall?" he asked.

"I got a really good grade on my portfolio," she said, "and someone from class asked if I wanted to be a part of a show. I'm hoping I might be able to sell some of these, this time."

Gerald handed her the clipboard.

"If you ever get famous, I want a signed picture," he said as she signed in. Ellen Craig. She had a BU ID with the name on it, though Gerald didn't ask to see it any more.

"You got it," she said and waved as she walked through the gate. The first time, she had had to wear a hard hat and stay with a chaperone to be on site, but with familiarity came complacency, and now most of the stable security guards knew her by sight. A mentor early in her career had told her that it was just like sneaking into a bar – as long as you acted like you belonged there, no one asked whether or not you did.

She ambled a little to make sure she still remembered where everything interesting was, then found an open door that lead to a stairway and another door, and she was on the roof of one of the warehouses. There really were some interesting pictures to take from up here. She glanced down at the warehouse across the street, then stood up and started shooting. She carried a bulky film camera with a fantastic lens and real capability to take good pictures, in case anyone who actually understood photography asked her a question, but she also carried a digital camera with an LCD screen and 'megapixels'. Some of the dock workers were hostile, and others patronizing or flirty, but, strangely, scrolling through miniature pictures of the dock seemed to put almost all of them off.

She glanced down at the street again, then froze.

Oddly, the tingling always started in her ears. Her breath stopped. After a moment, she remembered herself and slowly raised her camera. Her fingers tingled.

She took a picture of the mayor's car.

This was the reward good little reporters were told about in bedtime stories. She snapped the picture three times, just to be sure.

Then she zoomed out and took it again.

Mind abuzz, she settled down where she could take a steady stream of photos for the next hour. She captured everyone who so much as walked past the car, until finally, barely breathing, she took a series of pictures of a vaguely angular man she felt like she should have recognized as he escorted the mayor out to her car. Mayor Cromwell pointed a finger into his chest aggressively, and he responded with the casual carelessness of either the very powerful or the very drunk. Beth would have had a hard time putting money on one over the other.

Finally, the mayor's car drove out of sight, and Beth turned and sat down, her back against the concrete half-wall. She thought back to her winebottle post-it list. The mayor. The warehouse where a car was registered that was used by a pair of thugs taking protection money. In a photo on her camera. Why?

"... and the little twerp tried to give me the runaround, like I didn't know that he had been at the council meetings every single week while they were talking about the zoning decisions..." Kelly was saying. She frowned. "Dear Liza, I believe I'm having lunch by myself again."

"Why would the mayor think that she could get away with selling a multi-million dollar piece of jewelry without anyone noticing?" Beth asked suddenly.

"Because she found it in a lot of estate jewelry that was severely undervalued," Kelly said, taking a bite of her gyro and recrossing her legs. "If she wore it, she could even say she didn't know how much it was worth."

"I think you are in the competition for the smartest person I have ever known," Beth said. "How do you know that?"

"I am. The best. It's commonly known that she started going to estate sales and buying months ago." Kelly leaned forward. "Now, you tell me why she has a multi-million dollar piece of jewelry to sell."

Beth grinned, sipping her soda.

"You can't tell me that, too?"

Kelly shrugged and leaned back, draping her arm extravagantly across the back of her chair.

"If I did that, I'd have stolen your entire story, wouldn't I?" she said.

"Only if you can tell me who gave it to her, as well," Beth said innocently. Kelly tipped her head to the side.

"You want to go, this weekend?"

"Hmm?"

"To an auction. If you aren't going to tell me where she got it, we may as well go see her pretend to get it," Kelly said.

Beth thought about it. It was that or promotion records at the police office.

"Background research..." Kelly tempted. "I might even write a story about it, to give both of you a scare."

Beth brushed off her hands and folded up the paper from her sandwich.

"We both know you don't dredge the bottom of the barrel that badly."

"I don't dredge at all. Did you hear about the issues Aldrich is having coming up with the financial reports for his campaign office?"

And so it was settled. Beth walked back to the office with Kelly to drop off some photocopies at her desk. There was a folder of pictures that Beth had asked for from Keith the sitting there, as well, so she picked them up and headed over to the county clerk's office to continue her deep-dive on the company that owned the warehouse at the docks. Someone was playing three-card monte, there, and she was making real progress at untangling the strings, no matter how badly she wanted to go take pictures at the docks again.

By Friday night, she was ready to consider a career in cow tipping. Exciting, outdoors, and instant gratification, someone on her floor at her dorm had told her about it, and while she suspected it was a con on city kids, she'd always wanted to try. Kelly picked her up Saturday morning and they headed downtown to the auction Kelly had confirmed the mayor would be attending. Beth giggled in the passenger seat as Kelly unleashed her monthly indulgence of detailing the various rumors – factual and otherwise – of the inappropriate relationships Beth's government representatives were currently engaging.

"And you *know* that man is compensating for something," Kelly was saying.

"You know that light was red, right?" Beth asked.

"Pinkish," Kelly said. "Best guess is that his record is six different waitresses in a week. If he's ever actually successful in politics, some handler somewhere is going to be making a boatload. And her hair, Beth, it was orange."

Beth blinked innocently.

"Orange, not like, my-ancestors-lilted orange, not even orange like, can-you-guess-my-favorite-fruit orange. Orange like I-hang-out-at-sci-fi-conferences-on-the-weekends orange. You know how that would play on a front page?"

Beth covered her mouth with the back of her hand, grinning.

"And his wife! She'd split in two so that she could beat him and cut off his exit at the same time! Is 'my husband is a philandering idiot' a legal defense? Because if it isn't, 'I thought he just took a paternal interest in the careers of pretty young women' ought to be."

"If he had been at the office where he said he was, he wouldn't be dead?" Beth offered.

"I wanted to save our family from a painful divorce," Kelly rebutted.

"I killed him the same way he got her pregnant – I tripped," Beth grinned.

"It was *totally* an accident," Kelly said. "At least his wife is faithful. I'm beginning to believe the stories about Davis' wife and his lawyer. Not that I blame her. If I had to sit across a table from him for any serious period of time, I'd have to at least consider jumping him."

"Is that a fact?" Beth asked. Kelly shrugged.

"He's hot like I can't describe," Kelly said.

"You at a loss for words..." Beth said.

"I *know*. And he makes good money. He dresses the part..."

"You need a minute?" Beth asked. Kelly snorted.

"Whatever. You know what they say about lawyers."

Beth did not, in fact, know what they said about lawyers, but they had reached the parking garage, and Beth was watching the pedestrians and scouting for a parking spot.

"Did you have to dress like that?" she asked as they got out.

"Like what?" Kelly asked, her head up, scanning the crowd.

"Like Kelly K. Reporter, ace politico," Beth said, pulling a ball cap out of her backpack.

"Because I don't have a reason to not be noticed," Kelly said. "I'm upfront about my reporting."

"In-your-face, maybe?" Beth teased.

"When I want to be. But if a reporter shows up and people start acting nervous, that's when you know you've got a story worth printing. If you show up and they get excited, and you print it anyway, you're either an ambulance chaser or public interest."

Beth could see her point, especially since she'd heard it before. Kelly looked at her.

"I can pretend not to know you, if that helps," she said. Beth spotted the mayor, and pushed Kelly a step in front of her.

"Yes. Yeah. Please," she said, ducking a little. Kelly brightened, putting on her reporter face, and smiled at the mayor. Mayor Cromwell looked a little flustered, but righted herself quickly. Beth thought Kelly might have looked triumphant.

They got auction books and found a pair of seats in a crowded enough area of the seating to excuse them – complete strangers – from having to sit in adjacent seats, but with enough space to have empty chairs on both sides. Mayor Cromwell sat in the front row.

And the auction started.

First up was a clock. Then there was a moped. And a set of golf clubs.

Beth flipped through the book.

"This is just someone's old stuff," she said.

"Mmm," Kelly replied. "Most things are. Look, dear, she's bidding to impress me."

"Where are the paintings?"

"This is an estate sale," Kelly said. "They mostly sell old people's stuff here, not collector items."

Beth looked up at Kelly, who was in full hawk-attack mode watching the mayor.

"Why do you know that?"

"We've all wondered why she comes. She's not an aficionado of anything in particular. People talk," she said vaguely.

Beth settled in and focused. There was certainly an ebb and flow to the bidding, and the mayor had clearly participated before.

"That's a nice miter saw," she murmured. Kelly snorted softly.

Personal items were late in the auction, and Beth presumed that Mayor Cromwell would be most interested in those, so she quietly sneaked her notes out of her backpack. The folder of photos was still new. She slid them out and started paging through them.

"Oooh!" Kelly said, leaning over.

"Pay attention," Beth scolded, flipping to the next shot.

"She's bidding at random," Kelly said.

"She's unsettled. This is her greatest hope – that you, an upstanding member of the press, will be able to verify that she did indeed buy a lot of random jewelry at an estate sale. She's got to make a buy today, no matter how she likes the jewelry that's for sale."

"So?" Kelly asked.

"You need to actually witness it – her buying random jewelry to cover her tracks. It backs up my story," Beth said.

Kelly looked down at her, bemused.

"She needs me to back up her story and you need me to back up yours, despite the fact that they're completely at odds."

Beth shrugged.

"Your style of journalism is insane," Kelly told her. Beth smiled to herself, flipping another photo.

"Oh, for heaven's sake," Kelly hissed. "Why aren't you out stalking *them*? They look much more interesting."

Tank and Turbo. Beth shrugged to herself. They were more interesting.

Why wasn't she out stalking them? she wondered.

Because she didn't know who they were yet, she answered.

So?

Yeah, so?

She waited for a third voice to chime in and play the voice of reason, but none did.

"You ever see them before?" she asked impulsively. Kelly looked down harder at the photo, then shook her head.

"If they looked like that, I think I'd remember," she said.

"How long do these things last?" Beth asked after a minute. Kelly grinned, and twisted her hand so that Beth could see her book.

"We're still on page one," she said.

"That was the longest four hours of my life," Beth said, dropping her seat back and combing her fingers through her hair. Kelly shrugged.

"Try city council meetings," she said. She looked at Beth slyly. "How much did the stationary bike go for?"

"Thirty-five dollars to the man without any hair," Beth said. Kelly grinned and twisted in her seat to back out of the parking spot.

"And somehow when you tell it again in your story, it will be the most fascinating little detail dropped into a riveting story, and everyone will wish that they had as cool a life as you," Kelly said. Beth shrugged, pulling on her hat again and pulling it low over her eyes.

"It's a gift."

"It's something," Kelly replied. "You want to get some lunch?"

"I should probably get back to work," Beth told her. "Thanks for going with me."

"All work and no play..." Kelly said ominously, holding out a second chance.

"It's all play, no matter what I say about it," Beth admitted. "And I really should get back to it."

"You have a new lead?" Kelly asked.

"I know what I'm going to do next," Beth answered. Kelly nodded.

"Heaven forbid I get in the way of that..." she paused. "Who was that guy, anyway? He was kind of hot."

"He's so not your zip code," Beth said, laughing. Kelly shrugged expansively, holding a hand palm-up in the air.

"So? Change of clothes, a few more teeth, he could be downright presentable."

"The big one or the little one?" Beth asked. Kelly wrinkled her nose.

"The big one," she said as though it were obvious.

"You'd do better dating a bag of rocks – for conversation and etiquette," Beth told her.

"I've never tried that," Kelly said, thinking. "Ramifications?"

"I'm not sure I want to start on that," Beth said, grinning and turning her gaze out the window. She'd give herself the rest of the weekend to crack the warehouse owners, then Monday she was going to catch up with Tank and Turbo there and follow them out. They had to have lives outside of extortion – maybe that was where her next thread lay.

"Well, I could never take it to meet my parents, and my priest wouldn't approve, but talk about being able to go all night..." Kelly began.

She had hit the coffee-shop portion of her story.

It was late coming, but she finally had enough details to cogitate and enough tasks to keep straight that she found it useful to get up and walk down to the coffee shop down the street from her apartment and spend forty-five minutes drinking coffee and sorting things out. Often enough, it was just a matter of putting the wine-jumbled thoughts from the night before into an order that would be easier to remember. Any more, if she were at her computer trying to do this, she'd end up signing online out of habit and spend the morning talking to David and Kelly and Elliot, the weird guy she had met in a chatroom eighteen months before.

Elliot. She wrinkled her nose and smiled at the thought. She kept promising herself he was going to be useful, one of these days, but she knew she was just amused at talking to a twenty-three year old from Maine who was perpetually baked out of his mind and slept even less than Beth did.

She took her seat at the booth where she sat each morning and spread her notes out in front of her.

"Hi, Carol," the cashier called.

"Morning, Steve," Beth answered the boy.

She yawned and picked up a page of notes to scan as he made her coffee and brought it over along with the change for the $5 she was going to give him. Lazy and efficient are just a matter of perspective.

It was definitely time to follow Tank and Turbo. For as tedious as it had been, she now had a full story on the mayor. She had taken a bribe and planned to cover it by claiming luck at auction. Anything about what she had done for the bribe and who she had gotten it from could come just as easily from the other side of the relationship, and that was what Beth wanted – she was sure of it. More of the mayor's side of the story would just be politics. She nodded, putting down the page on the mayor and picking up one on the warehouse.

Ownership had been too hard to track down for it to be a law-abiding business, that much she was sure of. The fact that a pair of budding entrepreneurs were running a racketeering gig out of it seemed to scream that the warehouse belonged to people of a certain type, but Beth rejected the obvious until she could prove it.

Okay. Really, she didn't.

She just didn't write it down.

She had a lead on the mafia.

Her toes tingled as she looked at the yellow paper in her hand.

On paper, the warehouse was held by a long-defunct company that had declared bankruptcy five years prior. The note was held by a private lending company that had apparently overlooked foreclosure proceedings, and so the warehouse sat empty and forgotten.

In theory, anyway.

A warehouse, in Beth's deep and extensive knowledge of such things, should have trucks coming and going, picking up and delivering goods in such quantities that would justify the massive expanse of space that the structure protected from the elements. The elements being mainly thieves, of course.

This warehouse, though, acted like it was a parking lot to a small fleet of non-descript black sedans and one yellow Corvette. She would go back today and get pictures of all of them. She didn't ever see the drivers, but she would find her way into the warehouse, at some point. The connection was in that warehouse, and Tank and Turbo were her ticket in.

She sipped her coffee and put it back on the table, chewing a fingernail as she looked at the warehouse paperwork. She realized she was smiling. This was the top of the first hill of the roller coaster. Every reporter instinct in her body was certain of it.

Given that all of the sedans had tinted windows, Beth wasn't really sure what she was going to do to track down Turbo and Tank once they arrived.

She checked her watch. It was Tuesday, and given the driving distance... She did some quick math. The problem was, they weren't particularly reliable for when they were going to show up to start their cycle. Finishing it was worse yet. Some days, they'd sit at the park at the end of their rounds for more than an hour before the car came to get them; other days the vehicle would be waiting with the doors open and the driver leaning against it impatiently.

Somewhere in Beth's notes was written 'Turbo likes ice cream.'

She had just gotten settled, sitting against the roof wall to wait, when she heard an engine on the road below her. She turned and knelt at the wall, peering over it.

A truck had just pulled up.

A real honest-to-goodness shipping truck, with a shipping container on it.

She pulled out her camera and zoomed in on it, photographing the driver, the container, the wheels of the truck, whatever struck her. After a few minutes, the wide bay doors on the side of the warehouse opened and a large forklift came out. Another man followed it, signing the clipboard the driver handed him (Beth snapped shots of both men), then the container slowly trundled into the warehouse, a car slid out, the truck pulled away, and the doors jerked unsteadily back down to the ground.

Beth wondered if the most interesting part of her whole day was over.

"Lady! Hey, lady! You can't be up here!" a voice called behind her. Beth jerked.

"What?" she said, standing and turning, her heart rate jumping. A man in a grey security guard's uniform was climbing over the wall from the fire escape stairs. Relief flooded her body as she realized it was the building owner who had discovered her — not someone from across the street.

"This is restricted. Private property. You can't be up here," he said, approaching her with a not-unfriendly gait.

"But the skyline," Beth said, holding up the camera. "It's so pretty."

"I'm sorry, lady, but you can't be up here," he said.

"You said that," she said, smiling. "Gerald lets me in. I'm a photography student."

The guard looked skeptical.

"Doesn't matter, miss. It's dangerous for you to be up here. You need to come back down with me."

Beth looked back over her shoulder, keeping her head level with the skyline, but glancing down at the street level, again. Rats.

"Okay, okay. I'll come willingly," she said, putting her hands up playfully. The man rolled his eyes.

"Nothing personal, lady," he said, turning back to the stairway.

Beth's mind was racing. She couldn't make a scene; she didn't want anyone across the street knowing she had been here, but she didn't want to lose her chance to track Turbo and Tank when they got back from their route. She probably wouldn't even risk coming back here – having caught her once, the long arm of the law was going to be keeping an eye out for her. She sighed and snagged her backpack.

She still hadn't come up with a plan by the time the guard deposited her on the front sidewalk. She pulled her hood up as soon as he closed the metal door and started walking, just to be away from where the warehouse across the street could see her.

A block down, she finally looked up again, and nearly had to physically restrain herself from smacking herself in the forehead.

Tank and Turbo were getting into a cab halfway up the block going the other direction. Impulsively, Beth threw up an arm and dodged into the road, bringing another taxi to an un-amused stop. She dove in and the driver turned, clearly annoyed.

"I'm with them, but the jerks decided to leave without me before they told me where we were going," she said, shifting to get off of her backpack. The woman sighed and switched off her light. Better than 'follow that cab,' Beth thought. She stashed the cameras into her backpack and then leaned forward to make sure that the other taxi didn't leave them behind. How had they gotten out without her seeing them? Four walls, Beth reminded herself. Obviously there were other doors she couldn't see.

Less than ten minutes later, they were back downtown, and the other taxi pulled over.

"This is fine," Beth said hurriedly. "I want to surprise them."

The driver sighed again, and looked back at her.

"Six dollars," she said. Beth handed her a ten and got out, tempted to keep her head low. She got to the sidewalk without doing anything too spy-like and waited for the taxi to pull away before she slowly approached Tank and Turbo. They were talking to a couple of guys standing against a building, then ducked into a dimly-lit neighborhood bar. Beth waited a minute, then followed, leaving her hood up, but not pulled all the way forward. She shoved her hands into her pockets and went to sit at the bar. Tank and Turbo were sitting at a well-populated booth in the back.

"Help you?" the bartender asked, eying her with a slight bartender-ish suspicion.

"Bud Lite," she said, glancing up at the murky mirror behind the bar.

"Draft or bottle?" he asked.

"Bottle."

He clanked it onto the bar and popped the cap off, then stood looking at her. Beth eyed him back.

"What?"

"Two dollars," he said, sucking on a tooth, then smiling when she didn't blink. "All right, then."

She took the bills out of her pocket and put them on the bar, retreating with her drink to the far end of the bar.

It was turning fall, and the days were getting shorter, but even so, the sun hadn't set yet. Regardless, Tank and Turbo were drinking like they might run out of time. Beth watched quietly, leaning against the wall and crossing her legs as she drank her beer. Maybe thirty minutes later, the bartender brought her another bottle, and Beth settled in.

"You're new here," a woman said, throwing herself onto the next stool. Beth tipped the bottle in her hand back and set it on the bar.

"So?" she asked. The woman laughed too loudly.

"You don't go here," she said. Beth shrugged.

"Free country," she muttered, sinking into her hood as she evaluated the woman. Was this too much attention, or was this a source of information? She reeked of alcohol and her lipstick was streaked up nearly to her nose. Beth glanced quickly and found the matching mark on the back of the woman's hand.

"I'm Aly," the woman told her, slapping the bar.

"Go home, Aly," the bartender called from the other end of the bar.

"The night's young, Sid!" she yelled back, laughing again.

Beth picked up her beer and motioned to the back booth with it.

"I saw that guy at the park earlier today, and then I saw him here, and thought I'd go for it. He's hot, don't you think?" she prompted.

40

Aly wrinkled her nose, considering dramatically.

"Which one?"

"Leather jacket… the big guy," Beth said. Aly waved dismissively.

"Patrick? No, no… You can't get with that, anyway, but you picked the wrong one. You want Jess, the other one. He's… No," Aly said, turning back to Beth. "You go over there, they'll laugh at you. Always do, me. No, you want a gentleman, you talk to them."

Aly pointed dramatically, her arm straight, at a table on a side wall. A group of older men were sitting quietly hunched over their drinks. Even with the dim light of the bar confused with the long, orange beams of the setting sun, Beth could see dramatic scars on many of them. A couple looked up at Aly, but most ignored her.

Benign.

"Aren't they a little old?" Beth asked, digging a bit. Aly put her nose up.

"Refined. The young punks over there… You know, I used to go with Jacob, over there, and they used to…" Her eyes glazed a bit for a minute. Beth watched her, taking another drink of her beer. Why was it, again, that her stories tended to go places that people drank beer and scotch rather than wine and cocktails?

Because she wasn't Kelly, that's why, she thought. Shrugged slightly to herself. It made sense.

"You think I'm kidding?" Aly asked, coming back. Beth raised her eyebrows. "I'm not kidding. They're no joke. You see for yourself."

Aly stood and pitched toward the door, then changed her mind and headed back toward the end of the bar where the bartender was talking to a skinny man wearing a beat up hat. Gambler, Beth diagnosed. She sipped her beer.

A few minutes later, the bartender came back.

"You want another?"

Beth shook her head.

"Early to be that drunk," she said, motioning at Aly.

"She's harmless. Been mostly that way since her old dad died few years back." The man looked at her for a moment. "You look like a nice kid. Finish your beer and head out. This isn't a place where nice kids should hang out."

Beth shrugged, but did as he asked, taking her time to finish the beer, and heading out into deepening dusk.

She'd have to take her time to make her way in with Tank and Turbo. In the meantime, she wanted to go back to the warehouse. She wanted to see if she could scout the rest of the building. Maybe there was an opportunity to sneak in and take a look around after everyone left.

The sun had finally finished setting as Beth got out of a taxi a couple of blocks down from the warehouse. She cut back behind the buildings, furtively watching for anyone who would identify her as out of place. She pulled her hood all the way forward as she slunk along the back side of the warehouse two doors down.

Suddenly, it sunk in what she was doing. Her heart raced, and she wasn't certain whether it was fear or excitement causing the greater part of it. She paused, to collect her thoughts.

She was sneaking up on a building that she was reasonably sure was owned by a mafia family.

With the intention of sneaking into it, if she could.

Her heart dropped two inches in her chest and rebounded.

This was the story of a career.

Maybe.

She leaned against the building, mostly involuntarily.

She should consider the value of her own life before she did this, she knew.

But she leaned forward, trying to see down the dark alley further, and then took another few steps forward, as though drawn downhill.

Her heart felt like a squeezed fruit, and she wasn't sure if she was breathing. But she was grinning.

She darted another few feet, wishing there was more moonlight and less cloud cover.

Halfway down the next building, a service door had a single light bulb spilling a small pool of orange light onto the littered ground of the alley. Beth had to avoid looking at it to pick her way through the trash and debris that had accumulated behind the warehouse. A long building ran along to her left, and she hugged against it as she passed the lamp, feeling exposed. She wouldn't want that behind her, making her a silhouette, she thought, feeling her chest squeeze again.

She couldn't quite see the corner of the next building, *the* warehouse, yet, and she moved forward again, listening hard. Around her, the normal sounds of night in a city could barely compete with the sound of her heartbeat.

An engine turned up the alley between the two warehouses, and Beth nearly sat all the way down in her effort to be inconspicuous. A white van stopped and a trio of men in uniforms got out, then started pulling equipment out of the back. Beth eased forward, pressing her lips together, eyes never leaving the men as they worked.

Another few yards along, she could read the side of the van, and she turned back, picking her way back through the trash, ready to go find her car again.

Apparently the mafia were just like the rich. If you want to learn their secrets, you ask the cleaning staff.

Beth pulled her hair up and through her baseball cap, then walked into the cleaning service's economical front lobby. A man speaking on a phone motioned a greeting to her, then indicated one of three chairs against a wall. Beth sat and picked at her nails until he hung up.

"Can I help you?" he asked.

"I'm looking for a job," Beth said, standing.

"Not interested," the man answered. Busy, no nonsense, and authorized. Beth glanced at the floor then back up at him.

"No, I really need this job," Beth insisted, going to sit in the chair in front of his desk. He looked at her with uncompelled eyes.

"So?"

"It means I'd work really hard," Beth said, trying to gauge the right pace. Charity or greed? "And... um... You wouldn't have to pay me that much..."

The man raised an eyebrow.

"You ever done industrial cleaning before?"

"No," Beth answered truthfully. "But I learn really fast."

"You wouldn't be worth anything I'd pay you," the man said, and opened a drawer, pulling out a ledger. He glanced up at her. "We're done."

"Please," Beth said, emphasizing the hunger of the word. "Give me a chance."

43

"What's your name?"

"Anne."

"Where did you hear about us, Anne?" he asked, leaning on his crossed forearms.

"Um…" she said.

"We clean industrial spaces. Where did you hear about a company that cleans warehouses and manufacturing facilities?"

Beth looked at her hands. She hadn't prepared an answer for that, and one didn't seem to be forthcoming. In retrospect, that might have been an oversight.

"My uncle…" she started. He shook his head.

"Don't. You heard that we clean for mobsters and thought that would be sexy. Maybe you'd catch Edmond's eye, sexy maid and all that, while he's at one of his all-night poker matches at the warehouse. No. Get out of my office and go get a waitressing job," he said, turning back to his ledger. Beth sat for a moment, a little stunned.

"I didn't know that," she said, her surprise coming across quite well as sincerity.

The man looked up at her from under his eyebrows, not un-hunching from the ledger.

"Then you don't belong here. Girls around here are always looking for a way to get attention from Edmond. You look like a nice girl. You've got a pretty face. Get yourself away from here," he said, then muttered something under his breath that Beth didn't catch.

When he didn't look up again, Beth finally stood and walked out, headed for a nearby park where she could buy herself an early lunch from a street vendor.

While that certainly hadn't gone well, she had learned a couple of important things. One, she had been right about the mob. Check one off for reporter insight into the obvious. Two, the warehouse stood a reasonably good chance of being occupied at night, and she was going to get herself killed if she wasn't careful. She took a bite of her gyro and nodded. Check one off for astoundingly bad reporter insight into the obvious. Third, there was a guy named Edmond who was important.

She chewed thoughtfully.

She was pretty sure she should know what Edmond the cleaner had been referring to, but her keen reporting mind was apparently not the steel trap she had grown to expect. 'Over her head' really did exist. She took another bite and thought it through. She didn't have the good sense to be afraid, she knew, but she had been... what, wound up? Nervous? Anxious? It might have been fear, but here she sat in a park with a lettuce burrito, like nothing had happened.

Usually she was at least a little more careful.

She wrinkled her nose at the gyro. She was frustrated. Her leads were converging, and her instinct was to push it. She was going to have to watch that.

Going back to the bar had been on her list for tonight, if she wasn't going to be able to get into the warehouse, but she finished her lunch and nodded resolutely. She was going back to her desk, she was going to get her notes updated, and she was going to stay away from the bar for at least three days while she tried to figure out who Edmond was.

Two.

She made it at least two days.

She'd caught Kelly on her way out to lunch and thought, what the heck. She had the metabolism for two lunches.

She'd sat with appropriately wide-eyed interest while Kelly recounted the scandal of the morning, then casually dropped into conversation: "Can you list the Edmonds of note in the city?"

Kelly's jaw dropped and she slammed the front two legs of her chair down to lean across the table.

"Make me the happiest woman in this restaurant *including* that hostess who just came back from the coatroom with the... seriously muscle-bound busboy... he does look like fun..." she paused, then looked back at Beth again. "... and tell me that you are investigating Edmond Hughes, only son of James Michael Hughes."

Jimmy Hughes was a name Beth absolutely did know. She even recognized him, in the face of his son, flipping through her photos after she had made Kelly swear not to tell David, and ran out of the restaurant as casually as she could. There he was, Jimmy

Hughes, drunk, twenty-three years old, and called 'Edmond' in a photo with the mayor.

"Beth," she had said sternly under her breath. "You're slipping."

Which left the impossible three-day oath.

She had snuck into city hall for no real good reason she could come up with, wandering around and simply seeing things to keep her mind from racing about too frantically. Act like you belong there and carry a huge stack of files, and people will open doors for you anywhere. Even city government.

That burned a good three hours, so Beth headed home, determined not to get herself killed *tonight*, and spent the rest of the evening talking to Elliott. David had signed on for a few minutes, but he was busy, so beyond discerning that Kelly had refrained from telling him anything about Edmond, Beth let him be. She drank her wine, ate her Doritos, and went to bed early.

And didn't sleep.

She'd woken up. She'd gone to get her coffee, then went to sit over land grants all afternoon, but as the sun started to set, she found herself standing outside the bar again in a giant hoodie, inspecting the three skinny men standing outside. She thought about trying to bum a cigarette to establish rapport, but these didn't look the type. She shuffled past them and took the same seat at the bar instead, and ordered a beer from the same bartender. He snorted through one nostril, but otherwise refrained from comment.

She watched.

She listened.

Patterns were beginning to form by the time she took her third beer to a more out-of-the-way booth. Like most places where men routinely gathered to drink, there was a social order here that was only just held together. The older men thought that the younger men were idiots – they were – and the younger men thought the older men pretentious and stuck in the past. Beth hadn't formed an opinion there, yet.

A figure in black swept across the bar, a long, matte black jacket almost radiating shadow. A large black hat suggested the figure was a woman, but the jacket didn't give anything away. Beth watched with disguised interest as the bar fell silent. Aly slipped off of the bar stool three down from where the jacket had sat down, and, casting around for a friendly place to land, came to sit across from Beth. She gave no sign of recognizing Beth, but had no more aversion than the first time.

"Who is that?" Beth asked. Aly's eyes got wide as she dramatically didn't look at the woman at the bar. She shook her head. Beth gathered she wasn't supposed to look.

"That's His Dark Mistress," Aly hissed too loudly. The head turned slightly in recognition, but couldn't be bothered to twist far enough to see Beth and Aly. Beth sat deeper into the booth, staring at the woman's back, her tongue playing over her back teeth

Did the Easter Bunny drink here, too? Or just Jack the Ripper?

"No," Beth said softly. "She doesn't exist."

The silence in the bar called her a liar. Aly's eyes got wider. Beth shrugged.

"Myth," she said. "Someone everyone knows but no one's seen? Not possible."

Aly's head shook back and forth slowly

People didn't talk about His Dark Mistress. Reporters didn't write about her. She didn't exist, but somehow everyone knew that she did.

It was overstepping to say that everyone knew who she was – no one did, in point of fact, but the new gravitational center of the bar testified that while no one knew who she was, they *all* knew that *this was her.*

Beth only knew a few things about His Dark Mistress, and most of them involved how literally everyone was afraid of her. She was like the grown up version of the naughty child's imaginary scapegoat. When someone turned up missing, His Dark Mistress might have done it. When someone turned up dead and there were no promising leads, His Dark Mistress had probably done it. According to legend, she killed at whim, and had a massive temper.

And, yet, the bartender knew what she drank.

"She's imaginary," Beth whispered. Aly's poor eyes hadn't dropped back, yet. She just continued to shake her head. Mythical creatures don't just order a beer. They don't sit at the bar and drink it. That's not how things work, in the real world.

Slowly dredging the bar with her eyes, Beth wondered if she had left the real world.

She looked back at the back of His Dark Mistress and consoled herself that she'd gotten a piece of it right. Mythical creatures didn't order beer. They ordered whiskey.

Slowly, the demeanor of the bar had lightened, and conversation had returned. Beth sat, holding an empty beer bottle, and watched the tables come back to life in fits and starts. At first, every time His Dark Mistress lifted or sat down her glass, the bar silenced again, but eventually, even small humanoid motions – a sigh, shifting her weight from one hip to the other, a small foot twitch – were tolerated. Even the boisterous table of younger thugs – Tank and Turbo at one end – was reasonably subdued. The older men hunched lower over their drinks.

Outside, a scuffle of feet was enough to draw disproportionate attention, then suddenly Aly leapt up. Beth nearly dropped her beer.

"You want another one?" Aly asked too loudly. "I'm going to have another."

The entire bar froze as Aly looked at Beth. The dark head at the bar dropped slightly, listening. Beth froze solid. Aly shrugged.

"She hasn't killed anyone yet. She isn't going to. She's just here to drink," she announced, meandering back over to the bar and signaling two fingers to the bartender. Beth waited, but Aly didn't bring the second beer back. Instead the too-skinny woman wormed her way onto a stool and apparently lost her train of thought looking at herself in the mirror.

Another minute was plenty. Beth left her beer bottle on the table and headed out onto the street.

A couple of the guys at the door sniggered at her, more bold with more alcohol, but she made her way to the curb, feigning looking for a cab. Her car was parked six or seven blocks away, off the main road. She wouldn't expect to find a cab that quickly this time of night, anyway, so she set off toward her car.

Three blocks down, she turned off the well-lit streetfront and down a darker alley, pulling up her hood to appear as ambiguous as possible. Well-versed street training on how to avoid interest was instinctive now. Walk with a strong gait – not drug- or alcohol-

HIS DARK MISTRESS

addled – but without a direct, purposeful direction. People with purpose had money. Head up, but not visible, hands pulling the hoodie down and out slightly to disguise the size of her body. Watch the ground, not eye-level, to avoid eye contact with people who would find it a challenge. Her worn shoes and slightly hunched shoulders would get her past most anyone without a problem. She only carried a handful of bills this late at night, anyway, in case she did get mugged. Hand it all over and keep walking.

A full block off the main street, standing under a small lit doorway at an unused intersection, something triggered an animal instinct and she stopped walking. A glass bottle clinked off to her right. She pushed her face forward in the hood to get more peripheral vision, but the gray darkness was unforgivingly useless. She put her foot over the curb to step down and cross the street, when a soft voice behind her jolted her upright.

"Don't turn, don't move. We don't have much time," the voice said. Beth fell the six inches to the asphalt straight-legged and off-balance. Something in the voice had a sinewy seriousness that her primeval mind had no choice but to obey. It would take a solid, conscious effort to turn, and Beth didn't muster it.

"Every word. Remember every word if you want to live. Understand?" There was a pause. "Nod."

Beth did so, her heart shaking her ribcage. There was a sound of bird taking flight somewhere. Her eyes jerked up, looking for it, without her neck giving at all. Her teeth were clamped against each other.

"When you fall, fall knees, hips, shoulders. Cover your face with your arms. Don't!" the voice commanded as Beth's head inched around. "You'll wake in a room with no doors, and you will fear for your life. The less you are able to tell them, the longer you will live. Do what you must to survive."

Now, Beth heard footsteps.

"I am coming for you. That is why you will live. I am coming."

There was a flutter of heavy cloth, and Beth spun. The small pool of light behind her was empty, but she heard more footsteps behind her. Heavy steps. Men's boots. A figure came free of the corner of the building across the street, and a short man in glasses approached Beth. Beth backed up onto the curb, something deep in the palms of her hands tremoring, even as her her reporter's mind squinted at the man. He was familiar. His face split in a grin and he nodded exaggeratedly putting up an open hand even with his shoulder, some hybrid of a wave and a 'stop' signal to anyone behind him. Something bit Beth's chest, and she thought that she had been shot. Her heart shrugged and her chest caved involuntarily in pain and surprise. She put her hands to her chest and tried to find the hole, but her fingers were numb. Her weight was too far forward, but her feet felt heavy and too big as she tried to step forward to correct. Something whispered *knees, hips, shoulders* and her arms flew up toward her head, a combination of poor balance and self-defense, as the dark pavement came up at her face.

That was all.

She was breathing. The sound of air rushing back and forth through her nasal cavity filled her head as though her ears were plugged. The terror of her last moments rushed back and her body jolted, trying to protect itself from the unknown, but her wrists and ankles were locked and her body was against something hard. The animal in her mind thrashed again, and she shook her head, trying to see where she was. Her mouth was sealed shut, and her breaths became louder as panic laid hold of her.

Cloth ripped along her face, and her hair flew up with it, thousands of points of sensation lit up along her scalp, bewildering her. She tried to yelp as a cluster of hair at the top of her head pulled out, and suddenly light hit her eyes.

It was much too much light. Her brain was still fuzzy and dense with unconsciousness, and she thrashed backwards against it, closing her eyes hard.

"Who are you?" a calm voice asked. Her body convulsed in surprise and the gasp that should have come out of her mouth choked her instead. The tape over her mouth was ripped off, and Beth whimpered at the instinctive desire to comfort the skin with her hand. She pulled at her wrists again, but they didn't move enough to suggest they would wiggle free if she pulled harder. She was held tight. She forced herself to look up. Her conscious mind was waking up, and she was certain she thought she was stronger than this.

"Who are you?" the voice asked again. It belonged to a slight man in jeans and a gray dress shirt. Beth shook her head.

"I don't know."

It was the truth, in that moment. She didn't know who he thought she was, or who she had said she was, or what he thought – or knew – she had done. A heavy-set man in black pants and a dark jacket detached himself from the wall and took two steps to where Beth was tied to a chair and hit her, all in one motion. Backhanded. Insulting, but painful enough to make the point just as well as a fist would have. Beth's head cracked back, her jaw hitting her shoulder, and her vision dotted with electric yellow and black spots. The man in the gray shirt sighed.

"If you break her, I can't ask questions," he said. "Patience, Will."

Gravity pulled Beth's chin against her chest as she wrestled with reality. The spots cleared at the center of her vision first, and slowly retreated. This wasn't possible. She hadn't even done anything particularly dangerous, yet. She'd done so many risky things before and nothing had gone this wrong. Didn't that mean it couldn't?

She looked back up at the gray shirt, her fuzzy brain still confused. What did he want? How could she possibly be this interesting? No one ever actually saw her, but he was looking *at her*. He crossed his arms. She shook her head, trying to clear... everything. The chair, the room, the man. They weren't there. It wasn't possible. He still looked at her.

"Who are you?"

"Beth," Beth answered. The man in the gray shirt looked to his right, where, Beth saw, the man with the glasses was standing. The interrogator looked unimpressed. The man in the glasses shrugged.

"She was at the auction, city hall, and the bar. You draw the lines," the man in the glasses said. The man in the gray shirt sighed again and looked back at Beth, the clear muscles in his forearms shifting slightly.

"Care to explain it?" he asked. Beth looked around.

"This room hasn't got any doors," she said, tipping her head to look behind her. She was becoming hysterical, a sense of unreality blooming low in her chest and making her legs tingle. It couldn't possibly be real.

The man in the gray shirt tipped his head at her and blinked.

"Why were you at city hall?" he asked.

"Can't fight it..." Beth said, a random neuron firing and trying to find the other half. "Join it?"

The man in the gray shirt dropped one eyelid and rolled his eyes.

"Hit her again, Will."

The same landslide of motion punched her in the stomach.

That was pretty real.

Her body seized and her breath stopped and she felt her eyes bug out as she tried to recover. Her ears rung and finally she hung limp from her shoulders, tears running down her face involuntarily as she pulled the first breath back into her body.

Very real.

I am coming for you.

In something that almost felt like a physical wind, the room and the men in front of her became a clear reality.

Other people had sat here. The floor showed signs of half-heartedly cleaned blood, and the table the man in the gray shirt was leaning against was covered with glittering steel. Small, steel tools. And a room with no doors.

They could ask her questions for as long as they wanted. She wasn't going to get away, and they had all the time in the world to inflict pain and make her regret silence or lies.

The burden of that would have been immeasurable, Beth knew, but... *I am coming for you.* She looked at the man in the gray shirt. He was reading the clear consciousness in her eyes, and, there, in that tiny muscle twitch under his eye, that was pleasure at the reality she was taking in. Even with a promise... She looked around again. *There weren't any doors.*

"Tell me what I want to know," the man in the gray shirt said, his voice even softer. This was a soft, gentle promise. An offer of peace and mercy. He pushed off from the table and knelt in front of her. He showed her a gun, the same glittering steel as the rest of the tools on the table. "This is easy." He shook his head. "You close your eyes, and then... nothing. That's all."

He stood. His eyes kept hers, pleading for her to take his mercy. *This is your best interest,* they said. *I care about you.*

I am coming for you.
Beth looked down.
Do what you must to survive.
What was her life worth to her? She looked at the table, then up at the man and sighed.
She pressed her lips together in an apologetic smile, and he nodded.
"I understand."

He stood silently behind the table, his fingertips brushing the implements.
"I'm no sadist," he said, but the affection in his eyes called him a liar. "All I want from you is what I need to know. I don't want your pain. When we're done, it will be over. I make you that promise."
"Just so that we're clear," Beth said, wishing she had cleared her throat first for the huskiness of her voice, "what is it precisely that you need to know?"
He looked up, his face showing pleasure that surprised her.
"Everything. When all three of us are convinced that you've told us everything interesting that you know, then I will give you death," he said. Beth internally wrinkled her nose at that, trying to keep her face still. There was serious illness under that calm, gentle face. He enjoyed pain, she was sure, but he enjoyed fear more. Power. *No doors.* How many people had opened their eyes in this room to this man? There was no way out, there was no way to overpower all three of them. They would be offered two choices: a fast, painless death, or a drawn-out, excruciating end, and regardless of the one they chose, they would die screaming that they had said everything they knew. The man's face was placid, still looking at his tools. She squirmed, feeling ill, and found that she hadn't yet realized that her hips were bound, too.
He looked up, as though he had finished collecting his thoughts and picked up a coil of wire from the table.
"Pain isn't that complicated a thing," he said. "What makes it so… powerful is the anticipation of it. So I like you to be able to watch what I'm doing."
He paused in front of her.

"This is piano wire," he said, holding it up. "Nothing particularly gruesome about it. It's relatively soft, as wire goes, but it's plenty strong enough to go through tissue, especially at this thickness."

He paused, kneeling next to her, and looked up. Beth found herself transfixed by the genuine concern in his eyes.

"I need you to be very still after I put this around your wrist. I'm going to untie your hands, but if you pull against it too hard, it will go right through your skin and sever the veins and arteries in your wrist like they weren't there. Okay?"

Beth nodded, her stomach coiling with the threat of vomit. Her skin felt cold.

She felt the wire loop around her wrist and draw tight – too tight – and then felt his warm fingers on her forearm.

"Okay," he said gently, "I'm going to move your arm now. Just move with me."

He brought her arm around the back of the chair and placed it palm-up on the arm of the chair, then looped the wire around her wrist and the chair arm once and twisted the end in a knot. With practiced, methodical motions, he did the same at her elbow and below her shoulder. Doing the same to her other arm, he stepped back.

"So. Now you get to watch me work. You need to be still, though, because that will go through to the artery at your wrist pretty quickly. At the elbow you've got a little more room before something really bad happens, and, well, the bicep just hurts a lot. You don't want to cut that open if you don't have to."

He returned to the table and picked up a blade. It was an elegant little piece of metal, a handle and long, flat blade formed from a single piece.

"If you decide to try to bleed out on purpose, I should warn you: it won't happen fast enough. I'll put a tourniquet on it before you can bleed out, and then you'll just have to watch your hand die." He paused and grimaced a fraction. "It smells really bad after a couple of days."

Beth gagged, and looked at her hands. He nodded, and put his hand on her shoulder.

"Last chance," he said.

I am coming for you.

"I publish as E. Stanton," she said, her eyes unable to pull away from the blade that the man in the gray shirt held carelessly between two fingers, resting against her skin. He drew in his breath and smiled widely – she could hear it. He came and knelt in front of her. And waited.

"Yes?" he said. His eyes were wide, encouraging, and just the faintest bit manic.

Beth shook her head.

"You don't know what that means?" she asked. He raised his eyebrows, then his body slacked slightly and he sighed.

"I don't play games. You give me real information, or we get to work," he said.

Beth hadn't intended to play games. She realized, rudely, that not everyone knew her stories by byline. Or was it possible he didn't know her stories at all?

"I read the paper," the dark man against the wall said. "She's a reporter." The man in the gray shirt stood.

"Who knows where you are?" he asked.

"No one," the dark man answered. The man in the gray shirt glared at him for a fraction of a second.

"Who knew where you were?" he revised.

"No one," Beth said, regretting it the moment the words were out of her mouth. He saw it, and nodded.

"And what are you investigating?" he asked.

"It's just a bar," she said, feeling at a loss. She should have told him she worked at the cleaners... or for Casper... or... her mind cast for a story that wouldn't get someone else killed. The man in the gray shirt nodded, then sighed and dragged a knee forward so that he was directly in front of her.

"Do you want to see how your hand works?"

Beth tried to close her hand, but it tensed her wrist and the immediate, sharp warning of the wire at her wrist made her involuntarily relax her hand again. Her animal mind nothing more than to thrash, kick, bite, and her reporter mind had stalled, slack against the fact of a blade held just above the center of her palm, describing the shape of the cut he intended in quick practice motions.

They all jumped at the loud noise above the ceiling. Had that been a gun?

Beth's whole body jolted with adrenaline as the man in the gray shirt stood and looked at the dark man. The dark man shrugged.

There had to be a way out. *They got in.*

She strained against her ankles, and only the deepest discipline kept her from doing the same against her arms. Stupid little wires that she could break with her hands... She bared her teeth and looked up at the man in the gray shirt, but he wasn't looking at her. A ceiling tile had moved. The man in the gray picked up the gun from the table and the dark man pulled a gun from his waist. The man in the glasses moved away from everyone else, out of Beth's range of vision.

The man in the gray shirt slowly walked toward the hole in the ceiling, pointing the gun up at the darkness, then there was a loud noise and his body went limp. The gun clattered to the floor next to him, and Beth tried to pull back away from the gun and the body. She had heard gun shots before, even at closer range, but somehow it was louder, here in this room. The dark man stepped toward her slowly, pointing his weapon at the hole in the ceiling. A dark body fell through the ceiling and the dark man next to Beth shot it as it fell, one, two, three. He walked over to check it and Beth's stomach sank as it didn't move. He shot it once more, then pushed it with his foot. The shot that killed him nearly stopped her heart, and she choked on a sob. A metal ladder lowered from the ceiling at an angle and a figure draped in a dark jacket walked down it backwards.

His Dark Mistress turned to look into the room, finding something over Beth's shoulder. A look of annoyance crossed her face, and she raised her arm and shot the man in the glasses. He died with a whimper. Beth sat, rigid, searching the woman's stony face for a clue of what was happening. His Dark Mistress holstered her gun and finished climbing down the ladder.

"You can walk?" the powerful voice from the alley asked. Beth nodded without thinking. The woman bent over Beth, looking at her restraints.

"That's twisted," she commented, going back over to the table. She returned with a set of wire cutters and a stack of gauze. Beth looked down and realized that she was bleeding.

Badly.

She replayed the previous seconds, and realized that she had jumped every time a gun had gone off, the adrenaline blocking the pain response in her forearms and upper arms. Only her wrists were relatively clean of cuts.

She started to shake as His Dark Mistress cut the wires and pushed gauze against the deep cuts on her forearms.

"Hold it together," the woman ordered. "We aren't done yet."

When His Dark Mistress cut the nylon strap across her waist, Beth stood, ignoring the restraints on her ankles, and fell forward, tipping the chair with her. His Dark Mistress grunted, grabbing firm hold of Beth's calf to cut the strap there.

Beth found herself face to face with the man in the gray shirt. She turned away, swallowing sick-tasting saliva, and saw the blood that now spilled down the inside of her arms. She coughed and gagged, then kicked at the chair with one free foot. Cursing under her breath, His Dark Mistress grabbed the chair and Beth's leg together and slit the last restraint with a single motion. Beth scrambled free and lunged into the far corner, vomiting violently. His Dark Mistress came and grabbed her by the shoulders.

"Look at me," she ordered. Beth looked up at her weakly.

"You survived. It's over. We have to go."

Beth nodded, waves of nausea passing over her as though purging themselves from her body. Somewhere underneath them was calm and reason. She gagged again, her head hanging, and His Dark Mistress waited, then pulled Beth's arms forward for her to look at them.

"These will heal. Keep them covered. It's not as bad as it looks."

The dark woman looked at where the wire had pulled along under the skin on her upper arms.

"These are going to hurt a lot, tomorrow, but they're mostly superficial."

Beth looked at her arms, her insides still shaking. His Dark Mistress returned to the table and picked up a roll of tape. She showed it to Beth.

"Here, or outside?"

Beth looked at her arms, and the nausea cleared. Cuts. They were just cuts, and she was bleeding, but they were just cuts. She'd done worse with a knife, cooking. It was a lie, but it helped.

"Outside," she said. The dark woman nodded and led the way up the ladder. Beth didn't look over her shoulder as she followed.

His Dark Mistress bandaged and taped Beth's wounds in the yellow light of a streetlight. Beth fought sagging against her as the gaping flesh disappeared with a brutal efficiency.

Finished, the woman looked critically at Beth.

"You need to make it to the car with me," she said. Beth pointed wiltedly.

"My car is that way."

"It won't be for long."

Feeling like a lost, and beaten, puppy, Beth followed, trudging behind the dark coat. She crossed her arms in front of her, hugging her chest as much as she could before her bandages warned her off, and dropped her head.

Just to the car.

The coat snapped like a living thing at her in the turbulence of the still air churned up by His Dark Mistress' solid black boots. Beth blinked at it, intimidated.

To the car.

She stumbled and the dark woman paused, glancing at her.

"Stay awake," the woman ordered, and Beth nodded.

Of course.

The jacket beckoned at her again, and she followed, her chestfalls dragging her head lower and lower as she walked. Her tongue tasted of sickness, and she wished she had something to wash her mouth out with. Her eyes kept falling lower, and she blinked in rhythm with her steps.

She had no idea how far they'd gone.

A curb surprised her, but she remembered it hadn't been the first one.

She sped up to keep pace with the jacket, idly wondering if she should wonder why she was following it.

A little way further, she staggered into the side of a building and dry heaved at her feet some more. The dark woman stood a ways away from her, watching with her arms folded, but remained silent.

Beth's fingers played with the gauze bandaging at her elbow, and she shoved herself off the wall with her shoulder and followed again.

They walked more.

Beth wondered what they looked like, what someone would think, watching them.

Finally, a car door opened in front of her, and Beth looked up. His Dark Mistress had unlocked the passenger door to a small, sleek coupe that Beth would have been able to identify on a better day. Out of the corner of her eye, Beth noticed the license plate: HDM.

Her car.

She got in gingerly and let her head roll back, halfway to unconsciousness when the slamming of the driver's door brought her bolt, screaming awake.

The dark woman watched Beth for a moment as Beth panted, then took off her hat and tossed it into the backseat.

"You are in my care, Beth, and as long as that is the case, you are safe."

When Beth woke, her mouth tasted like death.

She shrugged under the covers and tried to remember if she had had too much to drink last night.

She remembered when the seatbelt held her tight.

For a terrifying moment, she thought it wasn't over yet, and she thrashed against the seatbelt, but her vision cleared from its morning fogginess and she recognized the car.

She slumped deeper into the seat, letting her heart rate come back down, and found that she was huddled beneath her sweatshirt, arms crossed as she faintly remembered them from the night before.

How do you cope with the most traumatic experience in your life, she wondered, when no one else is going to be able to understand?

Where had that come from?

Surely she wasn't supposed to be having insightful, introspective thoughts — self-pitying ones, at that — this close to being in shock.

Was she?

If there was no such thing as normal...

She frowned, trying to get her mind under control.

Where was His Dark Mistress?

That was the right first question.

The car was empty, parked in a dimly-lit drive-in under a dawning sky.

The lot was empty, but Beth heard another car approaching behind her over the rough gravel, and the car shifted as a weight came off the trunk.

There was a door slam and vague voices, and Beth struggled between the desire to see what was going on and the momentary shelter of sitting under her hoodie in ignorance.

Where had the hoodie come from? She hadn't had it in the room with no doors.

Her mind wandered and her eyes glazed across the parking lot, trying to understand what the posts were for. Her intellectual mind identified them and dismissed them, but her eyes were confused and waiting for an explanation.

Her door opened.

Cold, damp, morning air poured into the car, and she shifted the sweatshirt to cover where the air hit exposed skin.

"Hello, Beth," a man said gently. "I need to have a look at your arms."

Beth looked up at him, and obediently extended her arms out of the car. The man looked at His Dark Mistress, who had leaned against the car.

"How much blood has she lost?" he asked. His Dark Mistress shrugged.

"Don't know. I got there as fast as I could."

The man looked back at Beth, then bent over and unbuckled her seatbelt. He took the hoodie from her and folded it and put it reassuringly in her lap. Beth shivered in the morning air, looking up at the man without understanding why she trusted him. He helped her pull her feet out of the car, then carefully removed the improvised bandages from the night before.

Beth wondered how long ago that had actually been.

She hadn't actually looked at her arms yet. Her brain knew what would be there, and hadn't bothered to check, but as he pulled the first bandage from her right elbow, the suction noise as sticky blood pulled away from the wound jarred her attention.

Her forearms had spill marks down them from dried blood that had rubbed off in flakes. Her hoodie was dotted with red-brown specks that had caught there.

Beth was certain that should bother her.

She was also certain that the shooting pain up her arm as the man cleaned the wound on her arm with a cotton ball should be somewhere near the center of her universe, but she drifted on past it, dragging it along like a satellite. Yes, her arm hurt. It was attached to her, and that was why it hurt. If someone else's arm were attached to her, it probably wouldn't hurt at all.

"Beth, can you tell me your mother's name?" the man asked.

Beth looked at him suspiciously, narrowing her eyes at him. Why would he want to know that?

"She won't tell you," His Dark Mistress answered. "She's made a career out of lying to everyone about who she is."

"Okay, can you tell me what year it is?"

"1997," Beth said. "September 17th, 1997."

"Eighteenth," His Dark Mistress corrected. Beth checked. Yeah, that was right.

"And what did you have for breakfast yesterday?" the man asked.

"Coffee," Beth said.

"And lunch?"

Beth thought.

"Half a hot dog," she told him. He had pulled out a needle and was threading it.

"And dinner?"

Had she eaten dinner, she wondered.

"Beer?" she guessed.

The man looked up at His Dark Mistress.

"Feed her," he chastised. His Dark Mistress shrugged, shaking her hair and looking up at the sky.

The man stitched closed the wound on her forearm, then glued shut the one on her upper arm and switched sides. Beth watched him passively, then turned to watch the sunrise over his head.

Maybe fifteen minutes later, he wrapped all four spots in stretchy elastic athletic tape and stood.

"She's in shock," he said softly to His Dark Mistress. "Needs a lot of water and sugar, and then more sleep."

Beth figured that sounded okay.

Her head was tippy and sound was coming at her through a tunnel.

"The top cuts were surgical quality. What caused them?" he asked.

"You know better," His Dark Mistress said sternly, then stood and held the car door as Beth pulled her feet back into the car and cuddled back into her sweatshirt. She lost the rest of their conversation after the door closed, but her mind had already shut back down. She was long gone by the time His Dark Mistress opened the driver's door and started the engine back up.

There was a crowd gathered around the door to one of the practice rooms as Neil made his way out of the lockers. The gym had a large, central sparring mat and half a dozen private practice rooms off of it, but he was only here for the workout room, today. He practiced with his trainer on Tuesdays; he worked out on his own four more days a week.

He grunted under his breath at the gathered crowd, but paused when he recognized several of the men. This wasn't a gym for amateurs or tourists. Lynx couldn't stand them, and she picked who was allowed to pay dues. Police, security, military, and militia trained alongside mafia and dealers of various illegal goods, with a few genuine athletes thrown in as part of the gym's reputation.

Even among that crowd, though, some of the men standing on their toes to see into the third training room were men that were abnormally dangerous and introverted. Men who used real knives for sparring. Neil dropped his bag against the wall and reluctantly waded into the crowd. Curiosity. Who knew.

He spotted one of his sparring partners, a retired police officer who could lay out most anyone who didn't absolutely see it coming, and he jerked his chin at him.

"What's going on?" Neil asked.

"His Dark Mistress," Daniel told him.

Neil stood on his toes, but was still behind several men who had him beat by more than a couple of inches.

"Liar," he said.

"I'm not kidding," Daniel said. "She just walked in and went in there. I don't know what she's doing."

Daniel was great at what he did, but he was too nice. Neil had enough sharp edges on him to push his way through the rest of the crowd to find himself standing in the open doorway.

He saw a solid woman practicing forms.

"His Dark Mistress doesn't exist," he said under his breath, looking at her. "And she doesn't look like that."

As though she had heard him, her head snapped to the door, to look directly at Neil. His breath stopped like she had put a blade to his throat.

Her eyes smiled, like a cat that had caught wind of her prey, and she returned to her forms.

There was food, there was soda ("I don't drink soda." "Today you do."), there were car doors, and other voices, but all of it was part of the dream. When she woke, she couldn't make sense of any of it, nor could she determine what day it was.

She tasted of Sprite and potato. Funky, day-old sprite and potato, but it was better than death.

Her body ached as she sat up, finding herself on an army cot in a room that her writer's mind found difficulty attaching many words to.

It was dim, brown, and empty. There were two doors – she checked – and a window, which was also dim, brown, and empty. His Dark Mistress watched her from where she was sitting on the floor in the middle of the room.

"What day is it?" Beth asked, rolling her back to produce a chorus of pops.

"Tomorrow," His Dark Mistress answered. Beth nodded. It made sense, but she was pretty sure it shouldn't have.

"I need to brush my teeth," Beth said.

"Bathroom's behind you," His Dark Mistress said. "Take your time."

So there were two doors.

Beth stood and walked to the bathroom, her gait evening out as her knees remembered what they were designed for.

The bathroom was small, but clean, and there was a free-standing tub occupying the entire far wall. The toilet had a folded white towel and a toiletry bag sitting on it, and Beth found toothbrush, toothpaste, soap, shampoo, conditioner, and a hairbrush in it. She raised her eyebrows. That was certainly more than she had expected.

Not excited about having her bare feet on the floor, she went ahead and showered, anyway, once she had brushed her teeth thoroughly, only really remembering the stitches on her arms when she found them under the hot water.

They were red and warm to the touch, but not disproportionately tender, she thought, considering. It didn't look like any of them had gotten infected. She worried for a moment about the glue, but he hadn't told her *not* to shower (had he? no… she was pretty sure) and surely they planned on people showering in the stuff.

In all, she seemed to be in a reasonably small number of pieces for someone who had been abducted and threatened by a psychopath maybe a day before. Her stomach still quavered when her thoughts even brushed up against what had happened, but the shower felt good, and she could focus on that, for now.

She toweled off and pulled her shirt on over her head, now much more aware of the irritation as the fabric slid over her arms, then looked at her socks.

Boy, I wish I had new socks, she thought, then scolded herself for being ungrateful. Alive was good, clean was better.

New socks just would have been a nice touch.

She finished dressing, entertaining no more thoughts about clean undergarments, and walked back into the main room as she rubbed her hair dry. His Dark Mistress didn't appear to have moved. Beth sat back down on the cot and looked back at her.

"What does it mean, His Dark Mistress?" Beth finally asked.

"What do you want to accomplish?" the dark woman asked, her eyes blinking to indicate annoyance as she ignored Beth's question. Beth shook her head and shrugged.

"Great story, told well," she said. A writing professor's mantra from college that had stuck with her. His Dark Mistress' eyes narrowed slightly.

"Then go home, burn your notes, and move on. This isn't it," she said. Beth jolted.

"Are you telling me to walk away from my story?" she asked.

"If that's all you want out of it, yes," His Dark Mistress said.

"What else should I want?" Beth asked.

"To expose and destroy evil," His Dark Mistress said. Beth considered.

"Does 'bring truth to light' get close enough?" she asked. The woman frowned and stood. It might have been closer to a glare.

"You have two choices before you. You can go home, resume your life, and pretend nothing about your story ever happened. No one outside of that room knew who you were; they will not find you. Or." Her long pause made Beth uncomfortable. "You can root out true evil and see that it is destroyed. I can help you get the facts you need, but I cannot make you safe. You take your life in your hands."

Beth had difficulty taking this seriously, but sensed that doing otherwise would push a very thin temper further than she wanted to. Besides.

"You can help me with my story? I have so many questions," she said, sitting forward despite herself. His Dark Mistress held up a hand.

"I will not be a resource to you in gathering your evidence. I will not be available to prove what you say, later, to the police. You need to be able to prove everything on your own."

Beth sat back.

"If you already know it all, why don't you do something about it, yourself?" she asked. His Dark Mistress paused, her eyes never leaving Beth's.

"You have two options in front of you. Which do you choose?"

"No one is going to talk me out of my story," Beth said. Something in the back of her mind added, *especially now.* His Dark Mistress nodded firmly and began to walk for the door.

"Let's begin."

They drove someplace out of town, in awkward silence, winding south along the coast, and finally stopped in front of a set of small storefronts. Beth wondered if she had actually agreed to anything as she followed His Dark Mistress into a beauty salon and, feeling like a child, sat down in a waiting chair as His Dark Mistress arranged something with a stylist.

"Is this really necessary?" Beth asked as the stylist led her back to a chair.

"Is this not what you want?" the woman asked. Beth waved at her, without looking away from His Dark Mistress. "Fine. Seriously, though."

His Dark Mistress ignored her, flipping through a magazine.

"Here," the woman said, handing the magazine to the stylist. "Eyebrows, too."

"We don't do eyebrows. You don't want those chemicals in your eyes," the stylist said, pulling Beth's hair away from her head.

"Eyebrows, too."

Despite repeated protests, eventually, Beth had cotton balls taped over her eyes and petroleum jelly smeared around her eyebrows, and she sat, smelling her hair basting in the dye chemicals. Once or twice, she tried to start a conversation, but the stylist had wandered off to do something else, and His Dark Mistress may very well have driven off without Beth, for all Beth could tell. Finally, Beth just sat in darkness, her mind still to avoid touching anything sticky, and answered 'fine', every time the stylist came back to check on her. She thought for a moment about ranking the longest forty minuteses of her life, but that got crossed off the list of diversions immediately.

Finally, the stylist came back and rinsed off her eyebrows, then, with her vision restored, led Beth back to wash out the rest of the dye.

"You have amazing hair for a natural blonde. It's almost a shame," the woman said as she massaged Beth's scalp. Beth rolled her eyes, wondering what she hadn't-quite-agreed to. "I think your ... friend? ... has good taste, though. This color with your skin tone is going to be really striking."

Beth settled a bit in the chair. Striking. Was that one of those words that people used to say 'whoa' politely?

With her hair rinsed out, Beth started to go back to the chair, but His Dark Mistress held up a hand.

"Nails, next," she said.

"What?" Beth squawked.

"A style comes with the color," the stylist said, shaking out the cape. His Dark Mistress shook her head dismissively.

"Just the nails," she answered.

"Are you kidding me?" Beth asked.

"Nails," His Dark Mistress said, settling back into her chair and flipping a page.

Beth and the stylist looked at each other, and Beth finally rolled her eyes and shrugged. The stylist shrugged back.

"Tonya will take care of you, then," she said, holding up her arm to show Beth over to the corner where a table sat. A woman looked up from a magazine.

"You done already?" she asked. The stylist shrugged. Beth sat.

"Acrylics, right?" the woman asked. Beth frowned, spreading her fingers out in front of her.

"Can we just paint them?" she asked. Tonya the manicurist looked over Beth's shoulder.

"Look, girl, I know who she is. I'm not playing," she said. Beth glanced over her own shoulder at the dark woman in the chair. His Dark Mistress glanced up without moving her head, her dark eyes flashing a warning.

Tonya the manicurist took out a set of acrylic nails and set to work on Beth's hands.

Beth had had her nails done twice before, so at least now she had an idea how long she was going to have to sit. She slumped down in her chair and crossed her legs, eyes wandering to avoid being too personal with the woman working on her fingernails. Tonya didn't speak. Beth didn't try to induce conversation.

The blank, full-length acrylics went on, and Tonya pulled out a set of clippers.

"How long?" she asked. Beth started to motion on the thumb, the length of her nails making her awkward and self-aware.

"Longer," His Dark Mistress said without looking. Beth's mark inched outward. Tonya raised the clippers.

"The longest you've done this month," His Dark Mistress said. Beth heard another page turn. Tonya glanced at His Dark Mistress, reset the clippers, and set to work again. Beth tapped the finished nails on the tabletop, the feeling of touch that far from her fingertips strange and unsettling. She held them up in front of her and looked over her shoulder at His Dark Mistress.

"Is this actually necessary?" she asked. His Dark Mistress didn't give the slightest indication of having heard.

"How do people live like this?" Beth wondered out loud, waving the nails at herself.

"You get to the point that you can't imagine not having them," Tonya said. "Paint?"

The question was directed over Beth's shoulder.

"Not today."

His Dark Mistress stood, and Beth rose to find a mirror.

"Not yet," the dark woman said, intercepting Beth. "Put these in."

She handed Beth a contact case, and Beth dropped her head to the side.

"You couldn't have given me this *before* the nails?" she asked. His Dark Mistress shrugged and took a step back, waiting.

It took Beth a minute to figure out how to work around the nails, but she eventually got the first cap off. A dark brown lens stared up at her. She looked at His Dark Mistress and sighed.

"I've been told *my* eyes are pretty," she said. His Dark Mistress didn't blink. Beth took the case back to the manicure table and, with agonizing slowness, worked through the process of getting them into her eyes. She was grateful she had used colored lenses before, because otherwise she never would have managed without stabbing her eyes out. As she recapped the second contact chamber, and as she blinked the contacts into place, she felt a hand on her shoulder.

She allowed herself to be steered to a mirror, and blinked at the woman who met her eyes. Her hair was a deep, mahogany red, and her eyes nearly black.

"Hello, Sabrina," His Dark Mistress murmured. Beth blinked.

Beth stared at the paused screen.

"This is unreal," she muttered, looking down at the pile of papers on the floor in front of her. Notes. Lots and lots of notes.

This will be where you stay until you're done," His Dark Mistress had said, handing Beth the keys after she unlocked the door. She opened the door to an elegantly-furnished apartment and let Beth past her.*

"I have an apartment," Beth had contested, gawking despite herself.*

"The closets are full, the kitchen is stocked, and the name on the lease is a company in Miami."

Beth turned and looked at His Dark Mistress. The woman had almost looked amused.

"You have no idea, yet," she'd said, then went and turned on the TV.*

Beth picked up the photo. The girl had been heavy in middle school, with unkempt hair and too-bright lipstick. The image on the screen was the same woman in her mid-twenties, stick thin with blotchy skin and hair that indicated persistent poor health. She had varying levels of lucidity in the tape, even after it had been heavily edited.

"Sabrina Margaret Hughes-Matthews," His Dark Mistress *said, pausing, as the woman began to speak on the tape.*

"Hughes-Matthews," Beth said, approaching with undisguised mistrust.

"Cousin to Edmond Hughes," His Dark Mistress said, turning to watch the screen again.

"My mother married an Italian," the girl started. "Uncle James freaked. Disowned her. After Dad died. No, wait. She married my step-dad after she married my dad... After my dad died." She nodded uncertainly, as though the sequence hadn't been entirely clear to her. Beth raised an eyebrow.

"You are going to be what Sabrina could have been," His Dark Mistress instructed, handing her the remote. "Learn her story, know her speech. There is much more than this. You have two weeks."

Sabrina, her mother, and her step-father had moved to Tampa when she was twelve, starting a new life. It sounded like Sabrina had done okay for herself through high school, but was long gone by the time her parents had died in a car wreck a little more than a year ago. She hadn't had contact with her Boston-based family since they had left, nor had her parents.

Or so she thought.

Beth looked at the photo again, flipping the remote in her other hand. That was the risk of the thing. That Sabrina's mother had reached out to a member of the family, or an old friend, after Sabrina had lost touch with reality. The girl in the photo could easily have grown up to be the woman Beth found in the mirror. They may not recognize her spontaneously, but with the information Sabrina was providing about herself, Beth could convince any of the Hughes and most of their close friends that she was Sabrina.

"Your boyfriend in Miami is married, and his wife just got pregnant. He offered to send you anywhere, and to support you for as long as necessary, as long as you agreed to never come back and risk his wife finding out about you," His Dark Mistress had instructed after Beth had gone through the video the first time.

"Bastard," Beth said, softening her vowels to imitate the coherent portions of Sabrina's speech. His Dark Mistress might have smiled.

"The apartment is paid for by a company he controls. Anyone who checks will be able to tell that it's a shell. Your boyfriend is a money launderer for groups you know better than to identify."

"That's sexy," Beth said, smiling a little.

"You graduated high school in Tampa, never applied to college, never held a job. Lived in a company apartment in Miami. There's very little story for anyone to check, but it all checks. Sabrina has a single drug possession arrest from three years ago."

"It happens," Beth said, interrupting. His Dark Mistress scowled.

Beth went to the bathroom and sat on the stool in front of the vanity mirror. She watched her eyes.

"I took a few months, got my stuff together, and came home," she said, pulling the words around the way Sabrina did. Manipulative eyes. The kind of expressions a professional mistress would use instinctively. Beth opened a drawer and found a hairbrush and hand mirror. She opened another and found makeup.

She took the lipstick out and put it on.

"Well, that's bold," she said. Beth really wasn't used to calling attention to herself, but she was realizing that Sabrina was going to have to be a peacock if she was going to pull it off. She stared at her eyes, suddenly highlighted like they had never been with blonde eyebrows, and squinted slightly, smiling coyly. Yes, this would do.

"I need to get in touch with David," Beth said late the next afternoon. "He'll be wondering where I've been."

His Dark Mistress glanced up from the kitchen table, then went back to reading the paper.

"You won't contact anyone from your own life until you're done, here," she said.

"David will come looking for me," Beth said, not moving from her notes. "Besides, I want to add to my notes on my desk."

His Dark Mistress stood bolt upright, knocking over her coffee cup.

"You keep notes on your desk?" she asked warningly. Beth glanced up and shrugged, mildly pleased to have finally ruffled the dark woman. His Dark Mistress was bustling for the door.

"Reckless child," she growled. "How do I find your desk?"

Beth told her.

"David is your editor, yes?" His Dark Mistress asked. Beth nodded. "How do I convince him that you are safe and that he should not seek you out?"

Beth frowned.

"I'll just go with you," she said. "Or go by myself. It's not that big a deal."

"No!" His Dark Mistress said, standing by the door. "You do not go near your own life. Not looking like that. There must be no connection."

Beth considered.

"He was one of the youngest editors to ever get a major section at the paper. Kelly and I call him Baby Boy. Or Babe, or Babs, or Bees. He'll recognize all of them."

His Dark Mistress glared at her.

"You've already made plenty of mistakes. You don't have many left before you're going to cause someone's death," she warned. "Study, know that girl, and be ready. I'll be back in an hour."

And so Beth was on her own. His Dark Mistress would take the tape with her when she left at the end of the day, but Beth's notes would stash in a shallow floor safe under her bed. Beth was still relatively certain that His Dark Mistress was exaggerating the risks of what Beth was doing, *a floor safe?*, but she had been the one to pull Beth out of… Beth pushed the thought away. She would be more careful. She wasn't ever going to say that it was just a story, let it scare her away, but she could be more careful.

She stuck her tongue out at her reflection and went back to sit on the thick rug in front of the television, retrieving the remote from under the coffee table and restarted the video.

His Dark Mistress stood over the desk, fingering through the chaos of Beth's notes. It was clear there was a method to it, the way the papers were stuck together, but after a moment, His Dark Mistress began searching the desk drawers without ceremony, and, finding a manila folder, began to pull the note structure apart and push it into the folder.

"What do you think you're doing?" a skinny man asked, approaching His Dark Mistress with a self-confidence that she couldn't help but be impressed with. A few heads came up across the newsroom, but they ducked again when they saw the intensity with which His Dark Mistress and the editor named David regarded each other. After a moment, His Dark Mistress

reached down to the desk to pick up the last of the papers and jam them into the folder.

"We should speak privately," she said. David glared darkly.

"Give me that folder," he said. She handed it over easily. He turned.

"My office," he said. She followed, bemused, into a modest, cluttered office down the hall.

"Tell me why I don't call the police right now," he said.

"Your reporter is in over her head," His Dark Mistress said. "The less you know about it, the better, but I'm changing her methods. She won't be contacting you again for a while."

"That sounds like a threat," David said, putting his hand on the phone. It wasn't a bluff.

"You were young when you came into your job. Still are young, but she didn't mention that. Don't know any better than she does. She gave me four names that she calls you. You confirm you are who I think you are by giving me one, I'll tell you the other three," His Dark Mistress said, unfazed.

He thought.

"Baby."

His Dark Mistress smiled. He might be clever enough to keep Beth from getting killed, if anyone was.

"Baby Boy. Babs. Bees."

"She's okay?" he asked, sitting down. If he hadn't had so much dignity, it would have been a crumpling motion.

"The less you know," His Dark Mistress said, holding her hand out for the folder. "She wants those."

He tossed it onto the desk, pushing it so that it skid to the far side of the desk where His Dark Mistress could reach it.

"Who are you?" he asked. His Dark Mistress shook her head.

"The less you know," she said. "If anyone other than me comes asking about her, tell them she's hit a dead end and you haven't seen her in weeks."

"So... the truth," David said. His Dark Mistress smiled, then turned to go.

"I'll keep her safe," she said softly over her shoulder.

She wasn't sure, but he might have whispered 'thank you'.

The closets were indeed full. Beth tried much of it on the evening of the second day, playing with the idea of Sabrina's fashion sense. It was expensive, to be sure, but not highbrow. The apartment was a stroke of genius, she was realizing, because now she could have bilateral relationships with people – she could invite them into her life, rather than just inviting herself into theirs. She was a kept woman by a man with taste. Undoubtedly, he had a tasteful wife. What he had been looking for, she decided, was a woman who enjoyed taste without being run by it. One who owned black leather pants and backless shirts.

She went out, hailing a cab and getting herself into a club without needing the fake ID His Dark Mistress had given her. She played Sabrina.

She sat in laps, she talked too loud, she winked, she wiggled non-dance moves to music, she didn't pay for a thing.

By last call, she was sitting at a table with five men, all strangers to each other, who all thought she was going home with *him*. That she was seeing through all these other guys, and was playing with them, but *he* had a real shot. She drained her red, cranberry-flavored drink and stood, toppling slightly to the side with genuine tipsy.

"Which of you is going to call me a cab?" she asked, holding her hand over her head and flipping it dismissively. Five men reacted, two going to the bar to look for a phone, two dashing outside to look for a cab, and one – who was particularly attractive up close – putting his arm around her waist to balance her.

She leaned against him all the way to the street, feeling his body heat through the exposed skin where her shirt had rubbed out of the way at her side and where his forearm and palm held steady against her back. She had tossed her jacket over her far shoulder, and the air outside shook her. The man who had come up with the cab took her jacket from her and draped it across her shoulders, sneaking in a dirty look at the one who held her. Beth giggled. The third, coming up dry for a taxi, rushed up to open the door for her, and she sat on the back seat, turning and lifting both legs in at the same time, and closed the door. Three stunned faces looked down at her. She grinned at them and gave an address to the taxi driver.

"Where have you been?" His Dark Mistress asked as Beth leaned on the open door, recovering from the elevator.

"Out," Beth answered, tipping her head back.

"You're drunk," His Dark Mistress accused.

"So?" Beth answered, laughing. "It was boring here and Sabrina wanted to go out." She grinned at His Dark Mistress, daring her to be reactive. "Sabrina knows how to have a good time."

His Dark Mistress frowned.

"Did you get my notes?" Beth asked, straightening. Drunk was mostly about giving yourself permission to act dumb, Beth thought. And permission was just another decision. His Dark Mistress pointed to them on the table.

"David give you a hard time?"

"He's more careful than you," His Dark Mistress answered. "You reek of smoke and men and alcohol. Take a shower and go to bed. I'll be back tomorrow night."

Beth waited until His Dark Mistress was gone, then went to the kitchen to scrounge. There was a very nice wine refrigerator, but she had to settle for potato chips. She'd get Doritos tomorrow. She had work to do, yet.

Neil pushed open the front door at the gym and walked in, hoisting his bag higher onto his shoulder. A crowd had gathered in front of one of the practice rooms again, and he stopped. He considered just moving on — the gawking thing was disgraceful — but curiosity got the better of him, and he wandered to the back of the crowd.

"Her again?" he asked a face he vaguely recognized. Private security; no one Neil particularly needed to know.

"Yeah," the man grunted, straining to see. Neil sighed and rolled his eyes. Rumors were spreading around the gym about the dark woman who showed up periodically and unexpectedly, trained for maybe an hour, then left. Neil completely believed she was who they said she was, but didn't see why it mattered. A lot of notorious people trained here, and Neil didn't get much time off. She clearly trained much more than the few hours she had put in here; this was some stunt for attention and nothing more. He resettled his bag and started to head for the locker room.

Lynx came striding out of her office, and he paused. There was a woman he could profit from keeping his eyes open around. She was a force of nature, and there weren't many men at the club who wouldn't have gone after her, if they'd thought they had a shot.

She hissed at them, a harsh, inhuman noise through bared teeth, and the crowd scattered some.

"Tourists, out," she said, waving an arm. *Neil could see into the practice room, now, where the dark woman was watching the doorway from a crouch. Their eyes met, and he caught himself in the process of taking a step back, awkwardly resettling his weight instead.*

Lynx stood with her hands on her hips, glaring as the crowd broke up further, making muttered excuses about where they should actually be. The slim woman turned to Neil, and he tore his eyes away from the dark crouching woman to look at the nearer threat. He didn't think His Dark Mistress ever blinked, but he did, as he met Lynx's annoyed glare.

"Him," the woman in the practice room said, her voice low. *Lynx glanced over her shoulder and nodded. She glanced at Neil and smiled — up there on the list of the scariest things Neil had ever seen.*

"Good luck," she told him, stepping aside.

"I'm not changed," Neil said, shifting his weight to demonstrate the bag on his shoulder.

"You don't look like the type unaccustomed to fighting in jeans," the dark woman said, still unmoving. *Lynx raised an eyebrow, in effect calling him chicken. He sighed and stepped into the practice room, where Lynx closed the door behind him. The dark woman stood and stretched her back. He dropped his bag and leaned against the wall.*

"What do I call you?" he asked.

"You have no need for a title," she said, motioning him forward. *He grunted and pulled his jacket off, then unzipped his bag and pulled out a tank top, glancing at His Dark Mistress. She smirked, and he shook his head, unbuttoning his shirt to change into the other. She waited with her arms folded as he quickly stretched out, then motioned him forward again.*

"I'm not sure what's going on here," he said.

"They say you train hard. Harder than you actually need to," she said.

"What's your game, lady?" he asked, putting up his hands instinctively for an unexpected attack. *There weren't exactly any rules at the gym. She watched him with predatory interest.*

"Hit me," she said. *He glanced at her hands where they hung at her sides. They were battered, fighter's hands. Looking her over, he squinted slightly, calculating. She was a nose-breaker. The type who don't fight for anger. She would try to break her opponent's will as quickly as possible. He adopted a foot stance and tried his balance, feeling out the tension in his arms, his back. Her posture dropped into a relaxed guard as she watched him with open interest.*

"If it would help you get over hitting a woman, I could hit you first," she said, her mouth twisting in dark humor. He dropped his head a little and frowned at her.

"Not necessary."

He swung at her, just watching her reaction. She easily dodged, not moving anything below her waist. He swung again, with a little more commitment, wanting to push her off her feet, but she was more flexible than her size would have suggested. Dark eyes set in a pale face watched him calmly, humor making way for confident concentration. He stepped into her and she blocked the swing, but gave the step. She punched him in the gut, but his core was too tight for it to bother him too much. She was just observing he had left himself open.

Noted.

He dropped his right shoulder to get his elbow into position, and she swept her foot through his left knee, nearly dropping him on his back. He caught himself on his palm and looked up at her. She tilted her head to the side.

So it's like that.

He spun over his outstretched leg, aiming a mirror blow at her legs, but she swept around him, nodding at the athleticism of the recovery. He didn't feel like being patronized, and he stood with an intentional lack of grace to look at her again. He left his arms down.

"I still don't see what's going on," he said. She glared.

"Show me who you are," she said through gritted teeth as she rained a barrage of blows against defensive forearms and shins. Neil got lower, looking at His Dark Mistress with alarm for the first time. He had underestimated her. She wasn't just a charismatic myth. She meant to take the measure of him, and, looking at her in her radiant anger, he realized she would break him if he did not meet her standard.

A lifetime of dark alleys and men with weapons took over, and he dropped his civility, trading blocks with her in a whirlwind of back and forth that his mind remembered more clearly than he had lived it the first time. He met her attacks, fists, elbows, knees, and feet, and returned them, trying to draw her out with easy targets, looking for an overconfident mistake, or a misstep. She didn't make one.

Only instinct and muscle memory could keep up with her reflexes, and he felt the bruises to come on his forearms. She landed several more punches on his core, and he hadn't come in contact with any soft target on her at all.

"Damn," he said, realizing that she was better than him. She smiled, rewarding him with a renewed frenzy of attack that left him stumbling

backwards, looking for escape. He ducked, then finally rolled to the side, standing up several feet out of her range, his arms still up. He may be beat, but he wasn't done.

She nodded at his determination, and moved in, continuing to punish him. He didn't abandon himself to self-protection, and from time to time he did start to land hits; she was tiring, but not as quickly as he was. He cursed poker.

His skin began to grow slick, and His Dark Mistress was dripping sweat. His body had been shaken, but the muscle was well-founded on long years of training, and he kept up, swinging now and again at her face when he thought she might have lost her center of balance. His core kept him over his feet, and she did not throw him to the floor again.

For another length of time, the fight became one that someone else was fighting, as he hit his second wind and muscle soreness became a vague idea. Air scorched his throat as his lungs desperately pumped air in and out of his ribcage. She landed a powerful knee shot to his side, between his hip and his ribs, and he staggered back, putting his hands on his knees.

She waited, her own breath audible, amplified off the hard surfaces of the room.

He stood, dropped back over his knees for a moment, then stood again.

She nodded, and they began again.

Neil only remembered this portion of the fight in terms of what he felt. Her strikes might have been less strong as they had been, but his reactions were slower and his muscles less taut to resist them. His throat hurt, and his skin grew hot. His head wavered, balance becoming more difficult.

Finally, before she completely put him down, she withdrew.

He looked up as his heart rate slowly came back down to find her standing with her palms against the wooden wall, leaning hard with her head dropped.

He sat.

She turned and slid down to sit on the floor, resting her elbows on her knees and her head on her arms. His head bobbed up and down with his breathing.

"I know who you are," she said, her voice slightly muffled. He shrugged. Most people around here did.

"You believe in the city on the hill," she said, looking up at him. He raised his eyebrows helplessly. What kind of time was this to talk like that? She shook her head.

"Where the good people are. You believe that there should be good people."

He shrugged again. It might be like that.

"You need the good people to exist. Because without that, what's the point?"

He considered. He was too tired to think about philosophy, but it sounded about right. He took a deep breath, forcing his heart rate further down, and he stood.

"I don't know what you're talking about," he said, staggering to his feet.

"You aren't a bad man," she said, watching him with a slack frame. "You are a criminal, but you don't seek to destroy."

He looked at her, his mind clearing.

"What is this about?" he asked. She stood.

"Someone needs to organize the darkness, or it will invade the city on the hill," she said. He frowned. "You are a loyal man, but what if your loyalty is pledged to a man who destroys a higher virtue?"

"I'm not a philosopher," Neil said, hobbling over to his bag by the door. With sudden force, she walked across the room, stepping in front of him.

"Perhaps not, but you are thoughtful," she said, her voice now betraying none of the effort of the past half hour.

He met her eyes, too tired to be intimidated.

"You don't agree with what he does. He abandons the old ways, the old rules. For profit. For power."

He narrowed his eyes.

"I'm no snitch," he said. She shook her head.

"Let someone else tell the story. Just don't be there for it," she said. She stepped closer to him. "When evil shatters, there are other dark men who will grasp at the pieces. Someone needs to be there to put them back together the right way."

Neil looked her up and down, slowly understanding.

"Just go," she said softly. "Be somewhere else until after the storm passes. I choose you to be the one that I will save."

He watched her, his mind racing, for a long moment, then, almost against his will, nodded. She nodded back at him.

Suddenly, he was aware of how close she was standing to him. She was at least an inch taller than him, towering for a woman, and her chest still betrayed the intensity of their fight. There was a moment, as he knew his eyes registered his realization, where he had to decide either to step away or not.

He did not.

He watched her chest rise and fall for another moment, then brazenly looked back up into her eyes. They were inscrutable, watching him unflinchingly.

"I will sleep with you," she said, "but on the condition that you never seek me out."

He let a teasing smile spread from his eyes to his mouth.

"How could I argue with that?"

"I need you to not go out with uncovered arms until your stitches come out," His Dark Mistress said as Beth came yawning and stretching into the living room the next morning. Beth glanced down at her arms, covered again with pajamas, now. She realized that she was avoiding thinking about them. "I trust that won't be too hard, as it's not going to break sixty degrees again until May."

"Whatever you say," Beth said in Sabrina's voice, shrugging. She rubbed her arms. His Dark Mistress looked up at her from her newspaper with steady, dark eyes, making a decision. Beth shivered. After a long moment, His Dark Mistress returned to her paper. Beth sat down at the kitchen table and carefully watched His Dark Mistress. Her reporter's brain was screaming at her. *Who are you? Why do you care? What are we actually doing here? What in the world am I supposed to call you?* Somehow, though, Beth got up and made herself two slices of toast instead. Something about the deep foreboding of the woman kept Beth from speaking, but the woman's steady confidence kept her from leaving. She wasn't going to drop her story – she had too many pieces that didn't yet fit together – and her instincts told her that following this strange counselor was the best way to get to the end.

So she bit her tongue against the torrent of questions and sat quietly and ate her toast.

"The only people who would recognize your face are dead, but there are a few around who would recognize the work. The timing is suspect to begin with – you need to prevent rumors from starting about a woman with your markings at the bars. They will come for you again."

His Dark Mistress allowed the paper to drop slightly to gauge Beth's reaction. Beth did her best not to have one.

"You heard me," she challenged, stretching inside the idea of Sabrina. A woman who was used to dangerous men. "Whatever."

She couldn't tell if the answering expression on His Dark Mistress' face was a smirk or a snarl. She ducked slightly and ate her toast, still learning the nuance of holding it between the tips of two nails, with the rest of her fingers stuck straight out. She glared at her nails.

"Are you ready for the next video?" His Dark Mistress asked from behind her paper.

"There are more?" Beth asked, frowning at the crumbs on her fingertips.

"Six," His Dark Mistress said. Beth looked at her across the table through the forest of nails, feeling surreal again.

"How did you get these?" Beth asked.

"I don't answer questions. You can't keep them here, but I will return them to you before you submit your story. That is all that is relevant," the woman said, turning a page passively.

"You went and found her and interviewed her. After you knew that you were going to make me into her. Why?" Beth said evenly. The paper dropped and the two women stared at each other. Beth swallowed.

"You made your decision once. I will give you one additional opportunity. Do you want to go back to your life or do you want to pursue this?"

I don't understand why that means I can't ask questions, Beth thought, but she frowned and contained it.

"I will give you access to the information you need, but I am not the source of that information. That is final," His Dark Mistress said, reaching into her jacket and pulling out a video cassette. "I will be back again tomorrow morning."

Beth watched as the dark woman stood and walked out of the apartment, then, ignoring the twang of guilt at how easily she was led, eagerly grabbed the tape and trotted into the living room to start it.

A week later, His Dark Mistress had been at the apartment each morning when Beth woke, so she was surprised to find the kitchen empty when she wandered out of her room. She had started getting up earlier to try to catch His Dark Mistress coming in, but she hadn't actually expected to do it. There wasn't any coffee yet.

"Dang," she said to herself, going through the cabinets looking for the grounds. She was actually going to have to learn to find stuff in her kitchen. She missed Steve the coffee shop kid.

And his magic, effortless coffee maker. She scratched her arms absent-mindedly with the gargantuan nails that she was finally beginning to learn to work with. Use the thumbs sideways to pull open the cabinets, the sides of the pinkies to lower them closed, the palms for pushing, knuckles whenever more force was required. She still dug them into her palms every time she tried to close her hands, but she only needed about half an inch less length, and she would have been set.

She found the coffee and repeated the silly process to get the coffee maker up and running, then went to sit at the table to stare at it.

Coffee.

Coffee now.

Coffee.

Still no sign of His Dark Mistress.

The coffee maker started to drip, and Beth went over to watch it.

She nodded, waiting impatiently as the drips turned into a solid stream, willing the first cup to finish.

Half a cup was a good enough start.

She poured out the bottom of the pot into a mug and went and sat back down.

Still no sign of the woman. Beth tapped the coffee mug.

Had something gone wrong?

Beth realized that a lot of her working plans had assumed she would get a lucky break. There had to be a hole in Edmond's organization, and she had known she would find it. This ploy, though, that His Dark Mistress had dropped in her lap required a full background for her cover to work, which made her reliant on His Dark Mistress – at least until she got through all of the tapes.

The idea that she was just sitting here, though, waiting for someone to show up to signal that it was time for her to pick back up was startling to her. She tapped her coffee cup some more, growing increasingly annoyed. She needed to think. Put the facts in order. She had spent so much time learning Sabrina, this past week, that she hadn't taken the time to focus. His Dark Mistress had just showed up. What was her angle? What did all of this have to do with the mayor?

And that pin?

The door opened and a shrill, happy voice interrupted Beth's thoughts.

"Ohmigosh," a young woman said. "This place is beautiful. Who did your interior decorating? I'm always looking for names, you know, of people who do good work. You'd be amazed how many people drop serious money on places like this, and then have no idea what to do with it. Like, you have all that money, at least pay someone to make you look like you have taste, too. And if I recommended someone to them, and they did a good job, like they did in here, they mention it to their friends, and that's how I grow my business, you know?"

Beth stood.

"Are you suggesting I don't have taste all by myself?" Beth said, standing and looking at the woman with a coy, dark expression. The woman stuttered, then recovered.

"Of course not. Looking at you, obviously you could do this on your own. I was just asking because..." She looked over her shoulder at His Dark Mistress and thought better of it. His Dark Mistress looked taxed. Beth looked at His Dark Mistress, mixing exasperated and bored in response.

"Who is she?"

The return expression might have been the slightest of smiles.

"I'm here to keep your roots from showing," the young woman said, smiling obliviously. The annoyance on Beth's part was real now. She tried a few escapes, but couldn't find any credible ones for Sabrina. The woman would have demanded this type of treatment. She gritted her teeth and glared at His Dark Mistress, who took the victory and went over to the table with her newspaper. Denver, this morning.

"Well, let's get this done. I have stuff to do," Beth said.

"Fill ins on the nails?" the woman asked, pulling up Beth's fingers to inspect them up close. Beth sighed internally and nodded.

"Of course," she said.

"You should get them painted, too," His Dark Mistress called. Beth grimaced.

"Just don't let it take all morning," she said. The woman grinned.

"That's why I'm the best. You have a chair in the bathroom?"

As a matter of fact, she did. Beth spent much of the rest of the morning having her hair fussed over and her nails pampered, but she kept her focus better.

Edmond was the next key. He was doing something with the mayor, and assuming the mayor wasn't being bribed by multiple deep pockets in the city, it was a lucrative exchange. Her land studies hadn't turned up anything interesting, and she didn't have any other leads that were moving in the right direction, so going after Edmond was the best way to figure out what she was doing for him. His Dark Mistress, whatever her interest in it, had given her a custom-made way into the inner circle.

Which left one question: did Beth trust His Dark Mistress not to get her killed or – worse – get in the way of Beth's story?

The dark woman had saved Beth's life, on the one hand, but she had never explained why, on the other. *My life*, Beth thought, then dodged away. Was it enough to just accept that a woman who held mythical status in the city wanted to remain secretive? Did Beth need to know the why so badly that she would turn down the type of help His Dark Mistress seemed prepared to offer? She smiled to herself.

Kelly would never be able to let it go. That was what made Beth different. She already had her story. She didn't need to be distracted by the new one that His Dark Mistress was tantalizingly dangling in front of her.

She looked over at the woman sitting cross-legged at the kitchen table, seeping defiant power. Incredible as she was, there was another story at hand. Beth would trust, and let it go.

Later, as the girl was packing up her designer backpack with the few things she carried with her, His Dark Mistress stood and held out a small, folded stack of bills.

"And if anyone asks about her natural hair color," His Dark Mistress said warningly.

"Hey, I only do her nails," the young woman said. His Dark Mistress handed her the money and the young woman left. Beth watched disinterestedly, then returned to the interview with the real Sabrina on the next tape from His Dark Mistress.

"Lori will be back every week to retouch your hair and your nails," His Dark Mistress said. Beth resisted the urge to fight back, and just shrugged.

"She'll be fine," she said. His Dark Mistress nodded.

"I'll see you tomorrow."

Sabrina watched her back in the mirror. Dark brown eyes, dark burgundy lips, dark red hair. Beth put down the mascara and just looked. His Dark Mistress had just left, going to be somewhere from which she could get Beth out in the event of an emergency. That morning, His Dark Mistress had taken her down to the basement and shown her an old boiler room that her apartment building shared with the one next door.

"This is your bail-out," His Dark Mistress had told her. "When there's no salvaging it, and no going back, take the elevator up to the apartment, then take the stairs down here and the stairs up to the top floor next door. I will find you."

Beth shivered at the memory. The apartments had been renovated in the last three or four years, and the building had a new-posh feeling, but the basement was still a maze of rusted steel and cement harkening back to the sixties, at least. The boiler room had a huge, steel door, blackened with soot and age, and looked like the gateway to hell. Beth hadn't gone in.

Sabrina didn't look that concerned. She held her eyes wide, challenging but pretty, and her mouth pouted mockingly. Beth smiled, and the woman's mouth curled cruelly.

Closing her eyes to focus, Beth stood and slowly walked out of the bathroom, picking up the purse that she had originally found in the front closet, and putting on a knee-length black jacket. She tied the belt around her waist and pulled her sunglasses out of her purse. She checked the effect in the hall mirror, then made her way downstairs and outside to hail a cab.

The cab dropped her off at an address just outside of the city at a large house with an elegant spread of land around it. Beth tucked her purse in between her elbow and her hip and walked down the front walkway, Sabrina's hips sashaying slightly. She took a breath, then knocked on the door.

And waited.

Her heart raced as she stared at the hallway inside of the glass door, and she found herself smiling. A woman in her mid-fifties came into view, and Beth's heart stopped for two solid beats. This was it. The door opened.

"Yes?" the woman asked.

"Aunt Lily?" Sabrina replied.

The woman looked stunned for a minute.

"Sabrina?" she finally asked. Sabrina smiled. Lily put her hands to her mouth. "Oh my goodness. Come inside."

"I didn't expect you to answer your own front door," Sabrina said as she crossed the doorway and looked back out.

"Always have," Lily said, looking at Sabrina strangely. Sabrina smiled awkwardly.

"I just thought... you know."

Lily crushed her in a hug.

"I'm sorry things ended up like they did," Lily said in her ear. Sabrina hugged her back, then sobbed, once. Lily took a step back.

"What's wrong?"

Sabrina pushed at the inside corners of her eyes, trying not to smudge her mascara. She shook her head.

"It's good to be home." She looked around nervously. "I didn't think I'd ever be back."

"Come sit," Lily said. "James won't be home for a few hours, at least. I'll make some tea."

Sabrina took a step back, then firmly shook her head.

"I'm not my mother. I won't own her mistakes," she said. Lily squinted slightly at her, then nodded.

"You're family," she said. "He'll see that. Come sit. Let me take your jacket."

Sabrina followed Lily through the wide entryway into a white-and-glass sitting room and took an offered chair. Lily went into the kitchen and put a kettle onto the stove, then came back.

"Have you had lunch?" she asked. "Can I offer you anything?"

"I'm fine," Sabrina said, crossing her legs and leaning back in her chair, looking around the room. "This is beautiful, Aunt Lily."

"Thank you. We redid the whole house a few years ago. So. Tell me what's happened to you."

Sabrina shrugged.

"I've been in Miami the past few years. Things changed, and I decided to come home." She paused. "Mom died."

Lily gasped.

"Oh, I'm sorry. How?"

"Car wreck with Peter. She didn't feel anything."

They sat in silence for a minute.

"I'm sorry," Lily said again. Sabrina nodded.

"I didn't want to betray her, coming home like this before, but now…"

Lily nodded.

"You did the right thing. This is where you belong."

Sabrina smiled and nodded again.

"I'm actually looking for Edmond. I didn't know where else to start."

Lily looked pained.

"Is something wrong?" Sabrina asked.

"He's not really the boy you'd remember," Lily said. Sabrina frowned.

"Oh?"

Lily wiped her hands on her dress – a quick, nervous motion – and sighed.

"He and his father… They're different people." Lily looked up at her, apparently remembering the bitterness Sabrina would have had toward James. Sabrina shrugged.

"Boys grow up," she said, then lowered her head toward Lily. "So do little girls." Lily sighed, then smiled wanly.

"I suppose that's the way of things."

The kettle sang and Sabrina sat back again as Lily quickly walked back into the kitchen and assembled a tray. She brought it back into the living room and set it on a glass-topped coffee table.

"Sugar?" Lily asked.

"Please," Sabrina, selecting a fruit-flavored tea out of the basket and holding the cup for Lily to pour water into it. Lily smiled.

"It was never quite the same, after you left," she said. "The rest of them, they aren't family. Not like you and your mother."

Sabrina nodded, stirring the water with the tea bag.

"I missed it."

Lily smiled suddenly.

"Edmond missed you a lot."

Sabrina laughed.

"I imagine he did."

"The way he used to try to tag along with you and your friends…" Lily trailed off, smiling happily.

"I felt bad about that, looking back," Sabrina said. "Maybe if we had been a little closer in age, we might have been better friends."

Lily shrugged.

"Or he would have annoyed you more, because your friends would have actually dated him."

Sabrina widened her eyes in humor and sipped at her tea.

"So what *has* happened here since we left?" she asked.

Lily made a small hand motion.

"Oh, you know. Nothing a lot different. People came... and went. James keeps talking about retiring, but you know how he is. He won't ever really give it up."

"Do you still have the parties here in the summer?" Beth asked. Lily lit up.

"They get bigger every year," she said. Sabrina grinned.

"I can't wait to see it."

They were quiet for a moment. Sabrina drank her tea.

Finally, she set the cup back down on the tray and opened her hands in front of her.

"I really do want to see Edmond," she said. Lily tilted her head to the side.

"Stay. Have dinner with us here," she said. Sabrina sighed and shook her head.

"A lot has happened, Aunt Lily. That's where I want to be."

Lily sighed and set down her own teacup.

"What time is it?"

Sabrina looked around for a clock.

"I don't know."

Lily stood to see a clock in the kitchen.

"A little after four." She looked back at Sabrina. "They'll be at the warehouse now, I expect, but they'll head to Alan's place before too long."

"That place is still open? I didn't think anyone went there," Sabrina said.

"Edmond and his friends started going there when he decided he didn't want to drink with his father," Lily said. "He owns it now."

Sabrina nodded, impressed. She slowly stood.

"Aunt Lily..."

"I understand."

"I missed you," Sabrina said, stepping forward. Lily smiled and hugged her.

"I missed you, too. Go on."

Back outside, Beth shook her hands out. Lily had acted like Beth was reading the subtexts correctly. Beth felt bad, even a bit manipulative, to have taken sides against the woman in the inevitable power struggle between her husband and her son, but Sabrina needed to be on Edmond's side. That was where the story was.

She had called for a second cab to pick her up at the house, and she watched it pull up as she reached the street.

"Alan's Pub," she said, giving the driver the address. After watching Sabrina's interview tapes, she had less than a dozen bars to pick from that the core members of the family might have frequented – Alan's had been owned by a distant cousin, but had been out of vogue fifteen years ago – so she could have just started looking, but she and His Dark Mistress had agreed that this lent her story more credibility. If she could demonstrate real fluency with Sabrina's family history with Lily, she wouldn't have to worry so much about James and Edmond believing her.

She had just been lucky that James hadn't been home, though. Lily on her own was inevitably going to be easier.

She reviewed, watching out the window as they headed back into town. It had gone well, she thought. Awkward, certainly, but the groundwork of who Sabrina was had been laid admirably. Beth smiled grimly to herself. One down. One to go.

The table could have just as well had a spotlight on it. The other tables were moved subtly further away from it, and the early patrons gave it a safe buffer. Sabrina had felt a bit out of place at the house, but this was where she belonged. She strode confidently across the bar, peeling her jacket as she walked, and tossed her hair as she sat down at the forbidden table. She set her jacket and purse down, pulled a lip gloss out of her purse and retouched her makeup, then got up and walked to the bar. The bartender watched her, a combination of stunned and impressed.

"Cranberry juice and vodka on ice," Sabrina ordered, waiting for her drink, then returning to the table. A well-meaning man approached the table nervously.

"You can't..." he started.

"Keep walking," Sabrina told him, taking a large swallow of her drink and turning her head to look at him.

"No..." he said, then wilted and returned to his table where he and his companions continued to stare at her. She ignored them, hinting at drinking her drink, but mostly just putting up a display of vain confidence. She crossed her knee-high boots at the ankle, tapping one against the other.

Time crawled.

Several more patrons tried to warn her out of the booth, and she sent all of them packing.

She finished her drink and ordered another. The bartender watched her with interest, but didn't try to talk her out of her behavior.

No one, she noted, told her she looked like a nice girl.

She pursed her lips and smiled at no one.

Finally, someone cleared his throat at her.

"Clearly you don't know where you are," he followed up. Sabrina turned sideways on the bench, pulling her feet up onto it in front of her, and smirked.

"I figured you'd be here an hour ago," she said. It wasn't flirty. That fact seemed to confuse him. She held her space, not inviting Edmond or any of his entourage to sit.

"You've got balls," he said. "I'll give you that. Get out."

Sabrina rolled her tongue in her mouth, amused.

"Your mom wouldn't like you talking to me like that," she said. Edmond smiled an angry, predatory smile and leaned in over her legs, getting as close as the edge of the booth allowed him to.

"Not many people survive talking about my mother."

"*She* had the good graces to be happy to see me," Sabrina mocked, leaning in slightly. His brow creased, and he stood.

"Who are you?"

Sabrina pouted, her eyes teasing.

"You don't recognize me?"

"You want me to move her for you?" one of the men behind Edmond said impatiently. Edmond held up a hand.

"Who are you?" he asked, jerking his head. Genuine curiosity.

"Sabrina."

She left her mouth open, not quite smiling. Waiting. His eyes lit with recognition, finally, and he tilted his head to the side. A salute. He grinned, every feature still that same angry, predatory quality, then raised an eyebrow.

"You come here to drink alone, or are you going to move over?"

Sabrina dropped her feet to the floor and slid along the booth.

"This is such a cliché," she said, her eyes indicating the round booth. He grinned as he sat down next to her.

"But it's awesome, right?"

She laughed.

"You really saw my mom?" he asked.

"She told me where to find you," Sabrina told him, sliding her drink back over in front of her and giving a careful warning look to the man who slid into the booth on her other side. The man made a kiss motion at her and intentionally slid all the way up against her. She gave him a scathing glare and he laughed to himself as a waitress approached with drinks. The men sorted out the drinks and one of the men motioned to Sabrina with his glass.

"Who is she?"

There were grunts as several others agreed with the question.

"Darin, get a chair. You look like an idiot," Edmond said. "This is my cousin."

The table looked collectively skeptical, but the man sitting next to Sabrina gave her a fraction more room.

"Where have you been?" Edmond asked her, turning in to talk to her.

"Miami," she said, sipping at her drink and glaring at the man behind her again.

Edmond's eyes dimmed a moment, and he took a drink of his beer.

"Dad know you're here?" he asked.

"Don't care," Sabrina said, daring him with her eyes. He grinned.

"Yeah," he said.

"No," Sabrina said, taking another drink. She shook her head. "Mom and Peter died in a car crash about a year ago."

He watched her, waiting for her to show weakness. She didn't. He waited for her to go on. She shrugged.

"I took some time, got my stuff together, and came home."

He nodded thoughtfully.

"It looks like you've done okay," he said, looking her up and down shamelessly. She nodded.

"I know what I'm doing," she said. He grinned.

"Here's to new beginnings," he said. Sabrina lifted her glass.

"Here's trouble," one of the men grumbled. The table collectively turned as His Dark Mistress entered the bar.

"Who's that?" Sabrina asked. The entire table turned to look at her. Edmond gasped.

"You don't know who His Dark Mistress is?"

Sabrina grimaced at him.

"Why would I?"

The table gaped. Sabrina shrugged and finished her drink.

"I need another," she announced. She glared at the two men to her left, who grudgingly stood to let her out.

The bar was still in the shock-recovery stage of His Dark Mistress' entrance as Sabrina sauntered across to the bar. His Dark Mistress glared at her and grabbed her arm.

"You're drinking beer tonight. I'm not drinking pink cocktails," she said. Sabrina pulled away, confused. His Dark Mistress jerked her close again. "You run drinks all night. Every time you're up, trade it with mine."

Sabrina looked His Dark Mistress in the face, much too close.

"Do it," His Dark Mistress menaced audibly. Sabrina staggered to the bar, looked over her shoulder at the booth, then ordered a beer to match the one that already sat in front of His Dark Mistress. She walked back to the booth, glancing over her shoulder at His Dark Mistress once. The men at the table were laughing silently. One made to stand, but Sabrina just waved him over.

"Who *is* that?" she asked, leaning in as she sat on the edge of the booth.

"What did she say to you?" Darin, the man relegated to a chair, asked. Sabrina glared at him.

"I told you. It's His Dark Mistress. No one knows more than that," Edmond said.

Sabrina glanced at the bar.

"Obviously you do."

The men chortled. Sound and life was slowly returning to the bar.

"You're afraid of her," Sabrina accused. Edmond rolled his tongue, grinning.

"So are you," he said. Sabrina thought, then nodded. The table broke into grins, and she was in.

"Anyone need anything?" Sabrina asked, standing. Sean tipped his bottle at her, and Matthew tapped his glass. Sabrina tipped her bottle back, draining what was left of what she had traded with His Dark Mistress about thirty minutes before.

She was having a good night. She was playing the guys one against another, allying with one now, and against him moments later, commanding attention from all of them. Like holding court. She had embarrassed Darin by making him dance with her, then come back and gotten another round of drinks. Someone lined up rows of coke on the table. As the alcohol went down, the conversation got louder and livelier and warmer, and Sabrina was actually smiling a real smile as she went to the bar, bumping brashly against His Dark Mistress at the bar. There were loud gasps and laughs back at the booth.

"Excuse yourself and go to the bathroom. Say you don't feel well," His Dark Mistress said. Sabrina made an exaggerated face at her as she told the bartender which drinks she wanted then took a drink of her new beer, set it down, presumably to pick up the three drinks at once, but snagged His Dark Mistress' half-empty bottle, instead, leaving the new one. She staggered once as she made her way back to the booth, and put the drinks on the table. She laughed.

"I'll be back in a minute."

She made her way back to the bathroom, a dimly-lit room with two stalls and a single sink, and stood washing her hands. A few minutes later, the door opened and Beth turned, expecting to see His Dark Mistress.

"Don?" she said, finding one of Edmond's mid-level officers. He leered at her, perhaps not quite as drunk as some of the other men at the booth, but not completely steady on his feet, either.

"What's going on?" Beth asked. He pushed her toward the stalls, and she pushed back.

"What do you think you're doing?" she demanded. The sound of authority in her voice nearly put him on his heels, but he looked down at her skirt again and grinned. She slapped him. He let it pass, grabbing her shoulders. Beth snarled at him, thrashing and hitting his chest with the arm she broke free. He put his mouth against hers, and she bit him. He laughed, his hands pushing their way into her clothing. She hit the wall between the two stall doors and tried to push him off, but his lean kept too much of his weight against her. Two buttons popped loose at the top of her blouse, and she bit him again, still trying to get a solid grip on his shoulders, this time to angle him sideways. If she could rotate him sideways, he might lose his balance and give her a window.

He kept a hard grip on her hips as she pushed, then stood slightly and slapped her across the face. His breathing was hard, and now he looked angry.

The door behind him opened and before he managed to look over his shoulder, his eyes went fuzzy, and he sagged against Beth. His Dark Mistress closed the door, pulling a hypodermic needle out of Don's back as he slumped to the floor. She handed it to Beth, then reached into her coat and pulled out another two.

"Keep these in your purse."

Beth bent over her knees, breathing hard. She looked up at His Dark Mistress, not taking the additional two syringes. She made to ask a question, but couldn't find the right one.

"I didn't get you into this to get raped. If you can defend yourself, they'll leave you alone. Be intimidating."

Beth shook her head, looking down at the man on the floor.

"He'll know," she said finally.

"No, he won't remember anything about tonight at all," His Dark Mistress said, pushing the syringes into Beth's hand. "You did this."

"How did you know?" Beth asked. His Dark Mistress frowned at her.

"He spiked your drink. I can tell… But I knew this was what they did. Aly…"

Beth watched her, anger, panic, and bewilderment running a wild flurry in her gut.

"Edmond's thugs used to drug her and pass her around for rough sex. They broke her," His Dark Mistress said.

"Why don't you get her out?" Beth asked, anger flickering up higher to win out. She remembered the tragic, desperate woman at the other bar.

"She's gone. They can't hurt her any more. Besides, she hangs out with the older guys, now. They treat her better because they remember her dad," His Dark Mistress said. Beth glared.

"You know what they do to her, and you leave her there?"

"She's the one who told me what was going to happen to you that night," His Dark Mistress said warningly. Beth fell silent.

"I'm going out the back door. They won't know I stopped in here. Go make them pay," His Dark Mistress said, turning and, her jacket flicking the air behind her, walking out of the bathroom without looking back. Beth pulled herself back together and stood for a moment above Don's unconscious form. She kicked him once in the ribs, hard, with the toe of her boot, then stepped on his back and walked out the door.

She walked up to Edmond's table like a train. She pushed Darin to the floor and leaned over the table with her hands spread palm-down.

"One of your miserable lackeys is laying on the floor of the women's bathroom unconscious. The next one who tries it won't survive the encounter," she said, glaring around the table with genuine fury. Everyone, including Edmond, looked stunned.

"My boyfriend back in Miami was very – very – familiar with pharmaceuticals. Get it?"

She looked directly at Edmond, rage pulsating through her body.

"He's only alive because he's associated with you. Make sure he knows that."

She snatched her jacket and stood, glancing down witheringly at Darin, who hadn't bothered to get up off the floor, then strode out the door, her heels clicking soundly on the floor.

"Wait!" she heard Edmond call. She ignored him, heading for the curb to look for a taxi.

"Sabrina!" Edmond called from the door, jogging to catch her. She glared at him and threw up her hand for a cab. He grabbed her shoulder and she violently shrugged off his hand.

"They asked me if you were fair game. I thought he meant he wanted to make a pass at you. I didn't know."

She glared at him, stepping to within two inches of his face.

"Don't ever *ever* lie to me like that. You know *exactly* what your men do. *Anyone* who runs a crew like that does. I didn't just hang out on the beach in Miami. You can't just lie to me, because I *know* better."

She snarled at him, then stepped back to the curb.

"The fact that he thought that he could do that to a member of my family means he doesn't respect me like he ought to," Edmond said with a dark calm. Sabrina looked at him and the hatred she showed him on her face softened slightly. "He won't make that mistake again."

She nodded once, then took a breath and turned to step up to the cab that had pulled up to the curb. He grabbed her elbow.

"Come see me at the warehouse tomorrow," he said. "This didn't go right."

She shook her head.

"I don't know what that means," she said. He started to tell her the address, then shook his head.

"Where are you staying?"

She told him, grateful that she had an answer.

"Someone will be there to pick you up at noon," he said. She narrowed her eyes at him and he held up his hands.

"Bring a gun. If the driver acts up, shoot him. No loss to me," he said, then grinned. Sabrina wasn't ready for humor yet, but she nodded, then let him open the door to the cab for her.

Beth made it all the way up to the apartment before she fell on the floor and cried.

"You okay?" His Dark Mistress asked as Beth walked leadenly into the kitchen and poured herself a cup of coffee. Beth looked at her, glared silently for a long minute, then returned to her coffee.

"You still have the stomach for this?" His Dark Mistress asked as Beth sat. Beth glanced at the banner for a Houston newspaper, then turned away. His Dark Mistress folded the paper and set it on the table. Beth rolled the coffee cup back and forth between her hands.

"I get to destroy them – all of them – at the end of this?" she finally asked. His Dark Mistress nodded.

"I see no reason why not."

Beth stared at her coffee. She was angry. Deep, soul-burning angry.

"This isn't how I do stories," she said. His Dark Mistress waited. Beth glanced at her, then turned away to stare at the black television screen, sipping at her coffee. "I sit outside. I wait. They make a mistake, or I find someone unimportant to talk to, or I find the paper trail. I take the right pictures, I get the right quotes. I close the net."

"You don't swim with the sharks," His Dark Mistress said. Beth didn't turn.

"No."

There was a long silence. Beth drank her coffee.

"You're good enough," His Dark Mistress said.

"I know."

"They didn't even challenge you."

"Idiots."

His Dark Mistress laughed softly.

"There's a point in life where you realize that all you have to do is identify the idiots and you can get anything you want."

They were quiet again.

"I think Edmond is going to have Don killed."

"How do you feel about that?"

Beth drank her coffee. Something tightened in her chest.

"I don't care."

"I agree."

Beth looked at His Dark Mistress, then turned.

"Why me?"

"Pardon?"

"You want someone to use to destroy them. Why me?"

"Because you're capable."

Beth nodded. His Dark Mistress laid her hands out on the newspaper.

"You should know that I don't care if you live or die, as long as you are successful."

Beth narrowed her eyes, considering.

"Does that bother you?" His Dark Mistress asked.

"You'd make sure it got published?"

His Dark Mistress closed her eyes.

"I'd see that David got everything."

Beth nodded, slowly, rolling the thoughts, her eyes drifting down to the table. She looked back up.

"I can accept that."

His Dark Mistress nodded.

"So what is your next step?"

"Edmond is going to send a car over around noon to take me to the warehouse."

"So you're in."

"Yeah. I blend in to the background, as much as Sabrina can, and I keep my eyes open."

There was a pause, then His Dark Mistress stood.

"Once you go in there, you're on your own. Good luck."

Beth was a little surprised at how final that sounded on ears that were used to always working alone. She shrugged.

"Back to normal."

His Dark Mistress laughed.

"I've read all of your stuff. You've got it, but this is not going to be anything like normal."

Sabrina shifted in the back seat of the black sedan that had been sitting outside her apartment building when she came downstairs. She stared out the window, trying not to think about who else might have been ferried about in this car. The driver had looked at her with fear as he opened the car door for her, and she had smiled at him – the pretty girl he couldn't touch. She pulled at her skirt, then tapped her fingernails on the windowsill. The nervous kid in the front seat looked up at her in the rearview and she narrowed her eyes at him. He looked back at the road.

She picked at her fingernails, then yawned.

"How long have you been working with Edmond?" she asked the kid.

"Two years," he answered, glancing at her like he had tried not to. Sabrina's lips curled.

"He been in the same warehouse the whole time?" she asked. He nodded, licking his lips. Sabrina nodded.

"Uncle James has more taste, I think," she said. "Why would he pick a warehouse over a bar?"

The kid looked over his shoulder at her. She raised her eyebrows.

"It's awesome," he said, flicking his gaze back forward. "Better than a bar."

Sabrina laughed.

"Only because they actually let you in."

He licked his lips again.

"No, it's definitely better," he said. "You'll see."

She raised her eyebrows higher at him in the rearview, the humor dropping from her mouth, and he snapped rigidly back forward, risking one small glance at her then leaving his eyes fixed forward for the rest of the drive.

Edmond was waiting outside for her, leaning against the brick at the foot of the stairs that went up to what passed for a front door. He opened his arms and smiled. Sabrina grinned at him.

"Everything forgotten?" he asked as he hugged her.

"For as long as you've earned it," Sabrina answered, pulling away to twist her head coyly. He grinned.

"Miami was good for you," he said. She shrugged.

"I would have done better here," she said. He frowned, nodding, then put his arm around her waist and escorted her up the stairs.

"Wait 'till you see," he said, opening the door and letting her breeze past him. She looked over her shoulder at him and then went on as he closed the door. She pretended not to notice as it latched.

The front of the warehouse was exactly what it had suggested from the outside – a wide garage with scattered cars across the floor, and a small office with walls that didn't even attempt to reach the ceiling. A single shipping container sat askew in the back corner of the warehouse next to the fork truck that would have carried it there. Edmond's hand found the middle of her back again, and he whisked her on through a door on the right side of the open space, into a smaller, dim space with a dropped-ceiling and thick carpet.

"This is my cave," Edmond said, putting a hand on each of Sabrina's shoulders and speaking into her ear. Sabrina nodded.

Encourage or dismiss?

"It suits you."

He clapped her shoulders, and she slowly took her jacket off.

"Brian, take her coat," he ordered. A lanky youth detangled himself from the couch and held out his hand limply. Edmond smacked the kid in the back of the head.

"This is my cousin. You treat her with respect," he said. The kid looked dourly at Sabrina, but held his hand up slightly higher. Edmond was already headed for the prime feature of the room – a solidly-built table with a green-felt top. Four men were lounging at the table drinking beer and smoking.

"Sabrina, this is Casey and Jimmy, and you remember Matthew and Sean."

Sean jerked his head at her and Matthew touched his temple. Casey and Jimmy looked less convinced.

"This is my cousin Sabrina. Martha's kid," Edmond said. Sabrina shifted over one hip.

"Martha that married the outsider?" Casey asked.

"My mother's mistakes are hers, not mine," Sabrina said. Casey took a drag of his cigar, considering. Sabrina narrowed her eyes at him, sticking out her lower lip thoughtfully.

"You're Casey Martin. Your big sister married a black guy and moved to New Orleans," she said. "You wanna talk about loyalty?"

Casey lurched from the table. Matthew and Sean moved to hold him back, but Sabrina flew into Casey's face, index finger first.

"You know what, too?" she asked, baring her teeth. His momentum changed and she nearly tipped him backwards over his chair. She jerked her chin at him. "I bet I've seen her since you have. That first year, when I was still little and sad that we weren't here anymore, she came to visit us, and she told me that you weren't worth it."

She sat Casey down in his chair, standing over him.

"She said that you were a bunch of sniveling, incestuous, beasts, and that she hoped she never saw you again." She stopped, finger hovering less than an inch from Casey's paling face. "I came back. You know you have at least one niece? She stayed away."

Casey glared up at her, bubbling fury, but Matthew laughed.

"She's a Hughes, all right," he said, clapping Casey on the shoulder. After a long pause, Casey shrugged.

"Welcome home, I guess," he said.

Having initiated her to his core table, Edmond indicated the corners of the room.

"That's my office," he said, waving at a door. "The kitchen and bathrooms are through there, help yourself, pool table... television." He opened a door to a well-lit gym. "You're welcome to use this, but the girls usually don't."

"The girls?" Sabrina asked. Edmond grinned and shrugged.

"They'll be here later."

He opened a final door to a darkly-furnished, dim room that strongly resembled the main room.

"For privacy," he said, knocking on the much-thicker door, then grinning. Sabrina rolled her eyes at him.

"So you only hang out with the classy chicks, huh?" Sabrina asked. He grinned wider.

"I haven't got time for classy."

He wandered back over to the center table, slapping on it for Matthew to deal, and Sabrina made her way over to a couch to sit next to a heavy-set teenager in braces who glanced at her before continuing to channel surf. Someone offered her a joint, and she took it, reclining to smoke and observe. The kid who'd chanced coming over to talk to her waited for her to give it back, or speak to him. She did neither.

About an hour later, other girls began to drift in, one and two at a time, as did older men – in their twenties and thirties – who joined the population on the couches, or signaled for one of the younger guys that it was time to head out. Sabrina gathered that most of the younger men were drivers, and she wondered at that. The heavyset teen was summoned, and she stretched her legs across the couch, lying on her hip with an arm draped along the arm of the couch, and she watched. There weren't any women there even her own age; most were much, much younger. She watched in disgust as men in their thirties sat with teenage girls in their laps, then dragged them, giggling, into the next room.

Another pair of girls entered, and one of them – maybe sixteen years old – walked directly to Edmond, who tipped his head back for her to ladle her tongue into his mouth.

"Making your mom real proud there," Sabrina commented loud enough for both of them to think she was talking to them. Edmond looked at her with unconcerned surprise. The girl looked up with embarrassed rage.

"Who the hell are you?" the girl asked. Sabrina stood, letting her hips swivel more than necessary as she rose from the couch to emphasize her femininity.

"He knows that my name is Sabrina," she told her, coming to rest a hand on the back of the next chair over. "Does he know yours?"

"It's okay, Stephanie," Edmond said, amused. He took a drink of his scotch and eased back further in his chair. Stephanie possessively put her arms around his chest.

"He's all mine," she said. Sabrina could see in Edmond's face that it had been the wrong move. He squirmed loose of her arms.

"Go get me another bottle," he said, motioning with his glass to the mostly-empty bottle of scotch on the table. Stephanie rose, stung, and trotted over to the shelves of liquor on the wall. Sabrina watched the girl fight with her tiny tube dress before she reached up for a bottle, and Sabrina turned and eyebrow to Edmond. He laughed silently, draining his glass.

"Have a seat," he said, motioning to the chair. For a moment, the room paused, then went on, pretending as though nothing had happened. No one had sat at the central table but the men who had been there when Sabrina had arrived.

"She's nothing," he said, waving Stephanie off as she returned. She pouted, but went to sit next to the girl she had arrived with, who seemed – Sabrina noted – to be trying to attract the attention of one of the middling enforcers.

"She's statutory," Sabrina said. Edmond shrugged.

"There are more girls her age who say they've slept with me that are lying than are telling the truth," he said. "They may be young," he tipped his head back to look at Stephanie sideways, "but they know what they're getting themselves into."

He grinned and reached for the bottle where Stephanie had abandoned it. Sabrina shook her head.

"What, you didn't chase guys like me when you were sixteen?"

Sabrina shrugged and closed her eyes.

"I graduated high school with good grades. Ma didn't lose track of me until after graduation."

He grinned and stretched, then slid in his chair to rest his elbows on the table. He glanced at Matthew and Casey, indicating they should lean in. He looked at Sabrina, and she resisted the pull to lean forward further than she had when she first sat.

"What you should know, though, is that I don't care what my mom thinks."

He waited a moment. Sabrina coughed back a laugh. He looked at her, eyes patient with the rest of the secret.

"You're either with us or with them," he said. Sabrina widened her eyes with mock drama. "My parents. My dad."

Sabrina sat back with genuine surprise. Edmond ducked lower and Sean had the decency to look nervous.

"There's nothing open, yet, but... There are things. You need to pick a side."

Matthew, Casey, and Sean collectively breathed out and looked at her. Sabrina stifled the urge to shrug. She looked at Edmond.

"They're family," she said. It was the most important thing. It was the one rule.

"I won't let anything happen to them, but he's standing in my way." Edmond snarled. "Either I do this now, or I live in his shadow my whole life, as he gets old and even more senile."

Sabrina looked at Matthew, then Sean.

"You are... in?" she asked. Matthew nodded and Sean, watching Matthew, echoed it. Casey glared at her with determination, even though she had intentionally left him out. She sighed and sat back.

"He banished us. It seems poetic to be here to oust him."

Edmond nodded with finality and leaned back, motioning to someone on the wall.

"Caleb," he called. A skinny blond boy appeared. Surely he wasn't old enough to drive. Edmond looked at Sabrina. "What do you want?"

"Hmm?"

"To drink."

She checked her empty wrist where a watch would have been.

"Always night here," Matthew said softly. Sabrina scanned the wall.

"Vodka tonic on the rocks," she said. Edmond grinned.

"That's my girl."

He leaned in toward her confidentially.

"Mom insisted that I bring you for dinner tonight. I wanted to get things settled with you first. We good?"

Sabrina nodded, a bit bewildered.

"Yeah."

He grabbed her forearm, squeezing her still-tender stitches through her shirt with firm fingers wrapped all the way around it, and nodded.

"Yeah."

He slapped the table abruptly.

"Whose deal?"

Sean knocked the cards on the table in answer as Sabrina's drink arrived, and Sean motioned to Sabrina.

"You playing?" he asked. Sabrina sat back in her chair, crossing her legs at the knee and folding her arms across her chest.

"I have to learn the table, first," she said. "You never join an established game cold."

"They'll skin you alive," Matthew said, grinning at her, and shifting in in preparation to lean over his cards.

"Caleb," Sabrina said, snapping her fingers over her head. The boy appeared. She handed him her glass.

"You guys keep any girl beer around here?" she asked. Edmond groaned loudly. Sabrina shrugged and laughed at him.

"You may be able to drink from the crack of dawn to the crack of dawn tomorrow," she said.

"Like he ever sees sunrise," Sean snickered.

"But I have to pace myself," Sabrina finished. She motioned Caleb away. "Something fruity that comes in a bottle."

He darted away and Sabrina looked at Edmond.

"Whose is he?" she asked. Edmond waved at hand.

"He's one of mine," he said.

"He's actually old enough to drive?" she asked. Edmond laughed.

"Amazingly."

"Can I have him?"

Edmond laughed loudly, startling Caleb as the boy returned and put a bottle on the table in front of Sabrina.

"Caleb, you want to work for Sabrina for a while?"

"Who is she?" Caleb asked. Had his voice just cracked? Edmond looked at him levelly, his mouth implying a joke that Caleb didn't trust.

"She's my cousin."

Caleb looked at her, his slightly-blemished face working through his advantages and disadvantages. Sabrina could do the math. Edmond probably had a flock of teenagers all trying to prove themselves, so being on his own would make him stand out more, but he had probably had to fight for the spot he had already gotten.

"You going to make me go shopping for you?" he asked. Sabrina's eyes flew open at his spirit.

"As if I would trust your taste," she said. "Pick me up in the mornings, take me where I want to go, get my drinks, and make sure no one spits in them. From there, we'll see."

Caleb looked at Edmond, who, apart from being amused, wasn't giving anything away in terms of guidance.

"Choices, boy," Casey said, impatient for Edmond to ante or fold. Caleb nodded.

"Yeah, okay," he said. He waited. Sabrina raised her eyebrows.

"Go sit," she said, waving him away. Edmond returned to his cards, and Sabrina sat back, watching Matthew. He had the best poker face. Edmond had a suite of tells, but his officers seemed to let him win slightly more than he lost, out of diplomacy. Casey was hasty and Sean hesitant. Matthew could have cleaned the floor with them, if he had chosen to. He glanced at Sabrina and winked.

"She gets a car?" he asked. Edmond looked up from his cards.

"Hmm?"

"If she gets a minion, she'll need a car," Matthew said. Edmond looked at Sabrina craftily.

"You're right," he said. "She can have Don's for now."

He raised his head and looked around the room.

"Who has Don's keys?" he called. Someone produced them. Edmond jerked his head. "To Caleb. It's Sabrina's car now."

The ripple in the room said that something important had just happened. Sabrina guessed that she had been right about Don, and that this was Edmond making the official announcement. Matthew, Casey, and Sean seemed unsurprised.

"What was Don driving?" Casey asked. Edmond yawned, tossing chips into the pile in the center of the table.

"Ford, I think," he said. Casey snickered. Sabrina ignored him. The door to the garage opened. Her heart stopped.

Tank and Turbo approached the table, putting a bag next to Edmond. Edmond glared at them.

"What's this?" he asked.

"Who's holding for Neil?" Turbo asked. Sabrina did her level best not to stare, but the entire table was watching. *Don't stand out.* Edmond sighed.

"Put it in my office," he said. Tank went and sat down next to one of the girls with presumptuous familiarity, and Turbo disappeared into Edmond's office.

"Idiots," Matthew muttered.

"Late, too," Sean said, glancing at his watch.

"They can't be late. They don't bother to keep a schedule at all," Casey said. Sabrina looked at her finger nails, every fiber of her body stretched to feel the first indication that Tank had recognized her. She suddenly felt very surrounded. She didn't have to look hard to be able to count a dozen visible guns, one openly stuck into the side of Edmond's pants' waist. She took a drink.

What was she *thinking*, agreeing to this? She should have been one of the groupies. At the edge of the room, silent.

She heard one of the girls squeal – pleasure, anger, or fear, she couldn't tell – and realized why that wouldn't have worked, either.

Turbo returned from the office and settled in to watch television. Tank and his girl left for the next room. Sabrina settled a bit further in her chair, then sat up straight. Confidence. She belonged here, and no one was going to suggest otherwise. She glanced once at Turbo, but managed to focus on the game for most of the rest of the afternoon.

Later that evening, the rest of the crew from the bar arrived, and the poker game took a more serious bent. Sabrina cat-called and cajoled, making a nuisance of herself because she could, and not at all because of the steady stream of alcohol supplied by Caleb.

For a while, the room became crowded, and the pool table had a steady line waiting to play, then eventually the girls went home – some with escorts – and the men headed out for more serious drinking at bars. Edmond checked his watch.

"You ready?" he asked. Sabrina shrugged.

"Send the kid home, at least," Matthew said, motioning. Caleb sat, nonchalantly alert, on a couch. His head jerked, but he didn't look.

"Oh. Are you waiting for me?" Sabrina asked. Caleb looked at Matthew, then Edmond, and said nothing.

"Normally he'd sneak out with one of the kids with a car, but having a car will be new for him…" Matthew hinted quietly to Sabrina. Edmond looked amused.

"I say you let him sleep here. Break him in right."

"Go home Caleb."

"Frankie picked her up this morning. Get her address from him and be waiting outside her building whenever she's ready tomorrow," Edmond broke in as the boy sprang to his feet.

"Yes, sir," he answered, nodding as he loped sideways past them and out the door.

Edmond held his elbow out to Sabrina.

"Sean, Jimmy, Matthew, Darin, Casey, Eric," she said, looking at each of them, then winked. "Have a good evening."

The inner circle muttered their replies, and she took Edmond's arm. The warehouse was faintly orange from the fading light outside and the weak ceiling lights. He led the way across the warehouse floor to his Corvette. Sabrina watched the taillights of the just-another-black-car as Caleb drove out the garage doors, then let Edmond help her into the car.

"Ostentatious, isn't it?" she asked before he closed the door. He grinned and walked around the car, playing with the keys.

"It's the boss's car," he said then started and revved the engine. Sabrina rolled her eyes.

"So that's what you do all day, huh?" she asked, tipping her seat back slightly and settling into it. He peeled out, swerving through the jumbled cars left in the warehouse and broke the rear wheels loose around the turn out of the garage.

"On a good day," he answered, glancing at her as he straightened the car out. Sabrina looked over her shoulder.

"You going to close that?"

"Someone else will get it."

Edmond apparently felt that traffic signals were something that happened to someone else.

"That apartment building you're staying in," he said, hitting a gap in cross traffic to turn left. Sabrina took deep breaths, careful to keep her hands relaxed. "It's a nice one."

"Yeah."

"Your mom come into money down in Florida, somehow?" he asked. Sabrina glared at him.

"Do I not look like a girl who knows how to get what she wants?" she asked. He grinned, passing a line of cars in the empty oncoming lane.

"Sure, but why pay for it if you can get it for free?" he asked. "We've got a place not far from here where a lot of the guys stay."

"Who says I'm paying for it?" she asked darkly. He looked at her and laughed. She watched the road.

"You can't actually drive like this all the time," she said. "They'd have put you in prison by now."

"Who's paying for it, then?" he asked. Sabrina gritted her jaw. He pulled the car over and parked it.

"Why do you think you deserve to know?"

"I don't like when people around me have secrets," he said. She narrowed her eyes.

"I don't care," she said.

They stared at each other for most of a minute, then he grinned suddenly and dropped the brake.

"You're new," he said. "This is going to be fun."

The silence was more defiant than awkward.

"Your parents always eat this late?"

"No. I told them I was busy."

"You were playing cards."

"So?"

Sabrina paused.

"Is it really that bad, between you?"

Edmond shrugged.

"It's never been great. I'm not James Michael Hughes."

"You wanted to be just like him, when we were kids."

"I wanted a lot of things. I learned better." His moody glare at the steering wheel perked sarcastically. "I learned how to want a lot more."

Sabrina shrugged, looking out the window.

"I missed this drive," she said. Edmond bounced his head side to side slightly, re-gripping the steering wheel.

"One day will be the last time I come out here."

Edmond pulled into the driveway and stopped at the sidewalk to the front door. Sabrina paused. He noticed. Raised his eyebrows.

"I don't know if I actually want to see him," she said.

"The last time was the wedding, wasn't it?"

"Yeah. Ma hadn't told me there was drama."

Edmond pulled his head back slightly, surprised.

"You didn't know?"

Sabrina smiled stretching her hands and feet out in front of her.

"It was love, and we were family. I assumed." She glared out the windshield. "I trusted too much."

Edmond shrugged.

"If it were just her, sure, but sending you away, too? He should have let her stay, just because of you." He paused. "He yelled the whole morning." There was a longer pause. "Mom had to talk him out of bringing a gun."

Sabrina frowned harder. Edmond shook his head, clearing the memory.

"Let's get this over with. Get in, get out."

Sabrina looked at him, trying not to show anxiety.

"I've got you," he said. Sabrina smiled darkly.

"I'd be more worried about him," she said. He laughed, opening his car door and coming around to get her. She took his arm, smiling flamboyantly. He grinned at her, and they walked up the walkway to the door where his mother was waiting.

"Aunt Lily," Sabrina said warmly, dropping Edmond's arm to hug the woman.

"You're late," Lily said to Edmond. He shrugged, hugging his mother.

"There was stuff," he said. She smiled a tight little smile and opened the front door.

"Edmond?" a masculine voice called from the kitchen.

"Hey, Dad," Edmond answered, heading through the foyer. Lily held Sabrina's hand as the two of them followed. Edmond and James were facing each other.

"You made your mother wait," James said.

"I know. I'm sorry," Edmond answered. They looked at each other for another moment, then hugged. Both men leaned in as far as they could without looking comical, but it was still uncomfortable to watch. Lily squeezed Sabrina's hand.

"Come help me get the food out."

Sabrina followed her to the far end of the kitchen, where Lily handed her mitts for a ceramic dish. Sabrina took a minute to figure out how to use the mitts with her fingernails and finally followed Lily back to the table with her fingers stuck straight out, using her palms to hold the mitts. Edmond laughed.

"You're not very domestic, are you?" he said. She cocked her mouth to the side and shook her head. He snickered again. She sat and looked at James. He waited.

"Hi, Uncle James," she said.

"You look good," James told her. She pulled her hair to the side.

"Thank you. The years have been good to you, too," she said. It was true. He had always been on the heavy-set side, but his flesh had held firm in the past decade, and he was still built like a grizzly bear. Lily smiled.

"James, will you say grace?" she asked. Edmond sighed, and tipped his head to the side as Lily and James bowed their heads. Sabrina watched Edmond for a moment, then nodded slightly, waiting for James to quickly finish. Lily began serving the food.

"Lily said Meagan died last year?" he asked. Sabrina looked at her lap and Lily sat back, waiting.

"Yeah. It was fast. They don't think she ever knew what happened," Sabrina told him. He crossed himself.

"How have you been taking care of yourself?" he asked. She frowned at him, considering.

"I had a boyfriend in Miami," she said.

"Had?" he asked. She frowned harder, making it clear that this was her personal business, but answered.

"His wife got pregnant and he wanted me gone."

Edmond looked impressed. She wasn't just a girlfriend – she was a mistress. Sabrina shrugged at him. James looked satisfied.

"You did the right thing, coming home. Family will see to you," he said. Sabrina jutted her chin.

"I'm just fine, thank you, Uncle James."

He pretended not to hear her.

"Your mother's decisions shouldn't count against you. We'll welcome you back in as family, and I'll make sure you're taken care of."

Sabrina sighed. Lily made a small hand motion; Sabrina wasn't sure who it was actually directed at. *Silence, everyone*, most likely. Sabrina smiled with a small measure of pity and looked at Edmond, who was watching her with amusement. Like a confidant. She winked at him and he grinned. James took a bowl from Lily and served himself, then handed it to Sabrina.

"There are lots of young men that you might be interested in seeing," he said. "Nicholas has a son about your age that you might remember, Ryan?"

Sabrina shook her head and shrugged.

"I'm not really interested in seeing anyone," she said.

"What do you plan on doing, Sabrina?" Lily asked before James could. Sabrina smiled at her.

"For now, I'll hang out with Edmond's crew, see where I might fit in, there. I'd like to start going out with some of them, to see how they work, if you'd let me," she said, looking at Edmond. He raised his eyebrows and nodded. How could he say no? James looked at her.

"You'd work?" he asked. Sabrina bit back a sarcastic remark, reminding herself who she was sitting at the table with. Lily watched her with urgent eyes.

"This is my family, too, Uncle James. That relationship goes both ways. I'd like to help out, if I can."

He scratched his chin and nodded.

"Wouldn't hurt to show that clan of monkeys my boy keeps around him how to treat a real woman," he said. Sabrina smiled, taking a sip of her wine.

"I intend to," she said.

"You're welcome to stay here, of course, you know," James said, getting down to the business of eating, now. She shrugged.

"I'm quite happy in my apartment, thank you."

"I offered to put her up downtown, and she turned me down, too," Edmond said, devouring his own plate of food. "She's independent."

"Nothing wrong with that, I guess. Your place really nice enough to suit you?"

"It's lovely, thank you."

"We'd love to see it," Lily said. Sabrina nearly choked, but swallowed as gracefully as possible and nodded at her.

"I'd love you to visit. I don't cook much, but I know I could find a caterer for dinner some time," she said. Lily smiled a tight-lipped smile and continued to pick at her meal.

"If you ever want someone to show you how to cook a real, traditional meal..." Lily said.

"Of course. You are the first person I would ask," Sabrina said. "I just never had the knack for it."

"Or the interest, I bet," Edmond teased. Sabrina glared at him.

"Show some respect, boy," James said. Edmond winked.

"So do you miss Miami, Sabrina?" Lily asked. Sabrina shrugged.

"I had friends, a life down there. I can't say I don't miss it. Boston just had this mythic quality to it for all that time, though, and I'm still overwhelmed to be home," Sabrina told her, pausing. "Maybe once this gets to be regular, I'll miss it, but I'm still excited to be home, more than anything."

"Florida," James spat. Edmond snorted.

"Lotta business going on down there, Pop."

"Bad business, the lot of it. No one respects anyone. Just grab what you can take."

"Nothing wrong with that, if you're the one who gets to grab everything."

Edmond looked defiantly at his father for a minute, then suddenly looked at Sabrina.

"What did you say your boyfriend did, down in Miami?" he asked. Sabrina looked at him cautiously.

"I didn't."

"Mmm," he said, waving his fork at her. "We should talk about that."

She waited.

"I'm always looking for new business opportunities."

"Who says you'd be interested in his business?"

Edmond shrugged.

"Business is business."

Sabrina stared at him for a moment, then returned to her dinner. James and Edmond looked at each other, then simultaneously pushed their plates away. Lily picked at her dinner quietly. Edmond looked at Sabrina and raised an eyebrow. She shrugged, setting down her silverware.

"Well," Edmond said. James cleared his throat.

"Well."

Lily looked up.

"You just got here," she said. "I made pie."

"I understand if you need to go, Edmond. Sabrina is welcome to stay and catch up a while longer," James said. "I can give her a ride back into town later."

"As much as I would love to, I'm still getting settled in." Sabrina stood. "Thank you, Aunt Lily, it was lovely."

Lily stood.

"Another time, then," she said, hugging Sabrina.

"I'll call you about dinner," Sabrina told her. Edmond and James shook hands, then James moved in to hug Sabrina. Sabrina's first reaction was to step away, but she steeled herself and hugged him. He clapped her back.

"We're glad to have you back," he said. She pressed her lips together and nodded at him, then Edmond put his arm around her back and whisked her to the front door, retrieving her jacket and opening the front door for her. Lily and James stood on the front porch and watched them out to the car, then headed back inside.

"You want to get a drink?" Edmond asked after he started the engine back up. Sabrina considered.

"Not tonight," she said.

"The boys will want to know how it went. You still with us?"

"He always frightened me as a child," Sabrina said and looked at him. "I picked my side before I knew there were sides to pick."

They rode in silence back into the city and Sabrina gave him directions to the apartment building.

"I'll see you tomorrow, then?" he asked. She nodded, leaning down to see him as she stood on the sidewalk.

"I was serious about going out with some of the guys," she said.

"We'll see," he said. She grinned.

"No one ever actually manages to say no to me," she said, then turned and walked into the building. She waved at the front desk attendant and took the elevator up to the top floor, unlocking and opening the door to her apartment to find a bottle of wine and a fresh bag of Doritos sitting on the table next to a blank pad of yellow legal paper.

Beth grinned and got to work.

Several hours later, Beth sat among a cluttered pile of papers at the table and her wine was half gone. She was happy with her progress, but she wanted nothing more than to go turn on her computer and tell David that she had had dinner with James-freaking-Michael-Hughes. To tell *someone* that she had managed it. Instead, she sighed, collected her papers, and went to crawl under the bed to slide them into the safe. She came back and took the wine bottle to the couch with her, laying on the couch thinking until it was drained, then made her muggy way to bed.

The next morning, Beth was sitting at the kitchen table, completely zoned out when the door opened. Absent-mindedly, she flapped a hand at the doorway.

"Morning," she mumbled. The path forward was forming in her mind and her brain tingled. She heard a man's voice and spun, startled.

"Hello," said the kind doctor. Beth's hands flew to her forearms instinctively, and he smiled.

"Yes, let's have a look at those, shall we?"

Her sleeves wouldn't roll up high enough so, still reeling a bit from the shock of her transition, Beth quickly went to her room and changed into a tank top. His Dark Mistress leaned against a counter as the doctor first inspected and then removed the stitches from Beth's lower arms. He seemed happy with the healing at her upper arms, and after about twenty minutes, he sat back in his chair.

"I think you're set," he said. Beth realized she hadn't yet spoken to him.

"Thank you," she said. His Dark Mistress moved from the kitchen to shake hands with the doctor and murmur something to him softly enough that Beth couldn't hear it. Beth looked quietly at the purplish puckers across her arms, newly annoyed by the removal of the threads, but still a multi-colored flag from the original injury. She had avoided looking at them – in the shower, when she changed, while she was sitting around the apartment in short sleeves – so effectively that they still surprised her, now. She ran a thumb across them self-consciously, feeling the texture the stitches had left behind and the long ridge along the cut. She remembered the feeling of wire across her skin and shuddered, turning back to look at His Dark Mistress as the woman closed the door.

"You're alive," the woman observed.

"He should be careful," Beth remembered suddenly. "My ride might be outside, already."

"The child deafening himself in the car across the street? I'm relieved he was supposed to be that obvious. I made him three hours ago."

Beth waited.

"I don't come and go through the door to this building. The doctor is safe."

Beth nodded.

"How did yesterday go?"

"I had dinner with James and Lily Hughes," she said. "Dinner. At their house."

"And?"

Beth considered.

"It's strange. It's like they're fighting over me. I expected to have to work hard to get them to accept me, but…"

She wandered off, waving her hands. His Dark Mistress sat down across the table from her and folded her hands under her chin.

"Tension?" she asked. Beth nodded.

"Edmond asked me twice if I was on his side or theirs."

His Dark Mistress smiled.

"You legitimate them," she said.

"I what?"

"Without you, this is a father-son power struggle. You showed up to cast the deciding vote on who is family and who is the rebel."

"How convenient," Beth said, raising her eyebrows at His Dark Mistress sarcastically. The woman smiled slightly.

"Sometimes things just line up."

"How much work did that take?"

His Dark Mistress smiled widely, her pinkies shrugging up and out.

"I don't know what you're suggesting."

Beth balled her fists in the new method – fingernails wresting along the inside of her palm most of the way to her wrists – rested her chin on them, and frowned at His Dark Mistress for a moment. "You are on my side, aren't you?" she asked. His Dark Mistress made a disappointed face at her.

"Of course not. I'm on my own side, and that alone."

It took Caleb a good thirty seconds to notice Sabrina standing on the sidewalk, staring at him in the Crown Victoria. It took him another fifteen to figure out that she wasn't going to cross the street to get into the car. He found a hole in traffic and turned the car around, pulling up to the curb. Sabrina waited, and he leaned across the passenger seat and made a *really?* face at her. She ducked to look in the car at him, and he watched her with his head tilted forward. Finally, she laughed and got in the passenger seat.

"We're going to have to work on that," she said, settling in. He gave her an artful innocent look and started driving.

"Seriously. When I want to make an entrance, you're going to have to play the role," she told him.

"If you don't treat me like a servant the rest of the time, I'll act like one when it matters," he said, looking over his shoulder to change lanes. She nodded, considering.

"You make a little more effort than that, I'll teach you how to play the game."

Caleb glanced at her.

"You think I can't figure it out by myself?" he asked.

"If you were going to learn just by watching, you'd have stayed with Edmond," Sabrina said. "You want independence and unique opportunity. That's what I'm offering. Take it or leave it."

Caleb smiled.

"You could have your pick of the grunts, any time you wanted. Why take one?"

Sabrina shrugged.

"I like having a personal shopper."

He grinned.

"They said it was a Ford," Sabrina said, motioning at the car. "They didn't say it was a cop car."

Caleb shrugged.

"It's car. Better than you had before."

"Are you sure?"

He grinned.

Where to?"

"You know any routes that anyone is running today?" she asked. He looked nervous.

"Maybe."

"I just want to tag along. No one knows who I am, no one is going to get in any trouble. I won't cause any problems," she said.

"Edmond doesn't like the routes crossing over," he said.

"He said it was fine," Sabrina said. Caleb glanced at her, torn, then, coming to a stop at a light, looked at her openly.

"You have to pick," Sabrina said. "We're on the same side, him and me, but you have to choose who you listen to."

He glanced at her attire, starting back up again as the light changed.

"You don't know what you'd be getting into," he said. Sabrina laughed.

"What, because you can see my legs? Lesson one. This," she said, motioning to the fitted blouse and mid-thigh-length black skirt, "is part of what makes me powerful."

He glanced at her legs, then back at the road.

"You have a girlfriend, Caleb?" she asked. He narrowed his eyes at the road.

"I'm not going to talk bad about her," Sabrina told him. He shrugged and nodded. She nodded with him.

"You afraid of her?" she asked. He laughed.

"Sometimes."

"Why?"

He laughed again.

"I don't know what she's going to do."

Sabrina smiled.

"Exactly. Is she confident?"

"Not like you."

"Confidence and unpredictability will get you almost anywhere. As a man, certainly, but as a woman especially. Mix in a strategic temper, and I really don't have anything to be worried about. Not at this level."

Caleb considered.

"Besides. All I have to do is tell anyone who I actually am. I'm going to avoid doing that, but no one would mess with Edmond Hughes' cousin, and you know it."

He still paused. Sabrina let him think.

"I don't know," he finally said.

"Look, if you weren't going to do it, from the start, you'd have said no, and that would have been it. We'd have gone to the warehouse and I'd have traded you for someone who isn't going to tell me no. The moment you started arguing with me, you were negotiating. This isn't about you not being willing. It's about you looking for enough proof that I know what I'm doing."

He swallowed. Sabrina waited, picking her timing. Edmond had had an evening to consider what a bad idea it would be to let her see his entire business. He was only going to get harder to convince, but this moment was the wedge that would make it normal for her to take a strategic role. Not just the token vote in the family war, but a real member of the crew. She just had to flip a nervous sixteen year old.

"Okay."

He took her to a relatively low-rent part of town and they sat for about an hour waiting for the pair of mid-level enforcers to show up to start their route. He told her the names of the men and the small piece of the route that he knew, and told her – several times – that he would be waiting for her at the end of the route at a specific intersection about a quarter mile away.

"How long have you been doing this?" she asked.

"Four months," he said. "You have to have your license."

"Your friends all do it?"

He nodded.

"My brother did, too. He does errands for Sean, now."

Sabrina nodded.

"You ever have anything bad happen?" she asked. Caleb shrugged.

"Not really. People get in fights. I saw a guy get shot, but he deserved it."

Sabrina did her best not to gape at him.

"That easy?" she asked. He smiled grimly.

"I didn't grow up like you did." He looked at her, cocking his mouth to the side. "If I'm going to make anything out of my life, I'm going to have to fight for it. My brother got stabbed last year, by a guy who didn't want... well, he stabbed him, anyway. You suck it up and you move on."

There was silence.

"If anything happens to you, Edmond is going to shoot me in the face," he said. He was quiet, serious.

"I understand."

He smiled bitterly and opened his mouth, then closed it.

"What?" she asked.

"You may understand, but you don't care. None of the high-levels do."

"That's not true. The rule is family. If Edmond says you're in, you're family. I'm not going to betray that."

Sabrina tried not to think about that hard enough for it to be uncomfortable.

"That's them," he said, pointing. "I'll be at the end. If you have to ditch them, ditch them."

Sabrina smiled.

"If they get themselves into any real trouble while I'm tagging along, I intend to make them pay for it."

Caleb smiled at that, then she got out of the car and crossed the street to approach the pair of men in dark clothes that Caleb had pointed out.

"You two lack situational awareness," she said after a minute of following. The bigger of the two turned, and Sabrina realized that she had never seen either one of them before. She was going to have to sell who she was to a pair of thugs who had never heard of her.

"Beat it," he said to her. She grinned.

"That's not going to happen. I'm auditing the two of you," she said. The other glanced at her, but kept walking.

"You really don't want to be here," the speaker said. She nodded.

"I really do."

He grabbed her arm and hustled her into a gap between buildings. He raised his hand to hit her and she sighed.

"You've failed to ask the key question," she said. The second man was watching at the mouth of the alley, out of earshot. The hand began to descend, and she raised her voice.

"I'm!" He paused. "Sabrina Hughes-Matthews."

"Hughes," the man said, still digging his fingers into her shoulder. She watched him unflinchingly.

"Hughes-Matthews."

He watched her, his hand drooping only slightly.

"Boy, you're a sharp one, aren't you," Sabrina said, reaching over to peel his thumb off the front of her arm and twisting away. "Hughes-Matthews means that my mother was a Hughes and my father wasn't."

"There aren't any other Hugheses," the man said. She raised her eyebrows at him and nodded encouragingly.

"I just came back from Florida. I told Edmond I wanted to shadow some of the work going on, and he said it was fine. I'm surprised he didn't tell you," she said. "Did he tell you?"

The man wasn't actually that much of a Neanderthal, but Sabrina had disrupted an established behavioral mode, and he was clearly having difficulty transitioning. He squinted at her.

"You shouldn't be here."

"I'm tired of people telling me that. Get on with it," she said, ducking under his arm and walking out of the alley. The lookout seemed surprised to see her.

"We're square," she said. "Let's go."

"Go call the boss," the first man said, coming out of the alley behind her. The lookout nodded and scrambled down the block to a payphone. Sabrina stood with the talker for a couple minutes, waiting, then the second man returned, grunted a nod, and they were off.

Sabrina followed from shop to shop through what turned out to be an uneventful mid-afternoon, finding Caleb exactly where he had said he would be. She shrugged at him playfully as he opened the door for her in front of the two men. He got in.

"You want to get lunch?" she asked. He laughed.

"What were you expecting would happen?" she asked.

"Worst case – someone chasing you down the street, and me having to get you out of here before the cops showed up," he said. She tossed her hair back and laughed.

"Not me getting shot?" she asked. He shook his head.

"If you never came back, I could at least go back to the warehouse and pretend it didn't happen," he said. He grinned at her.

"What do you want for lunch?" she asked.

"You buying?"

"What did you do?" Edmond demanded as Sabrina and Caleb made their way into the lounge off of the warehouse. Sabrina stepped between Edmond and Caleb.

"You talk to me," she snarled. Edmond stepped up onto his toe and tried to get another good look at Caleb. She pushed his chest hard and stepped into him.

"You talk to me," she said. He looked at her.

"He had no right," he said. "To put you into that situation, or to show you where the route was."

"You said it was okay," she said, five fingertips still planted in his chest.

"I did not," he said.

"Yeah, you did," she said. "I'm not going to sit here and be a pretty bird for you."

He went up on his toes again to look at Caleb, and Sabrina stepped over in front of him again. She licked her lips.

"You're just being angry to make a show of it," she said softly, so that only he could hear. "If you were going to send me away, you would have done it when they called you. Own what happened. Make it yours. We're a team, right?"

He glared directly into her face for a minute, then softened his features.

"Make it right," Sabrina said, stepping away. To his credit, Caleb seemed to have held his ground not far behind her. Edmond looked at Caleb for a moment, then held out his hand. Caleb looked at the open hand, then tentatively shook it.

"If you're going to let her pull stunts like this, I need to know that you're going to watch out for her," Edmond said. Caleb shrugged.

"Like to see you stop her," he muttered. Edmond snorted softly, then reached to his waist and pulled out the gun there, handing it to Caleb by the barrel.

"Learn to use this," Edmond said. "She's your responsibility."

Caleb looked at the gun for a very long time. Sabrina and Edmond left him standing there to go back to the card table, and she glanced back once, smiling just a little, to see him still looking at the gun in his hand. He caught Sabrina watching him and shoved the gun into his waistband, scrambling over to the wall where he was less conspicuous.

"You're going to make a mess of everything," Edmond said, watching. She grinned at him.

"So?"

He shook his head.

"That's all. I don't mind messes, as long as I don't have to clean them up."

She nodded.

"Fair enough."

She sat and watched the inner circle play cards for the rest of the afternoon, first with just Edmond, Sean, and Darin, but eventually, as the room emptied out and presumably darkness had fallen outside, everyone in the core group joined in, and the game got intense.

Sabrina could tell Matthew was sandbagging, but other than that, the play was intense and for keeps. Thousands of dollars changed hands every hand.

Eventually, Sean took a set of keys out of his pocket and threw them on the table. Grins passed around the table as Sean called his bet.

"See your bet and raise you the Acura," he said. Sabrina raised an eyebrow as keys came out of pockets around the table and players looked harder at their hands.

"Impala," Jimmy said adding his keys and a fifty dollar bill.

"The Merc," Eric said, throwing out his keys. Darin reconsidered.

"Fold."

"I'm out," Edmond said. Sabrina was watching closely now.

"Out," Matthew said, throwing his cards, but leaning forward on the table.

"The 3," Casey said, tossing keys and a hundred into the pile. "Call."

"Three tens," Sean said, dropping his cards. Jimmy cursed.

"Two pair, queens over sevens."

Eric grinned.

"Straight."

"Three aces," Casey said, shrugging.

Four hands reached into the pile to retrieve keys, then Eric pulled in the stack of cash.

"You mean I can ditch the cop car?" Sabrina asked. Edmond grinned, motioning for Casey to deal again.

"Any time you want to swim with the sharks, they'll take your money and you can take your chances," he said.

The next morning, Beth was waiting for His Dark Mistress at the kitchen table. She smiled as the dark woman closed the door behind her.

"I'm going to need cash," Beth said.

"That won't be a problem."

His Dark Mistress sat down at the table and opened her newspaper – San Francisco. Beth waited.

"You seem eager," His Dark Mistress commented, settling a bit in her chair. Beth looked up at the ceiling and thought about it. She was eager. What was wrong with that? She looked back at the outside of His Dark Mistress' newspaper.

"I went on a route with a pair of Edmond's thugs yesterday. And I know how to get a better car," she said.

"That's nice," His Dark Mistress told her.

"It's this clutching, writhing cesspool of subordinates. They're all completely dependent. They're just trying to improve their ranking under him." Beth shook her head. "He's just sitting there at the top of the pile, in complete control. It's amazing."

His Dark Mistress looked at her blandly over the top of her paper, then continued reading.

"Well, it would be if you were capable of being amazed," Beth commented to her toast. A moment later, His Dark Mistress absently reached into her coat pocket and set a banded stack of bills on the table. Beth stared at it.

"I'd wondered how long it would take you to need it," the woman said without looking. "It's a cash economy."

Beth twisted her mouth to the side, wondering how she was going to carry it. Her cute little purse was barely bigger than the stack of cash. She shrugged. Sabrina would certainly figure it out.

She stood from the table and quickly went to change, only checking briefly on the reduced swelling on her stitches, then grabbed the cash, pulled a thin stack of bills to put into her purse, and slid the rest into the front waist of her pants. His Dark Mistress raised an eyebrow at her and snorted softly. Beth tossed a hand at her.

"Don't wait up."

Caleb was sitting on the car when Sabrina arrived downstairs. He opened her door for her, and she grinned at him.

"Don't get too comfortable. I'm upgrading this tin can soon," she said. He scurried around the car and got into the driver's seat.

"On, James," Sabrina said, swishing her hand at the road. He swallowed.

"Edmond called this morning and said to bring you to the warehouse first thing," he said. Sabrina raised an eyebrow at him.

"And you think that matters to me?" she asked. He didn't look over.

"He meant it," he said softly. Sabrina shrugged. Looking at the kid, she realized that he was sweating. Her stomach clenched and she bit the inside of her lower lip hard to keep from showing fear. She shrugged, but kept her hands in her lap the rest of the drive to ensure that her fingers didn't tremble visibly. Caleb escorted her into the back of the warehouse, then quietly vaporized, doing his best to become invisible against a wall.

Edmond looked up, his eyes unfriendly.

"My office," he said. The room was quiet as Sabrina followed him into the next room. He didn't spend much time in there, but it had been apparent from the first that this was where the secrets were kept. He closed the door and motioned for her to sit.

"Did you not think I would find out?" he asked calmly, sitting behind his desk and setting a gun down on the glass desktop, pointed just past Sabrina's right arm. She swallowed and waited, her heart violently lurching against her ribs.

"I checked you out. You thought I would just believe you?" he asked, a finger tracing along the gun.

"You're going to have to tell me what you're talking about," Sabrina said. She had chosen the line carefully. No strong denial, no overreaction, no false innocence. Sabrina certainly had things to hide. She curled her hands around each other, the twitches reaching her elbows now, and tried to remember to blink normally.

"Your mom didn't die instantly in the wreck," he said, spinning the gun slowly. Sabrina bent over her knees, her throat closing as she choked on her uncontrolled breathing.

"Well?" Edmond asked. It sounded like a lifeline. Sabrina looked up at him.

"Yeah," she said, tears forming and quickly breaking down her face. She pushed at the corners of her eyes with unreliable hands, her fingernails scratching at her nose and eyebrow. She changed to knuckles. "Yeah. She spent three weeks in the hospital. In pain. Not knowing what was happening. Crying. Asking for Peter. You try telling a delirious woman that the man she loved got shipped to the morgue in three garbage bags."

She dropped her head to cover it with her hands.

"Yeah, I'm sorry I don't want to just bring that up every time."

She looked up suddenly, glaring at him, as power flooded back into her.

"How dare you. How *dare* you. Bring me in here and threaten me like this, in front of everyone. Over *her*."

Edmond looked slightly stunned, dropping his hand to cover the gun, now. She narrowed her eyes at him and shook her head, even as she cried.

"You don't know anything. Think you can take me in, use me in a stupid turf war with your own father, then treat me like your pretty bird to intimidate your crew. You don't know anything about my life."

She stood.

"I want the other set of keys to my car. I'm not going to keep riding around in that cop car as the butt of your dumb joke," she said. Mutely, he reached into the drawer of his desk and pulled out a set of keys, tossing them to her.

"The others were... destroyed. I had new ones made for you," he said – lost, he was remembering what he had planned on telling her before. Before, he would have expected gratitude. Sabrina stuffed the keys into the front pocket of her black pants, pushed at her eyes with her knuckles, sniffed twice, quickly, and left the office, slamming the door behind her. She flung herself into Edmond's seat at the table and glared at Jimmy.

"Deal."

His Dark Mistress tucked her paper under her elbow and used her key to open the door at the apartment. She closed the door softly and turned, then smiled. There was a stack of loose bills sitting on the table next to that morning's Boston Globe. She picked up the note.

"Am financially independent. With new car. Out hunting wabbits.

-S"

Several weeks passed and Sabrina developed a routine again. She left in the late mornings with Caleb and audited another pair or trio of low-level crew members as they went through their relatively simple task of extorting money from merchants. It was ruthless, it was efficient. It was entirely disappointing.

"I wanted so bad to walk into that and say that it lacked organization and insight," Sabrina complained, looking between the toes of her crossed boots on Edmond's desk as he worked. He laughed.

"That wouldn't be Neil," he said. "He's a pro."

Sabrina dropped her feet on the floor.

"Let's be straight. We both know if I'm going to pick up a market segment, it's going to be by displacing someone else or creating my own, and while you have an obvious lack of a drug element, here, that's just not my style. Where are you weak?"

Edmond shrugged.

"If you wanted to shake someone up, it would be Casey and his real estate stuff." He glanced up at her and grinned, showing a perfect row of white teeth, from canine to canine. "I mean, look at us. We should be able to turn a profit at running a business, and he loses money every quarter."

Sabrina rolled her eyes.

"You're just trying to put a match to gunpowder because you like the explosion," she said.

"You calling yourself fiery?" he asked and looked back down, laughing. "If the shoe fits."

She pushed her hair off of her temples and watched him for a minute. His fine, strawberry-blond hair was so thin and so short she could actually see the entire top of his head.

"You ever think about growing your hair out more than that?" she asked. He grunted.

"Too much work," he said, glancing at her. "Besides, who am I trying to impress that I can't get anyway?"

She shrugged, then stood.

"If you want to watch the fireworks, I wouldn't hang out in here too long," she said. His chair hit the wall as she opened the door to the main room and walked across the open space to the table where the card game had never quit. She put her hand on Casey's shoulder and leaned over him, resting a palm on the table in front of him.

"You're up next," she said playfully.

"What is that supposed to mean?" he asked, not looking up from his cards.

"I want a list of properties and the paperwork on all of them," she said unflinchingly. He jerked, then looked up at her, bewilderment transitioning into fury.

"What gives you the right?" he demanded, standing. She let her hand fall away, leaning her hips against the table he had abandoned, and smiled.

"My last name," she said, then winked. "Anyway, I'm wagering that I'll be better at your job than you."

"What, you couldn't leech on through Neil, so now you're after me?"

She pursed her lips and clucked at him.

"This is what makes you a bad card player," she said. "You let your emotions get the best of you."

She turned and sat down in his seat, propping one boot up on the table and picking up his cards.

"Neil did abandon his post, but he was actually good at what he did, it turns out," she said.

"Does," Edmond corrected from the doorway to his office. "He's good at what he does."

Sabrina shrugged, re-sorting the cards.

"But I was going to find the weak link eventually."

She tipped her head back to look at Casey crookedly. He raised his hand to strike her, and Matthew and Sean sprung from their seats at the table to grab him. Sabrina heard more scuffling around the room, but didn't react. She watched Casey wickedly, then threw his cards back down on the table.

"He's got nothing," she said, standing. Matthew and Sean relaxed their grips on Casey tentatively as she narrowed her eyes at the fuming man and approached him, getting close enough to put her mouth to his ear.

"You really should be careful making enemies," she said in her best coffee-and-cream voice. "Sometimes they don't forget."

He screamed something creatively obscene at her, but she was pointedly not paying attention to him.

"Who keeps his books?" she asked, dramatically turning to sweep the room. A mid-level in his early twenties glanced at Edmond, then stood.

"Figured he wouldn't do it himself. Get them for me."

The young man paused, glancing from Casey to Edmond. Casey visibly deflated as Edmond nodded, and the bookkeeper darted into the next room. Everyone waited, frozen, as he returned and handed them to Sabrina. She motioned a salute with the stack of paperwork, then looked at Edmond.

"You mind if I use your office for a bit?" she asked. He shrugged and spread his hands. Casey had fallen back into his chair at the table, staring at his own knee absently. Sabrina swung her hips around Edmond and helped herself to his desk. He watched her with open amusement as she started the process of arranging the documents around her, then laughed softly and made his way back over to the poker table, leaving the door to his office open. Sabrina glared at it for a moment, then got to work.

"We're going to the bar," Edmond said, sticking his head into the office. Sabrina looked up, then stretched and yawned, pulling the paperwork in front of her back into the spiral-bound notebook the bookkeeper had given her. She nodded at his raised eyebrows and stood.

"You find anything?" he asked. She grinned and tapped the side of her nose.

"You don't give away hints until the big reveal," she said. He put his hand behind her arm as she walked past him, then pulled the office door closed behind her and walked her over to the table, where everyone was shuffling money and cards into stacks. Casey pointedly didn't look at her, but Sean looked up and grinned, sticking his tongue out at her.

"The 750 keys were in play," he told her, grinning wider, "and you missed it."

Sabrina's eyes widened.

"What?"

She looked at Matthew.

"I'm going to get them," she said. She looked down at Sean. "He kept them, I assume?"

Sean nodded. Matthew grinned at her, shifting as he put his wallet back into his back pocket.

"Of course."

There was a second Mercedes that was just assumed to be out of play because Neil used it as his personal vehicle, and he had a pocket full of keys. He didn't have to put it in play unless he was doing it to show off, the way Matthew would have. Apparently 'Neil wouldn't' was the punchline to any number of jokes.

Sabrina had traded her way up to the Audi that she had won from Sean several nights before, but she was aiming for the BMW 750... letter, letter, something. It was simply the top car, and Matthew had it. It was silly how motivating that was.

Sabrina motioned to Caleb, who took a moment to excuse himself from the conversation he was having with a pretty girl on one of the couches. Sabrina raised an eyebrow at him.

"Is that her?" she asked. He flushed.

"We're just talking," he said. Sabrina opened her jaw sideways and nodded.

"Sure. Put this out in the car for me," she said, handing him the books.

"You aren't leaving without me?" he asked. She frowned, then shrugged.

"I wasn't going to make you stay out, but that's fine."

He nodded and walked quickly out of the room. Matthew was putting on his jacket from the back of his chair, and leaned over to her.

"I expect you didn't notice it, but he pulled a gun on Casey when he was threatening to hit you," Matthew said into her ear. He backed up far enough to see her eyes, watching quietly for a reaction. Sabrina wasn't sure what her face showed, there at first, but she closed her instinctive reaction and twisted her mouth to the side.

"Wouldn't have thought he even had that much in him," she said. Matthew squeezed her arm — when had he first touched her? — and nodded.

"He was a good pick. More loyal than just about any of the rest of the boys. If you treat him well…"

Sabrina nodded.

"Yeah, he's a good kid."

Matthew got his keys out of his pocket and spun them around his finger into his palm.

"I would have offered you a ride," he said, spinning the keys again. Sabrina grinned.

"Don't worry too much. I'll be riding around in that car before too long, anyway."

He laughed and went to grab her coat off of her chair to help her into it. Caleb returned as most of the rest of the inner circle was heading out, following their drivers out to the cars. Sabrina shrugged at him and he turned back around.

"When you drop me off at the bar, I want you to take the books to my building and leave them with the concierge," she told him. He nodded, then swallowed.

"Um."

"Speak," she said.

"Are you done with the early morning work for a while?" he asked. She shrugged.

"Why would I want to get up before noon, if I didn't have to?" she answered. He smiled into his collar, then cleared his throat again.

"My ma, she rides the bus to work in the mornings. Takes her an hour to get to work. My brother used to drive her, but…"

"What time does she start work?" Sabrina asked.

"Seven."

Sabrina snorted.

"You don't even need to ask," she said. "I only want to see seven o'clock in the morning from the other side."

He grinned and ducked his head.

"Thanks," he said, running ahead to get her door.

She sat, thoughtfully, as he walked quickly around the car and got in.

"Caleb, how old are you?" she asked.

"Seventeen."

"You should be in school, shouldn't you?"

He shrugged.

"What are they going to teach me?" he asked.

Sabrina laughed wryly and shrugged.

"What, indeed. Were you any good at school?"

"Not really. It was dumb. Do this, do that, solve this problem."

"Yeah. Now you've got it down to 'do this, do that'. Much better."

He grinned.

"But I know where this goes," he said.

"Tell me."

He looked at her awkwardly and ducked his head, then straightened.

"Well, I drive you around, learn how to do what you do, then you put me in charge of something and I *do* it, and when I do it well, you put me in charge of more. You get another boy to be your driver, then you get someone to be *my* driver. I make money. I take care of my ma. Like my brother."

"You think I'd do that for you?" she asked.

"If you won't, someone else will. I'm smart."

He glanced at her, then back at the road.

"Not school smart, but I'm smart." He nodded sharply. "Someone will."

He looked at her again, longer this time.

"But you're going places. If I'm the first one on your side..."

"Ground floor, so to speak."

He grinned.

"Exactly."

"That's a big bet you're taking on me," she said, watching the headlights go by and settling into her coat.

"You better pay off. My ma wants to retire in style."

She laughed, but frowned out the passenger window. He'd pulled a gun out and pointed it at perhaps the third-ranking officer in Edmond's little army, just because the guy had threatened to strike her for mocking him openly.

"Listen. Don't get yourself killed, okay?"

"Mmm?"

"I've invested a lot of time training you to get my door," she said. "I'd hate to start over with someone who isn't nearly as good at it as you are."

He looked at her and laughed, rolling up to the curb outside the bar.

"Yes, Lady Hughes-Matthews. Of course," he said, jumping out and darting around the car to open her door. She laughed at him as he held out his hand to help her out of the car, but took it.

"I'll be back in less than an hour," he said. She waved him off and headed into the bar.

Edmond was sprawled out on a couch when Matthew got to the warehouse the next morning. Matthew stifled a yawn; Edmond had sounded tense on the phone, and his expression staring at the ceiling was murky.

"What's up?" he asked.

"Alan and Greg got hit yesterday," Edmond said, taking a drag at the cigarette Matthew hadn't noticed in his hand. Matthew's stomach tightened. "Took the cash and beat them. They didn't recognize the guys who hit them."

"You call him, yet?" Matthew asked.

"No." Edmond sat up and took another very long drag on his cigarette. "No, he's just going to pay. I'm tired of pretending to believe his lies."

"Neil picked a hell of a time to go on vacation," Matthew said. Edmond nodded.

"Things are always bad. He couldn't have known it would go sideways this fast."

"He should have told you where he was going," Matthew said.

"I told you. He said he didn't know."

"Doesn't know a thing about loyalty."

Edmond's eyebrow told Matthew that he had found the line. Again. He shut up. He pulled a chair over and sat down, waiting. Edmond leaned forward, elbows resting on knees, and stared moodily at the floor.

"War's coming."

"We'll win."

Edmond looked up and nodded.

"I know. Just be ready."

Sabrina sat at Edmond's desk for the third day in a row, eyes straining over rows and columns of numbers. She glanced up at the door, barely cracked today, and, holding her breath, slid open the top drawer on the left side of the desk. Her mind quieted, going into a deeper detail mode as she quickly went through the mostly-random collection of frequently used things in the top drawer.

Stapler, paper clips, desk knife, pads of paper, gun.

She smiled a little at the idea that her life had gotten so interesting that finding a gun in a desk drawer was dull. The paperwork on top was interesting enough to pull out; she slid it on top of her stack of notes and closed the drawer, giving herself a shot at not looking out of place if Edmond stuck his head in while she was going through them.

Phone numbers, addresses. A few money references, but mostly hand-written payments for benign things. Promotions she already knew about, food, liquor, rent. She slid the drawer back open and darted a hand in, tearing a sheet of blank paper off of a pad as quietly as possible, and scratched a couple of notes on it, stuffing it deep into a pile of Casey's paperwork. She returned the pages and went down another drawer.

File folders full of potential goldmine data. She bit the inside of her lip. She really didn't have time for that. She scanned them quickly. Titles, bank documents, records of all manner of transactions. She glanced up at the door, then took a deep breath and closed the drawer again. She had to assume that he would only keep the most legitimate paperwork at the warehouse. Even Casey's books suggested no impropriety that tracked back to Edmond or a larger network. There were a few things... She laid her hands flat on the paperwork and listened carefully to the tone of conversation in the next room. Girls squealed and laughed, men talked softly; the poker table boasted and cajoled. Nothing out of the ordinary. She opened the top drawer on the other side and found a long knife, three or four sets of car keys, a stack of post-it notes (her fingers itched, but she didn't touch them) and a mirror.

A mirror.

She wished she could own up to going through his desk so that she could make fun of him for that.

The second drawer on the right was completely full of boxes of ammunition. Sabrina pulled the scratch paper back out and quickly jotted down the labels on the boxes that she could see without moving any of them, then stashed the paper and closed the drawer, opening the last drawer.

She leaned down to look closer at the envelopes laying in the bottom of the drawer.

And almost fell out of her chair.

She slammed the drawer shut and sat bolt upright in her chair, heart racing.

What did she just do?

"Falling asleep in there?" Edmond called. There was laughter, and she started breathing again.

"Could you blame me?" she called back, blinking quickly. She pulled the drawer back open with her toe.

Yeah.

Those were inter-office folders from City Hall.

With the mayor's name on the last line.

"Call," Sabrina said, tossing chips out toward the middle of the table.

"See his hundred, raise another hundred and fifty," Casey said, looking at Sabrina. She glared at him. Part of the game. She had him, but she was going to let him drag her kicking and screaming.

"Fold," Sean said. Jimmy calculated, then added his chips to the pile.

"Call," Darin said. Edmond watched Sabrina – he was already out – as she considered. She sighed. Fidgeted her chips. Felt a little bad that lying to Casey was this easy. Picked the chips up, then set them down and re-sorted her cards. They expected her to be insecure, because she was a girl. Threw her chips in.

"Call," she said, more emphatically. They needed to play poker with more girls. Matthew knew. She could tell. She glowered at him.

Someone walked up to Edmond as Casey dropped his cards on the table. Sabrina had to give it to him – he had a better hand than she had expected.

Apparently better than Sean had expected, either. He sighed and leaned away from the table as he sailed his cards into the middle. Sabrina winked at Casey and rolled her cards onto the table, her finger nails clicking on the edge of each card as it slid onto the green felt. He refrained from making any verbal reaction, but leaned out from the table, as well, crossing his ankle across his knee and folding his arms. She grinned and pulled the chips in.

"Matthew, our guest is here," Edmond said. Matthew stood and nodded, making a few motions. Activity picked up, but without any real urgency. It appeared that all of the underage girls were being herded into the next room, and some of the weapons were being stored, but other than that, no one seemed that interested. Sabrina kept her head up, absently stacking chips from her pot.

"Will you please take Sabrina to get dinner?" Edmond asked. Matthew glanced at him, then looked back at him again, harder.

"What?"

Edmond didn't repeat himself.

"You're serious."

Edmond's stare didn't change – passive but unyielding. Matthew sighed.

"What's going on?" Sabrina asked, glancing once around the table for clues, but finding none. Maybe a little surprise for a few of them. Edmond smiled at her, tight lipped.

"Go. Have a nice dinner." He paused, then grinned. "You drink too much. Should be eating real food."

She looked at Matthew to protest, but he was already moving to grab her jacket. He was resigned. She sighed, then looked at Edmond with threat.

"I'm not your pretty bird. You can't just dismiss me any time you want," she said. He stood and walked around a chair to stand nearly chest to chest with her, leaning his head down so that his cheek brushed her temple.

"Are you unhappy with the level of access you've gotten to my business?" he asked. "Because I find it generous. Unprecedented."

She shook her head.

"No. You're right."

He nodded, the stubble on his jaw scratching her cheekbone.

"I will send you away whenever I choose," he said. "Do you understand?"

She swallowed, gripping the back of her chair. Stepped away from him.

"Cash me out," she said to Sean. He nodded. She realized that the room had gone silent. Matthew slid her jacket over one arm, cueing her to move away from the table so that he could reach her other arm, and she watched Edmond. Matthew swept up the stack of cash Sean had counted out. Edmond smiled a little.

"Don't look at me like that. I wasn't going to do this tonight, but..." He reached into his pocket and pulled out a set of keys. The table leaned in to see what set Edmond was adding to Sabrina's set, but he shook his head.

"Not on rotation. This one is yours," he said, handing her the keys. Sabrina looked at him for a long moment then reached out to take the keys.

"No hard feelings?" he asked, genuine. She sighed, the nodded.

"Yeah. I understand. Well, I don't, but I don't need to," she said. She looked at the keys. Looked harder at them, then tipped her head to the side.

"Ford?"

He grinned.

"Trust me."

He put an arm behind her back and walked her to the door, not opening it.

"Have a good evening. We'll see you at the bar later."

She nodded, still holding the key up in her line of sight. Matthew raised an eyebrow at Edmond, who smiled again and headed back to the table. Matthew opened the door for her and they stood on the ledge above the warehouse floor, looking for the car that didn't fit. Matthew drew breath, then laughed and pointed.

"Mustang," she said, grinning and running across the warehouse to where the car was parked against the wall.

"Should have been red," she said, running a hand along the hood.

"No," Matthew said, standing back. "Black suits you."

She motioned at the garage.

"They're all black."

"Come stand here," he said, jerking his head at her. She went and stood next to him.

"First, that is a damn sexy car," he said. She grinned. It was. "Second, I don't know if you'd noticed, but that is a coupe."

"Mmm?"

"Two doors."

She laughed.

"I can count."

"No. That is *your* car. That's not a car for Caleb to drive you around in." He paused. "None of us have our *own* car."

"Caleb could drive this," she said. He laughed and shook his head.

"You don't see it, do you? Everyone thinks you're bucking tradition on purpose, riding around in the front seat with him... You just don't know."

"It's weird and stupid," she said, shrugging. "You all look like idiots, sitting in the back seats by yourselves."

He laughed harder.

"More power to you. We're keeping someone waiting outside. You ready to go?"

She nodded, grinning again. He caught hold of the keys.

"May I?"

"You are *not* driving my car," she said. He nodded.

"I know."

He took the keys and unlocked the driver's side door, standing to the left as he did it, then swung the door open for her. She got in and he handed her the keys, closing the door for her. She grinned and settled into the seat, readjusting it three or four times by the time she realized he was waiting on the passenger side for her to unlock it. She looked around for the unlock button, finally letting him in, and readjusted the seat again, pushing her shoulders back and forth into the seat. He laughed again.

"A chauffeur you are not. Are we getting close?"

She nodded, starting the engine and laughing at the noise.

"I don't even like cars," she said. He grinned.

"You don't say."

A teenage attendant at the garage door opened it for her and she drove out, glancing at the car parked outside of the smaller garage door.

"Who is that?" she asked – a queued, planned question that popped out before she realized that she knew that car.

She snapped her head back forward.

"I don't think Edmond would want me to tell you," Matthew said, glancing over his shoulder.

"Why did he send you away, too?" she asked. He turned to face the road.

The mayor's car.

The mayor's car the mayor's car the mayor's car.

Sabrina looked at Matthew, pure, innocent curiosity. He leaned his shoulder against the car door and rested his elbow on a bent knee, mostly facing her.

"I don't know. I could guess... but." He nodded the punctuation – end of thought – and smiled and shrugged. "I'll just go with it, and be grateful for the chance to take you to dinner."

She rolled her eyes at him.

"I don't know if I remember any of the good places to eat," she said. "Only the ones my mom would have taken me to."

"Turn here," he said, motioning.

She followed his directions through the main portion of downtown, pulling in to the valet station in front of a well-lit restaurant.

"If I'd have known I was going someplace like this, I'd have dressed better," she said. He shook his head.

"You look great."

She rolled her jaw to the side as she handed the keys to the valet and got out of the car. She waited for the valet to pull away, then walked across the drive to take Matthew's arm.

"I know, but you should see how I look when I *want* to look great."

He grinned.

"Then we'll have to do this again. On purpose."

She dropped her head back and to the side.

"Look who's got moves."

He winked and approached the hostess desk. The woman smiled at him.

"Reservation?" she asked.

"Hughes," Matthew said. She glanced down her list, then looked up, eyes widening and smile going to wax.

"Right this way," she said. Matthew glanced at Sabrina.

"Is that supposed to impress me?" she asked, not looking at him. He laughed.

"Should have, the first time," he said. She shrugged.

"If you can't get into a restaurant that Edmond owns, I'd have been convinced I picked the wrong side," she said lightly, glancing up at him. "And, yes, that *is* supposed to impress you."

He laughed.

"Casey's books," he said. She shrugged.

The hostess led them through the spacious restaurant to a table where a server was placing fresh candles.

"The chef's table is also available," the hostess said, turning. Matthew looked at Sabrina.

"This will be fine," she said.

"Thank you," Matthew said. Sabrina knew that the next motion was an exchange of cash, but the hostess mostly just looked eager to get back to the safety of her desk. Matthew helped her out of her jacket then, hanging it on the discrete coat rack on the wall by the table, pulled out a chair for Sabrina. The maître d' arrived as Matthew finished hanging his own coat.

"Wine list?" the elegant man asked.

"Please," Matthew said, accepting it once he had settled into his own chair. Sabrina reached for it.

"I love wine," she said, glancing up at the maître d' to let him know he could move on. Matthew smiled.

"Why don't you say so? We can put it on the list for the warehouse."

"Not the right environment for wine," she said, indicating the restaurant with her eyes. "This is where you should drink wine."

She gave the menu to the next passing waiter and told him which bottle she wanted. Matthew's eyebrows went up.

"You are used to the finer things, aren't you?"

She grinned, then frowned and leaned out over the table.

"Speaking of Casey's books, though..."

He leaned over the table slightly, and nodded.

"Careful."

She considered her words.

"How much... loss... would Edmond consider normal?"

"What kind of loss?"

"Pocketed loss?"

He frowned.

"How much are you worried about?"

"A thousand... maybe two... per week."

He leaned back and shook his head.

"Don't worry about that. That's just operating expenses. Salary."

She sighed and leaned back into her chair.

"Okay. I wanted to make an accounting of, but..."

"He has a temper. It's good to see it coming," Matthew said, nodding.

Another waiter returned with a pair of wine glasses and the bottle. As the man finished pouring the second glass and returned the bottle to the far side of the table, Matthew touched his elbow.

"Can I get a glass of bourbon, please?" he asked. "Tell Alexsander it's for me."

Matthew sat back in his chair, crossing his legs and rolling the wine in his glass around.

"So... As long as we're going to do this..."

Sabrina raised her eyebrows.

"No shop talk tonight?" he asked. She smiled and nodded, once.

"Okay."

She put her elbows on the table and looked at him.

"What would you like to talk about then?"

He shrugged.

"How does it feel to be home?"

She laughed.

"I'm going to need to get a heavier coat. I'd forgotten how cold it gets here."

"This is still fall. You a Florida girl, now?"

"Miami. Worse still."

He jerked his head at her and leaned forward.

"What did you *do* there?"

She sighed.

"I actually had a great life. I was seeing a great guy who bought me anything I wanted. All he wanted was for me to be happy."

"How did you meet him?"

"I have a Hughes mind for business. You can't run in those circles forever without running into Javier." She shrugged. "We just clicked."

Matthew's face ticked.

"Do I know that name?" he asked. Sabrina twisted her mouth slightly and tipped her head back and forth.

"If you pay any attention... probably," she said, hinting with her eyes.

"Huh."

He paused.

"Does Edmond know?" he asked. She shook her head.

"Not specifically." She waited. "Are you going to tell him?"

"I don't keep secrets from him. And that would be a big one. Personal stuff, I wouldn't volunteer it; only if he asked."

She nodded. Fair enough. He watched her for a minute as she smelled her wine, waiting.

"How did it end?" he asked. She laughed and took a drink.

"His wife got pregnant, and he decided that his on-the-side wasn't worth the risk, any more."

"I'm sorry," Matthew said. She shook her head.

"No, not at all. For a girl like me, it's kind of the lottery, you know? I have plenty of stuff to prove we were together, so he'll pay for the rest of my life, now. He was really good to me, but it wasn't like we were in love."

"For a girl like you..."

She shrugged.

"It's all a game, Matthew. Even here. Everywhere I go, I'll be someone's pretty bird. That's what he called me. I make some money, I play the power games as good as anyone else, but it's always with some man's permission." She tapped her glass. "Maybe not here, though. Maybe not forever."

He raised an eyebrow at her, waiting. She shook her head.

"I don't want to run the whole crew. Frankly, you guys are disgusting. Maybe I could get to a point where Edmond wouldn't be able to just take what I have away from me, though. Like he trusted me, and we were equals."

Matthew picked up his glass.

"Here's to that," he said. They touched their glasses together, and Sabrina finished the rest of her glass. He poured her another.

"Anyway, you said no shop talk. How about you?"

"Hmm?"

"You got a girl?"

He shook his head.

"No. I saw a girl for a couple years after high school, but..." Sabrina rolled her eyes.

"Lots of fish in the sea, huh?"

He laughed. She couldn't tell if he was playing embarrassed or if he actually felt it.

"You have no idea."

She realized how much she had let the girls at the warehouse fade into the background of her awareness. They were just… normal. He shook his head and leaned forward.

"The truth is, a lot of us have kind of been on best behavior since you got here," he said.

"That's what you call best behavior?" she asked, taking a drink. He shrugged, sipping his bourbon.

"No, I know, but… After what you did to Don," he said. She nodded.

"Powerful and angry has always played well for me."

"A lot of us have been hoping we'd get a shot with you."

"Define us," Sabrina said, glowering slightly and sipping her wine.

"You know… Sean, Jimmy…" he tipped his head to the side a bit, "Casey, though I can't imagine what that would look like… me…"

He looked at her, teasing, and their waiter arrived with menus. Sabrina and Matthew watched each other, neither looking up at the waiter. He started to list the specials.

"You know what you want?" Sabrina asked. Matthew shrugged. *Sure.* She handed the menu back to the waiter unopened.

"Prime rib, rare, mashed potatoes, and the house salad, dressing on the side," she said. Matthew's mouth twitched in amusement.

"Lobster tail, seasonal vegetables, and another bourbon," he said, handing the waiter his own menu. The man left and Matthew and Sabrina kept watching each other.

"Steak?" he asked. "I'd have taken you for, what, quail's egg salad and grilled salmon."

She stuck her tongue out. He laughed.

"Okay, then."

There was a long pause and he finished his bourbon, sitting back and meeting her eyes again.

"So," she said, folding her arms. "Pitch me."

He raised his eyebrows.

"What?"

"If you want a shot at me, why should I consider it?"

He grinned.

"Well, what are you looking for in a guy?"

She shook her head and laughed.

"So I can tell you which lies to feed me?" She jerked her head. "Impress me."

He leaned forward and put his elbows on the table, reaching out for her hand. She sighed and leaned in to let him have it. He played with her fingers and looked at her hand, smiling.

"But it's so simple. All I have to do is divine from what I know of you: are you the sort of man who would put the poison into his own goblet or his enemy's?"

She laughed.

"Princess Bride. Excellent." She paused. "You're trying to trick me into giving away something. It won't work."

He grinned widely at her, still playing with her fingers.

"It has worked. You've given everything away."

The waiter returned with two plates and Matthew released Sabrina's hand so she could sit back and allow the waiter to place their meals.

"I think we just stole someone else's food," Sabrina said softly as the waiter gave them his compliments and left. Matthew grinned.

"So? Obviously we're more important."

"Why do you know *The Princess Bride*?" Sabrina asked. He shrugged, downing his wine and refilling his glass, then emptying the rest of the bottle into hers. He motioned at a waiter.

"We're going to need another bottle," he said. The man nodded and took away the empty bottle. Matthew looked back at Sabrina.

"My little sister was a huge fan. She made me take her to see it three or four times in the theater." He leaned in. "Don't tell anyone, but I actually liked it a lot."

Sabrina turned her head to the side slightly.

"I don't know. I might have to tell Edmond. We don't keep secrets."

Matthew snorted.

"I deserved that."

They ate for a moment, then Sabrina looked up and wagged her fork at him.

"I'm still waiting."

"What?"

"For your pitch."

He grinned.

"I thought I'd gotten out of it."

She pressed her lips and shook her head, taking another bite of her steak. He sighed dramatically.

"So I'm torn. I could appeal to your desire for power by pointing out that, other than Edmond, I'm the best power play you've got going, and you aren't going to end up with Edmond for obvious reasons. I could tell you that the prestige of being with me is probably even better than Edmond's girlfriend would get, because I have a reputation of being relatively serious. With a lot of the other guys, no one would take it seriously – you would just be the right-now chick. I could try to buy you with sheer cash." He paused, taking a bite and chewing thoughtfully. "But I don't think you're looking for any of those things."

"Paralipsis. Very clever."

"What?"

Sabrina laughed.

"Mentioning by not mentioning. It's a rhetorical device."

"You've studied rhetoric?" Matthew asked. Sabrina shrugged and curled her mouth sideways.

"You'd be surprised what I've picked up." She waited. "Go on. If I'm not looking for any of those things, what am I looking for?"

He squinted at her and sat back, holding his bourbon in front of him.

"It's closest to the seriousness. You want someone who isn't going to embarrass you. The power and the prestige actually is important, but not because you need them. Because the absence of them would be embarrassing." He read her face, the way he did when they were playing cards, and took a sip of his drink. He pursed his lips. "But you had that. And you have your own power. And your own prestige. And your own cash." He smiled, as though striking on it. "You want someone who is going to be fun, on top of all of that. Why would you date someone if you have everything they could give you, unless it was fun, too?" He nodded, then grinned. "So that's it. I'm the least embarrassing of your options, and I'm a hell of a lot of fun, too. I'm the guy."

She stuck her lip out, considering, and shrugged noncommittally.

"We'll see."

He grinned. They ate for a few minutes silently, he pausing to open the next bottle of wine and fill her glass again. She sighed at him and he grinned.

"Anything to improve my odds."

Finally he looked up at her again.

"You don't remember me, do you?" he asked. She looked up at him and frowned. Reviewed everything she could remember. Shook her head slowly, suppressing a small surge of panic.

"Should I?"

"I was a year older than you at school. I just remember you. Everyone knew who you were. You and Edmond. Back before we had shaken out the power structure with all of us, you two were the only ones that were definitely important," he said, his eyes remembering many years ago as he slowly chewed. Sabrina thought.

"I don't think I ever knew that," she said. He shook his head.

"I don't think you did."

She narrowed her eyes at him.

"You guys were really mean to me, back then," she said. He grinned.

"Yeah, we were. Everyone at school walked around on eggshells, around you, but us. The boys in the family took you for sport because you were so..." He had gone too far, and he heard it too late. She waited.

"Go ahead. Say it," she said. "I was weak."

He shook his head.

"No, you were..." He stopped. "I'm sorry. You were. You were weak."

She nodded.

"Yeah."

He bit his tongue, remembering.

"I'm sorry."

She shook her head.

"Don't apologize to me. Everything that has happened to me in my life has made me what I am. Can you imagine what would have happened to me if I had gone to Miami actually understanding what it meant to be Jimmy Hughes' niece?"

He snorted. She nodded.

"Yeah." She considered, then grinned. "I'll see what I can come up with, though, as penance."

He laughed.

"That, I can't wait to see."

"Besides," she said. "How could you have known I was going to end up so hot?"

Sabrina snorted into her wine.

"Nuh uh," she said.

"No, I'm serious. He was just lying there, completely naked, snoring," Matthew said. "Oh, she got him. He never messed with her again."

"I need to watch my drinks more carefully around you people," Sabrina said. Matthew raised an eyebrow at her.

"I think you've proved you're just fine, either way," he said. She shrugged, then grinned.

"You didn't like him too much, did you?" she asked. He wrinkled his nose.

"He needed to shower a few more times a week, if you ask me." He leaned across the table conspiratorially. "He and Darin were actually kind of close, I think."

"How close?" Sabrina asked. He grinned.

"Well, you didn't hear it from me..."

She laughed.

"He's just such a sad sack. I catch him watching me sometimes. Makes my skin crawl. What does he do?"

"Runs some of the cleaning crews. Generally cleans up after all of us." Matthew paused, smile fading a little. "I do feel bad. He's actually not a bad guy. We just give him a really hard time. He's..."

"He's weak," Sabrina said. "And unwashed."

Matthew picked up his glass and tilted it toward her.

"Here's to strong and well-groomed."

She tilted her glass to him and emptied it.

"Another?" he asked, then looked at his watch. "What time is it?"

She held up naked wrists.

"We should probably head over to the bar," he said. Sabrina finally took in the restaurant. Most of the tables were empty and the serving staff that was left was discretely cleaning up.

"Huh," she said. He nodded.

"I know."

"We don't have to go, do we?" Sabrina asked.

"What? Where?"

"To the bar. We could just hang out here and then say it got late and we didn't notice the time," she said. He looked at his watch again.

"That's kind of what already happened," he said.

"What time is it?" she asked.

"Midnight."

She blew air through her lips.

"Early, still."

He grinned. She rested her chin on her fingertips for a moment and watched him.

"Why did he send me away tonight?" she asked. Matthew shrugged.

"I honestly don't know why, but you know I wouldn't tell you if I did."

"No, I know you wouldn't tell me who. But you should know why, and I want you to tell me," Sabrina said. She folded her hands over her knee. He shrugged.

"I don't know."

"They were hiding the girls, but no one else had to leave. Does he not trust me?"

Matthew leaned his elbows onto the table and folded his arms.

"Honestly, he doesn't trust anyone like he's trusted you." He paused for a long time. Sabrina waited. "Okay, if I had to guess, I'd say he was protecting you."

"Who says I need protection?" Sabrina asked. He shrugged.

"Who needs to?" He spread his hands. "Look, you're pretty, you're saucy, you're sexy as hell, and we all like you a lot. Well, maybe not Casey, but… I like you a lot. You can't blame us if we want to take care of pretty things."

"I don't need it," she said. He grinned.

"I don't think anyone actually doubts that." He lifted a finger at one of the waitresses and shifted to pull his wallet out of his back pocket.

"Listen," he said as the woman left with the card. "Do you like to dance?"

Sabrina shrugged.

"I guess."

He grinned.

"That's a lie. You're from Miami, near as matters, and I remember that first night, you dancing with Darin. You were having fun." He leaned over the table and eyed her. "You can do better than that, can't you?"

She dropped her head to look at him through her eyebrows.

"Don't tempt me. You don't know what you're getting yourself into."

They spilled out of the elevator onto her floor, hands, arms, legs a tangle, still high on the music and the contact and the tequila. She tipped her head back to catch her breath as she tried to remember what she had to do to open the door to her apartment. He kissed her neck, her chest, pulling her waist up into his ribcage as he bent her backwards.

Purse.

Her keys.

They were in her purse.

She bent forward and met his mouth, losing all sense of where she was for another moment. Her back hit the wall and she swallowed hard, pushing his shoulders with the heels of her hands, trying to get the space to find her key. They slid along the wall, his mouth running up and down the soft side of her forearms as she pulled her purse open. Where had she lost her jacket? She turned and hunched her shoulders, closing her eyes and resting her forehead against the door as she tried to figure out how the key worked. His lips left cool wet spots at the base of her neck.

The lock clicked and the door fell open. She turned and he kissed her hard, their unsorted four feet stumbling into the apartment. She bit his mouth and pushed him back and away. They stood, watching each other, for three long, deep breaths, then she smiled deviously. He started toward her, hands up to take hold of her again, but she kept her palm solidly in the center of his chest.

"Good night," she said, running her tongue over her lower lip, then closing the door on him. She turned and leaned against it, laughing. She tipped her head back and arched her back so that the crown of her head rested against the door, and just leaned, feeling her body buzz and the cool air rushing up and down her open throat.

"Good night," she said again, softly, finally standing to look out the peep hole. He was leaning against the far wall, head tossed to the side, hands open, palms flat against the wall, with his eyes closed. She grinned, then skipped, best she could on drunk feet, to bed.

Where had her shoes gotten to?

Beth lay in bed wondering how long it had been since she woke up hung over. She wrapped her arms over her eyes. She tried to tally everything she had had to drink the previous night, but abandoned that as a bad idea. She sighed and slowly sat up in bed.

She grimaced.

She'd forgotten to change out of her clothes last night.

She heard a page turn in the kitchen and sighed. She needed to get cleaned up before she went out there. No doubt, she was a reeking mess.

She showered in the dark and brushed her teeth twice before she finally got dressed and headed to the kitchen. His Dark Mistress appeared not to be paying her any attention at all. Beth sat at the table for a moment, then went and got herself a cup of coffee, appreciating the silence as she continued to piece together the previous evening. His Dark Mistress turned the page. If the paper hadn't had the state printed on the masthead, Beth wouldn't have known where the city even was.

She leaned her temples down to her fingertips and rested there, smelling her coffee for several minutes.

"Rough night?" His Dark Mistress finally asked. Beth glared at her through the newspaper. The woman laughed at the lack of response.

"Lots of things you could lecture me on, right now," Beth said after another minute. The paper rustled as His Dark Mistress shrugged and settled into a new posture.

"I don't think you need to hear any of them. You're doing your job. I'm doing mine."

"What is your job, exactly?" Beth asked, picking up her coffee cup with both hands and sipping at it. Hot was good, but her throat was sore from shouting over the music for so many hours.

"It would be much more difficult to accomplish if you knew what it was," His Dark Mistress said. The woman folded her paper and looked at Beth for a moment. Beth became conscious of how hunched she was over the table and considered sitting up, but discarded the idea as too much effort.

"You are doing well, though. You should probably hear that," His Dark Mistress told her. "Better than I thought you could."

Beth smiled sarcastically at her coffee. Hung over and acting like a silly child. Sure. Now was when she was doing a good job.

"Oh," she said, remembering. "I mentioned Javier last night. Edmond has been hinting he'd like to get in touch with him to talk business, but I never said who he was, before. Matthew is definitely going to tell him."

"Good."

Beth waited, eyebrows up. His Dark Mistress shrugged and straightened out her paper into neater folds.

"He'll confirm your story. Call you a lot of rude things for not keeping your end of the bargain and staying out of his life. Make them defensive of you. He knew it was coming. They could have figured it out before through the shell company paying for your apartment, if they'd tried hard enough."

"Might have, already," Beth said. His Dark Mistress shook her head.

"I'd have heard from him, if Edmond had contacted him."

"Figured it out, I mean," Beth said. His Dark Mistress tipped her head side to side agreeably. *Maybe.*

"I don't remember if I told you," Beth went on. "The thing about Sabrina's mom dying instantly... Edmond called me on it. I think it worked."

His Dark Mistress nodded.

"Good."

"I thought he was going to kill me," Beth said softly, taking another sip of her coffee. His Dark Mistress watched her.

"Do you regret it?" she asked. Beth shook her head and shrugged, hunching further over her coffee. The heat on her face was refreshing.

"I don't know. What if he hadn't given me a chance to explain?"

"Risk. Reward. You're alive, so far," His Dark Mistress said, leaning back in her chair and folding her arms. Beth nodded.

"Only because of you, though, really," she said. His Dark Mistress nodded.

"Risk."

They were silent for another couple of minutes as Beth finished her first cup of coffee and went to get another, shuffling through drawers for a minute to find aspirin before she came back to the table.

"It's going to get worse," His Dark Mistress said as Beth sat.

"Why? I'm in, I thought. I thought we agreed I was past most of it."

His Dark Mistress nodded.

"Yes. It's going to get worse, though. I need you to keep that in mind. Keep your guard up."

"Why?"

His Dark Mistress shook her head.

"Be careful."

Finally, Beth nodded.

"Okay."

She stood and went back to the bathroom to finish her makeup for the day, taking her coffee with her, and when she returned to the main room, His Dark Mistress was gone.

Caleb would be a rotten card player.

Sabrina told him so as she got into the car. He continued to drum nervously on the steering wheel, anyway.

"So..." he said. Sabrina raised her eyebrows at him and waited.

"They said you didn't end up at the bar last night," he said. Sabrina smiled.

"You young boys and your gossip," she said, shaking her head and clicking her tongue at him. He blushed.

"No... Um."

"My car is still at the valet from last night. I'd like to go get it," she said. He looked at her and swallowed hard.

"Um."

She rolled her eyes and waited.

"I'm not going to tell you what happened last night, if that's what you're waiting for," she said. "It's grown up stuff."

He blushed harder, then swallowed again.

"No."

She tapped her fingernails on the doorframe and turned to stare at him.

"It was good you weren't at the bar."

She continued to wait, her fingers resting still.

"We have our own place where we hang out, down the street," he said. She nodded. She knew this.

"First we were just talking about… you know…"

She sighed. Nodded her head to indicate him to move on.

"Then…"

She waited some more.

"Something bad happened last night. Word went out this morning that no one is supposed to drink anywhere but Alan's, now. Until… whenever."

Sabrina closed her hand and took a deep breath.

"Tell me what you know. In order. Slowly."

Donnie and Gerald stood outside the liquor store where a pair of Jimmy's older enforcers were making a purchase. Donnie crushed one fist into the other palm, stewing a dark, numb anger while Gerald bounced on his toes. The skinnier man was quick-witted and a dead shot, much more menacing than his hundred and thirty pounds would have suggested. Neil tended to separate his working pairs into fast and smart matched against slow, willing, and massive. Edmond knew better than to question Neil's judgment. Where Gerald went, Donnie went, even when they were working for Edmond instead of Neil.

Donnie didn't like working for Edmond all that much. He had the feeling of a snake charmer, calling a tune for his underlings to follow, first this way, then that. Neil was a guy who, if he was going to shoot you, he'd shoot you between the eyes, unblinking, with a short, but complete explanation. Donnie figured they owed him at least that much. Edmond was the kind of guy who put you in front of a bus.

Gerald, though, was buzzed.

"This is it, man. This is the day. Donnie, man, we're born today."

Donnie thickly wondered how much stuff Gerald was on, switching hands when his knuckles got hot. He wanted to hit something. Anything, really. Just point and pull the trigger. Pain wasn't something he was particularly afraid of. His dad had beat him most days, growing up, until Donnie put him down in early puberty. Pain was just life. Inertia, though. Standing and waiting and watching the machinations of other people planning. It was like trying to bend light. If he couldn't put his hands on it, his mind wouldn't connect with it. Gerald bounced.

Donnie was angry.

He was always angry.

There was a plan, here.

He didn't like plans.

He liked schedules. Loose schedules with lots of time for hitting people who needed it. And a little time for hitting people who didn't.

He liked it when Neil slapped him on the back and told him good job.

Even Gerald never said he had done a good job.

"Donnie. Donnie, man. Get ready."

He bent his knees a little.

He was ready.

The enforcers, one of whom had gotten drunk with his father routinely, in the old days, walked out of the liquor store towards their car. The man recognized Donnie. Smiled in the limited way that a man who has seen more death than he signed up for smiles, and Donnie stepped in front of him.

"What's going on, son?" the man asked. Donnie pushed him.

Just warming up.

Feeling out the man's weight. His balance. His reactions.

"What the hell?" the other man said, stepping toward Donnie, ready to chastise him like a child. Donnie leveled him, his closed fist making contact with the second man's cheekbone with a devastating crunching feeling. It hurt. It was supposed to hurt.

Many years ago, he had stopped shaking out his hands after a hit like that. He didn't now.

The first man, his dad's friend, looked darkly at his downed companion and back up at Donnie.

"What's up is this, man. You're told," Gerald said. Donnie recognized the gun in the tone of his voice.

"This is really dumb, son," the man said to Donnie. "You don't want to start this."

The man looked like a bus, to Donnie, but Donnie had always known that if he was going to get hit by a bus, he wanted to at least punch it, first.

It began.

"The guy shot Neil's guy, and the other guy shot the first one and just ran, and they found them, and the other first guy, and they came looking for Gerald because everyone knows Neil's guys, and the showed up at the bar and a bunch of other guys got shot, and a couple of them died, and then the police came and everyone ran, and a couple of them got arrested, and…" Caleb paused, trying to remember if there were any other details that came after that. He looked at her, wide-eyed.

"If you aren't at the warehouse, you shouldn't be where they know where you are," he said.

"You really think that in the light of day, James Michael Hughes and Edmond are going to decide to go to war?" Sabrina asked. Caleb swallowed.

"They've been hitting each other for weeks," he said, his eyes telling her that he wasn't supposed to know that. "Coupla guys here, coupla guys there, taking money, trading licks. Like that. But last night… Don't be where they can find you. Okay?"

"Why do you care?" Sabrina asked. He looked at her, confused, missing the light in front of them turning green.

"You're my job," he said. "Edmond said to protect you. I can't protect you at Alan's." He looked at the steering wheel, remembering something he had seen. "Or anywhere else, where they know where you are."

"Why do you think I'm important to them?" she asked. He shook his head.

"You are but…" He braced himself, letting off the brake and watching the road again. "That's not why. You're just important, and that's all."

"Your girlfriend and your mom are safe?" Sabrina asked. He looked as though he hadn't considered it, then shrugged and nodded.

"They aren't important. They stay out of it, they'll be okay."

"And your brother?"

He shrugged harder.

"He lives his own life. We both understand."

"That's the order, okay?" Sabrina said. "Your mom, your brother, your girlfriend, then me. Only in that order do you get to be protective."

He looked like he was going to fight with her, then just nodded.

"Okay."

You're seventeen! she wanted to shout at him. *Get a life, get a job, run, live! Live!*

She watched the road silently as they made their way to the warehouse.

The mood in the main room was somber. A few men lay passed out on couches and against walls with visible injuries, but mostly men brooded and spoke softly to each other as Sabrina approached her chair at the card table.

"Lily called," Edmond said without looking at her. "She wants you to call her back."

Sabrina sat.

"What do you want me to do?" she asked. He eyed her.

"I guess you heard?"

"Yeah, you started a war."

"Who says I started it?" he asked, turning sharply to her.

"Tell me you didn't."

She waited.

"What do you want me to do?" she asked again.

"Call her. We stay civil. This doesn't have to go any further than he wants it to."

Sabrina looked around the table at the moody faces, then stood and walked to the wall where the phone hung. She dialed, then sat on the couch next to the phone and waited.

Lily picked up on the second ring.

"Aunt Lily?" Sabrina said.

"Sabrina!" Lily said. That was definitely relief.

"Hi. Edmond said you called?"

"Yes. Dear, James and I were talking last night... We thought we'd like to take you up on your offer for dinner. Are you available this evening?"

"Of course," Sabrina said, without thinking. Another moment and she was sure it was the right response, but the pause would have given away everything. She hadn't been able to afford to think.

"What time would work for you?" Lily asked.

"Eight?" Sabrina suggested. Surely there wasn't anything she had to plan around. She looked at Edmond, who was pointedly not watching her talk on the phone, since everyone else was.

"Dear..." Lily said then paused. Point, Sabrina. "Dear, we'd like to have dinner with you... alone."

Sabrina continued to look harder at Edmond. Let Lily wait. Lily had broken decorum first, she could stew.

"I can't do that."

"Dear."

"You know I can't do that, Aunt Lily. Don't ask."

Matthew's face. She hadn't noticed it yet. He watched her with intensity as he tried to decipher the other side of the conversation from Sabrina's expression. She met his eyes and smiled a little despondently, then brightly, for everyone else's benefit. She shrugged and grinned at the phone. Morale. Morale was what won wars. She looked back at Edmond. He glanced at her, then away again. Anywhere but at her.

The long pause dragged a bit longer, then Lily sighed.

"I understand, dear. Eight o'clock. Would you like me to bring anything?"

"Nothing," Sabrina said, then reconsidered. "No, a bottle of wine would be nice."

Hostess gift, save face, wine. Not a bad combination. No loss, at least. Plus a bottle of wine.

"Okay. We'll see you tonight."

Sabrina hung up and slowly walked back to the card table, sitting down between Edmond and Matthew. Edmond finally looked at her.

"We have dinner plans," she said nonchalantly.

"They know where you live?" Caleb demanded, behind her. She jumped. Cursed herself for it. Caleb planted his palms on the table, addressing Edmond, not Sabrina.

"They should not know where you live," he said. "I thought Edmond, Matthew, and I were the only ones who knew."

Sabrina tilted her head to the side.

"It would be rude to keep it a secret," she said, moving her head across slightly to get far enough into his field of view to draw his attention. "I'm not going to be rude to my aunt and uncle. Is that clear?"

Caleb looked at her wretchedly, real desperation clear on his face.

"Edmond…"

"She's right, Caleb. I'm sorry."

"You have to put people on her building," Caleb said. "I'll stay there as much as I can, but…"

"Caleb," Sabrina cut in.

"No, he's not that wrong," Edmond said. "I should have a couple of guys keep an eye on you," he said.

Sabrina glared at him.

"That will not be necessary. I did not leave Miami to sacrifice all privacy to yet another tiny despot."

He looked startled, then amused.

"It's fine. Just in case something goes wrong. The rest of us are clustered, and hard to get to. We'll just keep guys around in case we need to be able to react."

She glared at him, but his face sterned and she sighed. Looked at Caleb.

"Happy?"

He wasn't, but he didn't have any more arguments. He dropped his shoulders, looked at her once pleadingly, then made his way back to the outside wall.

Sabrina glanced at him, then looked at Edmond.

"Deal," Edmond said. She watched Sean reach for the cards.

"As long as we're burning time, you want to go through my numbers on Casey's stuff?" she asked him. He grinned. Diversion.

"Sure. Casey, Matthew, let's go."

Sean, Jimmy, Darin, and Eric leaned in to play the more intense game of cards that would result from half the table leaving. Sabrina realized that every chair at the table was full. Eric almost never showed up, here. They were circling the wagons.

Edmond lead the way into his office, thinking about it for a moment before he closed the door behind them.

"So?" Casey asked. Sabrina shrugged.

"I finished last night, but the numbers had started making me dizzy. It's there on your desk," she said to Edmond. He opened a manila folder. "Executive summary on top."

"The big numbers make you dizzy? That's too bad," Casey said. "Edmond, why are we wasting time on this? Obviously she has no idea what she's doing."

Edmond ignored him, reading the first page of text, then holding up the summary page of financials next to it. He grunted, picking up the next page and handing the first two to Matthew. "What?" Casey said. Edmond sat. Matthew sat. Sabrina leaned her hips against the wall and folded her arms. They were a few of them basic cons she had found in court filings, but...

"These are legit," Matthew said softly, taking a new page from Edmond. Casey snatched the first few pages out of Matthew's lap and turned his back to read them. There was silence. Pages fluttered.

"These are legit," Matthew said again. Edmond sat back in his chair and put his heels on his desk, reading the last page. Casey shoved the papers at Sabrina.

"Fine."

He shook his open hands over his head at her.

"Fine."

She frowned.

"What are you thinking?"

"I have too much dignity to deal with you. I'm out of here."

Sabrina grabbed his arm.

"What are you thinking?"

He glared at her.

"Do you want to do this?" she asked. His mouth and nose wrinkled up with contained disgust. "Because I don't."

His face dropped and Edmond, at the far edge of her field of vision, tilted his head to the side. She glanced at Edmond, then looked back at Casey.

"I'm serious. I'll admit I had fun, because you're a jerk, but I don't want your job." She grinned maliciously back at Edmond. "I want his."

Matthew glanced up at her with what might have been a spark of humor, then started through the pages again.

"Not today, you don't," Edmond said, handing the final sheet to Matthew. Sabrina's smile faded.

"Yeah."

Edmond considered her for a moment.

"Casey, go get Eric and have one of the boys bring more chairs," he said. Matthew handed him the rest of the paperwork, and looked up at Sabrina, pushing the second chair in front of the desk with his foot. She pushed his foot out of the way with her knee and sat.

"I thought I was going to get another shot at that 750," she said, the play mostly gone out of it. Edmond sighed, leaning forward and resting his forearms crossed on the desk. He hung his head.

"No. I need to do my job." He laughed once, his head bobbing over his wrists. "If I don't want you to take it from me."

He looked up and wiped his hands down his face. Casey and Eric appeared in the doorway.

"I wish Neil were here," Edmond said softly enough that only Matthew and Sabrina could hear. "Sorry, Matt."

Sabrina looked at Matthew quickly.

"He'd talk you out of it," Matthew said, barely audible. Edmond looked at him dangerously.

"Exactly."

Someone showed up with chairs and Sabrina pushed herself over to the wall, trying to get more room to observe. Edmond folded his fingers together and rubbed his woven hands over the back of his head.

"So," he said. Chairs stopped shuffling. "Look, you guys know what we did."

He looked at the core of his leadership, sitting there in front of his desk. No one spoke.

"I did it the way I've always done everything – the way I thought best." He paused again. "I'm not sorry that I didn't consult with anyone. I'm not going to apologize."

He looked around the room, waiting for anyone to challenge him.

"I will give you a chance to object now. If you want out, now is the time to say it. You guys are the only ones who are going to get that chance," he said. Sabrina tried to watch the various faces, but kept coming back to Matthew. He had known. She wasn't sure what he had known or when, but he had known. He was on the verge of twitching, he was so eager.

Edmond was looking at Casey.

"So?"

"I'm not going anywhere," Casey said.

"To the end," Eric said.

"Yeah," Matthew said when Edmond looked at him. They all looked at Sabrina.

"Does it matter what I do?" Sabrina asked. Let herself be drawn intentionally.

"You belong here," Edmond said.

"You know I've picked my side," she said.

"All right. You all need to know that we didn't start this. I was fine picking up where he left off, but he couldn't stand for us to have our own power. They've been picking at us for weeks, maybe months, and we had to stand up for ourselves. We're in the right, here."

"Is anyone going to call Neil?" Eric asked. Matthew glanced at him, then looked back at Edmond blankly.

"No way to," Edmond said. "That's it. I need to talk to Eric."

Sabrina stood when Casey did. Eric stayed in his chair against the wall and looked at the back of Matthew's head. Sabrina and Casey stood awkwardly.

"You, too, Matthew," Edmond said. Matthew paused, then dipped his head and stood, motioning for Sabrina to go ahead between the chairs. He followed her out. She looked at him as they headed back to the table. He shook his head. Not now. Sabrina glanced at the room, pulling in details again. The girls were beginning to show up, spooning out attention and laying claim to couch space. The room was crowded. Caleb watched her around his shoulder from where he was sitting on the back of one of the chairs at the bar. She met his eye and shrugged. Nothing new.

Sabrina wondered who Eric actually was. She had assumed he wasn't very important, from the way he was never around, but she was reconsidering. She waited for the current hand to wrap up, then as Darin started to deal again, she put a hand on Sean's shoulder. He looked up at her with open happy surprise. Sabrina winked at him.

"You have a minute?"

She motioned him away from the table and went to stand by the front door where there was some space. He watched her. How had she not noticed how cute he was before? She internally frowned at herself. That was not helping.

"You're up," she said, leaning her hip against the wall and straightening her sleeve.

"What?" he asked.

"I finished with Casey's stuff this morning. You're up."

"What do you mean?" Sean asked. Sabrina raised her eyebrows at him.

"Sabrina... um," he paused. Opened his mouth. Closed it. "I work for Matthew."

"Doing what?"

He laughed, his throat croaking as he struggled to answer.

"I can't tell you that."

She raised her eyebrows at him.

"I'm going through all of the operations. I'm good at this."

He shook his head.

"If Edmond and Matthew are okay with you going through Matthew's work, um, I'm happy to work with you but... You need to talk to Matthew, first."

His eyes were trying to tell her something, but she couldn't figure it out. She wrinkled her upper lip.

"If you're just another subordinate, why do you get to sit at the big kids' table?"

He dropped his eyes, then looked up at her, amused.

"We do big stuff." He nodded at her, cueing her to nod with him. "Matthew is ideas; I'm execution. Big. But I work for him. I can't talk to you unless he tells me to."

"What if Edmond told you to?" Sabrina asked, trying one more angle. He smiled shyly, confidentially, then looked at her with resignation.

"Even he doesn't know everything we do, and he knows it."

Sean touched her arm, nodding again.

"Talk to Matthew. I doubt he'll let you, but if he says you can go through everything, we'll talk."

She glared at his back, then walked back over to the table. Matthew was watching her closely. He'd have figured out what she was doing, and if he hadn't, Sean would tell him, she had no doubt. The corner of his mouth curled with malicious humor and she sarcastically jerked her head sideways. *What?* He grinned openly. Winked. She sat.

"Get out those keys. I'm taking them from you today."

Sabrina had him. She had him. They'd been trading licks all afternoon, when he wasn't in plotting with Edmond, and he thought he had her on the ropes. She'd bought her way up to the A8 a few rounds back after she'd lost the Lexus on a bad bet earlier, but she was playing flustered. Matthew watched her, reading her. It was intimidating. When he was playing hard, it was a challenge not to crack under that gaze. He just *knew*. She glared at her cards. She had him. He was going to give her a swing at the keys to the 750.

It wasn't going to be when he could crush her – he knew she wouldn't bite. He'd have to wait until there was no hope she was going to beat him, but when she thought there might be. Push her to just the level of frustration for her to take a dumb risk, then pull the rug out from under her.

She needed another car. She liked the 5-series, and would have kept it in her pocket if she could, but she had to keep her car in play, just to stay in the game.

Caleb kept casual track from the little cluster of drivers over in one corner, keys changing hands every time they did at the poker table. He knew she was after the 750, and he was teasing Matthew's prime driver that it was only a matter of time. Her eyes wanted to find him, to let him know it was close, but she kept her eyes on her cards, glaring at them as though willing them to be better.

Not this hand. Maybe the next, or the one after that.

It changed the game, having the keys in the pot. You couldn't fold without condemning yourself to the lowest car on the table. Someone who figured out they had the best hand at the table could bleed a lot of extra cash out of the remaining players, as they stayed in in hopes of picking up a better car than last place. She denied a smile. Two hands, maybe three.

Something flagged at the back of her brain as important. She set her cards down. Didn't need to keep staring at them. She didn't look at Caleb. That would be a giveaway. Something had been important.

Very important.

She called absent-mindedly. Stay in one more round, then fold.

Pain.

It had meant pain.

What had meant pain?

She tried not to roll her eyes up into her head as she tried to recall everything from a few moments earlier. She watched the hands at the table, the peripheral motion around the table.

There was lots of pain in the room. There were two bullets still lodged in flesh, within twenty feet of her.

She hadn't triggered on any of those, all day.

But it still itched.

Bad.

She folded.

She sat up rigidly. That was it. The whimper. She had heard it. She jerked her head to look at the closed door to the next room. Did a rough count of the men on couches. The ratio was wrong. She jerked back to look at the table. She had drawn some attention, but no one had figured it out, yet.

Suddenly the realization of what she knew hit her in force.

She stood up, knocking her chair over backwards and simply materialized at the door to the next room, not remembering the intervening space. She threw the door open, knowing what she would find, but unable to see it at first.

The girl was laying on the ground on her chest, sobbing, a man standing over her, adjusting his clothing. Someone froze three or four steps away from the girl at the intrusion of light.

"Get out," Sabrina growled. No one moved.

"Get out!" she screamed, her voice cracking. Her body shook with unexpressed rage, and she began to swing at unidentified bodies, punching, kicking, pushing, trying to punish them and push them behind her and make her way through the dark shapes to the girl laying still on the ground.

"Get out!" she screamed again. There were noises. She didn't know what they were. Someone grabbed her. She pulled away with a sharp, practiced motion and elbowed the mass attached to the grasping hands. They gave up and went away. She knelt by the girl. The young woman was still.

"Can you hear me?" Sabrina asked. The girl mumbled something incoherent.

"Here, take one of these," she heard in her memory. The girl in the electric purple top and short black skirt sitting in his lap. She

looked around wildly for the man she remembered, but wouldn't have recognized him in the dim light, even if she had found him.

The girl had bruises up and down both arms. Sabrina grabbed a particularly dark one and squeezed. The girl moaned loudly. Pain response. She could work with that. Her mind went blank with a clinical level of fury that would later seem strange to her. Don't move spinal injuries. Was this a spinal injury? She prodded the girl's neck and back, generating only slight protests, her stomach turning itself a full rotation at the sight of the dark purple blood on the girl's thighs. Someone got too close and Sabrina swung at him. He caught her arm and she jerked it away, swinging again, trying to connect elbow to chest. Pain. They all deserved pain. She turned to add her other fist to the attack, and Matthew caught her wrist. Eye contact broke the distance between Sabrina and reality, and she choked on the taste of her saliva. He didn't say anything, but the chaotic noise behind him registered for the first time. He waited. She jerked her arms away from him and turned back to the girl on the floor.

Sabrina rolled the girl over and brushed her hair out of her face, Sabrina's mouth spasming with disgust and rage at the mix of dark makeup and bruise there.

"Can you hear me?" Sabrina asked again. The girl's eyes rolled, unfocused, and the sounds that came out of her mouth weren't even trying to be words. Sabrina looked at Matthew. He was watching her, not the girl.

"She needs a hospital," Sabrina said, picking the girl's head off of the ground and putting her arm under her shoulders. Matthew held up his hands and started to argue.

"She needs a hospital," Sabrina said, louder, and looked back down at the girl. She heard Matthew stand and leave, noticing another set of shoes in her peripheral vision a few seconds later. She looked up at Edmond. He had his arms folded across his chest.

"Someone needs to call an ambulance," Sabrina said. He shook his head.

"I'm sorry. That's not going to happen."

"Look at her!" Sabrina screamed, shaking the girl. She hadn't meant to; her hands tingled with a desire to shake Edmond, instead. He frowned and looked over his shoulder.

"Call Ben," he said to someone, then came and squatted in front of Sabrina, hands folded.

"Don't pretend with me," he said through his teeth. Sabrina's mouth pulled, her nose flaring at the edge of control.

"This is not okay," she said.

"Don't pretend with me," he said. "She's nobody."

"You get her help," Sabrina said, "or I will."

"He's coming."

"Who?"

"Ben. He's already been here once this morning, but he'll come." Edmond paused. Was that humor? "There's nothing for him to do, anyway. She's fine."

"This is fine?" Sabrina asked through her teeth. Edmond shrugged. Stood. Walked a full lap around Sabrina and the girl sitting on the floor.

"Nothing broken, no open wounds. What do you expect him to do?"

Sabrina looked down at the still-purpling flesh, then back up at Edmond. He shrugged.

"I know injuries. She'll hate the world tomorrow and the next day, and then she'll be back again after that."

He paused for a long time.

"Honestly, you picked a strange day to suddenly care."

He turned and left, and the room was empty. Sabrina sat with the girl until a quiet older man came and took custody of her, then went and stood in a corner, the weight of her thoughts still too much. Had she really just ignored it, all this time? Had she *known*?

She strode out of the terrible room and motioned to Caleb.

"I need you to drive me to my car," she said as he scrambled over to her. Someone ducked a head into Edmond's office, and he and Matthew came out. She held up a hand.

"I'm going home to get ready for dinner tonight. I assume you won't be late?"

Edmond shrugged.

"I'll see you at dinner."

Matthew met her at the door. She shook her head at him. He grabbed her shoulder as she tried to brush past her.

"Hey," he said, putting his head by her ear. "I like that you expect more of us."

She narrowed her eyes at him, pulling away.

"That," she said, her eyes indicating the door to the other room, "shouldn't be something that anyone would accept."

He tried to answer her, but she pulled away harder and, locking her arm at the instinct to slam the door, pulled it closed quietly behind her.

Caleb had the good sense not to speak.

"So how are you settling in, dear?" Lily asked.

"Oh, very well, thank you," Sabrina said, pouring wine. Lily had expensive taste. Gauging by what she had found in the wine refrigerator, so did Sabrina.

"The guys all like her a lot," Edmond said. "The ones who aren't terrified of her."

Sabrina grinned at him, smoothing her skirt under her knees as he pushed in her chair for her. James was sitting at the head of her table with Lily next to him, and Edmond took the final chair next to Sabrina. The table was laid with food from a caterer that Lori the hair-and-nail girl had recommended.

"First real lady those shmucks have been around in a long time, I bet," James said, helping himself. Lily smiled.

"They are a bit rough."

"They've been great," Sabrina said. "It's an impressive setup."

Edmond had gotten there early and had made no apology. Sabrina found that she didn't really like having any of them in her apartment. No way she would have been home this early, but after this long being home, she would have had her hair washed of all of its hairspray and her pajamas on, long, flowing silk that whooshed when she walked. Instead, she had spent the afternoon making food arrangements and making sure everything in the apartment was where it belonged. When Edmond had gotten there, she had changed into an elegant black dress and redone her hair and makeup, missing her pajamas more than ever, and they had, with great efficiency of words, agreed to put the exchange at the warehouse behind them for the evening. Sabrina knew that they needed to be on the same side with James and Lily.

The evening was going to be strange enough all by itself.

They quickly exhausted the easy topics – the caterer was good, but not up to Lily's standards, the weather was warmer than that in Miami, Sabrina had a nice apartment (politely skirting how she had come by it), and Lily expected everyone to show up for her big Thanksgiving dinner, of course – and Sabrina found herself torn between staring at Lily, staring at Edmond, and staring at her plate.

She wanted everyone to eat faster so she could show them out. James seemed content to dish out seconds of everything, though, and Sabrina thought with an internal groan at the pie Lily had handed her when she and James first walked in. Hadn't been able to resist, indeed.

"Nasty business, last night," James said suddenly. Sabrina stopped chewing. Edmond didn't flinch.

"What's that, Dad?"

"Couple of my guys got ambushed, no good reason. Some upstart punk, I figure," James said. Lily's fork was frozen above her plate.

"Probably," Edmond said, reaching for more bread. "I've had some issues, lately, too."

"Is that so?"

"Yeah, someone crowding in. Gotta stand up for myself, you know? Might be the same thing."

James piled more potatoes onto his plate.

"Unfortunate business, really. Things have been going well, lately."

"Yeah, I had hoped they'd keep going like they were, too."

Sabrina took another bite, no longer tasting anything. This was Edmond's game. She knew he had a gun on his hip, and she knew that Caleb was sitting down the street in the car, watching specifically for James and Lily to leave. She knew that Matthew had asked one of his guys to keep an eye on Caleb to make sure that the boy didn't get into any trouble – Edmond told her that when she made to head downstairs to send Caleb away in fears that he would look like he planned an ambush. She knew she had a tunnel *out* if it came to that. Here, sitting in her apartment, eating a silly catered dinner, it would take something going massively wrong for her to be in danger.

And yet.

The feeling of being on a tightrope was inescapable. She looked at Lily, and again felt pity for the woman. This was her whole life, watching James balance risk and reward, escalating threat to meet threat. Always coming out on top.

So far.

She looked at Edmond, the cocky grin that she had nearly grown used to in full force as he waggled his fork at his father.

"You know, Dad, maybe it's a sign."

James stabbed meat with his fork and shoved it into his mouth.

"What's that?"

"Maybe it's time for you to retire. Someone gets the jump on you like that, maybe it's time to take the money off the table. You've had a good run."

"Don't talk to me like that, boy. I'll be putting bodies into the ground long after you and your mangy little band of overprivileged children have found the bottom of the river."

Lily somehow managed to further stiffen visibly. Edmond grinned.

"That's my dad." He spoke to Sabrina now. "That's the bull-headed attitude that won him this city in the first place."

Sabrina looked at James, then back at Edmond.

"Yes, we've met."

He grinned wider, downing a huge gulp of wine and reaching for the bottle. Sabrina stood to pick it up and pour him another glass. Lily coughed politely and smoothed her hands in her lap. Edmond held up his glass.

"To your success, Dad," he said, "and to the success of the Hughes line."

James eyed him, then picked up his glass. Lily was the last to join the toast.

"Cheers," Edmond said, drinking, then setting down his glass.

"I think you said there was pie?" he said innocently to his mother.

"Yes, I'll go get it," she said, making to stand.

"No, no, I insist. Please, let me," Sabrina said. "Does anyone want coffee?"

"Can I help?" Lily asked. Sabrina paused, then relented.

"Let me show you where the mugs are."

"None for me," James said.

"Wine is fine for me," Edmond said.

"I don't actually drink coffee..." Lily admitted. Sabrina shrugged.

"I guess I won't make any. I'll go get the pie."

She wished there were more than a counter between the kitchen and the table, but Edmond, James, and Lily could do little other than sit and watch her portion out slices of pie onto dessert plates and bring them to the table two at a time.

"You look good, even as a waitress," Edmond said.

"Edmond!" Lily said sharply. "That's inappropriate."

He snorted.

"She likes to hear it."

"I hang on your approval," Sabrina said, setting a plate down in front of him. He grinned.

"Don't disrespect your mother," James said. "I taught you better."

"I'm sorry, ma," Edmond said, leaning forward over the table to devour his dessert. Sabrina started to clear the rest of the table, but Edmond waved her into her chair.

"You can leave that until after they head home," he said. She shrugged.

"Old people," he said to her. "They just aren't up for late nights like we are."

Lily pressed her lips together. Sabrina thought that might have been going just a bit too far.

"No, he's right," James said. "I have work to get done, yet tonight. We can't stay too late."

Lily and Sabrina looked at each other, then at James and Edmond. Edmond paused chewing, then finished his bite.

"I probably have a late night, too," he said.

They finished their pie in silence.

After an uncomfortable number of minutes had elapsed over empty dessert plates, James stood.

"As you say, boy," he said. Edmond stood. They left the table and shook hands. Lily went to stand behind James' elbow and Sabrina stood at Edmond's shoulder. She met James' eye.

"Thank you for coming, Uncle James," she said.

"It was a lovely dinner, dear, thank you for having us," Lily answered.

"Good to see you, Aunt Lily," Sabrina said, hugging the woman. She and James watched each other awkwardly as Edmond hugged his mother, then James and Lily left.

"Where is your phone?" Edmond asked the moment the door closed. Sabrina pointed. He was halfway across the room when he stopped and turned.

"Someone is staying here tonight. No arguments. Matthew, Sean, or Jimmy is staying. Pick one."

Sabrina opened her mouth to argue, but found the steel in Edmond's expression dissuading enough to quit.

"Sean."

He nodded. Stood, listening to the phone ring.

"Put Matthew on."

Sabrina absently started to clear the table.

Lori actually had good taste in caterers. She'd have to remember the company, if she were to entertain again.

What a strange thought.

"Matthew. Yeah, tonight. I don't know. Get everyone ready..." Edmond said, listening to the answer. "Yup... yup... No, get them out of the store... Yeah... No, everyone is either at the bar or the warehouse... Tell Eric no exceptions. Keep everyone sharp... Yeah. I'm on my way... Yeah. Oh, send Sean over here. He's spending the night..." Edmond's gaze sharpened on Sabrina. "She didn't ask for you..." He grinned, all teeth. "I'm not your therapist, Matthew. Yes, she can hear me... Get him over here, now... Yeah, I'll tell him."

He hung up. Sabrina waited, setting down the silverware and putting a hand on her hip.

"I guess that means the rumors were true," he said. She played her jaw back and forth but didn't answer. He held up his hands. "You don't owe me anything, but..." He walked across the room and playfully put his hand on her shoulder. "Just don't hurt my friend, okay? It sounds like he's got it bad."

She rolled her eyes.

"He hasn't got anything bad. I'm just the latest in a long line of sparkly distractions, and we both know it."

Edmond laughed.

"I don't know about that." His face became serious and he dropped his hand. "Sean is on his way. I'm going to send Caleb home. We're going to keep you out of this, but until we know how bad it's going to get, that means you can't be alone."

"You really think that's going to work on me?"

He laughed.

"You're one tough broad, you know that? This is war, we're talking about. I'm willing to take one of my guys out of play to keep you safe, and you have the balls to resent it?"

"Then don't do it. Keep him. I don't need him."

Edmond took a step back and jerked his chin at her.

"Show me where you hide your guns."

She glared.

"You don't have any, do you? Not one. The steering-wheel monkey downstairs has a gun, and the spine to pull it, no less, and you don't even have one."

He sneered at her.

"You've lived your pretty little life as the lap dog of some cartel kingpin in Miami, and you think you know what life is. Sean is staying here tonight, and every night until my dad is dead, if that's what I say."

Sabrina didn't flinch.

"He shows up late, last thing, and gets up and leaves first thing. I sleep in, I don't even want to see him. I get up and Caleb drives me to the warehouse, same as always," she said. He dropped his head and waved her off.

"Fine. Fine! You die, I did my best, and you were too stupid to live, anyway. I need to get everyone ready." He looked at her fiercely. "People are going to *die* tonight."

"People die every night, when you're in charge," Sabrina answered. He paused, then laughed at the ground.

"Yeah. Yeah, they do."

He waved her off again and walked out of the apartment.

Beth had a moment of panic attack, wondering what would happen if His Dark Mistress walked in on Sean sleeping on the couch, but she resigned herself. She was out of time; what was going to happen was going to happen, and there was nothing she could do to prevent it.

Sabrina answered the door fifteen minutes later to Sean. She had taken her hair down and was wearing her pajamas with bare feet. He hefted an overnight bag uncomfortably and she stood aside to let him in.

"I don't want you here," she told him. He shrugged, looking around the apartment.

"I know."

"Nothing personal, but if I make this easy for you, I let Edmond push me around."

Sean looked at her a little sadly.

"You don't want to be here, either."

He shook his head. She sighed.

"You can put your bag down on the couch. There's only one bathroom, you don't get to use it in the morning. You sleep on the couch. I don't have a blanket for you. You leave in the morning by the time the sun comes up; I don't see you. You can eat anything you can find in the fridge. You don't get to bring anything to put in there. Don't drink my booze. I'm going to bed."

"Good night, Sabrina," he said. She walked into her room, then peeked out a few minutes later. He was sitting on the couch, elbows on knees, taking the clip out of his gun and clicking it back in. She sighed. It wasn't yet ten o'clock. She went into the bathroom and got a blanket out of the linen closet then walked back into the main room.

"Here," she said, handing it to him. "You watch TV?"

"Not really."

"Me, either. I guess we'll see if it's any good at burning time."

He moved over on the couch and she put her feet up on the coffee table, holding the remote in her far hand and eying him suspiciously.

"You don't get to hold the remote," she told him. He laughed softly and wadded up his bag under the blanket and laid back on it, putting his feet next to hers on the coffee table and stretching his arms behind his head.

Late night television wasn't any better than she remembered, but it made the time pass well enough. Sabrina went to bed around midnight, leaving Sean staring up at the flickering light, seemingly comatose. She left the remote where he could reach it.

His Dark Mistress was sitting at the kitchen table when Beth left her room the next morning. She had been awake since before dawn, paralyzed with the impending doom of what would happen when His Dark Mistress showed up before Sean left. But he had gotten up sometime after daylight, packed his bags, and gone quite uneventfully, then His Dark Mistress had arrived maybe thirty minutes later.

"You were late this morning," Beth said, pouring coffee.

"You had a gentleman caller," His Dark Mistress said.

"I had a babysitter," Beth said.

"Ah."

She sat down at the table. Bismark, this morning.

"I need you to get Lori here, today," Beth said. His Dark Mistress lowered her paper to look at Beth. Beth held up her hands.

She had lost four fingernails the day before, beating the men at the warehouse. Two had ripped clean, the others, she had band-aided for dinner. Lily had seen them, but been polite enough not to comment. His Dark Mistress nodded.

"I'll call her after I finish my paper."

That was all.

Beth drank her coffee, not feeling any pressure to push for further conversation, then went to shower. When she returned to the main room, His Dark Mistress was gone. Lori arrived thirty minutes later, clucking over Sabrina's ruined manicure, then insisted on pulling the rest of the nails and starting fresh.

In all, the morning felt surreal. Beth realized she had completely failed to tell His Dark Mistress that she had had James and Lily Hughes at that very table for dinner the night before, then wondered if the woman had already known, anyway.

She finally got downstairs sometime around noon to find Sean in the lobby. He ducked his head when she saw him and met her at the door, opening it for you.

"Sorry. They said I couldn't leave until you were in the car. Who was the girl?"

"Lori, my manicurist," Sabrina told him, waving her fingers at him. "I don't appreciate being spied on."

He ducked his head again, quickly waving at Caleb. He opened the passenger door for her, then stood and watched as Caleb drove away.

Sabrina sat back in her seat.

"So how bad was last night?" she asked. Caleb was stiff in the driver's seat.

"I'm not allowed to take you to the warehouse," he said.

"What?"

"Where do you want to go?" he asked.

"Why aren't you allowed to take me to the warehouse?" she asked.

"Edmond says you're staying out of it. Where do you want to go?"

"Alan's," she said.

"I can't take you there, either."

"James and Lily's."

He looked at her, stunned.

"Well, it wasn't on the list, was it?" she asked.

"No, but..."

"Fine."

She sighed.

"How bad was it last night?"

Caleb looked at her, then away.

"They called all the drivers this morning and made them bring in their cars. They sent all of us home. I'm the only one they let keep my car, and it's only because I'm supposed to keep you where no one knows to look for you."

"You didn't answer my question."

His eyes were wide when he finally looked at her again.

"No one will tell us. I can't find my brother." He swallowed. "I don't know if he's alive or not."

She sighed, putting her fingers to her forehead as she thought. *Could just let them all wipe each other out,* a small voice in the back of her mind thought. It wasn't what she wanted, though. She wasn't going to let herself get boxed out.

"My mom is frantic," Caleb went on. "I don't know what to tell her."

"Pull over here," Sabrina said. He looked at her, then followed her order. She got out, digging into her purse to pull out her apartment keys.

"Go back to my apartment. There's good wine in the little fridge in the kitchen. Get drunk. Stay out of my room. I'll find you there."

His face screamed panic.

"I'm not allowed..." he began.

"Can it. You have my directions. I'm not telling you where I'm going. No one, including you, is going to be able to find me. That meets your instructions from Edmond. Now, you either follow my orders or you don't."

She dropped the keys into the passenger seat.

"I may be counting on you being where I can find you, though," she said. Dirty blackmail, but it would work.

She walked down the sidewalk and looked back at him, sheet-white, still sitting in the stopped car. She got to the bus stop and got on the first bus that went by, hoping that the shell game of following her from bus to bus would put him off following her at all.

The next bus was more strategic; she had had time to think through her next move, and at least consider whether she thought she was making the right choice. Eventually, she arrived within walking distance of the warehouse. She snuck down the back alley and peered around a corner. There was a threesome of dark-clad men leaning against one of the buildings. She turned back and went up to the main intersection to catch a cab. She asked him to drop her off in front of the warehouse. No use risking exposing herself where she wouldn't trigger a confrontation, should someone stop her.

She banged on the door of the warehouse, standing well clear of the door when she heard footsteps inside. A heavy-set, mid-level grunt opened the door and pointed a gun at her. She was grateful that she had done routes with most of the mid-levels; he recognized her immediately. He grabbed her shoulder and pulled her inside. Three more men were standing just inside with weapons drawn. She held up her hands mockingly at them.

"I'm harmless," she said.

They lowered their guns and she looked past them. The garage was at capacity with all of the cars plus a shipping container. Matthew was standing in the far doorway, a handgun resting against his thigh. He looked resigned. She narrowed her eyes at him, brushing roughly past him at speed when she hit the doorway. The room was dim, quiet, and at alert. She charged directly at Edmond, who was standing at the center table, and slapped him.

Hard.

"No more of this little sister crap. I was going to let you be protective, but you don't get to cut me out just when things get interesting."

He didn't react.

"They're outside, watching the building," Sabrina told him. He shrugged.

"We're watching him, too."

He sat.

"Nothing should happen until tonight."

She looked around the room. It was strange to see it without the teenagers. She recognized Caleb's brother, crouched in one corner with a couple of his peers and internally sighed with relief.

"Then why are you cutting me out?"

He put his hands over his eyes and sighed loudly.

"I can't deal with this right now. Get her out of here."

Sean made a move to escort her out, and she put up a hand forcefully.

"I put up with you last night, Sean, but so help me, if you so much as touch me, I will break your face."

"Now! Get her out of here now!"

Matthew wrapped his arms around her chest, pinning her arms to her sides, and she thrashed. He paused and Edmond looked at him. Edmond jerked his head at him.

"Get her out of here."

Sabrina thrashed harder as Matthew dragged her out of the room and back into the garage.

"Sabrina!" Matthew said, squeezing her hard once then pushing her roughly away. She stumbled and turned on him.

"I'm coming," he said. "Let me take you get lunch. You haven't had lunch yet, I bet."

She paused, looking at him without trust.

"Give him some space," Matthew said. "Let me take you to lunch. I promise I'll bring you back here, if that's what you want."

"Doesn't that violate lock-down?" she asked, staying out of arms-length. He shrugged.

"Touche. Nothing should happen until tonight. Do you want lunch or don't you?"

"No."

He grinned, snagging her elbow. She recalibrated her idea of 'arm's length'.

"Too bad. I'm hungry and I want to get out of here for a couple of hours."

He gave her a chance to argue, but she rolled her eyes at him and sighed. He grinned again.

"You have no idea how much I want to get out of there," he said, walking her over to the ledge to look over the sea of cars. He paused for a long time, the silence of the space growing cool and calm against them.

"Well," he said finally, reaching into his pocket. "Since you're never going to actually get the keys outright, I may as well take you for a ride in it." He pulled out the keys to the 750 and twirled them at her.

"Bad taste," Sabrina said. He shrugged.

"Sorry."

He hopped down the four feet to the warehouse floor and reached up for her. She made a face at her heels and let him help her down.

He drove her to a café not three blocks away that she had never known existed, and a waitress quickly set up a table in a small, partially enclosed space at the back. Sabrina cocked an eyebrow at him.

"Sean and I come here sometimes to work," he said. Sabrina glanced at the door. "Not that often. No one would look for us here."

"They only have to look for the 750 outside," she said. He laughed, reaching for her hand to play with her fingertips. She pulled away.

"They don't want the police involved any more than we do," he said. "This is family business. It will stay that way."

"Right up until it doesn't." He started to protest, but she shook her head. "No, this I know. The rules in this business are only the rules until they aren't."

He sat back and smiled.

"I guess I, more than anyone, should respect that."

She folded her arms across her chest and leaned back, crossing her legs.

"So are you going to tell me what happened last night?"

"Sean came over to your apartment," he said, leaning forward, "instead of me. You watched television. You went to bed. It was pretty boring."

He looked down at his hands, then, leaving his head down, looked up at her.

"Why did you pick Sean?"

"Is this all just a joke to you?"

He curled his mouth sideways, then smiled up at the waitress.

"You eat burgers?" he asked Sabrina. She nodded, trying to emit impatience.

"Just the regular, then," he told the waitress, holding up a hand at the menus. The girl smiled and nodded, casting a curious glance at Sabrina, then left.

He looked back at her, lifting his eyebrows in despair, then sighed.

"A joke? No, it's not a joke. It's life. And I plan on enjoying it as much as humanly possible." He pointed at her. "And you can come with me, or you can get out of my way."

"Am I supposed to fall into a puddle at your feet, now?" she asked. He smirked and sat back in his chair.

"If you like."

"Tell me what happened last night."

Saul came running into Alan's, face speckled with blood, jacket torn.

"They were waiting for us," he said as the bar erupted into erratic action. The bar was packed past capacity, and chairs and tables scraped as men checked weapons and ammunition. Edmond's table was no different, but he and Matthew simply sat, first staring forward, then glancing at each other and turning to watch the room.

"How many?" Edmond asked.

"Should be one," Matthew said. Edmond nodded. They knew there would be losses. Edmond stood and the bar quieted slightly.

"Sit," he said. Someone produced a chair and put Saul into it. The story wasn't much. They had been walking to Alan's from one of the restaurants and a pair of James' enforcers intercepted them. His brother Gene was dead.

Saul said it started with a beating. It meant James had intended that to be the message, but Gene was a loudmouth and Saul was loyal. They wouldn't have backed down from the fight, even if they were boxing outside their weight class. Edmond weighed the option to escalate as Saul downed several shots. Matthew took the opening.

"They won't have gotten far. You four," he indicated, "go track them down. Call in when you find them. The four of you, head to McCarty's and pick someone off. I don't care who. I'm going to make an example of someone, tonight."

One.

Plus the two last night for three.

Probably one more tonight. These things happen.

Edmond sat back down at the booth, now emptied in the frenzy of anger and excitement that had taken over the rest of the bar, and watched the swirl. A few of the guys knew Gene pretty well and were reacting predictably. Rage, there. Panic, over there. Fear. Pity. All of it masked with a machismo that Matthew could orchestrate like an artist.

The first foursome was already out, the second was summoning teenage drivers to ante up a pair of cars. Were the boys driving? Edmond watched, mostly unconcerned. No, they were just turning over keys. Matthew protected them like children.

Saul drank another pair of shots and stood, screaming for blood. Revenge. He staggered toward the door and Casey caught him. Worthless. Saul slumped against Casey and Casey dumped him off into the booth around from Edmond. Edmond eyed him and shifted. He could still pop. Saul wasn't known for holding his liquor well.

Matthew had another three guys headed out to watch the bar at a distance. Did they know they were cannon fodder? That they were expected to show up, guns blazing, and get demolished as a simple alarm system?

The ones who survived would get what was coming to them. Edmond would move up in stature, and all of them would move up with him. It was the way of things. If they didn't make it, someone else would jump at the opportunity to ride Edmond's coattails. He was Edmond Hughes, and very, very soon the city would know what that meant.

"Two more dead, after that," Matthew told her.

"You're glowing," Sabrina said.

"We're winning," he told her. "It's just the first act. I have so much more. Once the guys get good at doing hits and doing kidnappings, we'll hit them all the time. Everywhere. We won't have to wait for daylight, because who's going to see? James Hughes has been picking at us for months, and Eddie wouldn't stand up to him. Now he's going to see that he kicked the wrong hornet's nest."

"Edmond isn't that much of a psychopath," Sabrina said. "Not like you describe."

"He isn't a psychopath. He's cool under pressure. Just like playing cards. You know what's in your hand, you can guess what's in the other guy's by watching him, then you bleed him out."

Sabrina thoughtfully chewed her burger. She had to admit, it was worth coming back for.

"Why did you send all of the drivers home?" she asked. Matthew shook his head, dropping his straw back into his soda. A passive part of the back of Sabrina's mind noted that she had never seen him drink something without alcohol in it, before. Collectively, their livers must be pickled.

"Unreliable. It was the easiest, fastest cut to make that would get the ones who are going to turn tail out of the equation."

"Caleb is really upset about it," Sabrina said. He shrugged.

"I'm sure they all are."

"You think he'd run?" she asked. He shook his head, then grinned.

"Not if you were around. Kid's got a crush, so bad… No, he wouldn't cut."

"Then why send him home?"

"Because at the end of this, I don't want to have told anyone that they're out 'cause they're a coward. They just didn't make the age cut. No big deal."

She considered.

"How long have you been planning this?"

He looked her dead in the eye, reading her. Blinked once. She held his eyes coolly. He ducked his head and grinned.

"Not this exactly, but… It pays to have your contingencies covered." He leaned forward in his chair, slightly around the table and nodded at her. "Edmond is my ticket, same as you."

She sighed.

"You're dangerous."

"Why is that?"

"You're the kind of guy who gets his guy to the top, then cuts him out," she said. She wondered if she would regret it, but the glint in his eyes concerned her. He watched her with a still expression for a moment, then a devious smile crept onto his face.

"I guess you'll just have to keep me close enough to get in my way, when the time comes."

She smiled at him.

"I guess so."

He sat back with his drink.

"No, I'm hurt, though, really. I'd never do that to Edmond. We've gone through too much together. His father started all of this. It would have never happened if James had treated Edmond the way he deserved."

Sabrina nodded, almost convinced.

"Sure."

He grinned.

"Hey, I'm not going to try too hard to convince you. Dangerous is sexy."

"I'm still not that easy," she told him. He jerked his chin at her.

"No, I noticed that, last time. You have to give me another shot, sometime."

"Don't expect it to end up any different."

"Why not? I always expect what I want. Means I get it more."

"Are you bragging?"

He pointed a finger at her around the side of his glass.

"You tell me what you want, Sabrina, and you'll get it. I don't care what it is. I can get it for you."

She rounded her lips, hinting to him that he'd made a mistake. His bravado didn't budge.

"I want Edmond to respect me," she said. He set his glass down on the table. Raised his eyebrows innocently.

"Doesn't he, already?"

She shook her head slowly.

"Not when he sends Caleb to take me shopping," she said.

"What if I told you I was the one who told Caleb to route you somewhere else?" Matthew asked. She narrowed her eyes at him thoughtfully.

"I'd believe you, but I'd bet you the keys to the 750 that it was because Edmond... let you know... that he wanted me kept out of everything."

The corner of Matthew's mouth curled.

"No bet."

She nodded.

"I'll get you in," Matthew said, suddenly serious.

"Right."

"No, he listens to me. He doesn't listen to anyone like he listens to me. I'll get you in."

She nodded for a moment, scratching her chin theatrically.

"You still won't get to go home with me," she said. He shrugged, reaching into his pocket to put a stack of bills on the table.

"We'll see about that."

Three bodies. Three nights.

Sabrina wouldn't let them send her home at night anymore, so she stayed at the bar with them until dawn, watching the ruthless efficiency with which Matthew conducted the war.

The war.

That's what he and Edmond had taken to calling it.

It made her physically ill, coming home, sitting on her couch, looking over at a passed-out Caleb on the other couch, and knowing that *the war* was happening. She sat still, trying to breathe out the stench of chaos and unexpressed fear and physical pain from the dark hours. Caleb slurped.

She laughed.

He sat bolt upright, scrambling for the gun that was laying on the glass coffee table. She made a barking noise at him and he blinked fuzzy eyes at her and collapsed back onto the couch.

"Seth is still alive?" he asked.

"Seth is still alive."

He sighed and nodded into the couch, dropping his arm over his head.

"You're supposed to be too young to be hung over," Sabrina told him. He nodded.

"I'm still drunk," he said. She smiled. He struggled up and blinked at the soft light that was making it through blue curtains. The curtains were always closed, now.

"Maybe I am hung over," he said. "I have a headache."

"Coffee?" Sabrina asked. He nodded. She stood, stretching a back sore from a bar booth that was never intended for that many hours of continuous habitation.

"Are we winning?" Caleb asked. Sabrina shrugged.

"Someone got shot last night. In the chaos, I couldn't figure out who it was. We disappeared another three of them," she said. "How does your mom feel about you staying at my apartment, right now?"

He rubbed his eyes, hanging over the back of the couch.

"She said if I'm just going to sit around and drink, I may as well not do it at her kitchen table," he said. "She..."

Sabrina looked at him, trying to read the expression through the drunk.

"She disapproves?" she asked. He considered, then nodded.

"She disapproves."

"How long is this going to last?" Caleb asked. Sabrina scratched her neck, remembering.

"When I was a girl, Uncle James got in a spat with one of the younger Italians." She leaned against the counter and looked at Caleb. "I don't really remember a lot. They didn't really tell me what was going on, but things at school were tense for a couple of weeks, really tense, and my mom kept me home a couple of days. After that, it felt more like... Look, did you follow Desert Storm?"

He nodded.

"We played soldiers."

She smiled, taking a moment to pull coffee mugs out of a cabinet.

"It was kind of like that. The first few weeks were intense. That was all anyone could talk about. Then it was just another part of normal life. I remember the big party at Uncle James' house when it ended, but I remember thinking that it was weird, that anything was still going on, really. I guess there were still people fighting, but for the rest of us... life just went on."

Caleb poured over the back of the couch. The attempt had apparently been to land on his feet, but his feet were slow coming over the couch and his hand was the first thing on the ground. Sabrina watched him silently as he found his feet and pushed himself up, leaning against the couch. She filled the mugs and joined him eventually at the table.

"Edmond didn't send you home, last night," he said, then apparently realized that that might have needed to be a question. He looked under the table tactlessly to see if she was wearing the same skirt as the night before.

"It's a glass table, Caleb," she said. He frowned and nodded, patting the surface with his palm. She hid a smile behind her hand.

"No, he didn't send me home," she said.

"I told you Matthew is as good as his word," Caleb said, sipping at the coffee.

"How much wine did you have last night?" Sabrina asked. He frowned, trying to remember.

"Two?" he asked. She sighed.

"Do you have anyone who will buy you alcohol?" she asked.

"Seth," he said. She nodded.

"Remind me tonight, and we'll get some groceries." She paused. "Strike that. Remind me tonight, and we'll get some groceries, and I'll cook you dinner."

"You said you don't cook," he said.

"You like macaroni and cheese?" she asked. He grinned.

"Pub food," he said. She laughed.

"Not exactly," she said, "but if you're just going to sit around my apartment all night and drink..."

"What else am I supposed to do? It's what you told me to do," he complained, apparently unable to decide between the two competing arguments.

"No, it's fine. I understand. But I can't let you live on alcohol. Not for more than a day or two, and you've hit your limit. I'm going to feed you real food. Macaroni, spaghetti, microwave pizza. The sky is the limit, as long as it isn't any more complicated than boiling water or turning on the stove."

He laughed, curling up over his arms again. She yawned.

"I don't know why I'm drinking coffee," she said, pushing her mug across to him. "I'm going to bed. I'll see you tonight. If you're going to sleep, sleep on the couch, not the table. Okay?"

He nodded his face against the table. She smiled and left to her room.

"Is the small boy-child going to be staying here much longer?" His Dark Mistress asked from the kitchen table when Beth came stretching out of her room.

"When did he leave?" she asked, yawning.

"A couple of hours ago. Looked pretty rough," His Dark Mistress said.

"Hard living," Beth commented. "Where's your paper?"

"I already finished it." His Dark Mistress leaned against the back of her chair and looked at Beth. "You do realize that most of the world considers sunset to be the *end* of the day, yes?"

Beth grinned and collapsed into a chair, rubbing her temples. "I'm so beat."

"You in over your head, do you think?"

"Who knows, anymore," Beth said.

His Dark Mistress watched her quietly. Beth got up and poured herself a cup of coffee. Hot. How did she know when to make coffee?

"Well, as long as you're here, would you like to watch the news?" Beth asked. His Dark Mistress shrugged and crossed the other leg.

"If you like."

Beth walked over to find the remote and turned on the television, paging through stations to find the news. It calmed her, somehow, to have the familiar statements of what was happening in the local world, dissected, de-animated, castrated of any visceral meaning. News.

This. Is. What. Is.

It was good.

If something particularly vast were to happen, these journalists would report it credibly, revealing the real humanity of news, she was sure, but a simple evening news segment had a cadence to it that Beth could almost sing along to. It was a shocking contrast, she realized, to suddenly understand how roiled she was day in and day out, underneath the thick oiled blanket of Sabrina's personality. Frantic, almost all the time.

"I'm not doing things my way, any more. I'm doing them her way."

She hadn't realized she had said it out loud until the transition from speaking to not speaking made the television seem louder. His Dark Mistress was watching her. She looked back at His Dark Mistress.

"I can't help you," the woman said. Beth nodded. It was the simplest truth.

"Yeah," she finally said, turning back to the television. She had stopped organizing her notes on her story. What would they say? she wondered. She suddenly stood and ran into her room to get a pad of paper. And wrote down the names and dates of every one of the men she knew had died.

"Do you know who the others are?" Beth asked. His Dark Mistress nodded.

"I do."

"But this is my story," Beth said. "I will find out on my own. I'll have proof."

She tapped the pen on the paper.

"I'll tell the story," she said. His Dark Mistress narrowed her eyes thoughtfully.

"If it makes any difference to you, I've never worried, ever, that you wouldn't."

Beth nodded.

"It does."

She closed her eyes and listened to the television for another minute.

"I really like Caleb," she said. His Dark Mistress didn't answer.

"He's a good kid. He cares... about... He cares about the people he should care about."

"Can I tell you something I've learned about villains?" His Dark Mistress asked. Beth's eyes flew open.

"Please."

"They're rarely uncomplicated," His Dark Mistress said, her gaze somewhere outside of the apartment that Beth couldn't see. "They want to provide for their families and protect their friends." Her eyes returned to Beth, now, slowly. That might have been sadness. "They generally have good reasons for what they do, and they didn't get to where they are today all at once."

Beth considered. It matched with everything she had ever written, actually.

"Most villains are neither dark nor light," His Dark Mistress continued after a time. "They're simply squeezed." The woman's wide, elegant eyes held Beth's for a minute. Again, Beth was struck by the power of those eyes. "It's the truly dark ones that are worth fearing. Are worth destroying. Don't underestimate them, Beth."

Beth was struck.

"Who?"

His Dark Mistress shook her head, shifting to lean her chin on her palm with her head turned to face the television.

"You know I won't answer that."

"You know who's dark and who's just squeezed?" Beth asked.

"Of course."

Beth sat back and considered. She'd never lumped people into those kind of categories. Bad was bad, and that was plenty to get her story. She could identify motives, but to her everyone just looked squeezed, by this new definition.

"The blond boy-child is sitting in a car across the street. He went home to check on his mother and his girlfriend and returned less than an hour ago," His Dark Mistress told her. Beth nodded absently then, returning, nodded again more decisively.

"I should get dressed, then."

Sabrina's morning rituals took much longer than Beth's ever had, but she had grown used to the grooming, the styling, the painting, and her mind wandered over her story as she got ready for her day. She had lots of details, but the critical links were still missing. She needed to push harder. She had the right people...

She just had to find the right opportunities to ask the right questions.

Caleb jumped when Sabrina knocked on the window. He had been dozing.

"How many hours a day do you sleep?" she asked, getting in. He swallowed hard and rubbed his eyes.

"Not sleeping very well," he said, glancing at her and starting the car. "Nightmares."

He said the last like he had hoped she wouldn't hear him. She ran her hand over her eyes. She actually knew what he was talking about. The blood. White bandages soaked with blood. The vagueness of his dreams must have been infuriating.

"They said you could come back with me, tonight," she said. He straightened eagerly. "Just to the warehouse. When we head to the bar, you either go home or to my apartment. Okay?"

He deflated.

"Okay."

"Food first. I was serious about cooking for you."

He nodded absently, then laughed softly and glanced at her.

"If I wanted someone to cook for me, I'd ask Ma to do it. She's a hell of a lot better than macaroni and cheese."

"And yet…"

They were silent.

"Have you eaten anything in the last few days? At all?" Sabrina asked. He shrugged and shook his head.

"Busy, I guess," he said. "Have you?"

She thought.

"I guess not."

They pushed a cart up and down aisles and picked out foods that looked good and that one of them thought they could cook, and Sabrina had to admit that having a refrigerator full of food, rather than a loaf of bread sitting on the counter and a fridge with a single stick of butter in it, was going to be nice. She had liked bagels once. He liked Captain Crunch.

She made fun of him for liking Captain Crunch.

He called her a wino.

They pulled random bottles of wine off of the shelves that Sabrina had never heard of.

Then they went back to her apartment and she made boxed macaroni and cheese and they sat and they talked. For a few hours, the war was outside, and they didn't think about it.

They talked about Caleb's high school.

Why he had dropped out.

They talked about his girlfriend.

With aspirations of being a doctor someday.

He was so proud of her.

Sabrina sat and just listened. She wondered how long it had been since someone had asked him about his life who cared. She refilled their bowls when they ran out, and between the two of them, they ate the entire pot of macaroni. Then two bowls of ice cream out of the same pair of bowls after Sabrina rinsed them out in the sink.

Finally, around eight, Sabrina put the bowls on the counter and stretched. Caleb was smiling. She was smiling. But it was time.

"I guess we should head out," she said. His face grew serious, and he nodded.

"Yeah, I guess so."

They took the elevator down to the lobby and walked down the street to where he had parked the car after she had taken the groceries out of the trunk. The drive to the warehouse was quiet.

The warehouse itself was quieter. The main room was beyond capacity as even the most tangential of Edmond's hangers-on crowded in, desperate for protection or eager for spoils. Glancing around the room, it was easy to tell who was who.

The center table was full, but there was no pretense of playing cards. The officers of Edmond's crew spoke softly to each other, giving Sabrina only polite greetings as she approached.

"I need to talk to you two," Edmond said, standing, before Sabrina could sit. He touched Matthew's shoulder. "Privately."

Sabrina nodded and followed the two men into Edmond's office.

"You're later than I expected," Matthew said to her privately. Sabrina shrugged.

"We made dinner," she said.

"You and the puppy?" he asked.

"It was nice," she said. He smiled incredulously.

"You aren't falling for him, are you?" he asked. She sighed and rolled her eyes.

"Jealous much?"

Edmond closed the door behind them and they sat in their accustomed chairs.

"We have someone playing both sides against the middle," he said. Matthew nodded. Sabrina sat forward in her chair.

"What do you mean?"

"They're picking us too clean," Matthew said. "Everything I think about Neil aside, his guys don't run on a clock. Ever. No one should know where they're going to be the way that Jimmy's guys do."

Sabrina thought very carefully. No, there was no reason they should either of them suspect her for something like that; she was under almost constant supervision, at this point, anyway.

"Right now, you two are the only ones I trust," Edmond said. "You're the only one I know who hates my dad more than I do," he said, looking at Sabrina, "and this was basically all your idea, anyway," he said to Matthew, "so for now, I need you two to keep your eyes open for anyone doing things they shouldn't be."

"You want me to carry a tape recorder?" Sabrina asked impulsively.

"What?" Edmond asked.

"It's something I did in Miami, once," she said, then shrugged as the two of them stared at her. "Men are fundamentally stupid. I smile at them, they tend to say stupid things that they didn't mean to say. I bring the tapes to you, you listen to them to make sure you aren't catching anyone in a lie – and believe me, you will – and then you burn the tapes."

Matthew and Edmond looked at each other for a long minute. Matthew shrugged cautiously.

"Could it hurt?" he asked. Edmond shook his head slowly, skeptically.

"The first rule is don't say it, and if you do say it, don't write it down. They don't even talk about recording it, because it's so obvious."

"But if you destroy them every day..." Matthew said. Sabrina sighed. The burdens of knowing more than she should have made her cautious when she didn't want to be.

"Javier talked to a lawyer before I did it," she said. "As long as I tell them that I don't know where the tapes have been and I don't remember who is on the tape, they can't use them in court."

"But they'll know whatever you were talking about," Edmond said. Sabrina nodded.

"That's your risk."

"I say we do it, Eddie," Matthew said.

"You always say we do it," Edmond said. Matthew grinned.

"That's why we're going to win."

Edmond looked at Sabrina for a long time.

"All right. Okay. Do it. I want the tapes every morning, in here, right?" he said. She nodded.

"Yeah."

"And no one outside this room knows we're doing this."

"Yeah."

Beth finished duplicating the third tape, scrambling out from under the bed after she closed the safe. She had had to measure the inside of the safe in order to find a duplication machine that would fit in it, but it worked perfectly. She looked at the tapes of yesterday's important conversations incredulously, shaking her head with amazement as she put them into her purse and walked out into the main room to get breakfast. Caleb was sitting on the couch with a bowl of Captain Crunch.

Liberating information from people came back to her like breathing. Edmond and Matthew listened to the tapes with amazement.

"He shouldn't have told you that," Edmond said.

"Or that," Matthew said a moment later. Sabrina shrugged.

"People tell me things. It's a gift."

Matthew eyed her.

"Remind me to be more careful around you," he said. She grinned. He grinned back.

Matthew popped the tape and handed it to Sabrina. She pulled the magnetic tape out of it, foot by foot, as Edmond started the second tape. She tipped Edmond's steel trash can over with her foot and dumped the contents on the floor, then dropped the mess of tape into it, picking up one of the loose sheets of paper and putting a hand out to Edmond. He handed her a lighter, continuing to focus on the tape recording. She lit the paper and dropped it into the trash can with the tape and watched with malicious contentment as everything burned.

She sat back in her chair and stared at the ceiling.

"You're going to create more of this than we're going to be able to listen to, aren't you?" Matthew asked. She laughed.

"If I'm any good at it, yeah. I didn't hear anything that sounded like a lie, though," she said. "Or anyone act like they had dropped a really big secret."

"So you're a human lie detector, too?" Matthew teased.

"Only keys I couldn't get were the ones in your pocket, remember?" she asked. He shook his head.

"And everyone just thinks you're a pretty face."

"The prettiest snakes are all poisonous," she said.

"The two of you are disgusting," Edmond said, leaning closer to the speaker. Matthew winked at Sabrina.

It was past midnight when they came out of Edmond's office. Most everyone had already gone to the bar. Sabrina identified three of Edmond's hand-selected body guards and two that Matthew had co-opted from Neil. *When is Neil coming back?* Sabrina wondered. *It's getting late, and everything I know about him his hearsay.*

She headed for the door, but Matthew touched her shoulder.

"We're staying for a while," he said.

"Oh?"

They were exposed, like this. Only eleven guns, including the four guys who were always at the warehouse, keeping watch. If the guys outside watching the warehouse had gotten a clean count, they would know that Edmond was here, which would make putting together a larger force seem worth it... She re-evaluated a little, considering that James' crew would have to break in and come through one of two doors. The garage doors were too thick to get through by surprise... She took a breath. It still didn't seem like Edmond's style to let all of the hotheads with guns abandon him.

"Leave the recorder in the office," Edmond said. Sabrina paused.

"You can get it before we head to the bar. We've got buyers coming, and they won't trust you, to begin with."

"Don't want to give them an excuse to want to shoot you," Matthew said. "I'd actually be upset."

"Touching."

He grinned and Sabrina returned her purse to Edmond's desk. They sat at the center table in the main room for maybe thirty minutes, without conversation, when one of the outside sentries walked in.

"They're here," he said. Edmond nodded.

"Bring them in," he said.

A minute later, five darkly-clad men entered. They zeroed in on Sabrina.

"Who is she?" the lead man asked.

"Sabrina Hughes-Matthews," Sabrina answered, standing, but not approaching. He squinted at her.

"I've heard rumors that say I shouldn't have even come, Edmond," the man said. Sabrina noticed that all five body guards had stood up from their couches.

"She's on my side in all this. Picking up a new role. Business, gentlemen," Edmond said, motioning to the center table. The new men paused for a moment, then the leader and one other nodded at each other and walked over to the table. The other three headed for couches. The posture of the room relaxed substantially.

"You'll understand, of course..." the lead man said as the second one stepped toward Sabrina. Her hand flew up into his chest.

"You don't touch me," she said. His hand went to his gun and she took a step back. Matthew moved to step in front of her, but she waved him off. She glared at the would-be frisker and lifted her shirt to her bra and turned.

"Anything else you need to see?" she asked. "There's nothing but me in *these* pants."

The man paused for a moment, eyes on her abs. She waited.

"We're good," the other man said, glancing at Sabrina as he sat. Edmond smirked and Matthew sent Sabrina a warning glance. She cocked an eyebrow, daring him to scold her, and smoothed her shirt back down, taking her seat at the table.

"Could use some toning," Matthew said to her.

"Let's see yours," she challenged. He grinned, pulling up his shirt. She should have known.

"Meathead," she said. He grinned wider. The visitor didn't appear to be amused.

"Sorry," Edmond said. "They're in heat."

Sabrina shot him a dirty look, then turned to look more closely at the buyers. They looked nervous. She could respect that.

"I'm only here because you promised firesale prices," the first man said. Edmond nodded.

"I just want them out of here. Five apiece," he said. The first man sat back in his chair.

"I was ready to pay seven," he said.

"I know," Edmond told him. "I don't want to play games, tonight. You take the last eight, hand me the forty grand, and we're done for a while."

"How long?"

"I don't want to move cargo in and out of here with James pointing a gun at it," Edmond said. "We'll see how it goes."

The man shrugged and nodded.

"Done."

He waved over one of the other three men and handed him four stacks of bills. The money went to Matthew, who stood.

"Let's get you packed up and out of here, shall we?"

They went out to the warehouse and Matthew opened the garage door. A van pulled into the garage after a pair of guards inspected it, and Matthew closed the door behind it. The van wove the chaotic path back to the container and stopped. Sabrina's heart rate picked up. She was finally going to get to see what was in the shipping containers. She'd asked Caleb about it, but all he could tell her was that Matthew, Sean, and Edmond kept it a close secret.

The men hopped off the ledge, and Sabrina let Edmond help her down. Stupid, stupid heels. They made their way over to the container and Matthew pulled out a key to unlock it. The doors swung open.

To a circle of hell.

Eight girls and women blinked at the light, pulling ragged clothes close against the cold warehouse air. Beth broke loose, gagging at the smell and grabbing hold of Matthew's jacket to stay upright.

"You okay?" he asked. Beth opened her mouth, but Sabrina closed it.

"How do you stand the stench?" she asked after a hard swallow.

"I know. Animals."

Sabrina forced herself to look. It was her job to see. Beth had to identify *these* girls. Her saliva tasted like bile, but she swallowed hard and studied each of them. The youngest was maybe fourteen, the oldest in her early twenties. All Asian. All skinny with thin, short hair. How could she possibly identify them again? They were hard to tell apart, just them. She worked harder, finding facial features that were distinctive. A mole, a jawline, the way the neck met the ear. She scrambled, standing stock still as the girls were loaded into the back of the van silently.

"What will he do with them?" she asked. Business. It had to sound like business.

"He's a wholesaler. A couple will go to salons, the rest will be cheap labor." Matthew smiled at her. "There's always demand for cheap labor. None of them could ever find their way back here. We make our profit and they take most of the risk."

"How many in a shipment?" Sabrina asked.

"Twenty to thirty. We tried to do more, but they started dying on us."

"How do you get them in?"

He winked at her.

"Ah, that's the trick of it. And it's not my secret to tell, either. Sorry."

Sabrina stuck her hands in the pockets of her coat, trying not to stare at the empty container. Matthew went and closed the doors as Edmond let the van out. How many times had she walked past it? How many times had she thought about breaking in, picking the lock, or just outright cutting it, her curiosity overpowering her?

"That's it. Now we head to the bar," Matthew said. "What do you think?"

"How much does it cost to get them here?" she asked.

"Fifty thousand for the container, but that isn't all we put in it. I gross most of half a million per container, in good weather."

She nodded.

"Good margin."

I cooked dinner for Caleb tonight, and I don't think I got everything completely done. I think I need to go home and sleep it off. The excuse tugged at her. She felt dizzy, sick. She pushed it away.

Gritted her teeth.

She had work to do.

"I'll go get my purse," she said. He nodded.

"Sure."

"I think I'll drive myself tonight," she said. "I might want to go home and actually get some sleep before the sun comes up."

He laughed.

"After all that to get on the inside track," he teased.

"You never told me it was going to involve not sleeping."

"Don't take too long," Matthew said. "We don't want to leave the garage door open any longer than we have to, tonight."

She nodded and walked down to the end of the walkway to take the stairs back up. She had to steady herself once on the stairs – her knees weren't up for the lift, the first time, but she covered it well enough, walking down the walkway to the door without any stumbles at all. She got her purse and pulled the tape recorder out of it. This was her version of heads on spikes. It was going to have to do, for now.

She went back out into the garage, where Matthew and Edmond were in a car with one of the body guards, waiting for her with the engine idling. She pulled out the key to the Mustang and went and got in, looking for a long time in the rearview at the shipping container.

Beth cried all the way to the bar. Guilt. She had been playing at this as a game. She had even had fun at it. She had forgotten.

These were monsters she was destroying.

She scrambled to get her makeup back in place as Matthew walked back to where she parked to escort her into the bar. More bodyguards accumulated as they walked, mostly from catching up to Edmond, and Edmond and Matthew spoke softly to each other, leaving Sabrina to her own thoughts.

She was thinking that it was a shame that she only had four tapes in her purse, because tonight she was going to finish her checklist.

She was going to get them all.

Sabrina hid under the table. Guns fired. A body fell in front of her that she identified as one of James' men. She looked at the face. Surprise. It was always surprise. She shifted further under the booth, listening to voices she recognized and voices she didn't.

She wondered why she wasn't afraid.

They had come for Edmond, but Matthew had sprung a trap, instead. Matthew was always two steps ahead.

She heard bullets hit the wall above her head, but she didn't drop her gaze. She needed to be able to watch what happened. Even from under a table, she needed to see. The tape recorder in her purse was running, sitting up on the table.

Her body held tense, coiled with a primordial fight or flight held ever so carefully in check.

Shouting as the two sides found cover on opposite sides of the bar.

They were dug in, but Matthew had picked his side.

It was over in a few more minutes.

Matthew walked around the bar, shooting survivors. Beth closed her eyes to this, but Sabrina forced them back open. Beth needed to see.

Matthew found an uninjured man cowering under the bar. He pulled him out at gunpoint and shoved him over to a pair of large men that Sabrina knew.

"Take him to the room with no doors. Then put his body on James' front lawn."

Sabrina burned.

Beth tapped her bagel against the plate.

And stared at the news.

It was just a wave of sound, now. Everything that wasn't going to pin a junior-league Irish mobster to the wall was just a wall of sound.

She tapped her bagel.

She didn't taste it when she took a bite, but she chewed on it maliciously, anyway.

And resumed tapping it on the plate.

She blinked slowly. Light and sound.

It was late. The sun was going down, and she had just gotten up.

She had made four tapes last night, though, all full to running over, and they were dubbed and ready in her purse.

She was eating breakfast in someone else's pajamas at sunset.

She wanted Doritos and wine and a computer.

And David.

Her brain shook clear of more of Sabrina's debris, thinking of David.

He'd be frantic.

By now he might think she was dead.

She tapped her bagel.

"Are you okay?" His Dark Mistress asked. Beth looked at her.

"You're quiet," the woman continued. Beth shrugged.

"You want to tell me what's going on?" His Dark Mistress asked. Beth shrugged again. His Dark Mistress nodded.

"Yeah."

She turned back to the television.

Sabrina was in rare form. The night before had been a decisive victory of sorts. Night before? Morning before? Day before? She'd lost track. At any rate, more of them were dead than us, and there was drinking and celebration. She found that the room had a sound system wired into the walls, and she called for music.

She danced with Darin, then she danced with Matthew. Then she danced with Matthew some more. Then she sat in his lap in the corner and smeared her lipstick all over his face as he held her mouth against his. Scouts came and left. Caleb was the toast of the rest of the newly-allowed teenagers. Tomorrow, Edmond said, a body of one of James' key officers would turn up on the Hughes' lawn, and then serious negotiation would happen. No more of this snatch and grab stuff. We had proven we wouldn't fold. Glasses were raised to whoops and cheers and Matthew pulled Sabrina against him harder as she held a beer bottle over her head.

"You two need to come up for air," Edmond commented at one point, pulling Sabrina's shoulders back so he could talk to Matthew. "There's business, yet, tonight."

Matthew nodded. What was that strange look he gave her?

Sabrina went to the bathroom to fix the clown mask she had made of her makeup, humming to herself. More toasts. There needed to be more toasts. She came back and started to walk to the center table, hips swaying with the confidence that every eye *should* be on them. But they weren't.

The room was watching Seth. Seth, the beautiful older brother of Caleb.

Seth was standing in front of Edmond with his hands up and his mouth open.

"No, Edmond, I swear."

Sabrina's throat collapsed into her stomach. She saw, but her brain kept it from her until later. The gun. The gunshot.

She heard the scream.

Caleb's voice.

It was Sabrina's reflexes that caught him, but Beth's voice that broke him.

"No."

He looked at her. He was taller than she, but in his state of partial collapse, he looked up at her. Eyes begging her to make it not true.

It couldn't be true, could it? Make it a lie. Make it a nightmare.

Sabrina glanced at the room. She couldn't comfort him. Not here, and not now. He needed to maintain as much apparent strength as possible.

Strong hands, capable, powerful hands took hold of his forearms and lead him out the door, not letting him pause. Not letting him see. Sabrina would not let him wallow. Not here. Not now. She stood him up straight outside. His spine slumped, but his posture was strong enough to hold him upright, at least.

"Don't think. Don't think, yet. You have your keys?"

He pulled them out of his pocket, arms limp like laundry swirling in a washing machine.

"Go to my apartment. Stay there until I get there. Don't think until you've locked the door behind you. Drive normal. Watch the road. Do. Not. Think."

He nodded, eyes lost somewhere on the floor between his feet.

"Go." Sabrina's voice was dark, husky. He couldn't not do what she told him. He shuffled down the walkway, shoulders slumped.

"I am so sorry, baby," Beth whispered at his back. Sabrina whirled back at the door, exploding it in front of her so forcefully that it slammed on rebound.

"Edmond Hughes, give me one reason that I should not disembowel you this second," she said. She stepped over Seth's body. Beth blanched, but Sabrina was on the warpath. Edmond's hand was still on the gun, casually. He looked at her.

"I knew you weren't hard enough for this business," he said.

"That kid has risked his life for me. I deserve an explanation why you killed his brother."

Edmond waved the gun at Seth's body.

"That's the guy."

"Oh, that's the guy. You just destroyed Caleb's life, depriving me of a valuable subordinate, because 'that's the guy'?"

Edmond shrugged.

"That's the guy."

Sabrina sat, looking from Edmond to Seth's body. Beth saw nothing but the hole in the boy's forehead.

"You're certain?"

"Certain enough."

She glared at him, then at Matthew.

"That's comforting." She stared at Matthew, reading him. "You knew, and you didn't tell me because... why?"

"Because you love the kid. You wouldn't be able to live with not warning him. That would have been complicated."

"Already is complicated," Edmond said. Sabrina looked at him, reading, understanding, dismayed.

"No."

Edmond jerked his head at Darin.

"You're up."

"No."

"Matthew, will you take care of her?"

Edmond looked tired.

"No."

"Sabrina, I need you to tell me where he's going."

Matthew stood and walked around the table to grab firm hold of her elbow. She didn't sacrifice her dignity to fighting him. Edmond's eyes watched her dully.

"Matthew will make you tell me, if I tell him to."

Sabrina jerked her arm away from Matthew. His body warned her that it was a favor – he wasn't going to let her go anywhere. She leaned over the table, intentionally ignoring the gun that was casually pointed at her stomach.

"If you force me to betray that boy, you will have made me more of an enemy than I ever was to James."

Edmond considered.

"He's going to her apartment. She wouldn't send him home. She's trying to protect him, and going home would just make him more upset," Matthew said. Sabrina didn't flinch, but it didn't matter. She didn't need a tell for Matthew to know he was right. Edmond, either. He jerked his head at Darin again.

"You're sure, Eddie?" Matthew asked softly enough that only Sabrina and Edmond could hear him. Edmond nodded, standing, speaking for the room.

"Caleb is a loyal kid. We all know that. But he considered Seth family above the rest of us. We have to take him out to protect ourselves. Best case, he comes back here angry, with a gun. Worst case, he goes to my dad."

"Just like his brother," Casey muttered. Edmond shrugged and nodded.

"I'm sorry, Sabrina," he said, then looked at Matthew. "Over there."

"Please walk," Matthew said into her ear. "I don't want to drag you."

She glared at him, but let him push her over to the bar. A chair on the wall where the teenagers generally sat stood next to a series of rings bolted to the wall. She understood.

The teenagers had scattered as soon as Matthew had taken custody of her. They knew what was going to happen.

Matthew held out his hand to one of the boys and the teenager approached with a set of handcuffs.

"Sit," Matthew said gently. Sabrina stood for a moment, evaluating. Darin left. She closed her eyes. Sat.

He handcuffed her to the wall and walked away, not looking back.

They didn't go to the bar at all that night. Sabrina sat in her chair and watched them until dawn.

They took Seth's body away. The officers sat and planned quietly. Sean and Casey glanced at Sabrina from time to time, but Matthew never looked at her.

At maybe five, Darin came back.

"It's done," he said.

"Took you long enough," Edmond said.

"Kid's squirrelly," Darin said. Sabrina felt a small triumph. Beth's hopes collapsed. Sabrina won the war of posture, but just barely.

"Her place clean?"

"Didn't happen there."

At seven, Matthew came over and unlocked her handcuffs. He held her shoulders and looked her in the eye.

"Go home. Sleep. Come back here tomorrow having forgotten everything that happened today." She glared at him without forgiveness. "It's the only way. I promise."

He waited for her agreement, but she wouldn't give it. Finally, he gave up and let her go. The room watched silently as she walked out the door. One of the sentries opened a garage door for her as she drove herself home in her Mustang.

She didn't sleep.

Around noon, Beth got up and threw out everything in the refrigerator.

The slurry of rage and disbelief wouldn't let her cry. When she didn't feel physically ill, she felt numb.

She laid down.

She got up.

The apartment was stuffy and hot and she hated the way her silk pajamas twisted up around her arms and legs.

She sat on the floor, missing sweatpants and hoodies.

She wanted to break things, but didn't want to have to deal with them after they were broken. She opened a bottle of wine and took the first swallow, then poured the rest of it down the sink.

She sat on the floor of the shower with her arms folded across her knees and ached.

The door opened and she coughed on a sob.

And then she cried.

Her chest hurt and her spine hurt and her entire head hurt, she cried so hard.

"Beth?" His Dark Mistress asked, knocking on the door of the bathroom. "Are you okay?"

Beth just cried. The door to the bathroom opened.

"Beth?"

"Get out!" Beth screamed, not moving. The water had long since gone cold, but she lay shivering on the floor of the shower and coughed sobs. The water turned off.

"Stand up."

She stood. Heaven help her, she didn't want to, but she did. A towel flopped over the curtain rail.

"Act like a grown up."

The blow stung like a physical slap. She heard the bathroom door close.

Beth stood, naked, shivering, but mentally quiet.

There was pain, and it was coming, but she still had a job to do.

She dried herself off and put on a robe, unwilling to either return to the bitterly pink pajamas or put on real clothes and accept the new day.

She walked into the main room, gliding on a sterile cloud of not-thinking, and sat down at the kitchen table.

"Caleb is dead," she said. His Dark Mistress looked at her.

"I'm sorry to hear that."

That was all.

The television was on, and Beth stared at it, taking in nothing. A day can be measured in any number of things, and by any one of those counts, it eventually ends. She would get through today.

Suddenly, the flag-waver at the back of her head went nuts. That part of her reporter brain had been dormant for so long that it took her a moment to recognize it.

"Wait, what?"

"What?"

"What did they just say?" Beth asked, trying to review what she had seen and heard to find what had itched. Something had plucked her attention uncomfortably. His Dark Mistress looked at her.

Dead. Someone was dead.

Someone important was dead.

Her heart ached, knowing who it was, but her brain jumped up and down impatiently. Suddenly, the face showed up from her reeling memory. She tried to stand, but her feet weren't where she expect them, and she nearly fell out of her chair.

"The gemologist," Beth said. His Dark Mistress nodded.

"That's what they said he did, yeah."

"He was here?" Beth asked. His Dark Mistress frowned and looked at the television.

"Is that how you got into this?" she finally asked.

"What happened?"

"They found him dead." His Dark Mistress paused. "Beth, the details were so limited… they may have tortured him. What could he have told them?"

Beth swallowed.

"I went to him to ask about jewelry that I saw Mayor Cromwell wearing. He said it was worth a lot."

"That's how you got into all this? Jewelry?" His Dark Mistress said, shaking her head. "Could he tell them who you are?" Beth shook her head.

"No. I used a fake name and told him it was my mother's."

His Dark Mistress relaxed slightly, but Beth shook her head harder, finally standing.

"No. No, no, no. That poor man just pointed me in the right direction, and they killed him for it." She looked at His Dark

Mistress with desperation. "I don't know who did it. I can't get them on this."

His Dark Mistress looked at her for a long minute.

"I can do it," the woman said slowly. "It puts you at huge risk, and it's the worst time for it, but..." His Dark Mistress stood slowly and pushed her chair in. "If it's what you want, I will go and find them."

Beth breathed, looking though the television, trying not to remember that room. He had felt the way she had felt, but no one was coming for him. Her body slowly stiffened with the effort of not feeling. She nodded slowly. His Dark Mistress put her hand on Beth's shoulder and squeezed it.

"I will end them, Beth. I give you my word. You need to stay safe and alive while I'm gone. I won't be able to watch over you. Remember that."

The woman was to the door before the words registered.

"You've been watching over me?" Beth asked. His Dark Mistress turned in the doorway, watching her with curious eyes.

"Of course."

Sabrina drove herself to the warehouse early, sitting in the driveway for a long minute while the sentries realized that she was out there. She felt numb. Too tossed to worry for her own safety. Whatever happened was already going to happen. There was no sense worrying about herself.

They opened the garage door, finally, and she drove in to an unusually empty garage. All of the teens had taken the cars home, and a few of the routes were starting back up.

The main room was nearly empty, just a few token body guards. Sabrina tossed her hair at them and knocked on Edmond's office door.

"Yeah," he called. She opened the door.

"Where's Matthew?" she asked. Edmond waved her in.

"Out. We're starting stuff back up."

He sat back and looked at her.

"Should I have a guard in here?" he asked. She sat.

"I think you were wrong. I think you should have told me what was going on, and if you ever, ever handcuff me to a wall again, I will find a gun and put you down," Sabrina told him. He smiled. "This is your show."

"You should have Matthew teach you how to shoot a gun. I think he'd like that."

She shrugged.

"Do you guys ever sleep?"

He grinned down at his desk and shook his head.

"Not much. Too much to do."

"You play poker all day."

He glanced up at her.

"You think that doesn't have a purpose?"

"Right. You want me to believe you're the magical puppeteer behind all things," she said. "You just like playing poker and drinking all night."

He shrugged.

"Whatever you want to believe."

She sat and watched him for a minute. Reached into her purse and turned on the tape recorder.

"So what are you working on, so early?" she asked. He glanced up at her and shrugged.

"He's going to bring you in anyway."

He flipped a stack of documents toward her.

Sabrina pulled the stack of manifests into her lap, her breath catching.

"We have an… arrangement with the mayor. Pay her in gemstones that she's supposed to fence through our guy later."

Sabrina looked up at him. He scowled.

"Fat cow is trying to outsmart us and sell them at market price. She got them appraised a while back. Trying to pass them off as a mistaken find at auctions." He snorted. "Worst part is, I wish I'd thought of it. I overpaid her."

Sabrina nodded, heart racing. The gemstones were listed on every manifest, but so was everything else…

"The problem is, the gemologist got curious and came looking for the point of origin of the stones. I need to figure out who he could have talked to, and wrap everything back up."

He jerked his head at the manifests in her hands.

"I'm looking for these three diamonds, right now," he said, turning a pad of paper toward her. "I think. They should have come in sometime in the middle of last year, separate shipments."

She nodded and started to page through the manifests carefully. He looked up at her after a minute.

"You like gems?"

She grinned.

"Of course."

He nodded.

"I'm kind of pissed at Matt this morning, anyway. Happy to steal his thunder. The business is yours."

Sabrina held up page after page of manifests, month by month. She found one of the diamonds and pointed it out to Edmond, breezing through the rest of the manifest while he copied down the date and country of origin.

"It was the damn pigeon bloods," he muttered. "I told Matt I didn't want stones like that, but he was obsessed with them."

"Hmm?"

"Eight of them, matched set. The seller couldn't get legal contacts to get them out, so he ended up with Matt's name, and Matt wanted them, bad. Had them out once and that fat cow saw them..." He looked up at Sabrina. "No stones that are that unique. You understand? I don't care how much they sparkle."

Sabrina nodded at him.

"Obviously. If someone could recognize them, they can track them."

He nodded, then rolled his eyes and shook his head.

"Neil would have never gotten himself into something like this."

"Where is Neil?" Sabrina asked. "I've been here more than four months, and he's like a phantom."

"That's right. He left not long before you moved up. I didn't realize you weren't here," Edmond said, sitting back in his chair and relaxing for a moment.

"His mom got diagnosed with something terminal, he told me. She always wanted to see the country, so he was just going to take her driving. I thought he'd be back by now."

"He hasn't checked in? Does he even know about what's going on with you and James?"

"Probably not. Neil's independent. Drives his own car and everything. Matt hates it. He'll come back when he's done what he left to do." Edmond misread the look on Sabrina's face, and sat forward, shaking a finger at her. "He's the best there is at what he does, though. Don't ever forgot that. He and Matt are at each other's throats all the time, so I don't expect you and Neil will ever get along. Fine. He is the best, and you will respect him."

Sabrina held up her hands innocently.

"Sure. You got it."

He nodded and crouched over the manifests again.

"I've got the third one, here," he said.

Someone knocked on the door and let themselves in.

"Off the security camera," the man said, nodding at Sabrina. She pressed her lips together at him, still defensive at how Matthew had treated her in front of everyone last night. Beth was furious that that was what Sabrina was defensive about. Sabrina ignored Beth, trying to remember... no, he hadn't been here last night. She smiled a small bit more generously at him as he left, then turned back to Edmond.

"What's that?" she asked as he opened a folder and paged through the contents. He glanced at her.

"The gemologist had security tapes going way back. Apparently never looped anything. Crazy. They found the day that the mayor went to see him."

Beth stood, slowly walking around Edmond's desk. He glanced up at her again, tilting the folder so that she could see it. Glanced up at her again, longer. Stared down at the photo. Looked up at Beth.

He was reaching for the drawer as she stabbed him with the syringe.

The manila folder sitting on the seat beside her bulged with the stack of manifests as Beth attempted to make the way back to her apartment without getting pulled over. Her foot kept trying to push the accelerator pedal all the way to the floor. The walk out of the building had been tortured. Her hands still shook. How long would she have? She couldn't assume anything more than minutes. Someone would go into the office and find him... they would know she had done it. They would come for her.

Don't look suspicious! her brain commanded as she parked the car. She was immensely grateful that she found two spots back to back, so she didn't have to parallel park. She was certain she would have hit the car behind her, if she had had to do something that careful. She clutched at the stack of manifests, trying to control her breathing.

Need help? Sabrina asked smugly. Beth closed her eyes and shook her hair out, tapping her fingernails on the folder. Sabrina got out of the car, carrying the folder carelessly under her arm, no interest in checking for sentries. No one was going to stop her, because she was Sabrina Hughes-Matthews. That was all that they were going to see.

All the way to the elevator. Sabrina watched the camera the same way she did every ride, letting the security guard know that not only did he see her, she saw him. She smiled at the camera as she got off the elevator, top floor. Only one apartment on this hallway. Hers.

Beth struggled with her keys, for a moment forgetting how to work around her fingernails to get the single key she needed to open the door. Finally got into the apartment and glanced around. Empty. She pulled a large bag out of the closet and ran into the bedroom to fill it with the contents of the safe.

Minutes.

Had there been someone downstairs who would come up looking for her?

She bolted back out the door, running to the end of the hallway to the door to the stairs and started the long trek down to the basement.

Her feet were numb. Her knees were numb, when she could feel them enough to know they were there. She kept licking her lips, as though her mouth had gotten less dry since the last time she had tried. She ran, tripping down the stairs in her ridiculous heels, the giant purse swinging recklessly as she tried to keep her balance. She should have changed shoes.

She was at the fourth floor when a door below her opened. She grabbed the handrail to stop herself, nearly falling down the rest of the flight of stairs, turning to go back up to the landing and through the door into the apartment hallway. She closed the door behind her as quietly as she could, then ran to the elevators, pressing her back against the metal doors. She turned her head sideways, body tensed for the doors to the stairwell to fly open. Seconds passed, and she remembered to breathe. The feeling in her chest couldn't have possibly been her heart. Her heart was supposed to have a beat. This was more akin to the tense vibration in her knees as they tried to stay straight. She pressed her forehead against the metal frame and looked down at her hand. She could still feel the syringe. The plunger as she pushed it. Her stomach turned. In the last moment he'd looked at her with hatred in its most unmasked form. She wondered if he would remember.

It didn't matter. She'd drugged him and taken the manifests. Even if he didn't remember the picture, they would come after her, and she had no explanation.

She finally concluded that they weren't going to break through the door, and she stepped away from the elevator, still half-convinced they would be standing there, waiting for her. He heart jerked as she looked around the corner, but the hallway was still empty. She took a deep breath and looked at the indicators above the elevators. Elevator or stairs? Would they still be on the stairs?

One of the elevators was on the top floor. She stepped back, hitting the opposite wall. Her back spasmed away from the contact, but her eyes didn't leave the lit floor numbers. The second car started back down and she inched away. Six... five... four...

Three.

The car kept going. Again, air rushed into Beth's lungs as though she hadn't ever felt oxygen before. She clenched her fingers closed once, twice, then waited. When both cars were on the bottom floor, she pushed the down button.

If someone got on in the lobby to go to the top floor, it wouldn't stop. She was certain. The car would be empty, or would only have someone in it who had wanted the fourth floor.

She was certain.

The bell nearly stopped her heart.

She looked at the empty elevator car until the doors started to close again. Made up her mind and rushed into the car, pushing the button for the basement. She didn't look at the camera. Would they be watching?

The doors took forever to close, now, finally sliding shut. She felt trapped. She measured out the size of the elevator with her eyes, then closed them. She had made her bet. The elevator started moving, and she involuntarily looked up at the floor indicator. Three.

Two.

L.

She didn't stop at the lobby.

The doors opened into the basement and she stuck her head out, jerking it back before she had actually seen anything. Shook herself and darted out into the concrete hallway. There was a laundry room down here, but everything was quiet, now. She made her way to the corner of the basement where the boiler room was and stood looking at the huge metal door before pulling it open and walking through.

The first day she had spent sitting in a closet, jumping at every noise, body strained with her readiness to react.

She fell asleep at some point, she didn't remember, and had dreams of blond teenage boys that she couldn't find, and tape recordings that would solve everything. When she woke, it was still dark, and her whole body ached. Immediately, she was alert, listening for the evidence of people in the room outside of the closet. Somewhere nearby a dog barked and something thumped, but it was downstairs. She breathed.

As the phantom dreams cleared out some, she relaxed against the wall of the closet, stretching out the muscles in her back quietly. Her eyes ranged the door, the ceiling, the back wall of the closet as she listened and thought.

If they were waiting for her outside, they knew where she was, and staying hidden would only help her if she thought His Dark Mistress would be showing up in the next few minutes or so. The realization that had been with her since the previous afternoon finally became conscious. Less than a day ago, Beth had asked His Dark Mistress to go and avenge the dead gemologist. Beth was on her own. She took a deep breath and stood, opening the closet door without peering out of it first. The main room of the apartment was empty.

She hadn't noticed much, when she had first gotten here. She had found the door unlocked and, after locking it behind her, found the first convincing hiding place. Now the room was lit by faint orange light from the street lights below. She left her bag in the closet, closing the closet door quietly behind her, and went looking for a lightswitch.

The one by the door lit the front entrance, and then another switch plate inside the entrance lit the kitchen and eating area. The room was sparse with old, but high-quality, hardwood floors and tan-painted walls with wood trim. The building was the same age as the one where Beth had been living, but it hadn't been renovated. The appliances were on the verge of being vintage again, and what little furniture there was was entirely wood or metal. From where Beth stood in the entrance, there was no fabric of any kind in sight. She stood, listening, again, before realizing that she was hungry. She went into the kitchen and opened the refrigerator.

It was empty, save for a bottle of red wine with a post-it note on it in His Dark Mistress' handwriting:

Drink this and be calm.

She snagged it and, on a hunch, went to a specific cabinet and opened it. She smiled at the brand new bag of Doritos. Of course. There was a single wine glass sitting upside down on the counter by the oven. She grabbed that and took her bounty back to the solid wood kitchen table, sitting in a folding chair. She worked at the cork in the bottle for a minute, then went back to the kitchen for a cork screw. The drawer it was in was actually empty, otherwise. She shook her head and finished opening the wine, sitting down and looking at it for a moment. She looked at the glass, then shook her head again, shaking her feet out of her shoes and putting them up on the chair across the table from her, sinking down into her seat and drinking her wine straight out of the bottle.

The second day, she ran out of Doritos. She left the lights off when she could, not wanting anyone to notice that the lights were on if they normally weren't. She left the television off, mostly sitting numbly at the table. She found a large shirt in one of the drawers in the bedroom and changed into that to sleep. Not that she slept much. When she lay down to sleep, the noises in the building kept her awake.

She knew they would be looking for her. They would have gotten a new copy of the pictures from the gemologist's office, and Edmond would know why she had drugged him. He would know she had been spying on him the whole time, and he would know what she knew.

From time to time she would look at the door, wondering why they hadn't found her yet. She thought of everything she had in the bag in the closet, but she couldn't bring herself to go through it all yet. The idea of having all of that spread over the table as Edmond walked into the room was the worst thing she could imagine. So she sat.

Occasionally she dozed at the table, jerking awake when her head dropped or when she heard anything that might have been a footstep. She thought of showering, but didn't want to be somewhere where they could sneak up on her like that.

She sat.

The third day, she peeked out the windows, trying to figure out whether she might be able to sneak out to find something to eat. She drank lots of water to forget that she hadn't had a proper meal in four days, and her mind started to wander. She knew better than to leave. They hadn't found her here, yet, and she was beginning to believe that if she stayed put, they wouldn't. His Dark Mistress would come for her. She believed that.

At the same time, maybe she could just go downstairs and ask for a sandwich. She drank more water.

She looked at the note from His Dark Mistress. Be calm.

Tried to remember why she knew that was His Dark Mistress' handwriting.

Laid down on the floor, trying not to listen to her stomach or the voice in her head reminding her how much she liked hot dogs.

Late the third night, a key turned in the door. Beth jumped like a caged animal and ran to hide in the bedroom, scolding herself the entire time that it wasn't changing anything.

"Beth?" His Dark Mistress called, flicking on the lights. Beth stuck her head around the doorframe. His Dark Mistress watched her without moving.

"I'm sorry," the woman said. "This wasn't how this was planned." She paused. "I got them."

Beth thought of the poor gemologist, completely unaware of what Beth had gotten him into. She nodded.

"Did you bring food?"

His Dark Mistress nodded, slinging a backpack off of her shoulder. She handed Beth a wax-paper wrapped sandwich from a vendor down the street that Beth recognized. Still hot. She tore into it, following His Dark Mistress to the table.

"Are you okay?" His Dark Mistress asked. Beth nodded.

"I spiked him," she said. His Dark Mistress raised her eyebrows. "The hypodermics you gave me."

The woman smiled darkly.

"Hence the emotional reaction," she said.

"Hmm?" Beth asked, mouth full.

"They're desperate to find you. They're searching the city, but they found the boiler room fast enough that they think they have you pinned. They're perpetually on the verge of searching room to room. I don't even know who the voice of reason would be, in that conversation."

Beth nodded, ignoring the oil running down her chin.

"Matthew. He doesn't make bad plays like that. He knows I have to come out sometime."

"We need to get you out of here. I'll come back for your safe later, if they haven't found it already," His Dark Mistress said. Beth motioned to the closet.

"It's all in there."

That look was probably as close as His Dark Mistress ever got to being impressed, but Beth was much too busy to care.

"How did you get in?" Beth asked. His Dark Mistress stood, glancing at Beth for a moment.

"You can't jump that far."

His Dark Mistress went into the bedroom and Beth ran out of sandwich. She followed, unable to come up with anything else to do. His Dark Mistress was in the bedroom closet on a chair. There was a large vent in the ceiling of the closet which, on second thought, was a bit odd, and His Dark Mistress was taking it down. She started pulling guns out of the hole, tossing them first onto the bed then, noticing Beth standing by the closet door, handed them to Beth.

Having once expressed a complete lack of interest in firearms, Beth had found herself sitting through a lesson on them from Matthew once, a little more than a week prior, and now she was disturbed both by the number of guns she recognized and by the number that she did not.

"How many of these should I fail to mention in my story?" she asked. His Dark Mistress paused from taking them down to look at her.

"Say that I was all Die Hard with just a pistol," she said. Beth nodded dutifully. *That* was a shotgun – she knew that without Matthew's help. After the guns came a series of harnesses that, in a different context, would have told a very different story. His Dark Mistress pulled her jacket off – Beth realized this was the first time she had seen the woman without it – and started taking harnesses back from Beth and putting them on. She put guns in holsters then went and got her bag and put the rest of the guns in the bag.

"Hold this," she said, handing it to Beth. Beth watched, overwhelmed, as His Dark Mistress climbed back up on the chair and started pulling down boxes of bullets. She dropped them into the bag, box after box, pulling one particularly tall box out, reconsidering, beginning to put it back up, then shrugging and tossing it into the bag as well.

"Die Hard, huh?" Beth asked.

"My body armor is in another apartment," His Dark Mistress observed, as though in non sequitur. She jumped down and went through the bag once, then patted various holstered guns, as though counting.

"I guess that's it," she said, shrugging back into her jacket. "You ready?"

"What?"

"Now is the time. We fight our way out of here or you die."

His Dark Mistress turned back in the main room and looked at Beth for a long time.

"You have three jobs. One," she said, ticking a finger, "stay alive. Most important, but only slightly more important and very related to job two: keep that bag with us. I'll carry it if I can, but you keep your eyes on it and if I drop it, you pick it up. There may be points where I can't take the weight, and I need to know – without checking – that I don't need to go back for it. Right? Three. Your stuff. Without it, this has all pretty much been pointless. Got it?"

"I think that's more words than you've said to me the entire rest of the time I've known you," Beth said. She could have sworn it was the shock talking.

"Stay alive, okay? I'd hate to see you die without getting an article out of it, at least."

"Are you flushed?" Beth asked. His Dark Mistress grinned and grabbed her bag.

"What can I say? I like shooting people in the face."

Beth ran to the closet to grab her other bag, then looked at her feet.

"I don't have any shoes," she said. His Dark Mistress twisted her mouth, then went into the bedroom and came out with a huge pair of combat boots and a pair of socks.

"Stick the socks in the end of the shoes. We'll try to find better soon."

Beth did as she was told, standing in the flipper-esque shoes and nodded.

"Elevator to the first floor. If you have to ditch those and run barefoot, do it. Cut up feet is better than dead," His Dark Mistress said. Beth nodded and His Dark Mistress turned off the lights, opening the front door to appear in profile, then nodded at Beth, waving her forward with a gun. Beth crossed in front of His Dark Mistress and went to push the button on the elevator, glancing at the woman for confirmation. As the dark shadow of a woman came to rest next to her, the world felt a lot more manageable. She was going to live, and they were going to pay. One way or another, they were going to pay.

The elevator arrived. His Dark Mistress pointed a gun at it as the doors opened, but it was empty. They boarded and His Dark Mistress pushed the button for the lobby with her gun.

"No staring at dead bodies, no screaming, no freezing in the open. Get something between your body and anyone with a gun. Metal is good. Concrete is better. Wood, Beth... Beth. Wood will not stop a bullet, nor will sheet metal. Got it?"

Beth nodded, watching the elevator count down.

"You stay in here until I say. Don't let the doors close, but don't be visible from outside. Yes?"

"Got it."

His Dark Mistress nodded firmly, checking various mechanical functions on the gun, then moving to the front center of the elevator and standing with the firm balance of someone who knew what they were doing. The elevator dinged and Beth pressed herself against the wall, holding the 'open doors' button. His Dark Mistress stepped forward, arms still at her sides.

There was a single gunshot, then two more, then someone cursed and someone else yelled. Gunfire answered and a bullet smashed the back wall of the elevator. Beth dropped to the ground, her back still against the wall, and heard several more shots. She fought the twin impulses to squeeze her eyes shut and to stick her head around the corner.

"Go tell Matthew!" someone yelled. There were more shots, then the elevator doors dinged and started to close. Beth reached up above her head, trying to find the open doors button. She stood and found it as His Dark Mistress stuck her head into the elevator.

"Were my instructions too complicated?" she asked. "Let's go."

Beth stuck her head around the edge to look into the foreign lobby of the-building-next-door, then quickly stepped over to where His Dark Mistress was retrieving her bag. The night desk attendant was frantically giving information to the police over the phone, somewhere behind the desk. His Dark Mistress sighed, then shrugged.

"More chaos is better, I suppose," she said. They walked quickly out the front door, where a car sitting at a curb across the street turned on its lights.

"Cover," His Dark Mistress said, holding out her bag. Beth scrambled for it, then raced to the corner of the building, shoes clomping unsteadily through fresh snow, looking for anything in the alley that might get her away from a car. There were more shots behind her and tires squealed. Beth turned back at the corner, keeping most of her body behind the building, but watching now as His Dark Mistress stood, shooting at the car that charged her. The woman was standing a few feet from a street light that she used to keep the car from driving straight at her, and she kept shooting as the car corrected back into the other lane and sped away.

His Dark Mistress looked over at Beth and made an exasperated face.

"That's not exactly what I had in mind," she said. "They had a clear shot at you."

Beth licked her lips, unable to come up with an answer. His Dark Mistress shook her head.

"Keep moving. Let's go."

His Dark Mistress led the way through a twist of alleys and abandoned warehouses. Beth was promptly lost, but His Dark Mistress kept muttering to herself as they would pause.

"He's good. He's very good."

They ducked down a stairwell and skirted a parking lot, when His Dark Mistress froze. The dark woman cursed under her breath.

"What's going on?" Beth asked.

"I doubled back once too many times. They're looking for us in the next building. Our tail hasn't had a chance to tell them where we are yet, but if he gets around us…"

His Dark Mistress stood on her toes, scanning the far end of the parking lot.

"I hate being chased."

She popped the clip out of her gun and checked it, nodding once at Beth as she started back forward into the same building they had been going toward in the first place. There was the sound of metal skating on metal, then a click, and His Dark Mistress kicked the door in to the next warehouse, dropping her bag as she ran in. Beth grabbed the bag, slamming into the doorframe under unsteady weight as she tried to get two bags settled on her shoulders and keep up with His Dark Mistress in duck shoes. There were gunshots and Beth struggled to identify which shape was which in the dark. Someone yelled, and His Dark Mistress' coat flapped as she turned a corner. Beth ran after her, head up, but not able to make sense of the shadows.

"There," His Dark Mistress said, pushing Beth back into a corner. "I'll draw them forward and come back for you here. Stay down."

Beth fell to the floor as much from shock as from willingness to do what she was told. Slowly her eyes began to pick shapes out, but it was mostly a flurry of chaos, even if she could see people. More gunshots, and occasionally the sound of His Dark Mistress' jacket. A man yelped, and someone else shouted. Footsteps on concrete. Footsteps on metal.

"Sabrina!" a man yelled. Beth stood, to push herself deeper into the corner. It was just a simple corner, one where the wall turned to make a small landing for a flight of stairs. Anyone could walk up to her, if they knew where she was. She looked down at the bag of guns at her feet and worked her hands.

"Sabrina!" the man yelled again. Beth peeked around the corner. At the end of the warehouse, silhouetted by distant street lights, a man stood in the center of a wide doorway.

"It doesn't have to go this way!" Matthew yelled. "You know I don't want you dead."

He paused and took a few steps into the warehouse, his shadow lengthening along the empty floor. The room seemed to pause.

"It can't be like it was, but you don't have to die tonight. Come back with me. We'll figure it out."

A man fell over the railing and thudded jarringly on the concrete floor. Matthew didn't look over, but rather up at the railing.

"Who's your banshee, Sabrina? I'd like to hire her."

There were more shots. All upstairs. Someone yelled instructions to someone else. Beth stared at Matthew. He didn't even have a gun in his hand. He was nearing the center of the warehouse, now, and the light was too weak to even cast a real shadow any more. He simply stood, head up, looking at the warehouse around him.

"We're going to tear this place down, Sabrina. And any place you hide. We'll find you. If you let me leave, you're going to die badly." He paused, still looking up at the second story. "Last chance."

Beth was grateful that His Dark Mistress put a hand over her mouth, because otherwise, she was certain she would have screamed. His Dark Mistress motioned, and Beth did her best to follow the tall woman up the stairs silently. It took forever, placing one shoe and then the next. She stopped at a landing halfway up and slid her feet out of the shoes, running up the stairs behind His Dark Mistress in bare feet. The metal grating of the stairs was enough to make her reconsider, but she wanted to be out of the building. His Dark Mistress led her to a window in an upstairs office that had a broken-out top pane and wordlessly disappeared through it. An arm reached down after a second and Beth handed up first the weapons and then the purse she carried. She tried to find with her fingers where the glass had pulled free of the frame completely, but her hands shook and she gave up. She was going up and out, no matter what.

She stood on the window sill and, a gust of freezing wind taking her breath, braced herself and put her torso out the window, turning to look up at His Dark Mistress hanging over the roof edge. The woman waited silently as Beth pulled her body out the window and hesitantly tried to get her feet under her. She clamped her mouth shut when she slit open her heel on a glass edge, but got the balls of her feet on the icy window frame. She wasn't sure how to stand. There wasn't anything outside of the building to hold on to. His Dark Mistress handed her the strap from the duffel bag.

"Around your chest," the woman whispered. Beth nodded, fingers trembling with strain as she tried to get the strap around her chest without dropping it. Gritting her teeth, she pinned it between her arm and her ribs and wound it around the front of her chest, dropping it behind her. She grabbed hold of the window frame again and took a deep breath, then, trying to hold the strap on the other side, reached behind her to find the loose end.

Her balance was impossibly far back, and she felt the wave of vertigo threatening to tip her body completely out of the window as she looked down for the strap. She closed her eyes and searched with her hand in open air. Touched it with her fingertips.

She caught hold after the third touch and pulled the strap around to the front. Looked at the clasp.

And didn't know what to do with it.

"Any day, Beth," His Dark Mistress whispered.

The mechanical function clicked like catching a falling leaf, and she slipped the clasp over the strap and handed the free end back up.

"I've got you," His Dark Mistress whispered, mostly disappearing over the edge.

Letting go of the window was the hardest part.

Her body tipped away from the building with the inevitability of gravity, and her arms flailed for the rooftop.

She couldn't reach it.

The strap pulled tight against her chest and her body swung back in against the building, her knees still bent against the window frame and snow swirling around her. Slowly, she stood and reached for the roof edge. It didn't come in reach until she was most of the way extended. How had His Dark Mistress done it? Standing on her toes, she could get her elbows onto the edge, but she didn't have the strength to pull herself up, even under the best of circumstances. His Dark Mistress pulled the strap tight and Beth's body slid over the edge, toes hanging free in the cold night air for a moment as she scrambled onto the roof. She landed elbows-first in a drift of snow on the other side of the wall around the roof and stood, brushing herself off as an excuse to rub her elbows.

The rooftop felt slick under her. Her heel was wet with blood, but she couldn't feel the cut yet. She looked at it.

His Dark Mistress unzipped her bag and pulled out a roll of cloth bandages and knelt in front of Beth.

"I expect you'll want to sit," she said. Beth looked around.

"Are we safe here?"

"For a minute. Sit."

Beth found a clear spot and sat for His Dark Mistress to bandage her heel, then, for good measure, wrapped both feet completely.

"Should have done that from the start," she commented. "You ready?"

Beth nodded.

"Why didn't you shoot Matthew?"

"He was the decoy. They wanted me to come out where I could get a look at him. Besides. He wasn't a threat."

Beth looked around.

"So what next?"

The snow started to come down faster and Beth rubbed her arms.

"We can't stay here tonight. I need to scout for a few minutes. Find a warm spot and sit tight."

His Dark Mistress turned and disappeared across the rooftop. Beth checked for both bags, then squeezed herself into a dry corner the wind had protected from the snowfall. Her light fashion jacket and skirt were both massive liabilities, now, but she didn't give herself space to think about it. Part of her knew that she should have been more worried about the gunshots earlier, and the fact that men wanted to kill her, but mostly she was okay just staring into the dark, waiting for His Dark Mistress to come get her. It was working, for now.

She listened to the snow fall and breathed cold air.

It was working, for now.

His Dark Mistress returned.

"We're going to have to flush again," the woman said, grabbing her bag.

"We're what?"

"Flushing."

Beth blinked and shook her head.

"Hunting term?" His Dark Mistress asked. "Usually game birds, but also applied to just about anything that hides?"

"Oh."

His Dark Mistress thrust Beth's purse at her.

"Keep close, move fast."

They went to a wall and His Dark Mistress peered over it. Beth leaned slightly. There was a fire escape below, but it stopped at the windows maybe ten feet below them.

"Don't think, Beth," His Dark Mistress said, hopping onto the wall and swinging her legs over. "Move."

Beth mirrored her, looking skeptically down at the landing. Her fingers were cold and she couldn't feel anything below her ankles.

"It doesn't matter what you do, this is going to be loud. Go fast," His Dark Mistress told her, then slid off the ledge, holding on with her fingertips until the last moment and landing on the stairs with a loud protest of metal. Beth closed her eyes and shut down her brain and did the same.

The grate was just sharp enough to manage to hurt her numb feet, landing, and she toppled toward the railing with bad balance. His Dark Mistress grabbed her and pushed her against the windows.

"You steady?"

Beth nodded.

"Move."

There were already shouts below as they ran down the stairs, and someone started shooting. Beth was too focused on one step and then the next to notice who. The metallic noises around her could have been the staircase groaning; they could have been bullets. She didn't want to look up. His Dark Mistress tipped down the final ladder and motioned to Beth.

"Go."

Beth eased past the dark woman and looked around at the alley below. She could pick out three dark shapes, two at one end and one at the other, crouched in cover. The noise of bullets winging off of the staircase was unmistakable, now.

"Go!"

The voice of authority drove her on. She turned her back on one of the gunmen and started climbing down the ladder. His Dark Mistress was returning fire. Beth looked up once to watch the flare of the gunshots over her head. She had thought that was just in movies. She moved faster.

From the ground, she could only see one of the shooters – the other two were behind a dumpster and a car. She looked back up at His Dark Mistress in time to see the woman throw her bag down to the ground a few feet away from Beth. For a moment, Beth wished she knew enough about guns to help. His Dark Mistress would have to stop shooting to get down the ladder, and they would both be exposed.

Her worry was misplaced.

The dark woman didn't turn to walk down the ladder. She jumped.

Beth covered her head instinctively as the three men shot at the dark target. His Dark Mistress landed in a flurry of rippling leather and rolled to a crouch.

"Keep moving."

Beth snatched the second bag and ran to the covered side of the dumpster. It was better than nothing, and strangely comforting. More men appeared at the head of the alley, but apparently the man behind the dumpster wasn't getting any backup. His Dark Mistress launched herself over Beth's head onto the top of the dumpster and the metal lids bent under her, the sounds reverberating inside the dumpster and against the alley walls. The number of guns firing at the other end of the alley spiked and Beth hunched lower, listening to all of the bullets landing as she heard a man scream on the other side of the dumpster. She grabbed hold of both bags, counting them as a dumb mental exercise to stop her from thinking anything more interesting, and ran around to the far side of the dumpster. His

Dark Mistress stood over the body of the man who had been shooting at them, crouched only slightly in acknowledgement of the number of bullets smacking into the dumpster, the walls, the ground. She pulled the bag out of Beth's arms and pulled her against the wall. Someone shouted.

"Against the wall and low. Run."

Beth found something sharp with her foot, but she scrubbed it on the ground and kept running, her bag banging against her legs on both sides as it swung wildly. She glanced back to see His Dark Mistress crouching at the front of the dumpster. The woman looked at Beth, calculating, then threw something down the alley and started after her.

The light at the explosion was blinding. Something went whizzing past Beth's head, but she was running much faster now, blind, desperately feeling for the end of the wall.

Corner.

There had to be a corner somewhere.

She stumbled and nearly fell sideways when she hit it.

"You watched," His Dark Mistress said, grabbing Beth's arm to keep her upright.

"My job," Beth mumbled. His Dark Mistress laughed and pulled her along.

"Keep moving. You're almost done."

Beth blinked and shook her head, trying to clear her vision. A gust of wind blew through her skirt as the storm intensified. Her legs were so cold that all she felt was pain. She ran.

"One more," His Dark Mistress encouraged.

"Tracks?" Beth asked, brain getting fuzzy.

"Not in this wind. We're almost there."

His Dark Mistress leaned Beth against a wall and pulled a padlock away from a door handle and looked at it. She pulled a set of keys out of her pocket and unlocked the padlock, then shepherded Beth in the door and pulled it closed behind them.

Beth sat in a disheveled heap on the floor, holding a blanket around her shoulders. His Dark Mistress was on high alert, breezing back and forth past Beth as they occasionally heard shouts outside. They were in a tiny kitchen, from all indications a completely abandoned one, but His Dark Mistress had pulled a huge blanket out of the freezer above the ancient refrigerator, and that had been all Beth really needed to know.

Finally His Dark Mistress returned, sitting with her back against a narrow wall by a doorframe.

"The building is secure. They shouldn't guess we're in here; all of the doors are locked."

Beth shivered. His Dark Mistress smiled and stood.

"I expect you've missed these," she said, pulling another bundle out of the freezer. She tossed it to Beth and Beth untangled her sweatshirt and jeans. A pair of tennis shoes fell out. Beth squealed softly and pulled the hoodie directly over her head. She stood to put on her jeans and stumbled back onto the floor. His Dark Mistress looked at the floor.

"You're tracking blood," she said. Beth frowned.

"I think I picked up piece of a bottle."

"Let me look," His Dark Mistress said, kneeling. Beth let the woman look at her foot for a moment.

"You pulled the glass back out already, but I'm going to have to rebandage this. You're going to need more stitches, I think."

"They can follow us, can't they?" Beth asked. His Dark Mistress shrugged.

"Sit tight. They come in after us or they don't, nothing changes now."

She returned with her bag and redressed Beth's foot, where sensation was just beginning to return – and let her know just how much her feet hated her. She winced as the final wrap of the bandage went on, then slid into her jeans. She finally felt like herself again.

"I recognized your handwriting," she said. His Dark Mistress returned to her section of wall, checking her gun.

"You know how to reload a clip?" she asked. Beth shook her head. His Dark Mistress snorted.

"You took notes from my notes," Beth said. "I watched you."

His Dark Mistress glanced up and shrugged, dragging the duffel bag close enough to root through it and find a box of bullets.

"You were the one who was feeding James Hughes all of the information about Edmond's guys," Beth said. "You got Seth killed, and then Caleb."

"I am genuinely sorry that the boy died, Beth. I am. But I didn't give any information to James. I picked them off myself."

She paused and looked at Beth again, then rolled her eyes and shrugged.

"I needed them to get going, but I was hoping they'd spin out another few weeks and completely cripple James before I pulled you out. The jewelry guy was just bad luck."

"It was all your fault."

"Beth, would you have spared him?" His Dark Mistress asked. Beth shook her head.

"I never saw him do anything illegal," she said. His Dark Mistress shrugged.

"But you would have given his name to the police, and they would have brought him in. What are the odds that he actually never did anything illegal?"

Beth hadn't thought about it. She frowned.

"He was going to end up dead or in jail. He was never your friend. You weren't going to protect him." The woman looked up at her and sighed. "I'm sorry."

"Who are you?" Beth asked. His Dark Mistress sighed again, reloading the gun and going fishing in the bag again for something else.

"I'm a shadow. Nothing more. After this is over, you'll never see me again."

"No. I'm serious. Who are you?"

His Dark Mistress tipped her head against the doorframe and stared at something far away.

"I won't tell you who I am, but maybe I'm willing to tell you what I am."

"Okay."

"Once upon a time in a very small but very wealthy kingdom, there were two brothers."

"What?"

"It's a story, Beth. I'm going to tell you a story."

Beth paused.

"Can I publish it?"

His Dark Mistress thought.

"Only if you could get it word for word."

"Can I record it?"

"What?"

"I have a tape recorder," Beth said. There was a long pause. "Get out." She stared at Beth. "You're kidding, aren't you?" Beth reached into her bag and pulled it out.

"You've been tape recording Edmond Hughes? You have more balls than I gave you credit for."

"He gave me permission," Beth said. "I'd been interviewing guys looking for a snitch for a couple of days."

His Dark Mistress shook her head and laughed, then laid a gun across her lap and settled harder onto her heels. She checked the gun in her hand and glanced behind her, then shrugged.

"Fair enough. Knock yourself out."

Once upon a time in a very small but very wealthy kingdom, there were two brothers, princes. They were well-loved and given anything their hearts desired because, though they were loved, their parents were often absent, tending to the affairs of the kingdom and none of the palace staff had the heart to deny them. As so often happens in these tales, one of the brothers grew up light and the other dark.

In this same kingdom was a pair of girls, sisters, of the aristocratic class, upon whom their father doted throughout their childhoods. No opportunity was denied them, no matter what the request, as he was quite wealthy and a widower. As also so often happens, one matured into a lady of darkness, and the other of light.

Once they had reached the appropriate age, they fell in love and were married – or at least were married, at any rate – dark brother to dark sister and light brother to light sister, and the kingdom rejoiced. They took up residence in the palace and began their married lives.

"What shall we do today, my love?" the light sister asked her husband one morning shortly after they were married.

"I don't know, dearest," he replied. "What would you like to do?"

"I wouldn't dream of suggesting an activity with which to occupy ourselves until I heard what you would like to do," she told him.

"Would you fancy a game of chess?" he asked. She made a face, sticking out her tongue prettily. "How about a ride around the grounds?"

"I don't like horses," his bride answered. "They smell bad."

They sat in silence for a moment.

"I know!" cried she. "I shall throw a party! We haven't had a ball since we were married." She clapped her hands, her blond curls bouncing against her shoulders. He smiled at her enthusiasm.

"Whatever makes you happy, my dear," he said, standing and kissing her forehead.

"Now, I shall need a new dress," she said, standing and beginning to tick things off on her fingers. "Oh! Who shall I invite?" She didn't wait for an answer, bustling happily out of the room.

"What do you want to do today?" the dark sister asked of her husband the same morning.

"What do I care?" he asked. "We both know you already have a full day planned, and that I have no intention of taking part in it."

"What will you do today?" she asked.

"I suspect I will shortly go back to bed and call for wine. I'll take until lunch to finish the bottle, then call for my lunch in my room. I'll take a nap after lunch, then call for an entertainer to keep me amused until dinner time. I'll have dinner with you and that will conclude my day."

She watched him for a moment, but it quickly became apparent he had no curiosity whatever about the activities of her day, and she stood and left.

Later that day, as he was out seeing to the construction of a new stone fence where he had the intention of grazing cattle, the light brother came across the dark sister.

"Good day," he said, trotting up to her on his horse and slowing to a walk. She nodded.

"And you." Any other would have taken her tone as a warning to accept the polite greeting and move on, but he was determined to forge good will between them, she being his wife's sister and his brother's wife.

"It's a good day to be out of the palace," said he. "Spring has broken early this year, I dare say."

She examined the still-bare trees overhead.

"The corn will plant early and be plentiful, but I don't expect the summer will get hot enough to satisfy the rest of the vegetables," she said. He looked startled.

"Are you a student of the seasons, then?" he asked. She frowned, straightening her mare's mane.

"I am a student of many things, and you do me a disservice to assume otherwise." Her waist-length black hair fell down to mingle with her mare's jet-black mane and he could no longer see her face, or how her dark eyes watched him through the tresses.

"Then please accept my sincerest apology," he said. "My wife does not seem to have studied as you have. Perhaps I have underestimated her as well."

The dark lady threw her head back proudly.

"Not at all," she said. The insult seemed to silence him, but he shook off the sting.

"What brings you into town, today?" he asked.

"Private business," she answered. Her silence smote him again.

"I am arranging to fence the field your father gave me as your sister's dowry," he said. She did not answer. "I plan to expand the dairy on the other side of the hill."

She looked at him, then back forward, urging her mount into a trot. He followed suit.

"You are a beautiful rider," he said.

"Thank you," she answered, her form perfect, but frosty.

"I've noticed that the adjacent land your father gave my brother yet lies fallow," he said.

"Unsurprising," she said. He silently agreed.

"If you would be interested," he said, "I would love to let it from you and expand my pasture further."

She slowed to a walk.

"In matters of finance, I am always interested," she said.

They discussed the details the rest of the way to the palace, and he quickly discovered that she was going to turn what he had meant as a half-serious offer for quick, easy profit on both sides into a shrewd business arrangement skewed as far in her favor as possible.

"You have a mind for numbers that rivals most of the men I've met," he said.

"I have a mind for numbers that easily surpasses all of them," she answered coldly. "Have the contracts drawn up and give them to me. I will sign them."

"It's my brother's land," the light brother answered.

"It will be his signature," she said. He stopped, holding his horse's reins in one hand as he inspected her. She sighed.

"Very well," she said. "I will have him sign them himself."

He paused for a moment, troubled and torn. Finally he settled with himself and smiled.

"That will do quite nicely," he said. "Now, you strike me as the type of person who knows how to enjoy a game of chess."

For the first time since he had known her, her face lit up, though she did not smile.

"I know quite well how to enjoy humiliating you at just such a game," she said, and took his arm to walk into the palace.

His Dark Mistress stood, stretching out her legs. Beth stopped her recorder. "Is that it?" she asked. His Dark Mistress shook her head.

"I'm going to go do another round. I'll be back in a few minutes."

Beth looked at her recorder for a moment as His Dark Mistress left, then sat listening to the quiet of the warehouse around her. The story was such an odd contrast to the dimly-lit abandoned room and the sound of footsteps outside, in ever-decreasing frequency. The outside world was far enough away from her second-floor kitchen waystation that she wasn't entirely certain that she wasn't imagining the footsteps, the shouts. She shifted in her blanket, closing her eyes to listen harder.

The night had taken on a surreal quality. All indications were that His Dark Mistress was going to continue telling her a fairy tale of some allegorical nature as men searched neighboring buildings and streets, trying to kill her. She tucked her arms into her hoodie, laying down on her side and enjoying the thick warmth of the fabric.

She wasn't cold.

She wasn't hungry.

Her feet weren't that bad, really.

And she was still breathing.

She'd had worse evenings.

She thought through the first piece of the story. This wasn't the His Dark Mistress that Boston knew. She thought back to the first day she had met His Dark Mistress. The woman had changed. It came to Beth as a shock, comparing her behavior back to that first day.

She wanted the truth. That was the whole of it, but His Dark Mistress was talking, and she wasn't going to take that for granted.

A few minutes later, the woman returned and sat on the floor. Beth waited.

And waited.

"So…" Beth prompted.

"Maybe tonight isn't a good night," His Dark Mistress said, staring off into the distance.

"I'm not letting you off that easily," Beth said. "Finish the story."

His Dark Mistress sighed.

"Very well."

The tale wandered. There was a party and an impending war. His Dark Mistress was apparently adept with swords. Beth found herself watching the gun the dark woman had left sitting on the floor, unsurprised by the relatively benign weapons in the story. Slowly, the point of the story began to dawn on her.

"You were in love," she interrupted. His Dark Mistress snorted and shifted her posture.

"Mistress," she said. "I didn't expect it to come as that much of a shock to you."

"Mistress doesn't mean love," Beth countered. His Dark Mistress sighed, then looked at Beth hard.

"You didn't think I could love?" she asked. Beth considered. "Would you?"

His Dark Mistress smiled and chuckled once, silently.

"Love is a squishy luxury that I find no need of," she said. Beth waited. "Unfortunately, it's hardly that simple, though is it?"

Beth shrugged.

"What is?"

"Shall I finish?" the dark woman asked. Beth nodded.

"Please."

Two days later, she arrived at the appointed hour in his training room, dressed to work. He was already warming up.

"I was afraid you would not come, after I spoke so poorly to you last we met," he said, his words measured, due to his audience. "May I offer my retraction, and my most sincere apology?"

"You may offer them," she said habitually, eyeing the walls. Much of the non-essential house staff, including her husband's entire staff, stood on the perimeter of the room to spectate the prince's workout.

"My sister has blown this all out of proportion, hasn't she?" she muttered to him. He smiled with some pain. The light princess had convinced much of the palace that he was marching to his death, going so far as to draw an intervention from the queen for his safety. The dark princess had understood that the queen had simply confirmed that he was taking no fewer men than were necessary, but it was evident that his wife had expected him to abandon

the enterprise entirely. She had been locked in her chambers crying for the past eighteen hours.

"Well, let's give them a show, shall we?" she asked, attacking the light prince with gusto. He fought back with energy to rival her own.

Her swordplay was in a new realm. Normally, she fought with training precision, watching for weaknesses and exploiting them, teaching him his flaws and correcting her own. This morning she was ferocious, attacking him as though to wound him, her will was taking him by storm. He stepped up with her, answering as though by instinct, his eyes watching her face more often than her sword. After three hard, resounding blows, each blocked with force, she stepped back, her eyes blazing.

"I hope you face an army that fights just as I do; it seems I cannot take you," she said.

"I would hope not, myself. I should be the only survivor," he said. Now he took the initiative, stepping into her and pushing her back. Her arm began to ache from the force of the fight and she gritted her teeth in anger, pushing him in turn. She might have growled at him, but it was not audible above the sound of the wooden swords and their reverberation off the walls. Her hair was falling into her face and she flung her head to clear it, moving faster than she had ever before found reason.

Abruptly her hand was empty and the floor greeted her unexpectedly. Hard. The floor was very hard.

"Yield," he said playfully, looking down his sword at her. She looked around, her concentration broken. Ceiling, walls. Crowd.

"If you have time to make sport of us, it is obvious you have not enough with which to occupy yourselves," she barked from the floor. The spectators looked uneasy, their enjoyment of the spar breaking as a spell.

"You heard me!" she commanded. "Make use of your hands or find yourselves removed of them," she ordered. The room quickly emptied.

"That was unexpected," the light brother said, leaning on his sword and looking down at her. "Have I pricked your ego that badly?"

"Not my ego," she said, ignoring his hand to help her up as she stood and straightened her clothes. She pushed her hair away as he watched her.

"You are stronger than I," she said finally. He shrugged.

"I bested you today," he said. "The statistics dictated it would happen some time."

She smiled, nervous. She weighed the many ideas that she had considered over the past two days, trying to find where to start.

"You are a good man," she started. He smiled easily.

"Thank you."

"You are complete unto yourself, and to wish you different would be to wish you destroyed." She swallowed and he waited, evidently unable to see where she was going.

"You have strengths I do not possess, and I respect them," she started.

"Thank you," he said, his face easing out of confusion, but she continued. *"But I have fewer limitations. I can do so much that you could not. You shackle yourself for what you believe."*

He made to speak, but she held up a hand.

"Now, you must give me your word that anything I say next is in the strictest confidence," she said, raising her eyebrows.

"Of course," he said, frowning.

"I have never known one such as yourself. Powerful, aware, cunning, and yet completely trustworthy. I see myself as from your perspective – weaseley, sniping about in the shadows, fearfully amassing a hoard intended either to buffer myself from danger or from which to launch some brutal campaign for power." She held up her hand again as he tried to protest. *"I know you would never be so unkind. But yet. I perceive what my motives and actions would look like from where you stand. And I have explained how your behavior appears to me. We are on divergent paths, paths that should they intersect, one of us would break."*

She paused, exhausting the thought.

"I find myself at a loss," he said. *"What are you trying to tell me?"*

"I told you once that I loved three people; my sister, my trainer, and myself," she said. Suddenly he understood, and was unable to look at her. *"I have found a fourth in yourself."*

He looked up and away, his mouth open as he searched for a reply.

"This would be a good time not to say anything," she said, moved to pity at his surprise. Suddenly she wondered if this was completely unexpected for him, if he had simply been treating her as a sister, but she shook her head, pushing her hair back again.

"It matters not if you reciprocate my feelings, for in truth you should not, and I would love you all the more for it. You must not consider me in competition with my sister; it would tarnish your character."

"But love must always desire to find itself returned," he said, almost a question.

"What business has love wanting?" she asked sternly. *"That which is motivated by love cannot want, and that which wants cannot be love. Even I know that."*

He pressed his lips together now, avidly watching her face.

"I have considered this for some time, now, and know what action I must take."

"What is that?" he asked.

"By simple elimination, I cannot stay here, because that would be to tempt you to love me, I believe, and I will not sacrifice what you are. I cannot simply move away and continue my life as it is, because that would abandon my love for you to a lack of will. I am not and will not be so weak. Therefore I will leave this place and do the things you cannot, but would, do. I will cheat, I will steal, and I will kill as necessary, but I will be doing the things that you would do, had you the freedom. I will love you more than myself."

He looked stunned.

"But you are my brother's wife," he said. "You will leave him?" She smiled sardonically.

"I am only his wife by law. I believe that, in the eyes of the church, I am not yet and never will be his wife, don't you agree?"

He furrowed his eyebrows together.

"You will leave," he said.

"Yes, today," she answered, gathering strength. His eyebrows shot up.

"Today? Where will you go?"

"I will not tell you, so that when my husband asks, you may tell him in truth that you do not know." She took a step forward, holding up a finger. "More importantly, remember that you gave me your confidence. Should — when — my husband asks if I have left him for another man, you must tell him that you know, but on your honor you may not tell him who. Your secrecy is bound in your oath, you should not need to lie to him or anyone. Your feelings you should keep to yourself, should you have any, and you must fight against them, if you do, for temptation is not itself a sin, is it?"

They looked at each other for several long minutes, then she nodded decisively.

"Mind my sister, you must care for her enough for both of us, now. You'll find the paperwork in my chambers giving you ownership of all of my legitimate local holdings. The foreign ones I will keep for convenience and the illegitimate ones I have agents shedding as we speak. Your brother will largely be living on your largesse, now; do what you will with him."

"In less than a year, you bankrupted him?" the light brother asked.

"In less than a year, he bankrupted himself. I stood by and collected the spoils because I was not about to allow him to become King independent of myself. You will undoubtedly be crowned, now, by the way. I have halted my actions to preclude it. It does not matter, for I care only for your success, but you will be a better king than he." She paused, searching for anything else she *desired to say to him that she would be willing to disclose. Finding nothing, she nodded again.*

"That will be all. I will take my leave," she said.

"Will you return?" he asked. She shook her head.

"No. I will go out into the world anonymous, nothing but your dark mistress," she said.

In the hall, she found the light prince's personal manservant standing against the wall. She started and then frowned deeply at him, but he shook his head.

"My master's confidence is my own, m'lady," he said. "But may I say that though you often abused us, knowing that we belonged to you and knowing how aggressively you defend what's yours has given the staff here great comfort. You shall be missed."

His dark mistress had raised her hand to strike the servant, but lowering it, slowly looked back through the door at the drooping posture of the prince she had left behind. She smiled softly and held out her hand to shake hands with the servant. He turned it and gently raised it to his lips.

"Goodbye, m'lady," he said. She smiled with more warmth.

"Good bye."

The recorder clicked.

His Dark Mistress stood.

"I'm going to check the perimeter again. You should sleep if you can."

"What happened to him?" she asked.

"Who?"

"The light prince?"

"As far as I know, he is ruling with great grace and wisdom," His Dark Mistress said. "There is nothing more to be said about it."

"What about the dark prince."

"Nothing more."

There was a stern silence, then Beth sighed.

"What happens in the morning?" Beth asked.

"We walk away."

"They're just going to let us? Why?"

"You don't know where we are? This is the building where I first caught sight of you. Up on the roof."

Beth tried to remember.

"Across the street from the warehouse?"

"In the morning, we walk out through the docks side. Stay visible and you should be able to make it clear."

"Why would they let me go?"

"We're across the street from their headquarters. They don't want police here."

"Enemies closer," Beth said softly.

"Sleep now. The days probably aren't going to get any shorter."

Beth didn't actually expect to sleep, but curling up in the blanket was attractive enough that she was willing to pretend.

She jolted awake tasting of iron and oil. His Dark Mistress was staring at her.

"You awake yet? I swear, they could have stormed the place by now."

"What?"

"It's daylight."

Beth glanced up.

"Is not."

"The dockworkers are here. It's time to move."

His Dark Mistress handed her a piece of paper.

"Wait fifteen minutes, then follow me out. Go straight away from the warehouse until you hit the water, then find a taxi and go there. I'll be waiting for you."

"You aren't coming with me?" Beth asked, sounding pathetic even to herself.

"If anyone is going to get ambushed, I'd prefer it be me, by myself. You know what you're doing, here." His Dark Mistress looked at Beth for a moment and cocked her head to the side. "It's time to blend into the background again. Just fade away."

The woman left and Beth sat on the floor in her jeans and sweatshirt for what felt like a long time. She could feel that walking was going to be a challenge, but she steeled herself to not limp. She finally pulled on her shoes and tested herself on them.

The glass had gauged the arch of her foot, and while it was easily the worse of the two wounds, the slice across her heel was going to be hard to ignore. She gritted her teeth and practiced walking across the room. She picked up her shirt and skirt and went to throw them out, but a red-brown color in the trash can caught her eye. There were stacks of gauze bandages in the bottom of the trash can with varying degrees of red. Beth looked over her shoulder. His Dark Mistress was injured. She threw her old clothes into the trash can on top of the bandages and walked back to the doorway. Had it been fifteen minutes yet? Sabrina had never worn a watch. Beth went and picked up her bag. Close enough. Her knee wanted to give on every step, but she braced herself firmly. If His Dark Mistress could take a bullet without saying anything about it, Beth could get across the docks with cuts on her feet.

She walked out of the kitchen and went looking for a window. She found one on the right side of the building without much trouble and stood looking at the warehouse across the street for several minutes. She knew better than to stand right against the window, and her reflexes were still on a hair trigger, but she refused to run away with her tail completely between her legs.

Sure, they had chased her off, but she had her story. She had enough on almost all of them, and the most important ones, she had on tape. She could tell her whole story.

She frowned.

That wasn't actually true.

She still didn't know how the mayor was involved, in the first place.

She sighed and adjusted her bag. The reporter in her was furious. She never gave up on a story. She told it beginning to end, and she hadn't figured out all of the pieces yet. And they had found her and chased her off.

She narrowed her eyes, determination percolating back into her. She wasn't done, yet. Her story wasn't written. She was still going to find all of the pieces and put them together.

She left the warehouse, emerging to a world of gray dawn light and deep, drifting snow, and made her way across the docks with a blind determination that precluded her from ever looking to see if she was being followed, if she had been spotted. No one stopped her, and no one was going to. She knew where she was headed, and most anyone would know to stay out of her way.

"I need to talk to David," Beth said, sitting on a couch that had probably been rescued from a curb more than once. His Dark Mistress had met her cab, as promised, and driven her several miles away from downtown, bringing her to another dark, dusty apartment. The woman ignored her now.

"I need a computer with an internet connection. I need to talk to David," Beth said, feeling her fingertips with her thumb. The first thing she had done when she had gotten to the new apartment was rummage the bathroom for clippers and cut her nails off. The skin on the tips of her fingers was feeling air for the first time in months, and the sensation of fingertip to thumb was a bit addictive.

"That isn't going to happen," His Dark Mistress said. "You are going to write your story. When they are all convicted and in prison, you can return to your old life."

Beth sat back in her chair, fully feeling the power of the hoodie, and folded her arms.

"The story isn't done, and I'm missing something. This is how I work. I need to talk to David."

His Dark Mistress finished checking the cabinets and returned to the living room. They stared at each other.

Beth blinked benignly at His Dark Mistress and shook her head, sighing. She smiled and shrugged. *Sorry.* She wasn't even slightly tempted to back down.

They stared longer.

Beth scratched the back of her head and re-folded her arms.

"I will not give you a computer. I don't want any information getting out before you publish your article and turn the rest of your papers over to the police," His Dark Mistress said, finally. "I will bring him to a meeting place exactly once. That is my only offer."

"I would need several hours, at least," Beth said. His Dark Mistress shrugged.

"Fine."

"He's kind of busy."

"What's your point?"

"I need to know when he has a few hours to not be at the paper."

His Dark Mistress blinked and shrugged.

"If he isn't available, he isn't available. I won't try twice. The risk is too great both to you and to him."

Beth sighed.

"Will you take me to the library, then?"

His Dark Mistress looked at her blankly.

"I'll sign online and ask him if he can meet me. If not now, when. Yes?"

"I don't like computers."

"Tell me something that surprises me."

Beth pulled the hood of her sweatshirt up over her head before she got out of the car. Most of her focus was still on not limping.

"They shot you," Beth said. His Dark Mistress' coat caught the breeze in the parking structure as they walked.

"Just another hole," His Dark Mistress said.

"When?"

"It doesn't matter."

Beth pulled deeper into the heavy jacket that had been at the new apartment and shook her head.

"I'm not sure I believe you're real."

"Probably healthy."

They walked the couple of blocks to the library and Beth filled out the form to use the internet with a fake name.

"Thank you," she said to the young woman at the counter, taking the computer password over to where His Dark Mistress sat.

"I've got forty-five minutes," Beth said and snorted. "Byzantines."

His Dark Mistress rolled her eyes.

"They never put AIM on these things," Beth said as she logged in. She searched for a moment. "Nope."

They also didn't protect admin rights very well. She downloaded the software she needed and logged in.

"AzuraThena?" His Dark Mistress read.

"Comic book geek gave me the name. I was researching a ring of thieves…"

"I remember the story," His Dark Mistress said. Beth shrugged, restraining herself from humming along with the modem.

"She was a warrior scholar named for Athena, sort of… I guess," Beth said. "I liked it at the time, so I used it."

AzuraThena: you around?

She waited. His Dark Mistress tapped her fingers on the desk.

BabyBoy2317: You're alive.
AzuraThena: you doubted?
BabyBoy2317: Where are you?
AzuraThena: undisclosed location
BabyBoy2317: Are you okay?
AzuraThena: i need help
BabyBoy2317: What do you need?
AzuraThena: im fine
AzuraThena: with my story

There was a pause. His Dark Mistress had stiffened when David asked where she was, but Beth had waved at her.

BabyBoy2317: You're still working?
AzuraThena: it's like you dont know me at all
BabyBoy2317: Well…
BabyBoy2317: Tell me about it.
AzuraThena: im not allowed
AzuraThena: you have a few hours this afternoon?
BabyBoy2317: What do you mean you aren't allowed?
BabyBoy2317: ...
BabyBoy2317: Yeah. Where should I meet you?

Beth looked at His Dark Mistress.
"I'll come get him."

AzuraThena: my friend will get you
AzuraThena: you remember her
BabyBoy2317: Not going to forget that one anytime soon.
AzuraThena: be nice
AzuraThena: shes reading over my shoulder
BabyBoy2317: Hi, scary lady.

"You two are children."

AzuraThena: shes on her way
AzuraThena: see you soon

Beth logged off and, after considering for a moment, deleted the software back off the computer.

"They need better security on here. Any teenager could do this."

"Perish the thought."

His Dark Mistress followed Beth back out of the library.

"I'll just wait in the car, right?" Beth asked.

"Hardly."

Beth glared at the man who sat across the room from her. He seemed impervious. She glared harder.

"Can you at least tell me your name?" she asked.

"I have strict instructions not to talk to you," the man said. She sighed.

"I don't need a babysitter."

"I have strict instructions not to talk to you."

"I would be fine on my own. It's not like I'd run down to the pub for a quick drink."

"I have strict instructions not to talk to you."

"Your mom is a pink cockatiel named Warren," Beth said. He didn't flinch. Didn't even blink.

"I have strict instructions not to talk to you."

She sighed and glared again. He crossed the other leg and shifted in his chair. He was scarred. Everything on him was scarred. With skin like leather, it was impossible to tell how old he was; with a clean-shaven head and face, she couldn't even tell if he should have had gray hair. It was possible. He might have been thirty. He might have been sixty. He just sat with his arms draped across the back of yet another dilapidated couch and watched her.

If she stands, make her sit, His Dark Mistress had told him. Beth believed he would do it, so she sat. Angrily.

It had been an hour since His Dark Mistress had left them in the little two-room office. Beth was hungry, she was thirsty, and she didn't want to sit any more. She leaned her face on her palm and watched the guy. He watched her, apparently content.

"She train you to do this?" Beth asked.

"I have strict instructions not to talk to you."

The key clicked in the door and Beth turned in her seat, eyeing the man to see if maybe he'd let her stand up. The door opened and David brushed past His Dark Mistress into the room.

"Beth."

She stood and he froze.

"Whoa."

"Yeah. It's been an interesting few months," she said. She wasn't wearing the contacts any more, at least. She hugged him.

"It's good to see you," she said privately.

"I worried," he told her. She laughed and hugged him harder.

"That's what you do."

His Dark Mistress dropped a backpack onto the table and Beth looked over.

"That's everything," the woman said.

"Who are you?" David asked.

"I'm called His Dark Mistress," she said, then turned to the scarred man. "Thank you."

The man stood, nodded a salute to His Dark Mistress, and went into the next room. Beth leaned to watch him, then grabbed David's wrist.

"You've got to see this."

She emptied the backpack out on to the table and started handing him things. She got to a folder she didn't recognize and opened it.

"What?"

"You're welcome," His Dark Mistress said. Beth fingered through a stack of photos. All of them were of her with different members of Edmond's crew.

"They can't say they've never seen you before," His Dark Mistress said and smiled.

"What do you call her?" David asked. Beth shrugged.

"Never had to refer to her before." He nodded.

"Working?" His Dark Mistress said. Beth grinned.

"We're only going to annoy you," she said. "You may as well go do... whatever it is you do for fun."

"Does it have fun?" David asked. Beth laughed.

"Working."

David sighed and started going through pages.

"You may as well get me caught up."

"So. I've got all of them," Beth said, finishing her outline and handing David the last of the tapes. "I just don't know how Cromwell plays into it. I mean, I saw her there, but I still don't know what she was doing."

"What do mayors do?" David asked.

"I know. I've made that list. It isn't that exciting."

"But you've got a complete story, outside of her?" he asked. Beth nodded.

"Yeah. The best one of my career," she said. He nodded.

"I think so, too." He looked at the photos again. "Can you just leave the mayor out?"

"No."

He sighed.

"Beth."

"No."

She watched his face. He knew that would be the answer. He just had to try it.

"So you think there's a hole here, still."

"I wish I could say that for sure," she said, "but I know they did a lot of things I didn't know about. It's possible I just don't have anything to tie the mayor to any of it."

She sighed and started paging through documents again.

"I guess I could start over at the hall of records," she said.

"No," His Dark Mistress said. "You aren't in public until this is in print."

"I won't print it if it isn't done," Beth said. David and His Dark Mistress looked at each other, and Beth almost laughed.

"Look, you both know I mean it. Maybe it's here. Maybe it isn't. I won't quit looking until I find it."

"Inter office mail?" David asked. Beth nodded.

"Yeah. They were sending her some kind of information that they didn't want traced back to them. She wrote her name on them herself, I would guess. It wasn't Edmond's handwriting, I'm certain. It was way to pretty."

"So what information do they send to the mayor, that they have to pay her to have?"

"Is it information, or is it money?" Beth asked.

"They're paying her in gemstones. Would you use interoffice mail to send gemstones?"

"The envelopes have little holes in them. No way."

"Could they be paying her in cash, too? Something else?"

"It would need to be something inconspicuous. That didn't look like a payment."

"Beth," His Dark Mistress said.

"So if they were paying her in some unnamed currency through interoffice mail, it doesn't get us any closer to why they were paying her," David said.

"No. What does a mayor do?" Beth answered.

"Beth."

"Yeah?"

"This isn't the address at the docks," His Dark Mistress said, handing Beth a manifest. Beth froze. Looked at David. Regretted that she'd be sending him back to work this quickly. Wondered where that thought came from.

"The municipal port."

Security at the Boston ports was federal. So was the labor. Everyone knew that.

"Getting into the Port of Boston would be hard..." she said. "Not unnoticed."

They waited. Beth's mouth felt dry.

"The city has a port," she said finally. "The mayor's office can clear shipments into it. Who inspects those, I wonder."

"The shipping containers," His Dark Mistress said.

"The girls." David picked up the list of descriptions Beth had written.

"The gemstones," Beth said. "All from the same place, all the same way. All they have to do is tell the mayor when they're supposed to show up, and she clears them."

Beth sat back in her chair and looked at the manifest.

"I've got you."

"Can we have a minute?" David asked as Beth finished up organizing her documents. Her brain was buzzing with *the story*. His Dark Mistress looked at him for a moment, and his face set into the impassible editor-face that Beth and Kelly had long ago learned not to mess with.

"Three. No more."

His Dark Mistress went into the next room and closed the door.

"Beth, I haven't been able to reach you," he said. She nodded absently, looking back down at her folder. She needed a nice, flat surface to glue everything together to with post-it notes. She needed post-it notes.

"That was kind of the point."

"Kelly missed you."

"I missed her."

"Beth, they decided you weren't coming back."

"Hmm?"

"Senior management."

She glanced up at him again.

"What does that mean?"

He sighed.

"For one thing, they gave away your desk."

Beth frowned.

"Why would they do that?"

"Beth, no one could find you. There's a strange woman living at your apartment. Everyone thought you'd died or just left."

"There's what who?"

"She looks a little like you, but... I don't know. She wouldn't talk to me. She wouldn't talk to Kelly."

"I'm going to..." Beth started, making for the door to the other room.

"Not yet," David said. He sighed and looked at her. "I'm sorry."

Beth shrugged.

"Not your fault."

His eyes widened. She smiled and shrugged again, then grinned.

"Look, I do what I do. Turns out I don't actually need a desk to do it. This just means I get to renegotiate how much they pay me for this story."

She paused.

"I guess I'll regret that I'm not working for you anymore."

He kissed her.

Looking back, she would decide that she should have seen it coming, that he was a little too desperate to have his hands on her face and his mouth on hers, but that it had been a good kiss, anyway, but at that moment her brain just shut down. It felt like taking her first breath after having been underwater until her whole body ached. Looking back, she couldn't remember what her hands had done, or how long it had been before His Dark Mistress had interrupted them.

But that had been inevitable.

Beth couldn't read the woman's face as she stepped away from David, who held on to her wrist until it was completely out of reach. Beth remembered she was supposed to be angry at His Dark Mistress for something, but didn't remember what it was. Had she wanted to kiss David? She glanced at him.

"Don't go," he said. His Dark Mistress was quiet for a moment.

"David, if I don't keep her where no one can find her, Edmond will find her and have her killed. They won't find her body. They will find pieces of it."

David looked aggressively at Beth then back at His Dark Mistress. Beth put her hands over her scars.

"I'd rather the police protect her," he said. His Dark Mistress shook her head.

"Fewer people keeping a secret means it gets kept better. I will be the only one who knows where she is, and David, I give you my word I will keep her alive. The danger is past, as long as she has no contact with anyone until this is done."

"Done," David said.

"Testimony and all," His Dark Mistress said. She paused. "I am sorry."

"I trust her," Beth said. Both of them looked at her. She rubbed her arms. She realized what she was about to say and gritted her teeth for a moment. "I'll do what she says."

Beth stretched and yawned. Ran her thumb over her fingertips as she looked down at the stretch of floor she had adopted for her story. It had taken her a long time to get it organized – much longer than normal. Twice she had woken up to find the man who wouldn't speak sitting on the couch.

"She's out," he said when he first saw Beth, then refused to answer any further questions. Beth was getting more creative at pestering him.

The post-it notes had truly gone wild on this one. It would have spilled off the edges of her desk and down the sides. She had transcribed the tapes. She was ready to write.

"You're sure you want her here?" Officer Chris Ward asked. Beth sighed.

"If she leaves, I do," she said.

"I can't take your testimony if you're under duress," Ward said. Beth shook her head.

"Ward, drop it. This isn't testimony."

Ward was the one she had brought her last three stories to. She trusted him, and His Dark Mistress hadn't been able to come up with any reason not to. Which seemed to frustrate the dark woman. This was the handoff that the woman was most concerned about. Beth wasn't that worried. She had copies of all of the documents and photos; the only thing she couldn't replace were the tapes, so she had kept those, for now. A thick folder of her organized notes lay on the desk in front of the police officer.

"Any crimes you committed getting this, that you're going to need immunity for?" he asked. Beth shook her head.

"As long as this counts toward my reporting-a-crime requirement, I'm good."

She paused and he caught the hesitation.

"What is it?"

"I guess…" She sighed. The thought had hit her at a time she truly hadn't expected it. "I probably contributed to the delinquency of a minor."

"What did you do?"

"I gave a seventeen year old alcohol," she said.

"What's his name?" Ward asked.

"Caleb. I don't know his last name."

"Do you know how I can find him?"

"He's dead."

Ward watched her, and she let him read her.

"I would have opened with that part."

She took a deep breath.

"Probably not the part you're most interested in, actually."

She indicated the folder. He opened the front cover to find a picture of Edmond Hughes.

"Oh, hell."

"I organized them by suspect. I thought that would help," Beth said. He looked at her.

"You're serious?"

She nodded. He stood and left. His Dark Mistress fidgeted. Ward returned several minutes later with two other men.

"These are RICO guys I work with," Ward said. One of them looked at His Dark Mistress.

"She shouldn't be here."

"Guys, the article on this runs tomorrow morning. Tick tock," Beth said. The second of the men was flipping through pages.

"Like hell it does. I'll get an injunction. We need to get warrants out first."

"Does it take more to get an injunction against a major newspaper, because I'd think it would."

"If you have anything here," the second man said, "we need to put together a case."

Beth shrugged and crossed her legs.

"I'm obviously not the expert, but I'll sign an affidavit that I saw everything I say I saw in there. I'd say that should be your probable cause on the lot of them."

"You watch too much television," the first one said. Ward cleared his throat.

"I'd look at what she's got before you say too much," he said. The three men hunched over Beth's notes, flipping slower and slower. Matthew. Casey. Sean. Jimmy. Eric. Darin. The high level enforcers. The errand boys. Names. Addresses. If she had printed just that folder, it would have been dry, but blockbuster all by itself. The last page was the mayor.

"Suzanne Cromwell?" the first man said, standing. "Last?"

"She's the least connected, but that's what I have," Beth said. The pictures of the mayor and Edmond outside of the warehouse. The picture of the brooch. The transcript of Edmond talking about her. The manifest of the container sent to the municipal port. Beth smiled. She got it.

"You'll testify to all of this?" the second man asked. Beth nodded.

"Of course."

His Dark Mistress stood.

"We'll turn over the tapes once the lawyers are involved. Right now, Beth is the only one who has had them." She handed the second man a business card. "You can contact this number when you start raiding looking for the girls. Beth will be available to identify them, but we'll have to discuss security. Leave a message and I'll be in touch."

"Who are you?" the second man said. Ward raised an eyebrow at Beth.

"She keeps me alive until this is done. No arguments, no other questions."

"Beth, you know we can keep you safe," Ward said. Beth shook her head.

"My story runs in the morning. You have," she paused, looking at her watch, "eighteen hours until it hits newsstands."

She smiled and allowed His Dark Mistress to whisk her out of the room.

It was a good story.

Her best.

They watched the indictments on television.

Beth ate ravioli.

Most of the low levels took deals. Beth went to a women's shelter and managed to find six of the eight women from the shipping container, out of the hundred-odd the police pulled out of various businesses. One of them was holding a baby in her thin, scarred arms, and Beth realized she had been pregnant when Beth had seen her. The woman looked away as Beth stared, the hollows of her cheeks casting shadows across her face.

The police didn't know where the last two women had ended up. Beth was sick that they'd gotten lost. The police were thrilled to have found as many as they did.

The trials took months. Beth was stir-crazy and bored. Spring came and went. She was still living in a dusty apartment that she wasn't allowed to leave. She spent a lot of time thinking about David and wishing she knew exactly what he wanted – or even what she wanted. Surprisingly, she didn't have any real desire to read newspapers or look for new stories. She read fiction.

Learned how to cook. Did yoga. Tried not to leave nailmarks on the walls. Made up songs about how bored she was.

Matthew's trial was the most interesting. Sean had cooperated in exchange for a prison sentence out west, and the ideas that Matthew had managed to execute were astonishing. Beth sat in the gallery at his verdict, still amazed at how sadistic he had actually been. They had found the new torture room and the sadist had taken a deal. They had tracked down more than a hundred fifty girls that Matthew had sold, and the trials of several of the 'nationwide wholesalers' would begin in the fall. They had found the bodies of dozens of them who hadn't survived to sale. Matthew looked placid, confident. Beth had to admit – he was gorgeous. The media had loved running his pictures and the stories about what he had done. Readership at David's paper was reportedly up three or four times normal, since the trial had started.

Edmond's trial was the last. James Michael Hughes had gotten a change of venue, and Beth wasn't on the witness list. Edmond, even now, seemed shocked that anything had gone wrong.

Guilty.

Guilty.

Guilty.

Beth cut the article out about Darin's verdict and kept it. That was the one that meant the most to her.

Summer.
The story, seeing it through to done, had taken her a full year.

Beth lay on Kelly's couch and stared at the ceiling.

She had no story. She didn't want to go back to her apartment, because it didn't feel like hers any more. David had offered her a spot on his couch until she figured out what she was going to do next, but that was weird. He was taking her to dinner.

Kelly was still picking through the stories that Beth had left out. A member of the zoning commission was under investigation. The mayor had resigned, but bought her freedom with her testimony. The political hounds were asking who knew what when. Beth ate lunch with Kelly a couple of times a week, but it was strange being the one with more free time.

There was a knock on the door and Beth went and answered it.

David smiled.

"You look great," he said. Beth laughed.

"I still don't know what to do with the idea of you not being in your office at six," she said. He shrugged.

"They make do."

They walked down the hallway to the elevator and stood awkwardly through the ride down.

"You miss your shadow?" David asked.

You'll never see me again, His Dark Mistress had said the last day, when she dropped Beth off at Kelly's apartment building. *Don't look for me in any of the places you've stayed – I won't be there.*

"It's weird how much I miss her."

"She was there for you," David said. Beth nodded. The Legend of His Dark Mistress had gone out in a literary journal in the late winter, and there were howls of protest at the quality of the writing – both inside the journal and among its normal readers – but the volume of sales generated by the tie-in to the trials made the publishing decision easy for them.

They got to David's car and Beth waited as he got in and unlocked her door.

"It's easy to be romantic about the whole thing," Beth finally said, giving voice to her thoughts just to break the silence.

"What do you mean?"

"She got what she wanted. That's all she ever said she was doing. She took care of me because she wanted those guys in prison. She wasn't really ever there for *me*."

"Do you believe that?" David asked. Beth looked at him.

"Why not?"

He shrugged.

"Maybe the stuff she did was all necessary to get what she wanted, but does that mean she wasn't there for you, too?"

Beth leaned back in her seat and smiled.

"Hopeless romantic."

"You tell Kelly that the next time you see her. She called me heartless today."

"You cutting up one of her stories?"

He laughed.

"Uh huh. You are heartless."

"What are you going to do?" David asked.

She chewed on that the rest of the way to dinner. He found street parking a ways away from one of the sidewalk cafes that she and Kelly routinely went to for lunch, and they walked through the cooling evening air for a while. Beth wasn't sure if it was awkward or not.

The hostess seated them and Beth leaned her chin on her hands.

"What should I do?" she asked. He shrugged, scooting his chair on.

"I don't know."

He paused.

"I don't think you've ever asked me that before."

Beth smiled and rolled her head to the side.

"I feel lost. Like I don't even know who I am any more. I played Sabrina for so long... I think maybe she was more convincing than I am."

He frowned and shook his head.

"You're a reporter. You follow the story, and you print it. Everyone who knows you knows who you are."

"Am I?"

He looked at her.

"I don't have a story, do I?"

He set the menu down on the table.

"I really don't know what to do with that."

"I know. Neither do I."

He laughed.

"I mean, I'm an editor. I could hire you and assign you a story."

"I think that would drive me crazy."

She paused.

"I'm afraid I already am crazy, though."

He shook his head, then looked up at the waitress as she brought them glasses of water. They ordered.

"What did you say, a second ago?" he asked.

"That maybe I'm crazy," Beth said, rolling her eyes. It had been a dumb thing to say.

"Give it some time," he said. "Something will click, and you'll know what to do. You always do."

She nodded.

"It's so weird," she told Kelly later that night. "He's just always been…"

"Babs?" Kelly asked.

"Yes. He's always been Baby Boy. How am I supposed to see him… like that?"

"Especially after Matthew," Kelly said, grinning deviously.

Beth hit her with a pillow.

"You're terrible."

Kelly grinned, then licked her lips and leaned in toward Beth.

"I don't know why you don't see it, though. He's a sexy beast."

Beth rolled her eyes.

"You say that about everyone."

"No, seriously. He is."

"He's a skinny nerd who writes for a living," Beth said.

"So are you," Kelly said. "Besides, you're in love with him, or else I'd have had him by now."

Beth opened her mouth, but found she was stunned into silence. She closed her mouth and opened it again.

"Ew. I can't believe you just said that. He's our friend."

"He's smart, he's employed, he's not-bad hot, and he's in love with you, too."

"Well, okay, that part might be true, but…"

"Beth, he sits at his desk at night and waits for you to sign online. You would come home and couldn't wait to sign on to talk to him. Have you ever imagined him, sitting in an empty office, waiting for you? Even when you were gone, he did. Every night."

"He's my friend. He might be my best friend."

"No, I'm your best friend. We talk *about* people. You just can't wait to talk *to* him. And he can't wait to talk to you. Please. Go have sex with him and then come and tell me all about it."

It had been so long, Beth had almost forgotten sitting at the computer with her bottle of wine talking to him. She had kind of believed it was the wine. She tossed her hair back and shook her head.

"I don't want to talk about sex with David, okay? That's creepy."

Kelly shrugged.

"If you say so." She paused and tossed her head nonchalantly. "So how long are you going to be living on my couch?"

"You throwing me out already? I've been here a week."

"No. Just. You have money, you just don't know where to spend it. Are you going to keep writing stories in Boston... do you want to move to New York... Are you going to move in with David and have lots of sex and babies?"

"Kelly!"

Kelly laughed.

"I'm getting wine."

The woman uncurled from the couch and Beth wrapped her arms around a pillow, laughing. New York.

She would never move to New York. Boston was home. That was just how it was.

New York.

Something itched.

Kelly returned with a bottle of wine and two glasses. She offered one to Beth.

"Unless you just want to pass the bottle, like the old days."

Beth took the glass.

A small but very wealthy kingdom...

"New York," Beth said. Kelly raised her eyebrows.

"Here's to new life decisions, I guess," she said, pouring wine into her glass.

"No, New York, Kelly. I'm going to find her." Beth paused. "I have to know who she was. It's the last part of my story. Even if I don't write it, I have to know who she was."

It took lots of wandering and wrong starts.

It always did.

But Beth stood in the lobby of a very expensive apartment building in New York City, watching the desk attendant politely. The woman had been dismissive, but Beth had out-stubborned her and managed to convince her to call up to the penthouse and at least ask if she should be allowed up. The woman repeated Beth's name twice, then, choking on her next words, smiled and hung up.

"The elevator will take you up," she said. Beth, surprised, smiled and thanked the woman. The building had a small enough number of tenants to only require a single main elevator, and Beth got into it, looking for a button. The doors closed and the elevator silently ascended, not even beeping to announce floors. It was disconcerting. Beth tried to stand relaxed, folding her hands behind her back, but she was nervous. She knew she was in the right place – she had found pictures that were conclusive – but she wasn't sure what she was going to say. Was even being here a betrayal to the woman who had saved her life?

Thirty-eight floors up, the doors opened and Beth started to step out of the elevator. Only that would have meant walking into the apartment itself. She stopped.

"Please," a man said, stepping into view. He offered her a hand, as if stepping off of the elevator required extra balance somehow, but she took it instinctively, and he walked her into the front foyer of a grand two-story apartment.

"I'm Bradley Dawson," he said. She knew him from his picture. Light hair in a modern executive style, solid build. He went by Brad.

"I'm Beth," she said. He smiled.

"I know. I've read your story. And the legend. Please don't mention them to my wife or my brother," he said. Beth raised her eyebrows. "Jane would be very upset if she knew that you were here, but Tricia will be relieved to know her sister is alive, and… Well, you'll meet Jesse."

"What would you like me to tell them, then?" Beth asked. Brad smiled at the sarcasm.

"Leave out who you are, they probably won't ask. Just say that Jane saved your life, and you wanted to thank her. Is that accurate enough?"

Beth shrugged.

"That's not really why I'm here."

He smiled.

"I doubt you'll have to say that much. Just leave out anything about her new identity. We'll talk upstairs soon."

"Darling, was that the elevator?" someone called. Patricia Dawson appeared around a doorway into the two-story entrance and smiled happily, her blond curls bouncing as she walked.

"Brad, I believe you need to introduce me," she said.

"Trish, this is Beth. She knows Jane."

Tricia's eyes widened and she grabbed Beth's elbows.

"Oh, Darling, tell me everything. Tell me what's going on in her life. How is she? Where is she? Come sit, have you eaten? I'll go find someone to fix something for us."

Tricia waved over her shoulder as she trotted back the way she had come. A voice from upstairs called down.

"She isn't dead, then?"

Jesse Dawson walked down the stairs carrying a decanter of amber fluid. For a moment, Beth was certain she was seeing the most attractive man she had ever laid eyes on.

"I thought he would be heavier," she whispered to Brad. Brad laughed softly.

"Jane is the most unkind to him," he said. As Jesse reached the landing, though, his age started to show in the details she hadn't been able to see at first. The skin under his eyes was soft and his jawline sagged.

Oh, Beth thought. His hair was dark brown, rather than black, and while Jane, Brad, and Tricia had very fair skin, Jesse had a slightly darker complexion. He wasn't unattractive, but the sneer in his slightly drunken eyes was off-putting in a way that made her question her first impression of him.

"I asked you, she isn't dead?" Jesse repeated. Beth shook her head.

"No... no, she's alive."

He muttered something into his drink and jerked his chin at Brad.

"No harm asking." He looked back at Beth. "Come talk to me when she's dead."

Beth looked at Brad with alarm.

"Seriously?" she whispered. He shrugged.

"It would be an ugly divorce, if he could figure out how to arrange it," Brad whispered back. "She bankrupted him."

Beth watched Jesse's back as the dark man followed Tricia out of sight.

"They don't know?"

Brad shook his head.

"No. No reason either of them should."

Beth had to shake herself from staring into Brad's eyes. There was a genuine sincerity there that was bewitching. He smiled at her again.

"Trish will be a bit. Would you like to come up to the garden so we can talk?"

"Garden?" Beth asked.

"On the roof. One of Trish's projects. I'll show you."

He offered her his elbow and she took it, feeling very out of her own world, following him up the stairs and across a broad, golden sitting area and out a set of tall double doors. Up this high, the crisp New York breeze was lovely. There was a set of stairs up the outside of the building to get to the roof, where what must have been several tons of earth had been imported for a lush, green garden.

"Wow," Beth breathed.

"As much time as she put into planning this, she never comes up here," Brad said, looking around at the space. "It's too bad. I think this may be the nicest place to sit in all of New York."

He showed her to a small patio space in the midst of ornamental trees and exotic flowers, and rested his hands on the back of a chair for her to sit in. He let her sit and enjoy for a few minutes before he spoke again.

"So. How is she?"

Beth looked at him.

"Should I tell you the truth? Honestly?"

"She wouldn't want you to, but I do manage to keep track of her. I knew she was in Boston and that she was tangled up with the Hughes, but I haven't gotten to talk to anyone who has actually spent time with her in a while. I'd appreciate it if you told me the truth."

Beth smiled, then laughed.

"She's scary."

He nodded.

"That sounds like her.

"I don't know what else to tell you," Beth admitted after a second. "I don't know what else she might have ever been."

"How did you find us?" Brad asked.

"Society pages. I pulled the microfilm at the library and went through the wedding announcements. Brothers who married sisters. Then there was a picture."

"She was beautiful, wasn't she?"

"Are you really...?" Beth asked.

"In love with her? We don't talk about it, she and I. I'd rather not talk about it with you, if that's okay."

Beth nodded.

"Sorry."

She stood to look at a vining flower.

"What was she like, before she was His Dark Mistress?" she asked. He stretched out on his reclining chair and put his hands behind his head.

"Ferocious."

Beth glanced at him, but his eyes were distant.

"It was supposed to be her and me running the company, not Jesse and myself," he said. "We were the heirs-apparent from the time we were seventeen. She was cutthroat and I was a builder. The pragmatics in the company figured we'd be unstoppable."

He paused and looked at Beth.

"I hated her. She would do anything to get her own way, and she was so rough on Trish. I called her selfish more times than I could count."

"I'm not sure you were wrong," Beth said. He laughed.

"I told Trish, once, when we were dating, that Jane was a dark wind that was going to destroy the whole family. I found Jane standing in the next room a few seconds later. I've regretted it, deeply, for the rest of my life."

Beth looked at him incredulously.

"You think that was enough to upset her?"

"No. I saw malice that wasn't there. I wrote her off too entirely, and she knew it. I mistrusted the one who should have been my best ally."

"I doubt she even remembers," Beth said.

"I suspect she remembers clearly," Brad told her. "She always did whatever suited her. She was capable of anything."

"Why did she marry Jesse?" Beth asked.

"Pretty much the reasons she told you. Power. Convenience. To spite him. I swear she always hated him. He knew she'd be his meal ticket, but she got their papers written so that if he cheated on her and divorced her, she'd get all of the property they held jointly. Same is true for her, but he has to prove it. She has a waitress living on Park Avenue who has video…" He paused. "I'm sorry, that was crude."

Beth shrugged.

"I spent half of the last year hanging out with much worse."

"That's not an excuse for me." He laughed. "It's strange, having someone to talk to who knows what she is, now."

"I'm not sure I actually know what she is…" Beth said.

"I believe you have spent more time speaking with her in the last year than anyone else has in the last three. Lady reporter, you know her better than anyone," he said.

"That's frightening."

"Isn't it?"

He paused, then turned in his chair.

"Why did you come, Beth?"

"I just needed to know. I needed to know who she was."

"You know who she is," he said. "I'm not sure anyone knew who she was. Will you look for her?"

"I don't know. I expect I will. I don't know what else to do."

"She has that effect."

Beth looked around.

"She actually lived here?"

"For about six months. My father gave it to us as a wedding present. Jane loved to look down at the city."

"It's hard to imagine her fitting, here," Beth said.

"In some ways she never did, but, just looking at her, you wouldn't have known."

Beth was dying to ask about Tricia, but she kept it to herself. Even a reporter had a hard time being rude to the elegant, earnest man who stood up and walked to the roof wall just past her.

"Is there any way she's happy?" Brad asked.

"I don't know," Beth said, then remembered something, and laughed. He looked at her. "I'm sorry. She was happy one evening… She told me she liked shooting people in the face." Beth swallowed hard. "I'm sorry. That was a terrible thing to say."

He looked away.

"But it sounds just like her."

Tricia came bouncing up the stairs.

"Everything is ready, if you want to come down," she said happily. Beth looked at Brad.

"I'm sorry, Dearest," he said, walking over to Tricia and kissing her cheek. "Beth has other plans tonight. She only stopped in to let us know that Jane is well."

"So soon?" Tricia took Beth's arms and kissed her cheek. "Of course, of course. I'm sure you have very important things you need to do. Thank you so much for taking time out of your evening to bring us word." The woman paused and looked Beth in the eye. The difference between Tricia and His Dark Mistress was staggering. "Beth?" Beth nodded. "Beth, if... when you see her again, please tell her that we would love for her to come *home* for a while. Even if it were just for a day or two..." The woman smiled bravely, but tears sparkled in her eyes, and she bit her lip. "Please. I miss my sister."

Beth nodded.

"I promise."

Tricia nodded firmly, shaking Beth's arms with her nod.

"Excellent. Of course. Thank you."

They walked down the staircase back to the sitting area and Brad walked her down to the elevator. He pushed the button and they waited.

"If you do see her again. Add my wishes to see her, as well. We all miss her."

Beth nodded at him.

"She's doing it all for you," she whispered, almost involuntarily. He sighed.

"I don't know. I wish she'd just come home."

The elevator arrived and Beth got on. Brad stood and held her gaze, a quiet uncertainty behind his eyes, all the way until the doors finished closing.

Brad stood at the edge of the rooftop, arms out, hands spread flat on the concrete, watching the lights in the city below. He was unsettled. The reporter showing up the week before had surprised him, and made him think about Jane in a much more immediate sense than his routine spy reports did. The woman had actually sat at a table with Jane and spoken with her. It made his sister-in-law back into a real person, an idea he had avoided for years, now.

There was a flapping noise behind him and he smiled.

"Hello, Darkness," he said without turning.

"Hello, Fraud," she answered.

"I could have sworn I had an alarm installed on the fire escape," he said.

"My name is on the deed, same as yours," she said. "A well-motivated employee at the alarm company was perfectly willing to add my code without mentioning it to you."

"I've heard that things are going well for you," he said.

"Don't be coy with me," she said. "I know Beth was here."

"She's clever," he said.

"She's going to make a nuisance of herself if I'm not careful," she answered. Brad smiled.

"Then she's more clever than I estimated," he said. The woman behind him snorted.

"More persistent, than clever, actually."

He grinned at the city.

"Will you come downstairs? Trish is desperate to see you," he said. She paused.

"Not tonight. I came to warn you about Jesse. He's in over his head, and if you aren't careful, he'll pull you down with him."

"I manage Jesse just fine," Brad said. "Please, Trish would really love to talk to you. Just for a few minutes."

"It's good to see you, Brad," she said. He turned. She was wilder than he had remembered. They looked at each other for a long time, then he looked down.

"We've been holding off telling anyone. I kept hoping I'd find a way to get you here." He looked up at her. "Trish is going to have a baby."

Jane froze, maybe the smallest hint of panic in her eyes, then her cold mask dropped into place.

"Be careful of Jesse. He will hurt you."

She turned, then looked over her shoulder.

"Take care of her."

He nodded.

"Always do."

She started to walk away.

"Goodnight, Darkness," he said.

"Goodnight, Fraud."

THE LEGEND
OF
HIS DARK MISTRESS

E. Stanton

Boston Monthly
Vol. 173   No. 2

Ed. Sam Knapp

Once upon a time in a very small but very wealthy kingdom, there were two brothers, princes. They were well-loved and given anything their hearts desired because, though they were loved, their parents were often absent, tending to the affairs of the kingdom and none of the palace staff had the heart to deny them. As so often happens in these tales, one of the brothers grew up light and the other dark.

In this same kingdom was a pair of girls, sisters, of the aristocratic class, upon whom their father doted throughout their childhoods. No opportunity was denied them, no matter what the request, as he was quite wealthy and a widower. As also so often happens, one matured into a lady of darkness, and the other of light.

Once they had reached the appropriate age, they fell in love and were married – or at least were married, at any rate – dark brother to dark sister and light brother to light sister, and the kingdom rejoiced. They took up residence in the palace and began their married lives.

"What shall we do today, my love?" the light sister asked her husband one morning shortly after they were married.

"I don't know, dearest," he replied. "What would you like to do?"

"I wouldn't dream of suggesting an activity with which to occupy ourselves until I heard what you would like to do," she told him.

"Would you fancy a game of chess?" he asked. She made a face, sticking out her tongue prettily. "How about a ride around the grounds?"

"I don't like horses," his bride answered. "They smell bad."

They sat in silence for a moment.

"I know!" cried she. "I shall throw a party! We haven't had a ball since we were married." She clapped her hands, her blond curls bouncing against her shoulders. He smiled at her enthusiasm.

"Whatever makes you happy, my dear," he said, standing and kissing her forehead.

"Now, I shall need a new dress," she said, standing and beginning to tick things off on her fingers. "Oh! Who shall I invite?" She didn't wait for an answer, bustling happily out of the room.

"What do you want to do today?" the dark sister asked of her husband the same morning.

"What do I care?" he asked. "We both know you already have a full day planned, and that I have no intention of taking part in it."

"What <u>will</u> you do today?" she asked.

"I suspect I will shortly go back to bed and call for wine. I'll take until lunch to finish the bottle, then call for my lunch in my room. I'll take a nap after lunch, then call for an entertainer to keep me amused until dinner time. I'll have dinner with you and that will conclude my day."

She watched him for a moment, but it quickly became apparent he had no curiosity whatever about the activities of her day, and she stood and left.

Later that day, as he was out seeing to the construction of a new stone fence where he had the intention of grazing cattle, the light brother came across the dark sister.

"Good day," he said, trotting up to her on his horse and slowing to a walk. She nodded.

"And you." Any other would have taken her tone as a warning to accept the polite greeting and move on, but he was determined to forge good will between them, she being his wife's sister and his brother's wife.

"It's a good day to be out of the palace," said he. "Spring has broken early this year, I dare say."

She examined the still-bare trees overhead.

"The corn will plant early and be plentiful, but I don't expect the summer will get hot enough to satisfy the rest of the vegetables," she said. He looked startled.

"Are you a student of the seasons, then?" he asked. She frowned, straightening her mare's mane.

"I am a student of many things, and you do me a disservice to assume otherwise." Her waist-length black hair fell down to mingle with her mare's jet-black mane and he could no longer see her face, or how her dark eyes watched him through the tresses.

"Then please accept my sincerest apology," he said. "My wife does not seem to have studied as you have. Perhaps I have underestimated her as well."

The dark lady threw her head back proudly.

"Not at all," she said. The insult seemed to silence him, but he shook off the sting.

"What brings you into town, today?" he asked.

"Private business," she answered. Her silence smote him again.

"I am arranging to fence the field your father gave me as your sister's dowry," he said. She did not answer. "I plan to expand the dairy on the other side of the hill."

She looked at him, then back forward, urging her mount into a trot. He followed suit.

"You are a beautiful rider," he said.

"Thank you," she answered, her form perfect, but frosty.

"I've noticed that the adjacent land your father gave my brother yet lies fallow," he said.

"Unsurprising," she said. He silently agreed.

"If you would be interested," he said, "I would love to let it from you and expand my pasture further."

She slowed to a walk.

"In matters of finance, I am always interested," she said.

They discussed the details the rest of the way to the palace, and he quickly discovered that she was going to turn what he had meant as a half-serious offer for quick, easy profit on both sides into a shrewd business arrangement skewed as far in her favor as possible.

"You have a mind for numbers that rivals most of the men I've met," he said.

"I have a mind for numbers that easily surpasses all of them," she answered coldly. "Have the contracts drawn up and give them to me. I will sign them."

"It's my brother's land," the light brother answered.

"It will be his signature," she said. He stopped, holding his horse's reins in one hand as he inspected her. She sighed.

"Very well," she said. "I will have him sign them himself."

He paused for a moment, troubled and torn. Finally he settled with himself and smiled.

"That will do quite nicely," he said. "Now, you strike me as the type of person who knows how to enjoy a game of chess."

For the first time since he had known her, her face lit up, though she did not smile.

"I know quite well how to enjoy humiliating you at just such a game," she said, and took his arm to walk into the palace.

The weeks passed uneventfully. The corn was planted, and the light brother oversaw the planting of the house garden – his wife showed no interest. The light sister planned her ball for the spring equinox, now less than a week away, and the household was in a flurry of activity, planning for an event the likes of which the kingdom had not seen in generations. The dark brother resumed his normal nightly carousing with his friends, the newness of his wife having worn off, and the dark sister kept her own company, attending to plans only she herself knew.

Each was happy enough with the method he had selected to entertain himself, and the time passed without conflict. The morning four days before the ball, the light sister entered her sister's chambers.

"I brought you a gift,"' the fair one announced.

"I have never enjoyed any of your gifts any more than your presence," the dark one answered, looking up from her writing desk.

"Ah! You're such a darling, sister. But look at the dress I've had made for you!"

"You didn't model for it yourself, did you?" the dark one asked, holding it up to the light. "You know you have a slighter frame than I."

"Of course not! I made her model it on your last set of riding breeches," the fair one said, wrinkling her nose, her pink mouth turned into a half-serious frown that could not overpower her permanent smile. "Not that she liked that, but I knew you would never stand for her."

The dark one showed no ripple of emotion or response as her sister went on about the arrangements of the ball. In truth, though, it was a fetching, handsome dress of black and green, and she couldn't help but to be pleased with it.

"Oh! Try it on!" her sister suddenly cried, hopping on her toes.

"No," she said sternly. "I'm busy."

"No, no, you must!" the pretty blond said, laughing. "I won't leave until you do."

At length she allowed herself to be persuaded, and she went into her dressing room to change.

"The night of the ball, I'll send my maid to help you dress. I just want to see how it fits."

"I don't need someone to dress me," the dark sister said, emerging.

"Oh, that fits perfectly! I was worried I would have to take it back to get refitted without you, but that will do nicely!" the blonde said, adjusting the fabric as the dark one turned in front of a mirror.

"It's about as good a fit as a ball gown ever will be," the dark one said. Her sister smiled broadly, then turned her attention to the dark locks tangled down her sister's back.

"What shall you do with this?" she asked thoughtfully. The dark one stood for a moment, enduring, then turned away to change back.

"I will come up with something, if I have to do it myself!" the blonde called, laughing, then traipsed out of the room to attend to more details.

In the front courtyard, the light brother was returning from an errand. He dismounted his bay horse and handed the reins to a stable boy.

"Did you have a good ride, sir?" the boy asked.

"He went well for me, thank you," the fair prince answered. He made to enter the palace, but was distracted by his brother exiting the barn with his arm around the waist of one of the maids. When she saw the light brother, she startled and tried to get away, but the dark one tightened his arm around her and smiled. The light brother nearly growled as he stormed back across the yard.

"The audacity!" he spat. The girl squirmed under the intensity of his gaze, but his brother continued to meet his eye innocently.

"Not six months wed, and you flaunt your infidelity thus? You are heir to the throne!"

"My activities are no mystery to anyone but yourself," the dark one answered, finally releasing his companion, who fled toward the kitchen entrance of the house.

"One of your character will never sit on the throne of this kingdom," the fair brother spat, feeling color rise in his face. His brother laughed.

"Why do you think I selected my bride?" The light brother was startled by this, and did not find words before the darker sibling shook his head, amused, and continued. "She did not marry me for love, brother. She will make me king, no matter what I do, because she would be queen."

Without waiting for a response, the dark prince brushed past his taller brother and strolled casually into the front doors of the palace.

The morning of the ball dawned lovely but uneventful. The dark sister vanished into town on business of her own, the light brother met with a pair of country landowners – his parents would be returning from a diplomatic visit to a close friend of the Queen's later that week, but he was managing royal affairs in their absence – the dark brother slept or otherwise amused himself, and the light sister immersed herself in grooming and last-minute details.

At lunchtime, the dark sister returned from her errands and retired to her chambers to manage her affairs. She sent for a minimal lunch and in her candle-lit, windowless main chamber for three-quarters of an hour before a maid – her sister's maid – announced herself by knocking timidly on the door.

"Your sister sent me to see to your dress," she said softly, peering around the edge of the door.

"Come back later. I'm busy," the dark sister said, waving her away.

"She said I wasn't to take no as your reply, madam," she said, not moving. The dark sister looked up sharply from her documents and the half a nose and eye dodged fractionally further behind the door.

"You have overstepped your place. Leave me!"

"M'lady said to find the worst I could imagine with which you could conceive to threaten me, and consider myself pre-emptively threatened," the woman said and blinked. The dark sister almost laughed.

"Can you read, woman?" she asked.

"No, madam," the maid answered, inching slightly further into the room.

"Very well. Be quick, and if I consider you to be unduly interrupting my work, I will throw you out."

The woman came quickly into the room, retrieving the new dress from the ottoman where the dark sister had discarded it and proceeded to aid her in changing for the ball. The dark sister held out her papers so that she could read them, and did not much suffer herself to be disturbed, despite having agreed to the intrusion.

After an hour and a half, she was dressed to her sister's maid's satisfaction, and the woman began to work on her face. The dark sister brushed her away.

"No, now, that will do," she chided, still reading.

"But my lady said…" the woman countered, persisting. The dark sister threw down her papers.

"I said that will do."

The woman stepped back, as though remembering herself.

"Yes, madam," she said, gathering up her implements and departing. The dark princess tried to settle back into her work, but was uncomfortably distracted by the bindingness of her party clothes. She had not many minutes to stew before her sister came bustling in unannounced.

"I told you," she said before her dark sibling could speak, "I was going to get you ready for my party if I had to do it myself. And you shan't find me as easy to send away as someone else." The dark one found herself speechless as her fair sister set to work. The color to her lips, cheeks, and eyes was as expected, if more tedious than she found profitable. Then, though, the pretty blonde opened a container and began to brush oil into her dark sister's hair.

"You're pushing me to my limits of patience," she said, attempting to stand.

"I care not. Sit," the fair sister said around a clutch of pins in her mouth. Stunned and slightly amused, she sat. It took the fair one more than an hour to exhaust the oil and finish detangling the long black hair.

"You have such lovely hair," the fair one murmured, pulling her slicked fingers through it cleanly.

"Get on with it. I have more important things to do," the dark one said.

"So do I," the light one answered, stuffing the pins back in her mouth. "I'm not even dressed, yet."

Next came a soft bar of wax.

"Are you making this up as you go along?" the dark one asked. The blond giggled, rubbing the wax along her sister's scalp, ordering the slick, shining black hair as she saw fit. She pulled a part far to the side and, pulling the hanging hair straight, pulled a damp reed out of a towel and turned it in the hair, wrapping it all the way to the back of her sister's head and tucking the ends of the reed into the hair against her head, then resumed with the wax.

"You're coming back tonight to undo this mess," the dark one glowered. Her sister smiled.

"You will have never looked better."

Finally, she was happy with the results of her labor. The wax was mostly gone, and her sister's hair held a sculpted, sleek shape, curling around her head to the knot at the back. The dark one reached up to touch it.

"Well, I'm fit for battle, with this helmet," she said. "Will you leave me in peace, now?"

"Jewels," the other answered, dropping a velvet bag on the dressing table.

"I'm not sitting in my room wearing those for the rest of the afternoon," the dark sister said.

"Just promise me you'll wear them?"

"If it will make you finally take your leave, very well."

The blond grinned, then glanced about.

"How do you tell time in here? I must go get ready, myself."

She bustled out, leaving half her implements behind, and the dark one leaned back in her chair, trying to recollect her thoughts. Her hair was pulled too tight, and she wandered if that was made her sister seem so dumb all the time.

She was still disoriented when, some time later, her husband allowed himself into her room.

"Your sister says it's time for your entrance," he said. She hurriedly threw on the jewelry, paying it no special attention, and resigned herself to his arm all the way to the ballroom.

The entrance to the ballroom was an event of some spectacle, but finally the four young members of the royal family claimed their seats at the head of the hall – the brothers in the middle with their wives beside on each side, down a step and slightly recessed – and the three of them who were inclined to socialization sorted themselves into their accustomed company.

The dark brother surrounded himself with the friends with whom he routinely caroused, and would make forays into the clusters of shy women scattered about the edges of the room, generally making a nuisance of himself.

"Dude, your sister-in-law is hot," one of his buddies said, elbowing him as he returned from talking to a tittering, blushing trio of brunettes.

"And completely inaccessible," the dark one answered, running his fingers through his hair.

"Only a matter of time, with you in the same house," another said, leering.

"Nah, I don't even think my brother gets any," the prince said, laughing and commenting on another woman who had just entered.

Meanwhile, the light brother stood with a close business associate and a childhood friend, greeting guests s they were announced.

"A fine affair, by any account," the friend said. "Too long since the last."

"My mother didn't care for arranging them. My wife seems to have a fair hand for it, though," the prince answered, excusing himself to shake the hand of a local noble and bow to his wife and of-age daughter.

"When do you expect the king and queen?" the associate asked as he returned.

"On the morrow, or maybe the next day, if their plans haven't changed."

"A shame they will miss this," the friend said. The fair one smiled.

"This was to be a welcome home gala, but you know my mother – diplomacy first. They sent word last week that they would be longer than initially intended. It was, of course, too late to change the plans. My wife is already planning another event for early next month as substitute."

"You'll make the dressmaker a wealthy woman," the associate teased, and they laughed.

The fair sister had repaired to her social group, the light daughters of the kingdom aristocracy, nearly a dozen in number.

"Ooh, it's so lovely to have a formal party to look forward to," one oozed. "You must do this again."

"I shall, but you should return my invitation," the princess answered. The first speaker's eyes widened.

"You would still attend?" she asked. The princess smiled.

"I would do everything in my power to see to it that my husband and myself, at least, would attend," she said, pressing the hand of her friend amicably.

"I doubt your sister would join you," another said, as she openly, but without malice, watched the dark princess.

"I suspect you are correct. I wasn't certain she would even attend this fete – in her own house," the light one answered.

"She does not look like she expects any enjoyment out of the event," a third one said with pity.

"Doesn't she look regal, though?" a fourth asked, momentarily silencing the group.

Up on her throne, the dark sister was watching the ebb and flow of the party dispassionately. If she had been willing to, she would have admitted that her coiffure made her feel more confident than normal. Those in the room would mostly cower before her under normal circumstances; now they couldn't even look at her. She held her head up, her neck twisted snakelike toward her angled shoulder, and she folded her hands coldly on her knee. The orchestra struck up a waltz and the room broke into dancing partners and still she watched, the slow, even rhythm of her breathing keeping her own time. The hours passed, the room nipped at food and each other. She watched. Parts of her mind wandered to various industries she was taken with, but she kept a mental presence in the room, learning to know her sister's attendants, her husband's cronies. At intervals, the royal family would seek their seats, but they refrained from speaking to the dark woman until, late in the evening, the light brother seated himself in his brother's throne. The lack of decorum surprised her.

"Do you dance?" he asked, leaning on the arm of the chair.

"With less flair but better form than my sister," the dark one answered, turning her head slowly to him. He smiled broadly.

"Would you dance with me, then?" he asked, standing. She considered for a moment, then offered her hand. He escorted her to the floor, her hand tucked under his arm in classic fashion, then swept her into the steps and flurry already in progress. She kept her eyes on his face, a gaze that withered men, especially during the waltz. Very few asked her to dance twice. He looked into her eyes, unconcerned.

"My wife has worked a remarkable magic with you," he said warmly.

"She made the best of me that there could be," she answered.

"You don't receive complements well, do you?"

"Me? I thought you were praising your wife," she answered. He dropped his head slightly, smiling harder.

"Well, then, let me try again," he said. "You look beautiful tonight."

"You are very kind," she said. He laughed, then his face settled slightly.

"My brother is very fortunate to have a poised and beautiful woman such as yourself at his side," he said. The bitter tinge on his voice confused her, and she let her eyes slide to his shoulder, considering. He feared he had embarrassed her, but before he could recover the conversation, they heard a shriek they both immediately recognized. Both heads shot up, searching over the newly-disorganized crowd, seeking the source.

In the forest, a skilled hunter may read the actions of birds to find the location of various animals. The dancing pair were such skilled hunters in a ballroom, and each quickly perceived, by the bent of the spectators' heads, where the disruption was sourced.

The light brother dashed across the room to his wife's side, where she stood in a small open space clutching her chest. At the sight of him, she collapsed into his arms and commenced sobbing. He glanced around to find both the source of her discontent and to find the dark sister, and again the motion of the crowd communicated to him what had happened and what was happening.

The dark sister, at the onset, had looked not for her sister, but for her sister's aggressor. She had spotted the big man wading across the crowd and made to interrupt him.

She hit a pocket of exited young women and blasted through them, leaving a wake of upset and tearful guests. Several men pushed out of her way, and she had a clear view of her target, owing to her height. The crowd put up a half-hearted resistance to the big man as he attempted to charge his way through to the door. She caught him in a few more strides and spun him roughly. As he rotated, his arm flung out and she saw the sparkle of a gold chain. His other arm flew up to block her, but his slightly inebriated reflexes were no match for hers. She put the heel of her hand into his nose and he staggered back. She pressed, striking him thrice more before he fell. She disentangled the jewelry from his hand and found a corridor had opened between herself and the other two royals. She strode composedly to her sheet-pale sister as the man on the floor struggled to sit up. She held out her hand to her sister, who hesitantly received the necklace.

"Oh!" cried she, suddenly clutching it and wandering several steps toward the thief.

"Oh!" she cried again, throwing her hands to her waistline and wringing them. The room was silent. The dark sister and the light brother stood shoulder to shoulder and watched her. The light woman's lip wavered.

"Oh, but what if he needed it? What if his family is starving and he had no other way to feed them?"

She approached, her hands spread.

"I want him to have it," she said, her voice nearly cracking as tears rolled down her cheeks. Her husband hesitated.

"Those jewels belonged to my mother. If he leaves with them, he will be dead by morning," the dark one muttered, turning her head down and in to speak privately to the light prince. He nodded confidentially, then opened his arms to his wife.

"Dearest, I'm sure we can find something of similar cost and much less value with which to feed his man's family, should they have real need," said he. "Keep your jewels."

She clutched them to her chest again, smiling through her tears and rushed forward to kiss his cheeks. The palace guard had collected the disoriented man from the floor and departed, and the orchestra tentatively resumed. A few couples returned the floor, and most of the crowd broke off into clusters to discuss what had happened.

"You highness," the dark princess said coldly to the light prince. "I believe the excitement has been enough for me tonight. I will take my leave."

He bowed formally, and she waded her way through the compliant crowd out of the ballroom, allowing the heavy doors to close behind her. Her black shoes clicked and echoed down the long stone hallway and her skirts ruffled in the still air. The door behind her opened and closed.

"He will be punished," the light brother called, slowing from his relaxed run as he caught her.

"Why do you assume his fate concerns me?" she asked.

"Doesn't it?" he asked. Her face was impassive; she did not answer. He sighed, leaning against a wall. She stopped.

"I had assumed that was why you left. You are much sturdier than my wife," he said and paused. "Thank you for catching him. The shame of being downed by a woman is worse than any punishment I could enact."

She pressed her lips together hard enough to force the natural color out of them, but the false pigment there was too robust for the symptom to show.

"You're welcome," she said, turning to go. She heard him draw breath and looked back at him. He paused, then shook his head.

"My brother does not love you," he said, sounding pained. She smiled.

"And my sister does not love you," she said pleasantly.

"How can you say such a thing? She is the most loving creature I have ever known!"

"She loves you as she loves puppies, dresses, and clouds. And by loving everything, she loves nothing," the dark princess said.

"Much like yourself," he said, stung. She shook her head, calm and still smiling.

"You are mistaken. I do not love my husband, true enough, but I love my sister better than you do, and two others, beside. My sister I love in a foolish, filial manner, as I grew up with her and know her weaknesses and have an instinct to defend her. You have no such excuse and are merely fond of her."

The light one opened his mouth to protest several times, then thought better of it.

"Who are the two others?"

"The first is my trainer," she said.

"Your trainer?"

"I have studied with him for ten years, with money from my own pocket," she said.

"Who is he?" the prince asked.

"A retired mercenary who no doubt has escaped your attention." She smiled privately. "I love him because he knows me and does not fear me, and has no reason to."

"And who is the last?" the prince asked, leaning harder against the wall and watching her. She smiled at him.

"The one of which you should already be very much aware. Myself."

She nodded her head in adieu to him and left him leaning against the stone wall in the torch-lit hallway.

The next morning, the dark sister found that her hair still hurt. She sat in front of the mirror on her dressing table and worked a brush through it. Despite herself, she was in a sunny mood. In all, she had enjoyed the party. She could still feel the man's nose on the heel of her hand, and the distinct crunch when she broke it. When she had gotten back to her room, she had found blood on her dress darkening one of the spreads of green velvet. It had made her smile wickedly.

There was a knock on the door and she turned her head from her work.

"Who disturbs me at this hour?" she called, the smile of memory barely fading on her face.

"It is me," the light brother answered hesitantly.

"Enter," she called, turning back to her mirror. She would enjoy his discomfort at being in her chamber. No doubt he had hoped she would come to the door. He opened the door and stepped just into the room, closing it behind himself and surprising the dark sister.

"I train each morning for an hour in my wing of the palace. Join me," he said. She startled, further surprised, and before her mind could come up with appropriate substitute words she had never before uttered flew unchecked from her mouth.

"My hair is a wreck."

His eyes widened and he laughed impulsively. Her hand flew to her mouth. They stared at each other for a moment.

"Clearly I wasn't expecting your question," she finally said.

"I genuinely don't care about your hair," he said with good humor. She considered for a moment.

"Very well. I could do with a new sparring partner," she said. She tied her hair up with a piece of string and dismissed him so she could change into her working clothes.

She made her way to the other wing of the palace where a manservant was waiting to escort her to a large open room with a hardwood floor and walls covered with a nice, but not exhaustive, selection of weapons. The light prince was practicing with a foil, one arm tucked behind his back. The manservant departed and the dark sister wandered to the wall, taking various wooden weapons in her hands and replacing them.

"I put out a foil for you," said he, the slender weapon in his hand cutting the air audibly.

"My mercenary friend calls fencing the sport of cowards who fear injury," replied she. He laughed.

"Very well. With what would you prefer to spar?"

She selected a pair of oak practice swords and tossed one to him. He deftly caught in and spun it in a figure eight down and over his head. She smiled approvingly and took her stance in front of him. They traded parry, parry, attack, attack for several minutes, the click of wood on wood the only sound of note.

"You're good," he said.

"I know," she answered.

"Why did you leave early last night?" he asked.

"I grew bored," she replied, stepping back to let him speak.

"I was enjoying our dance," he said, leaning on his sword. "Did I bore you that terribly?"

"I was disgusted," she said, scowling.

"With my dancing?" He was surprised.

"With your mercy," she told him. She stepped into him and he raised his sword again. She struck.

"What would you have had me do?" he asked.

"You promised to feed his family, making my sister a target for every hungry family in riding distance," she said.

"They don't have to attack her to win our mercy. With as much as we have, is it not right that we should feed those who are hungry around us?"

"I care not for right or wrong," she said. "It is weak to give what is yours."

"You care only for strength?" he asked.

"I care only for strength," she said, striking at him more forcefully. His breath started to come with more effort.

"And you perceive... our goodness as weakness?"

She was good, but he matched her.

"And your darkness is strength?" he asked, pushing an offense.

"Darkness is simply an absence of light. It does not make me strong. Witness the slovenliness that is your brother."

The light one grunted in humor.

"And then I am weak?" he asked.

"You..." she said, pushing him back. "You are strong... despite your goodness."

With her last word, she spun and, getting under his sword, landed a hard blow to his ribs. He grunted as his wind rushed out and he stepped back, conceding her victory. She rested the tip of her sword on the ground, still poised and ready should he resume his attack. He coughed several times, rubbing the spot with his opposite hand.

"It's a shame," he said, breathing deep to regain his energy, "that you shall waste your strength on yourself."

"It's a shame," she said, refusing to let her elevated heart rate show, "that you shall waste yours on everyone else."

That evening, the light brother lay in bed with his wife, very happy with his day. The princess was talking happily about tea with her friends when she found the spreading bruise on his right side.

"What's this?" she asked, her fingers on her mouth. "It was my wicked sister, wasn't it? She's hurt you."

"It was a fair blow. She bested me," he said. Tears began to leak from her eyes as she stared at the bruise.

"She has, she's wounded you. Oh, I wish she were dead."

He sat up sharply in bed.

"You mustn't say such things," he reprimanded her. She pulled the sheets up to her chin, still crying.

"But I do!" she said.

"She did nothing wrong. Have you ever known her to do something so wrong as to deserve death?" he asked.

"No," she pouted.

"Then you mustn't wish her death. It's poor character," he said.

"Then I wish she'd never been born," the blonde woman said. He smiled and shook his head.

"She cares for you too much for you to say such things, but I suppose I can't fault you for a lack of justice," he said, settling back into the warm sheets and trying to put his arm around her. She pulled away.

"Have you seen a doctor?" she asked. He frowned.

"No, it's nothing, Love," he said. She pulled further away.

"You must see a doctor. I'll call for him," she said, moving to rise. He caught her wrist.

"It's a simple bruise. You're overreacting," he said. The tears thickened and she wrung her hands.

"My wicked sister... I couldn't live with myself if there were something wrong."

He tried to interrupt.

"No. I shan't sleep until you call for a doctor," she said, pushing him off and getting out of the bed. "It's your decision."

He sighed and relented, motioning for her to fetch the doctor.

The next morning, the dark couple sat at breakfast. He drank a glass of scotch, huddled over the table, and she leaned over her stack of papers, taking notes.

"You spent time with my brother yesterday," he said.

"I did," she replied, not looking up.

"He'll be quite a tool in your tool box, won't he, Dearest?" he asked, smiling with his teeth. She slapped him so hard his entire face shook and then snatched up her papers.

"Don't call me Dearest."

The dark sister made her way to the other wing of the palace as the sun was rising and the staff was just beginning to stir audibly throughout the castle. It was her third week of training with her brother-in-law, three mornings a week. She hadn't since their first morning landed a bruising blow, but it wasn't for lack of trying. Each time they grappled longer, and now several of the light prince's personal staff would creep in to watch the pair at the end of the session.

"May I ask a question whose answer I have no right to hear?" he asked, whirring his sword through the air.

"I care very little for your supposed social etiquette," she said in answer.

"Why did you marry my brother?" he asked. She stepped into him, but without malice.

"I thought I had answered that," she said. "I love no one better than myself, and he was the greatest opportunity of which I was aware."

Parry, parry, attack, parry. Her feet were ever so slightly quicker than his, but his strength, with enough practice, would eventually master her.

"But how do you tolerate him?" he stepped away, uncomfortable. "He has so many mistresses."

She laughed and shook her hair out.

"You care for my honor more than I. He has not touched me, and he will not. Should I desire to bear an heir for him, I'll find a more suitable parent."

The light one was stunned at this admission. He found nothing to say. She raised her sword and they resumed.

"Well, why did you marry my sister?" she asked at a pause. He considered, then, as she blocked his attack, answered.

"She is a sweet person, trustworthy, suited to court, and pleasant company," he said.

"Not because you love her," the woman answered. "Interesting. Will she be a good mother?"

"I have many years to grow to love her, and, as you say, I am fond of her."

"But will she be a good mother?"

He was silent for some time as they battled.

"Raising an heir is a critical role of a queen, is it not?" she finally pressed.

"It is," he answered through gritted teeth as he strained.

"And?"

"She would raise excellent daughters, like herself," he said.

"But an heir?"

He didn't answer for several more minutes.

"She is too soft, is she not? You're afraid she would spoil a boy," she said. He winced almost in mourning. "How can you think that that treatment is acceptable for daughters and not sons? If all she would do is raise women who could not raise sons?"

At that point, two servants entered, and their conversation ceased. They battled on for another quarter of an hour and then were quits.

"You may return to your positions," the prince said in a not unfriendly tone. They bowed slightly and left. The prince dabbed his forehead with a handkerchief and looked at the dark sister, who was drinking water out of a glass left at the door.

"I have news of the northern border," he said. She looked at him in passing interest.

"The border farms have long faced occasional raids from our neighbors, but they have become more bold of late, and I will be organizing the nobles to go defend the land."

"Have you told my sister?" she asked, lowering the glass. He shook his head.

"You know her character too well," he said. "We both know what she will say."

"No!" she shrieked, her face reddening. "No!"

"I'm sorry," he said. "That's what's going to happen."

"No. You can't go. You can't," she said, running forward to clutch at him. He couldn't find words to answer.

"Do you want to leave me?" she asked, looking up at him.

"I'm not going because I want to be away from you. I'm going because it's my job," he said.

"Is your brother going?" she asked, her head still tipped back.

"No, I don't expect he will."

"Is your father?"

"Of course not."

"Then why do you have to go? Why can't you just send someone?"

"Because that would not make me a good ruler."

"But they aren't going," she said, pushing her head into his chest.

"My father fought in his prime. He passed that responsibility on to us. And honestly," he said, pulling her head back so he could look into her eyes, "would you really prefer I behave like my brother when it's easier?"

She slammed her face back into his chest.

"Yes," came her muffled reply.

He considered carefully his reply.

"If you loved me truly, you would want me to go, because my honor would be a critical part of what you loved about me," he said.

"If I loved you, I would send you away to die? Oh, I do not understand that!" she said, stepping away. "I love you so much that I would never see you taken away from me. You are too dear to me."

"Then you love only yourself," he said, sadly, "for you would sacrifice who I am for your own happiness."

"You are too cruel!" cried she. "How can you come here with this news, and then accuse me of such things?"

"I'm sorry, my love," he said. "I just must go, and I wish you could understand why."

"I'm sure I never will," she said, turning away and slowly, then all at once running to her bed and collapsing onto it, sobbing. He watched her for a full minute, helpless, then turned and left, returning to his own chambers.

He sat for a quarter of an hour attempting to write a letter, but was unable to escape the sound and image of his wife's misery. He refused to allow his resolve to be shaken – he had considered this step and all of its consequences before he had taken it, but in reality the soft voice of his emotions asked if he had not been too stern, if he oughtn't to have given her concerns more voice, or downplayed the danger to allay her fears. A soft lie was still a lie, he silently reminded himself, and a one-time excuse wouldn't help for next time. He would be going to battle for at least another ten years, fifteen if his body held up. She would have to learn to accept that part of his crown.

He threw down his work, giving up, and strode out of the palace to the barn and ordered his horse saddled. He needed motion, action, to clear his mind. He had been idle too long. His mind returned again to his young bride. He had been too hard on her. Pre-judged her. That was unlike him, he thought. He urged his horse into a trot, enjoying the spring-smelling cool air. Life was blossoming all around him, frail and sweet-smelling and full of promise, just like his wife. There was strength in her, she had just never been pruned properly to bring it out in her. Her father had doted on her and never developed the resolve that must be paired with her goodness. He loved the daughter that her father had produced – he did love her, he thought loudly – but she wasn't perfected yet. Who could expect that? She was still so young and had so much life to learn from. He had been unkind. He should be instructing her, growing her. He nodded to no one in particular. He had allowed himself to become over-excited by his sister-in-law. His mind was troubled at the conviction of this new line of thought, but he tumbled through it, the freedom of the riding lane enervating him.

Hadn't she poisoned him against his wife? Hadn't she placed each seed of mistrust that had now borne fruit? And for what purpose? There was no knowing, with her. At her own claim, she acted only in her own best interest. She seemed to enjoy his company tolerably well, but what did he actually know about her motives? Plenty, he told himself. Probably all he needed to. He had taken her word against her sister, and committed a grave sin against his wife. He would have to be more guarded against the counsel of the dark princess, he resolved.

The very same approached him in the riding lane, coming back from some errand that had occupied her morning. He was shocked at how glad he was to see her.

For her part, she was preoccupied with a complication one of her business endeavors had experienced, and she was nearly upon the light prince before she perceived him.

"Good day," he called. Her head jerked from her horse's ears and she realized the identity of the speaker. She smiled and checked her horse to a slow walk.

"Good day," she answered.

"What brings you out into our wonderful spring day, if it is not reason enough unto itself?" he asked.

"An associate sent me correspondence indicating that I had an affair the next town over that required my personal attendance," she told him. "Though I will admit that the season suits me well."

He nodded, stopping his horse entirely. She did the same.

"What of your own journey?" she asked. He shook his head, the smile at seeing her not fading.

"Just taking a constitutional," he said.

"Aren't you young yet for such activity?" she asked. His brow creased.

"I was occupied, but unable to focus..." he said.

"What has happened?" she asked, her voice toned to indicate not-excessive concern. He paused, apparently considering. She had nothing particularly pressing awaiting her.

"It may be shameful inactivity," said he, "but the sun and the blue sky beckon. Would you care to join me for a ride through the estate?"

She considered for a moment, smiling, then nodded.

"From you, I would not be ashamed to take a lesson on leisure."

They rode in silence for perhaps ten minutes before he spoke.

"I told your sister of my plan to depart for the northern border," he said finally.

"What did she say to that?"

He sighed.

"She wept. Begged me not to leave her."

"Did she offer to accompany you?"

"Beg your pardon?"

"Did she ask to go with you?" the dark princess asked again, pushing her hair off both shoulders and looking at him, letting her mount pick its own way across the broad pasture they were crossing.

"Of course not. The borders are no place for a princess," he said genuinely.

"'S'what I would have done. Insisted that if the danger were appropriate for you, it was appropriate for me, and if you were going, so would I."

"That makes no sense," he said. She laughed.

"And my sister's current stance does? You should wait to defend your territory until your territory only includes your person and her own? I don't have to make sense to get what I want, nor does she."

"You would be able to make such a demand because you are capable of taking care of yourself and could survive comfortably enough at the borders. She could not," he said.

"That's not my fault is it? Or yours?"

"It is your father's, but I intend to see to it," he said, his hands closing harder on his reins. She laughed heartily and his head snapped to look at her.

"Oh, not you, not so soon," she said, shaking her head as she laughed. He raised his eyebrows, his expression a mix of surprise and anger. She was unconcerned.

"How many husbands, and wives for that matter, have I witnessed exhausting boundless energy and optimism trying to 'fix' that which is at the core of their spouse? My sister was my father's darling, true enough, but he gave both of us the same opportunity. The difference between the two of us is simply who we chose to become."

"But something must have spurred you on to your accomplishments," he said. She widened her eyes dramatically, mocking him.

"Some single, life-changing event that made me want to be powerful, or secure, or victorious? There is none, my friend. Or if there is, it was that she was born blond and I raven-haired. Though I put no stock in that, myself."

They rode in silence for a few seconds when a new thought occurred to her, and she smiled again.

"Besides, my sister would be appalled if you said that her accomplishments did not compare to my own," she said. He opened his mouth and closed it.

"I find no profitable reply to that," he said. She grinned.

"I have never known anyone so accomplished at getting what she wants. For as hard as I work to accumulate tools and resources, she is out of my league."

He shook his head, not following her. She continued, enjoying herself. He had tapped into a deep well of thought concerning her sister that she had never voiced.

"She alternates between weak and aloof, as it suits her. Her world is comprised of people who are simply waiting for an excuse to give her what she wants. She cries or she pouts when it is withheld. She is vulnerable and pitiable, and people cannot help but love her for it." She laughed. "I will never understand it, but she does it even to me. She is the very best at what she does, and she got a crown for it. I don't even believe she does it on purpose." She paused and her eyes narrowed as she smiled darkly. "Tell me you didn't even consider sending the troops on their own."

He paused.

"Not seriously."

She waited and he slowly smiled. She laughed.

"The sad thing is, for as much surrounded as she is, I don't think she's ever had a real friend."

"Have you?" he asked. She tilted her head to the side, considering.

"I believe I do," she said gently. She let her gaze drift back forward, watching the world framed between her horse's ears. She felt his eyes on her, but didn't look to meet them, wondering quietly if she had said more than she cared to.

"You've been unusually talkative today," he said after a few minutes. She considered.

"Just at my ease, I suppose," she said, then clicked to her horse. "I've allowed you to take me away from my affairs for too long, though. It's time to be heading back."

His horse broke into a trot without any urging from him, the instinct of the animal to stay with its stablemate overpowering its inertia, and she pushed her mare into a canter.

"When do you expect to head north?" she asked as his gelding pulled even with her mount.

"It should take less than two weeks to get the supplies arranged," he said. She nodded.

"And after that I'll be on my own, training, again," she said.

"Unless you join us," he answered thoughtlessly. Her look shot to him and he looked as surprised as she felt at his words.

They reached the stableyard and she tossed her reins to a groom, ignoring the prince as she entered the palace and made her way to her chambers. There she sat at her desk with her papers laid out before her and a pen and her hand and stared at the wall for the rest of the evening.

Two days later, she arrived at the appointed hour in his training room, dressed to work. He was already warming up.

"I was afraid you would not come, after I spoke so poorly to you last we met," he said, his words measured, due to his audience. "May I offer my retraction, and my most sincere apology?"

"You may offer them," she said habitually, eyeing the walls. Much of the non-essential house staff, including her husband's entire staff, stood on the perimeter of the room to spectate the prince's workout.

"My sister has blown this all out of proportion, hasn't she?" she muttered to him. He smiled with some pain. The light princess had convinced much of the palace that he was marching to his death, going so far as to draw an intervention from the queen for his safety. The dark princess had understood that the queen had simply confirmed that he was taking no fewer men than were necessary, but it was evident that his wife had expected him to abandon the enterprise entirely. She had been locked in her chambers crying for the past eighteen hours.

"Well, let's give them a show, shall we?" she asked, attacking the light prince with gusto. He fought back with energy to rival her own.

Her swordplay was in a new realm. Normally, she fought with training precision, watching for weaknesses and exploiting them, teaching him his flaws and correcting her own. This morning she was ferocious, attacking him as though to wound him, her will was taking him by storm. He stepped up with her, answering as though by instinct, his eyes watching her face more often than her sword. After three hard, resounding blows, each blocked with force, she stepped back, her eyes blazing.

"I hope you face an army that fights just as I do; it seems I cannot take you," she said.

"I would hope not, myself. I should be the only survivor," he said. Now he took the initiative, stepping into her and pushing her back. Her arm began to ache from the force of the fight and she gritted her teeth in anger, pushing him in turn. She might have growled at him, but it was not audible above the sound of the wooden swords and their reverberation off the walls. Her hair was falling into her face and she flung her head to clear it, moving faster than she had ever before found reason.

Abruptly her hand was empty and the floor greeted her unexpectedly. Hard. The floor was very hard.

"Yield," he said playfully, looking down his sword at her. She looked around, her concentration broken. Ceiling, walls. Crowd.

"If you have time to make sport of us, it is obvious you have not enough with which to occupy yourselves," she barked from the floor. The spectators looked uneasy, their enjoyment of the spar breaking as a spell.

"You heard me!" she commanded. "Make use of your hands or find yourselves removed of them," she ordered. The room quickly emptied.

"That was unexpected," the light brother said, leaning on his sword and looking down at her. "Have I pricked your ego that badly?"

"Not my ego," she said, ignoring his hand to help her up as she stood and straightened her clothes. She pushed her hair away as he watched her.

"You are stronger than I," she said finally. He shrugged.

"I bested you today," he said. "The statistics dictated it would happen some time."

She smiled, nervous. She weighed the many ideas that she had considered over the past two days, trying to find where to start.

"You are a good man," she started. He smiled easily.

"Thank you."

"You are complete unto yourself, and to wish you different would be to wish you destroyed." She swallowed and he waited, evidently unable to see where she was going.

"You have strengths I do not possess, and I respect them," she started.

"Thank you," he said, his face easing out of confusion, but she continued.

"But I have fewer limitations. I can do so much that you could not. You shackle yourself for what you believe."

He made to speak, but she held up a hand.

"Now, you must give me your word that anything I say next is in the strictest confidence," she said, raising her eyebrows.

"Of course," he said, frowning.

"I have never known one such as yourself. Powerful, aware, cunning, and yet completely trustworthy. I see myself as from your perspective – weasely, sniping about in the shadows, fearfully amassing a hoard intended either to buffer myself from danger or from which to launch some brutal campaign for power." She held up her hand again as he tried to protest. "I know you would never be so unkind. But yet. I perceive what my motives and actions would look like from where you stand. And I have explained how your behavior appears to me. We are on divergent paths, paths that should they interesect, one of us would break."

She paused, exhausting the thought.

"I find myself at a loss," he said. "What are you trying to tell me?"

"I told you once that I loved three people; my sister, my trainer, and myself," she said. Suddenly he understood, and was unable to look at her. "I have found a fourth in yourself."

He looked up and away, his mouth open as he searched for a reply.

"This would be a good time not to say anything," she said, moved to pity at his surprise. Suddenly she wondered if this was completely unexpected for him, if he had simply been treating her as a sister, but she shook her head, pushing her hair back again.

"It matters not if you reciprocate my feelings, for in truth you should not, and I would love you all the more for it. You must not consider me in competition with my sister; it would tarnish your character."

"But love must always desire to find itself returned," he said, almost a question.

"What business has love wanting?" she asked sternly. "That which is motivated by love cannot want, and that which wants cannot be love. Even I know that."

He pressed his lips together now, avidly watching her face.

"I have considered this for some time, now, and know what action I must take."

"What is that?" he asked.

"By simple elimination, I cannot stay here, because that would be to tempt you to love me, I believe, and I will not sacrifice what you are. I cannot simply move away and continue my life as it is, because that would abandon my love for you to a lack of will. I am not and will not be so weak. Therefore I will leave this place and do the things you cannot, but would, do. I will cheat, I will steal, and I will kill as necessary, but I will be doing the things that you would do, had you the freedom. I will love you more than myself."

He looked stunned.

"But you are my brother's wife," he said. "You will leave him?" She smiled sardonically.

"I am only his wife by law. I believe that, in the eyes of the church, I am not yet and never will be his wife, don't you agree?"

He furrowed his eyebrows together.

"You will leave," he said.

"Yes, today," she answered, gathering strength. His eyebrows shot up.

"Today? Where will you go?"

"I will not tell you, so that when my husband asks, you may tell him in truth that you do not know." She took a step forward, holding up a finger. "More importantly, remember that you gave me your confidence. Should – when – my husband asks if I have left him for another man, you must tell him that you know, but on your honor you may not tell him who. Your secrecy is bound in your oath, you should not need to lie to him or anyone. Your feelings you should keep to yourself, should you have any, and you must fight against them, if you do, for temptation is not itself a sin, is it?"

They looked at each other for several long minutes, then she nodded decisively.

"Mind my sister, you must care for her enough for both of us, now. You'll find the paperwork in my chambers giving you ownership of all of my legitimate local holdings. The foreign ones I will keep for convenience and the illegitimate ones I have agents shedding as we speak. Your brother will largely be living on your largesse, now; do what you will with him."

"In less than a year, you bankrupted him?" the light brother asked.

"In less than a year, he bankrupted himself. I stood by and collected the spoils because I was not about to allow him to become King independent of myself. You will undoubtedly be crowned, now, by the way. I have halted my actions to preclude it. It does not matter, for I care only for your success, but you will be a better king than he." She paused, searching for anything else she desired to say to him that she would be willing to disclose. Finding nothing, she nodded again.

"That will be all. I will take my leave," she said.

"Will you return?" he asked. She shook her head.

"No. I will go out into the world anonymous, nothing but your dark mistress," she said.

In the hall, she found the light prince's personal manservant standing against the wall. She started and then frowned deeply at him, but he shook his head.

"My master's confidence is my own, m'lady," he said. "But may I say that though you often abused us, knowing that we belonged to you and knowing how aggressively you defend what's yours has given the staff here great comfort. You shall be missed."

His dark mistress had raised her hand to strike the servant, but lowering it, slowly looked back through the door at the drooping posture of the prince she had left behind. She smiled softly and held out her hand to shake hands with the servant. He turned it and gently raised it to his lips.

"Goodbye, m'lady," he said. She smiled with more warmth.

"Good bye."

ABOUT THE AUTHOR

Mindy Saturn is one of the many identities of Chloe Garner, a wanderer with a host of identities in her head fighting each other to get out. Mindy writes the dark, the sarcastic, and the mysterious. Her heroines tend to wear an awful lot more black leather than is really good for them. Find her at blenderfiction.wordpress.com on Twitter as BlenderFiction, or on Goodreads and Facebook as Chloe Garner.